A Taste of You

A Taste of You

Sorcha Grace

Praise for A Taste of You

"With a deliciously sexy hero, a heroine with unforgettable spice, and mouthwatering sensuality, Sorcha Grace's *A Taste of You* will have you begging for seconds. Absolutely delectable."
> —J. Kenner, *New York Times* bestselling author of RELEASE ME,
> CLAIM ME, and COMPLETE ME

"More than just a taste of sexy here. Scorching hot flames have burned up dinner! Witty and fun, *A Taste of You* by Sorcha Grace is a satisfying, sensual read not to be missed."
> —Raine Miller, *New York Times* Bestselling Author

"Fans of Sylvia Day and E.L. James will find a lot to like about the mysterious William Lambourne and will root for a heroine who deserves a second chance at love. An intriguing start to a saucy new trilogy."
> —Roni Loren, National bestselling author of FALL INTO YOU

"Yummy! Imagine Christian Grey with warm chocolate and you have William Lambourne. Add a complex heroine who gives love another try and you have *A Taste of You*. This steamy romance will take you through twists and turns and have you cheering for love to prevail. I can't wait to read what's next for William and Catherine!"
> —Aleatha Romig, Author of the bestselling CONSEQUENCES
> series

A Taste of You

To the men in my life: M, S, and D. You know why.

ONE

"Cat, you have to try this brioche. It's to die for, if I do say so myself." Beckett waved a thick slab of the warm, buttery bread he'd baked just before we left under my nose, but my stomach roiled at the mere thought of taking a single bite.

"Thanks, I'm not hungry." I turned my attention back to the scene outside the window of the cab: the gridlock of Chicago's afternoon rush hour traffic. We were on the Kennedy, and I hoped the traffic would clear once we got off at Randolph.

"Do not check your watch again," Beckett warned through a mouth full of bread. "We aren't going to be late."

I gave him a wobbly smile. He was a good friend and only trying to help me relax, but this photo shoot was my big chance and I didn't want to mess it up.

The cab crawled forward, and finally, we exited and headed west. The driver studied row after row of industrial buildings and warehouses looking for the address we'd given, and I clenched my hands on my black denim jeans. I wished I had driven instead of taking a cab, but oh well. I was still getting used to big city driving, and the Fulton Market neighborhood was not somewhere I wanted to get lost on a weekday night. All the buildings looked the same, and even though a few really hip art galleries and restaurants had opened in the neighborhood, it was still a pretty sketchy area. I hadn't been a Chicagoan for long, but I had quickly learned to pay keen attention to my surroundings and think about my safety.

"You'd feel better if you ate something," Beckett said. "You skipped lunch, and coffee and toast for breakfast only get you so far."

I gave him a rueful smile. He knew me so well. But when I was nervous or busy, I couldn't be bothered to eat. "My coffee had milk in it," I answered lamely.

"Skim," he chided me. "Not that you need it." He took another bite of brioche.

"You're going to have to start taking skim milk in *your* coffee if you don't lay off the carbs," I told him. "It's the week after New Year's. You're supposed to be dieting."

He gave a mock gasp. "Perish the thought!"

Beckett probably could perish the thought. He was naturally slim and gorgeous with wavy blond hair and light blue eyes. Even though he hadn't lived in Santa Cruz for years, he looked every bit the quintessential California boy I'd known since high school. He just dressed better these days. Today, he wore a stylish, black wool trench coat, open so I could see the collared shirt and V-neck sweater beneath. His matching trousers were pressed and crisp, and his shoes the best Italian leather. I honestly didn't know how he managed to keep so slim when as a pastry chef—a truly *amazing* pastry chef—he loved to sample his own creations. I was certain the brioche stuffed with juicy, fragrant peaches would be wonderfully sweet and filling if I allowed myself a bite. But I couldn't. I was on my way to possibly the most important photo shoot of my career, and though I appreciated Beckett's concern for keeping me fed, I was much more grateful to him for keeping me employed.

Once he'd finished culinary school, Beckett had spent time working in several impressive restaurant kitchens around Chicago, including two years baking at a Michelin-starred emporium of French haute cuisine. But he hadn't been happy, so now he was paying the bills by working as a food stylist. And thanks to him, I was reinventing my career by taking pictures of the food he made look so good.

I glanced at my watch and felt a stab of panic. It was almost five and we were going to be late. That was no way to make an impression on the owners of Willowgrass, the new restaurant which was our destination. And I needed to make an impression—a good one. In California, I had a reputation and was a known commodity with a following. But in Chicago, I was starting from scratch. I really didn't want to blow this.

Beckett took my hand and squeezed. "We're almost there, and that cheapo watch of yours is fast. We're going to breeze in at exactly five o'clock."

I glanced at the black men's digital watch on my wrist. Beckett and I had tons of disagreements over the years about what he called, "Cat Time," otherwise known as my chronic lateness. My "cheapo watch" was ugly, and it kept shit time, but I strapped it on day after day as my low-tech solution to my aversion to punctuality. It ran ten minutes fast, and it had saved me from disaster more than once. It was well worth the ten bucks I'd spent at Walgreens.

I heaved a sigh of relief when the cab slowed and the driver mumbled the address we'd given. I climbed out, shouldering my bulky camera bag, while Beckett paid the fare. I glanced at the brick building, its rectangular windows still papered over but glowing with warm light in the darkness of early evening. The building was old and original to the neighborhood, but the new owners had gone to some trouble to restore it while keeping its classic charm. Above the windows, a heavy wooden rectangle with *Willowgrass* seemingly burned into the dark, distressed oak, welcomed visitors. The letters curled playfully and a stalk of grass formed an extension of the W.

On a whim, I pulled out my camera and snapped a few shots. They would likely be too dark to use, but they might inspire me later. I wished I'd brought my Leica, but since this was basically a meet and greet, I'd brought only the bare essentials. A gust of wind whipped down the street, cutting through me, despite my layers of clothing. I was wearing a version of what I thought of as my urban winter uniform: tall boots, slim jeans, a long-sleeved T-shirt with a cashmere sweater over it—all in black. I'd thrown on a charcoal pea coat that had once belonged to my dad along with a scarf, and still I shivered at the bite in the air. This was my first Chicago winter, and I didn't think I'd ever get used to the weather. The sun and surf of Santa Cruz was in my bones.

Beckett strode beside me. "Ready?"

I smiled. "Ready." My breath puffed out at my words and faded into the darkness.

Beckett ushered me into the building, where we were immediately greeted by a petite woman with pale, porcelain skin and a sleek, dark bob, wearing a chic tweed dress. "Beckett!" She absolutely beamed, gliding forward on towering heels. "I'm so glad you're here." They air-kissed, and I stood back, more than comfortable in my role as observer. Beckett, with his fair-haired good looks, made a stunning counterpart to the woman. But then Beckett always looked good. People often assumed we were a couple. In fact, Jace had written me off initially because he thought I had a thing for Beckett. But Beckett wasn't my type, and I certainly wasn't his.

A quick peek in a mirror behind the woman who'd greeted us showed me my cheeks were pink from the cold, but my green eyes were bright, and my brunette hair was still tame in its ponytail. I wasn't quite as fashionable as Beckett, but I had my own look. I'd worried that I might be too casual, but I didn't want to seem like I was trying too hard to impress. This was an informal meeting after all.

I took a moment to study the space, noting there would be an abundance of natural light when the paper came off the windows, and nodded with appreciation at the simple, yet elegant, interior. The floors were distressed, burnished wood and I wondered if they were original or had been salvaged. The tables and booths were also wood, the chairs rustic and sturdy. The walls were an earthy green, juxtaposed by exposed brick and thick support beams. An open metal staircase led to an upper dining area that circled the main floor—

another led down, presumably to the kitchen. I knew immediately I'd get great interior shots.

"Amanda," Beckett was saying, "this is Catherine Kelly, the fabulous photographer I was telling you about. Catherine, this is Amanda Lee, one of the owners of Willowgrass."

Amanda held out her hand and smiled warmly. "Catherine, thank you so much for filling in on such short notice. You are seriously saving my ass."

I shook her hand, noting how warm it was compared to my frigid one. I was always forgetting my gloves. "I'm happy to do it. This is a great space."

She beamed a blistering, white smile. "Do you think so? We love it."

"It's going to photograph beautifully. Do you mind showing me around a bit?" I was anxious to get a feel for the place. The shoot was tomorrow, and normally I'd have walked through several times before now, done test shots, and mapped out my plan of attack. But since I'd only gotten the call this morning, I needed to cram three days of work into an hour. Not that I was complaining.

When Beckett called to tell me Jenny Hill, another photographer I knew in passing, had broken her wrist after slipping on ice the night before, I actually gave a squeal of delight. I was sorry for Jenny, but happy for me. Jenny had been hired by *Chicago Now* to shoot Willowgrass for a feature on its chef, who had recently won the top prize on a popular cooking reality show. The opening of his first restaurant was highly anticipated. The magazine was one of those oversized glossy ones filled with high-end ads and pictures of tons of parties and society events, so the photographs were paramount. This was a great opportunity, and I didn't hesitate to say yes when Beckett asked if I'd be willing to fill in.

Amanda walked us through the restaurant, pointing out the unique features, like a section of the loft that had been converted into a private dining room. I asked a lot of questions about what look and feel Amanda wanted the photos to capture, and then I asked about the food.

"Finally!" Beckett breathed. I wasn't surprised. All the talk of broad and diffuse light and light falloff bored him. Beckett's talent was making food look beautiful. He understood the essentials of photography, but his passion was making food look irresistible and his touch was magic. I'd seen him perk up wilted lettuce with nothing but harsh words and his magic spray. "Where's your brother?" he asked.

Amanda shrugged. "In the kitchen, where else?" She gestured toward the open metal staircase at the back of main dining room, and we descended and headed into the kitchen.

"Ben is doing amazing things with comfort food, using as many locally sourced ingredients as possible," Beckett whispered in my ear as we walked. "His specialty is unexpected twists on old favorites. You'll love it."

I'd done my research—well, as much as I'd had time for—so I knew this, but I suspected Beckett was reassuring himself. This was an important job for him too.

As soon as we entered, Beckett all but squealed. "Now this is what I'm talking about. Total kitchen O."

I'm not sure if Amanda heard him, but I did, and I rolled my eyes. Cooking and sex measured equally on the pleasure scale for Beckett, and though I adored his enthusiasm, I didn't share it. The kitchen was mostly white walls and floors accented with stainless steel counters, racks, and appliances—not interesting from an aesthetic standpoint—but clearly Beckett saw something I didn't. Of course, I still made scrambled eggs in the microwave so what did I know? I did know I smelled something truly delicious, something spicy and familiar. My mouth watered, and I was suddenly ravenous.

"Beckett!" A man with curly brown hair and warm brown eyes stepped from the open door of a large walk-in cooler, wiped his hands on his apron, and shook Beckett's hand and then mine. "Hi, I'm Ben," he said as his big hand enveloped mine with a hearty grip. He was as attractive as Amanda and broader of shoulder, but I could see the family resemblance.

"Nice to meet you," I said.

He gave me a genuine smile. "Likewise. You're doing us a big favor by stepping in at the last minute."

"Not at all. You're doing me a favor."

Beckett rolled his eyes. "Don't be so humble, Catherine. Ben, Catherine is new to Chicago—she's a transplant from Santa Cruz, actually—and she is absolutely one of the best in the business. We work together as much as possible. You know the Fresh Market billboards with the kebabs that are all over town? That's Catherine's work."

"Really?" Ben's brows rose, and I felt my cheeks heat. I never knew quite how to take a compliment. "Those are some sexy shots."

"They're kebabs," I said. "And Beckett was the one who made them look so good."

"Please." Beckett waved a hand to cut off any further protest. "The way she lit the beef, the way she angled the camera was genius."

"Very phallic," Ben said with appreciation.

"Ha! They look like huge cocks," Beckett bellowed. "I just about choked on my espresso the first time I drove past the billboard on Fullerton."

Oh, my God. I was so embarrassed. I ducked my head, wishing I had worn my hair down, so it would fall forward and shield my face. I *had* been going for a phallic vibe, but I didn't mean it to be quite so obvious. Still, the execs at Fresh Market had loved the shots and contracted me for more, so I guess I should be proud that my first commercial print assignment here was such a success.

"Now I see why you come so highly recommended," Ben said. "If you can make my food look half as sexy, you'll more than earn your fee."

Good. We were back to business. "What dishes were you thinking of having me shoot?" I asked. Just being in the kitchen, surrounded by the yummy smells, was giving me ideas.

"We'll do an assortment, but the ones I really want to play up are the starters and small plates. A lot of the entrees are big meaty items, and in a magazine like *Chicago Now*, I think the small and artful plays better. What do you think?"

I didn't hesitate. "I love it. Our goal is to make readers want to find out if your food tastes as good as it looks—and want to be seen tasting it."

"See?" Beckett chimed in. "She gets it."

Ben nodded. "I prepared a few of the dishes so you can taste them and get an idea of my style."

We sampled a dozen offerings, including deviled eggs with lobster, warm marinated olives stuffed with spicy sausage, a braised pork belly sandwich, white truffle mac and cheese, and a small charcuterie plate with several cured meats and cheeses and the best pickles I'd ever tasted. We studied the selection of food for another forty-five minutes or so and talked about how each dish might photograph and how Ben wanted the food presented. Everything was really delicious, and I was glad I had a chance to sample now, since tomorrow Beckett would cover them all in chemicals to make each dish look perfectly delectable for the magazine. By the time we wrapped up, I was exhausted and ready to sit back and sort through all the ideas flooding my mind.

We said our good-byes, and as I collected my coat and shrugged into it, I glanced through the glass front door at the night sky. I hated how Chicago got so dark, so early, in the winter. It made the nights seem that much longer. The stretch of lonely nighttime hours used to fill me with dread, and I could still feel a small pit of sorrow in my belly. But slowly, ever so slowly, that dread and loneliness and sorrow was finally starting to fade.

"Want to grab dinner?" Beckett asked. "I know a great tapas place not far from here."

I'd sampled a little bit of everything and was pretty stuffed, but leave it to Beckett to still be hungry. "Sure." It was the least I could do, given that he'd dropped this choice gig in my lap.

Beckett took my elbow and steered me toward the door, then dropped it. "Shit. I forgot I wanted to ask Ben for a copy of the menu. I'll be right back." He turned around and headed toward the kitchen, and since I already had my hand on the door, I pushed it open and stepped outside. The pavement was uneven, and before I knew it, I caught the toe of my boot on a jagged edge and stumbled forward. The weight of my camera bag did the rest, and the ground rushed at me, but before my knees hit the sidewalk, I was caught under the arms by warm, strong hands. My fall was aborted, but my camera bag spilled open, scattering my expensive equipment all over the sidewalk.

The hands released me and righted me gently on my feet, and I looked up. And up. And up… into the face of the hottest guy I had ever seen. I actually blinked, certain it must have been a trick of the light. He was simply too stunning, too good-looking to be real. He gave me a slow smile and said something I didn't hear because the blood was thrumming in my ears.

I knew men like this existed—with perfect lighting, makeup, and a little airbrushing—but this guy was the real deal. I couldn't seem to catch my breath, and I reeled, unable to catch my balance either. I stared up at him, vaguely aware he had been touching me a moment ago, and shocked because some part of me clearly wanted him to touch me again.

"Are you alright?" he asked, and from the tone, I knew he was repeating an earlier question. His voice was low and velvety, and I actually felt it rumble through me and slide seductively against my skin.

"I..." I tried to respond, but my whole body tingled with awareness and heat poured through me, making me suddenly too warm, even for January in Chicago. I couldn't think. I could only feel.

"Let me help you," he said, setting my bag back on my shoulder and bending so we were at eye level. *Oh, my.* That face—those eyes. He had dark brown hair, wavy and thick and tousled. It was sexy hair. The kind of hair a man sports after he's been rolling around in bed. I wanted to run my hands through it and feel its texture between my fingers. His cheekbones were high and sculpted, giving him an aristocratic air, but his chiseled jaw and his sensuous lips spoke of a masculine earthiness that caused my belly to perform a slow roll.

And then there were his eyes. I was staring blatantly now, and I couldn't quite get a fix on their color. I decided they were blue and then changed my mind and went with smoky grey. Whatever color they were, they reminded me of the skies above the beach just before a storm—wild, unpredictable, dangerous.

"Are you a photographer?" he asked.

That snapped me out of my trance. "Y-yes. Why?"

"An observation." He gestured to my equipment, now scattered all over the sidewalk. "It looks expensive."

"Oh shit!" I scrambled to my knees and shoved cameras, notebooks, and batteries back in my bag. "It is expensive. If anything is damaged, I am so screwed."

He was crouching next to me, and he didn't miss a beat. "I'd like to see that."

What? My mouth might have been hanging open at this point. *Did he just say what I think he said?* I took a camera case he held out and then a lamp. Our fingers brushed, just for a second, and I flinched as though burned. The tingle of electricity rushed up my arm and infused my body. I even glanced at the lamp to see if the heat that passed through me could have come from it. But no. It was dark and cold. That spark of charged current came from *him.*

He stood. "If anything is damaged, you should send me the bill. This was my fault entirely."

I shook my head, still on my knees, and painfully aware I was level with his crotch. This wasn't his fault. I had a hazy memory of an uneven sidewalk. "No. I couldn't." I peered in my bag, studying the contents. It was lacking my normal organization, but it appeared everything was inside. I wobbled to my feet, slinging my bag over my shoulder. "I tripped. You were an innocent bystander."

He grinned, looking almost boyish, and shoved his hands in the pockets of his wool overcoat. And then he did it again. "That's the first time in a long while I've been called innocent."

I was too stunned to respond. I felt my cheeks heat, but my schoolgirl blush was nothing compared to the heat coursing through the rest of me. My heart was beating so fast my stomach dipped again, and I actually felt a pull deep inside, something I hadn't felt in a long time. How was this possible? I kept staring, silent, watching his blue-grey eyes crinkle. Then he gave me a knowing smile, as though he could read every one of my thoughts, even the secret, naughty ones I'd never reveal to anyone. But this man looked as though he not only saw them, but he *liked* what he saw.

"Sorry that took so long." Beckett's voice was like a weight, bringing me down to earth and reality. I turned, trying to think of an appropriate response. I had no idea how long I'd been in front of the restaurant with this tall, dark, and handsome stormy-eyed Adonis, but it felt like time had stopped. Beckett blinked. "Cat, what's wrong? What are you doing?"

I faltered. "I… nothing."

"Your face is all flushed."

I put my hands to my cheeks. "It's the cold. I'm not used to it." I couldn't resist glancing at Stormy Eyes to gauge whether he could tell I was lying, whether he knew the heat in my cheeks was caused by him and his sexy innuendo, but when I turned, he wasn't standing there anymore. He was gone. Completely gone.

What the fuck? Where did he go? I craned my neck to see if I could spot him on the sidewalk striding away, but the block wasn't lit, and he'd disappeared into the darkness. Despair lanced through me. I'd lost him. I shook my head. We'd met for all of three minutes. I was making too much of it. Still, I couldn't believe he was gone so quickly. Beckett hadn't seen him. Had I imagined the whole encounter? I peered into my bag, studying the haphazard way everything was shoved inside. If I imagined it, then who helped me pick up all my equipment, and why were my legs still weak, and my center so hot and tender? I shifted uncomfortably from one leg to the other, feeling an unexpected warmth between them, which made my skinny jeans feel too skinny in certain places. Oh my God, I had been totally turned on by a random stranger. I lifted out the lamp he'd handed me, hoping I'd feel something of the connection in the object, but it was just a lamp. What the hell had just happened?

"Cat?" Beckett's voice was high and concerned. "You're scaring me, sweetie. What's going on?"

I tried to collect myself and explain. "I dropped my bag," I said, knowing I sounded a little too breathy to be totally convincing, "and this guy helped me pick everything up." Except he wasn't a *guy*, I screamed in my head. He was so much more than that. But how was I supposed to explain that to Beckett? And now that the mystery man had disappeared into the night, I was starting to feel the cold again. Beckett just stared. "You said something about dinner?" I asked, hoping to change the subject. My thoughts were too jumbled to make any sense right now.

"Sure. Let's get some food in you. I think you'll feel better."

*****

An hour later my thoughts were less scattered, and I was more relaxed. I was sipping my second glass of a really delicious tempranillo and basking in the warmth of the cozy Spanish restaurant.

"I still can't believe you didn't ask his name," Beckett chided me, topping off my glass with the last of the red wine. "He gave you the perfect opportunity."

"I wasn't thinking straight," I said. "I was too…"

"Horny?"

I laughed. "Yes, there is that, but I was going to say overwhelmed."

"I wish I'd be *overwhelmed* by a sexy stranger on the street. What are you calling him again?"

I felt the heat creep into my cheeks. "Stormy Eyes." I had interacted with the guy for like ninety seconds and I had already given him a nickname.

"I like it. Makes him sound all sexy and mysterious."

"I don't even know why we're still talking about him. I'm sure I'll never see him again. It was just one of those weird things. Memorable, but meaningless, right?" I could hear the breathiness creeping into my voice as I did my best to sound convincing. Again. Beckett seemed to buy it, but I wasn't sure I did. "Let's talk about something else—like the shoot tomorrow. Tell me what you have in mind for the styling."

Beckett launched into his ideas for arranging Ben's dishes in a sexy, mouthwatering way, what sprays and colorings he would use, and I tried to pay attention. I really did. I needed to pay attention, but my thoughts kept wandering back to Stormy Eyes. What had he meant when he said no one had called him *innocent* in a long time? It was so obviously sexual, but I suppose he could have meant it any one of three or four different ways. Was he just a smart-ass, or was he thoroughly debauched? And why should the thought of a man with a dark, sexual side turn me on so much? I'd always preferred the clean-cut type, and I liked guys with open smiles and all-American values. Then why did I have to press my legs together to ease the tension building there? My mind wandered to the vibrator a friend bought me as a gag gift for my bachelorette party. I still had it. Jace and I played around with it once or twice, but I hadn't ever used it on my own. But tonight, after Stormy Eyes and our sidewalk encounter, I needed to ease the ache between my thighs, and I knew my hand wasn't going to cut it.

*****

Beckett and I took separate cabs, and mine dropped me at my condo in Lincoln Park. I paid the driver and looked at my black windows, wondering when this place would feel like home to me. After eight months with a Chicago zip code, I still felt like a visitor. Santa Cruz was home. In Chicago, I had to remind myself the water was east, not west, and driving anywhere took double the time I anticipated. Some days I woke up and still couldn't believe I had packed up and moved halfway across the country. I'd never considered moving until Beckett called and suggested I come to Chicago.

I was a California girl at heart, but a move was exactly the escape plan I needed after my life in Santa Cruz had fallen apart. And

Beckett had helped me through it all. He was the one who found my condo, and I couldn't have asked for a better location. I was a few blocks from the lake, and the neighborhood was full of coffee shops and little boutiques. I could spend an entire Saturday browsing unique shops. My condo was fabulous as well. It was on the top floor of a converted nineteenth-century mansion and retained all the charm of that past era. I loved the stone foundation, the limestone exterior, and the floor-to-ceiling French windows. It was a remnant of the past nestled among the modern and new.

I usually enjoyed the exercise of taking the stairs to my floor, but tonight I was tired and drained. When I opened the door, Laird gave a low *woof* and bounded over to greet me. I dropped my bag, bent down, and gave him a huge hug. He was a big mutt with hints of Australian Cattle Dog. For an older dog he still had a lot of energy, but he didn't shed much and was happy and easygoing. Laird was the one thing I'd brought from my life in Santa Cruz. He'd been Jace's dog, and Jace had named him Laird after Laird Hamilton, a famous surfer and one of his idols. Laird licked my face and *woofed* again, letting me know he didn't appreciate these late nights.

Later, after I'd walked the dog, changed into flannel pajamas, and laid in bed listening to Laird's soft snores in his own bed on the floor at my feet, my thoughts turned to Stormy Eyes. I pictured his slow, sexy smile, the way his eyes darkened when they focused on me, the feel of his fingers as they brushed mine.

I pressed my hand between my legs. I felt swollen and tender there, and I thought again of that vibrator, wondering where I'd put it when I unpacked. But then I closed my eyes and fell asleep.

*****

I woke up thinking of Stormy Eyes. I'd dreamed of him, though the dreams were foggy in the morning light. It was what I was beginning to think of as a typical January day in Chicago—cold and sleeting. From my window, the sky looked dreary and ominous. It was a good day to stay inside, curl up with a copy of *Digital Photo Pro* or *B&W*, and eat soup with a grilled cheese sandwich. But I didn't have that luxury today, so instead, I took Laird for a brisk walk along the lakefront. My breath puffed out in great gusts the faster we walked. Despite my thermal leggings, multiple layers, and North Face boots, I was freezing and in a hurry to get back. But Laird romped and played and generally had a great time. He obviously didn't mind the cold temperatures.

The lake was iced over in places, and so calm and placid compared to the ever-churning waters of the Pacific. I told myself that was a good change for me. My life had been wild and churning the past few years, and I needed calm and placid. I did miss the vivid blue of the Pacific, though Lake Michigan could take on that color at times. But this morning it was grey, reminding me of Stormy Eyes. His eyes were such an unusual color. I would have liked to see them in another light to judge them better. I really had to stop fixating on this guy. Already his effect on me was the antithesis of the calm I wished for.

It was a random encounter, I reminded myself. I whistled for Laird, and we headed back.

We were wet from the sleet, and I grabbed a towel from my car and dried him off before we went inside. As Laird and I stepped into the warmth of the common foyer, he gave a happy yelp and ran to lick a handsome, older woman trying to collect her mail. "Laird! No! Sorry, Mrs. Himmler." I dragged Laird off. The Himmlers sometimes watched Laird when I had to be away overnight or on a long shoot, and he adored them. The feeling was mutual.

"It's quite alright, Catherine," she said, patting Laird on the head. I could hear the faint trace of her German accent. "You know I don't mind. What I do mind is your refusal to call me Minerva. *Mrs. Himmler* makes me feel old!" She gave me a warm hug.

"I'll try, Minerva," I said. But it was hard to call this refined, dignified woman by her given name. Minerva Himmler and her husband, Hans, were my first friends in Chicago, other than Beckett. They lived in the condo below mine, and Minerva welcomed me with chocolate-covered *baumkuchen* the day after I moved in. I think I ate the whole cake in less than an hour.

Since then, Minerva and Hans had become good friends. They invited me over for dinner once a month, and the food was always delicious. Minerva liked to point out how lucky I was to have a renovated kitchen that included an AGA stove—or cooker, as it was called. It was this behemoth, white cast-iron monstrosity with all these doors and compartments, and it wasn't anything like the Kenmore gas range I had grown up with. I still hadn't figured out how to use the

AGA, so I felt luckier that I was a master of my microwave. Minerva, however, made wonderful *stollen* in the AGA, and Beckett—well, Beckett just about creamed himself every time he looked at it. He found reasons to come over and bake in it all the time, which I didn't mind, since he usually left me half of whatever he made.

Having Minerva and Hans as neighbors was another great perk about the condo and completely unexpected. It was like having my grandparents living downstairs. They were sweet and funny and spoiled me. They also knew enough not to pry into my life. They minded their business when they could tell I was having a bad day and wanted to be alone, and they drew me out of my shell when I was lonely and wanted cheering up.

"I have not seen you much the last few days," Minerva said.

"I have a job. I'm doing a shoot for *Chicago Now*. It's to accompany a piece on Willowgrass, a new restaurant opening in Fulton Market."

She nodded. "I read about that one. Ben Lee's venture. He was on that cooking contest show, yes? He's quite the rising star and handsome too. And *Chicago Now*? I am impressed. You are making quite a name for yourself." This from a woman who was a celebrated opera singer in her day, the coloratura soprano famed for her brilliant performance as The Queen of the Night in Mozart's *The Magic Flute*. She still looked the part, with her grey and black hair coiled high on her head, her stylish navy trousers and white sweater, and her dramatic makeup. I hardly ever wore makeup and always felt pale beside Minerva.

"Thanks. I'm doing the actual shoot today, so I'd better get going."

"Good luck. Come for dinner soon, *ja*?"

"I will." Laird and I walked upstairs, and I changed for the shoot. It took me longer than usual to get ready because I tried three different outfits. I couldn't figure out what was wrong with me. Usually I threw on whatever I first grabbed in my closet, but I couldn't seem to make a decision. Finally, I decided on black suede boots, tights, a slim black skirt, a grey and black striped sweater, a cashmere scarf wound around my neck, and the diamond studs that were a gift from my mother when I turned twenty-one. And just for fun, I put on a lacy, red balconette bra and matching panties. It wasn't because I was hoping to see Stormy Eyes again. Even if I saw him, he'd never know what I was wearing underneath. But I would.

A quick check of the time told me I was running late, so I dashed out the door, stowed my equipment in my white Volvo SUV, and backed out of my parking space. It still felt weird to drive such a big car, but I needed a change, and now that I didn't have surf gear to tote, I didn't have to worry about scratching the paint on a nice vehicle. Plus, the design was touted as one of the most solid, and the car had all these high-tech safety features.

It was sleeting hard, and traffic was slow thanks to the icy conditions. By the time I reached Willowgrass, found a parking spot, and unloaded my gear, I was ten minutes late. *Cat time. Great*, I thought. I dashed into the restaurant feeling completely frazzled. I'm sure I looked it too, but Amanda was all smiles when she greeted me.

"Do you need anything, Catherine? How about a nice espresso to warm you up? It looks awful out there."

I ran my hand through my hair, hoping to smooth it down and undo the sleet damage. "Um, no thanks. How about a water instead?" I was already nervous enough, and the last thing I needed was to be bouncing off the walls with a caffeine buzz.

"Sure thing, hon. Let me go grab it. Beckett's in the kitchen with Ben," she added as she left to fetch my water.

I went to look for Beckett. He was in the back, working with Ben and the food, and after I checked in, I went into the dining room and set up. Amanda brought me the water then finished tearing the paper off the windows. I wished the sleet would stop so more light would come in, but I had brought extra lamps just in case. Except for a handful of Ben and Amanda's friends and what I assumed were financial backers sitting quietly by the bar, I was alone for a few minutes, which was perfect. I could really look at the space and the lighting and do a few test shots before making final decisions.

I started working, but every few minutes I found myself glancing over my shoulder at the restaurant's front windows. I knew it was because I kept expecting to see *him*. I had no idea who he was or why he was outside the restaurant the night before, but a part of me hoped he'd reappear today.

Ugh. I had to stop this. I pressed my cold palms to my frozen cheeks and tried, once again, to concentrate on my job. This was so unlike me. Usually, focusing was a non-issue for me. This was a fabulous space and a great opportunity. I was really excited about this assignment. I don't know why my mind wandered back to Stormy Eyes. Well, yes I did, but I tried not to think about it.

"Cat!" Beckett breezed into the dining room and gave me a hard hug. He was wearing slim jeans and a cable sweater with a white apron. I never knew how he managed to keep his apron so clean when he was working with food. "How's it going? Can I bring out the food for the first shots?"

"Yes. I'll finish positioning the lights while you spray and shellac. I wish I'd remembered my gas mask."

"Ha-ha. You know everything I use is all-natural."

"That doesn't mean it smells good."

"You're one to speak, Miss Reek of Darkroom Chemicals."

I grinned, relaxing now that Beckett and I were bantering. We'd known each other so long and were such good friends, it was easy to work with him. We knew each other's routines, likes, and dislikes.

"Ben is totally pulling out all the stops. You're going to love how everything looks," Beckett said as he retreated to the kitchen. "So sexy."

I smiled, loving that he was as excited about this as I was.

I checked my notes on the first shots, and my cheeks thawed and tingled. I bent to retrieve a camera from my bag, and as I straightened, I spotted a pair of expensive men's shoes—sleek black leather. I looked higher and saw grey flannel, tailored trousers, a suit jacket, a crisp white shirt, and a silver tie, loose at the neck. Slowly, already knowing who I'd see, I glanced into his face. His eyes were molten grey, like the suit he was wearing. His hair wasn't windblown or wet from the sleet. In fact, he looked like he just stepped off a page of a magazine.

I swallowed and felt my hands tremble. Our eyes met, and in that moment, it was all I could do to breathe.

TWO

I took a shaky breath and looked down quickly. My hands were trembling so badly I almost dropped my camera.

His look was intense and completely mesmerizing. My whole chest constricted and when our eyes met, my breathing became shallow, and my throat tightened. Everything inside me became soft, liquid, and unbearably hot. It was as though an internal furnace had been turned on, and I had no way of releasing the pent up heat. I averted my eyes and pulled at the black pashmina artfully wrapped around my neck. I hoped I wasn't flushed from the unexpected flash of hot raging through me, but I was pretty sure I was glowing.

I didn't know how I would concentrate with him standing so close, but I made a valiant effort to ignore him and go about my work. At least I knew who he was now. He had to be one of Amanda and Ben's backers or a friend.

I bent to grab a flash and sneaked a peek at Stormy Eyes. He'd retreated to the bar with the rest of the group, and I breathed a little easier—until I saw he was still staring. Then my pulse skipped, and I had to look away again. If he was an investor, I had better act professionally. I didn't want to make Amanda and Ben look bad by falling to my knees in front of Stormy Eyes and begging him to take me then and there. But that's exactly what was flashing through my mind. A vision of sliding down his front, rubbing myself wantonly across every inch as I looked into those turbulent blue-grey eyes and mouthed, *take me*. I was still too warm, but I shivered as if a cold breeze had brushed across my heated skin, and I felt my nipples pebble into hard, sensitive nubs. *Oh shit*. I was in real trouble here.

I smiled uneasily and tried to forget the heat of his gaze as it bored into my back. My skin prickled everywhere while I finished setting up. I was probably being rude. He was looking at me so long and hard. I should have introduced myself. I should have asked his name, but I feared that would somehow break the spell. And though I was so warm and tight that I was uncomfortable, I didn't want the feeling to end. It had been so long since I'd felt anything but numbness. And I'd never, ever, been this aroused from nothing more than a man's look.

And then Amanda and Beckett came out with Ben's first plate of starters, and Amanda practically stumbled when she spotted Stormy Eyes. Any woman would stumble looking into a face like his. He was male perfection—all hard lines and planes and chiseled features. But then, she did the impossible. She recovered gracefully—I had to give her credit—approached him and embraced him.

So he was not a god. He could be seen by others. He could be touched. He could lean down and wrap his arms around a woman. At that moment, I felt intensely jealous. Obviously, Amanda was his girlfriend. Watching them embrace, I think I saw red blurring my vision. I could hear the low murmur of conversation, but I was far enough away that I couldn't make out what they were saying. I heard Amanda laugh and watched as she put her tiny hand on his upper arm, which looked, even from where I was standing, rock-solid.

"Cat?" Beckett looked toward the bar then back at me. I realized I was straining to eavesdrop, and I was staring, so I quickly averted my eyes and focused on Beckett. "Are you feeling okay?" he asked.

"Great." I dug in my bag to give myself something to do. I knew who Stormy Eyes was now. He was Amanda's boyfriend. I hated her, and at the same time, I understood. She was beautiful and petite and dainty—the exact opposite of me.

I was plain old me. Brown hair, not much makeup, a veritable Amazon at five-foot-six with an athletic build, more curves than straight lines, and dressed all in black like most urban, artsy types, but really because I hated to draw attention to myself. I'd always thought my green eyes were my best feature, but they didn't stand a chance when Amanda was a tiny, perfect package. "Is this the first shot?" I asked.

"Yes. Are you sure you're ready?" Beckett positioned the food. "Do you need a minute?"

"Nope." I said too brightly. "I'm ready." I moved to the other side of the table, looking for the best angle. It put my line of vision directly with the bar, but I made an enormous effort not to look. I didn't want to see Stormy Eyes touching Amanda, playing with her hair, kissing her neck, or caressing her perfect perky breasts.

My camera slipped, and I had to crouch, pretending I was going for a closer shot. The benefit was that I finally noticed the food. And then, I had to smile. I couldn't remember what Ben was calling these, but they were essentially pigs-in-a-blanket, made with lamb merguez sausage, topped with a spicy mustard sauce, and then wrapped in flaky puff pastry. They were a clever take on an old favorite, and when I'd tasted them yesterday, they'd been delicious. The wrappers were golden and crispy, and the filling was colorful and savory. I loved how they crunched initially, then turned creamy and wonderful in my mouth. Ben had taken something fabulous and used his skills to make it irresistible.

"There," Beckett said, stepping back and admiring his work. "Let's see how that photographs."

I immediately started snapping pictures. After a dozen shots, Beckett and I studied them, and he moved in with a few tweaks. He pulled one of his sprays from his bag and spritzed the lamb rolls then added color to a couple spots with his vegetable-based paints. Regardless of the natural products he used, the food was inedible now.

"How's that?" he asked.

I put the camera to my eye and snapped a shot. Beckett and I studied it. "Looks good," I said. "Let me do a few more, and we're ready for the next dish. Two-minute warning."

This was our code for Beckett to start his final prep on the next subject. He didn't like to put the final touches on too early because, as he put it, food had a perfect window. Style it too soon, and it would wilt before I took the first shots. Timing was important, and Beckett and I had it down.

I snapped a few more shots of the lamb bites, and then the next dishes came in rapid succession. Beckett brought me venison tartare with foie gras, marinated stuffed olives, and herb-roasted chicken tenders. All the while, I kept my head down, talked only to Beckett, and ignored Stormy Eyes. I didn't forget about him. My skin tingled when he was near, making me hyperaware. My bottom chafed against the soft wool of the skirt, and my breasts were too sensitive against the silk of my bra. Yet the food had its own allure, and it was enough to keep me from forgetting my reason for being there.

"That's the last starter," Beckett said. "I'm going to prep the first small plate."

"Sure." I rubbed the back of my neck and moved my head from side to side, trying to loosen up. "Give me about five minutes."

"I'll plate it and bring it out." He leaned close and whispered. "You're doing great!"

Those were exactly the words I needed. "Thanks." I breathed, feeling relieved. He headed for the kitchen, pausing at the monitor to study the last shots.

"What do you think about the farmhouse table for the small plates? Maybe a larger stage and a different look?" He shrugged and disappeared into the kitchen.

I took a step back, studied my setup, and decided Beckett was right. The farmhouse table was perfect. I loved the knotted wood and honey color. But it was too far back to give me the natural light I wanted, so I set my camera down and moved to the end to give it a shove.

It barely moved.

I shoved again, and the next thing I knew *he* was beside me.

"Allow me."

Oh, God. That voice again. That low, seductive voice that rumbled through me and vibrated into the depths of me. He'd said nothing provocative, and yet my body reacted as though he'd murmured, *spread your legs.*

I looked up at him—geez, he was tall—and kept an unaffected look on my face, but I don't think it worked. I felt wide-eyed and bowled over, and I suspected I looked it too. "I can get it," I said. "It's my job." The truth was it was physically painful to be this close and not touch him. If he'd been mine, instead of Amanda's, I would have killed any woman who looked at him. I needed to keep my distance.

"Absolutely not." The way he said it, with such authority and finality, stopped my protest completely. In fact, I stepped back, out of his way, and he moved the table with little effort. A quick glance at the bar told me no one was paying attention. Amanda wasn't standing there anymore. Only this tall, well-dressed man had noticed that I needed help and had come to my aid. "Here?" he asked, pausing.

I glanced at the table and nodded. He'd placed it almost perfectly. "Yes. But I think…" I moved to the table and gestured to show him I wanted it closer to the window. The sleet had finally stopped, and I wanted to take advantage of the clearer skies and brighter light. I placed my hands on the wood, ready to give the table a shove, but as I was about to push, his hands came down on top of mine. I hissed in a breath, and my body reacted as though an electric current had traveled from his fingers to my very center. I'd thought I was hot before, but now, I was on fire. I couldn't move, I couldn't speak, and all I wanted to do was press my body against his and find relief from the unbearable heat.

Slowly, he slid his hands off mine, placed them on either side of my palms, and leaned his body into me, moving the table as he did. His body was warm and solid behind me. I could feel the steel of his biceps, and above the scents of the food and the chemicals, there was another scent, something masculine and exotic I couldn't place. All I knew for certain was that I could feel him touching me, and every nerve in my body was alive and firing.

"Here?" he asked.

I made an unintelligible sound.

"Do you like it here?" he asked with more directness.

I was rendered momentarily speechless as I looked into his stormy eyes. I watched them widen as I licked my bottom lip and thought how to answer. At least my mouth wasn't hanging open. *Do you like it here?* This sounded as innuendo-laden as the quick one-liners that had floored me last night, the ones about my being screwed and him not being innocent. *Oh my.* Maybe I was reading this all wrong, but I didn't think so. "Oh, yes," I finally stammered with my heart racing.

He chuckled, moved away, and gave me that knowing expression. Again. "Good," he said, and then he turned and walked back to take his seat at the bar.

His absence felt like the cold January air sweeping down. I wanted my warmth back. I squeezed my eyes shut and gripped the table. *Stop.* I no more needed his kind of warmth than I needed a huge slab of decadent dark chocolate cake. I might want both, but they were not good for me. I had to remember why I was in Chicago and stay focused on my goals. Right now, my professional life was paramount. My personal life, what little there was of it, was on hold. That was fine because it was still too early to start dating again. I wasn't ready.

When I released the table, my hands still shook and my belly still fluttered, but I felt a little steadier. I knew my face was warm, and I probably looked flustered. I didn't think there was a woman alive who wouldn't have been flustered by this man.

"Don't kill me," Beckett announced, holding a plate high as he strode through the kitchen door. "Ben threw together one more starter, and I couldn't resist. This one is mucho sexy! I've sprayed it within an inch of its life so it's really shiny and juicy."

He set the plate on the table with a flourish, and my eyes widened. The dish was gorgeous and undeniably sexual. "What is it?" I said, my voice huskier than I'd intended.

"Figs. They're supposed to be an aphrodisiac."

I didn't look at Stormy Eyes. I wanted to. I could feel him looking at me, but I kept my gaze on the figs. Beckett pointed to the dish he'd plated. "These are wrapped in prosciutto and have a touch of goat cheese. They've been baked." He moved his hand, indicating another group of figs. I couldn't help but notice that in their raw state, the figs bore a close resemblance to the female sex organs. "These are raw, but there's a little crumble of Danish blue cheese in the middle, then they've been drizzled with warm spiced honey. Well, if you order them, they're drizzled with honey. This is syrup and something akin to motor oil. But wouldn't all the gooey honey be perfect for licking off your fingertips?"

I couldn't stop myself then. It was as if my eyes were independent of my brain. I looked at Stormy Eyes, and our gazes met. He smiled slowly, his eyes twinkling wickedly, his lips full and sensual, and I felt the spot between my legs throb in response. *Get a grip*, I told myself and raised my camera. The food was gorgeous, the lighting perfect, the restaurant amazing. I could very well take some of the best damn photos I'd ever taken. I wasn't going to let some guy with gorgeous eyes and extremely kissable lips get in the way.

Steeling myself, I snapped the first shot of the figs. It was blurry and unfocused, but that was okay. It was a start. Beckett and I conferred, and he was kind enough not to comment on how blurry my shot was. He reached in and used his tongs to move one of the raw figs slightly, and as the fruit shifted, the thick, gooey coating dripped down the side. The dollop of creamy cheese on top was softening and spreading thanks to the heat of the lamp. The whole dish looked luscious and juicy, and I envisioned a thick tongue slowly flicking across the top, lapping up the sweet deliciousness. *Oh fuck.* I steadied my aim, took a deep breath, and the next shot was perfect.

Beckett and I slipped into our routine, and the work felt natural and right. I snapped photo after photo of some of the most mouthwatering food I have ever seen. And all the while, I was starving. I should have eaten before heading over. The irony was that even though I was surrounded by delicious food, I couldn't have even a taste because it had been handled and sprayed with products.

And then there was the added irony of Stormy Eyes. I could feel his gaze. I could feel it touching me, caressing me, arousing me. But he, too, was untouchable. I tried to push my X-rated thoughts away, but they lingered in the back of my mind, threatening to surface whenever I let my guard down. The air in the restaurant crackled with tension and attraction, but I kept my head down, my camera up, and worked until it became rote.

I was snapping pictures of apple-cheddar tartlets and lemon panna cotta with blackberries when my stomach growled loudly enough for Beckett to hear. "Cat, you're starving!" he exclaimed. I resisted glancing at the bar, mortified that he might have heard too.

"I'm fine." I waved a hand, not wanting to stop now that I had momentum going. Not wanting to allow my attention to drift, once again, to Stormy Eyes. "This is the last of it anyway, right?" I asked Beckett, who had leaned in with one of his tongs to push a berry a fraction to the left on the plate.

I glanced up to see Ben and Amanda standing beside the monitor and smiling. Ben glanced at the last shots, gave me a thumbs up, and I nodded and finished the final photos. "I'm going to take a few of the interior," I called out. I'd taken some already, but I wanted aerial shots. I also wanted to get away from the penetrating gaze of Stormy Eyes. "I'll take a look at these right away. I'd be happy to bring the proofs by tomorrow." This wasn't something I needed to do, but it was a little extra I liked to throw in. If Ben liked the shots, he might recommend me to his chef friends or request me the next time he was featured in a magazine.

"That would be great!" Amanda said.

"If *Chicago Now* wants more?" Ben asked.

"No problem. I'd be happy to come back and shoot as many photos as it takes. I want to make sure you're pleased and that the magazine is pleased. Whatever it takes."

"They won't need her to come back," Beckett chimed in confidently. "*Chicago Now* is going to be blown away."

As I headed up the metal staircase to the loft above the restaurant, I wished I felt as confident as Beckett. Normally, I didn't question my abilities. In California, my surfing photos had been featured in several magazines and on tons of surfing websites, and my career had been in high gear. But in the realm of food photography, I was a complete unknown, and Fresh Market's phallic kebab ads were my highest profile credit to date. I knew it was going to be like this here—all the insecurity and self-doubt that went along with starting from scratch and trying to make a name for myself—and I was ready. But today, I'd felt off. It had nothing to do with my abilities with a camera and everything to do with Mr. Mystery with the unsettling eyes, or more specifically, my reaction to him. I glanced at the bar. He was gone. My chest clenched with disappointment. I'd wanted… I don't know what I wanted, but I hadn't wanted him to leave. But maybe it was better this way. Now I could concentrate on my job.

I raised my camera and took a couple shots of the main dining area below, then stepped back to look at them.

"Do you ever take a break?" a velvet voice I recognized asked.

I looked up, holding my camera in front of me as a shield. There he was, leaning against the railing, his body long and loose, his posture that of a sleek cat ready to pounce. I noticed his eyes were blue rather than grey now—how could I not notice—but they were still the blue of a dangerous, turbulent sea. He smiled, and his smile was predatory, not reassuring.

"Sometimes." My voice was breathy, seductive. I didn't mean it to be, but this man's effect on me was unavoidable. He moved closer, and I thought about moving back, but I didn't. This close, he was as gorgeous as I remembered. His hair was thick and wavy, and I felt the familiar pull of wanting to run my fingers through it. His brows were an elegant slash over mesmerizing eyes, and he had more than a hint of a five o'clock shadow on his jaw. I wondered how it would feel against my skin. He wore his suit well, looking as comfortable as most men did in jeans and a T-shirt. It was an expensive suit, but he owned it. I didn't have to think too hard to imagine what his body looked like under that suit—broad shoulders, lean waist, narrow hips, and muscled thighs. I had felt his rock-hard biceps when he helped me move the table.

"Something you said downstairs intrigued me." His fingers played on the railing beside me, and my skin prickled as I thought of how just a slight movement on his part would have us touching.

Don't ask. Don't ask.

"What was that?" I couldn't resist. There was something about his eyes. I couldn't look away. They were going grey again.

"You told the chef you'd do whatever it took to please him."

My cheeks heated when he repeated my words. Stormy Eyes made them sound... erotic—up here, in the semi-darkness, just the two of us, alone. His eyes were locked on mine, and I couldn't look away.

"Do you have that same philosophy in bed?" He reached out, and his long fingers stroked my hand. They were aristocratic fingers, long and strong and beautifully manicured. I clenched my fingers tightly around my camera. Everything in me wanted to scream, *Yes!* My body was willing to do anything to keep this man touching me, looking at me, speaking to me, and I could feel myself responding, yet alarm bells went off in my head.

"What's going on?" I finally sputtered. "What's this about?"

"I should think that would be obvious." His direct gaze never wavered. "I want you."

I was stunned into silence. When I didn't answer, he moved closer. I swayed because I felt the heat of him, and there was that scent again—smoky and intoxicating.

"I want to fuck you. Hard. Long," he whispered. "Until you come and come and think you can't come anymore."

I felt like I was going to melt into a puddle. I didn't understand. I hated arrogant come-ons—not that I'd ever had a man come-on to me quite like this—yet my legs were quaking, my breath had been snatched away, and my panties were wet. I'd never been so immediately and so unequivocally aroused by a man. Not even Jace. But where was the basic civility, the: "Hi, I'm so-and-so. Nice to meet you." I didn't even know who this guy was and the fact that a part of me didn't care—and was screaming *oh yes!* in my head—well, all my alarm bells got even louder.

I shook my head and backed away. I had to put some distance between us, or I'd never say what I needed to. My heart thudded in my chest, racing so fast I felt as if I'd just run three miles, but I was going to say this. "I don't know who the hell you think you are, but your chances of getting me into bed are exactly zero."

He raised a dubious brow, and my heart kicked up a notch.

"I don't know you, and I don't want to know you. So why don't you just go back to your girlfriend and leave me alone?" I stomped away, tossing my hair over my shoulder for good measure. I hated girls who did that, but it seemed appropriate in this instance. And besides, I needed every trick in the book to prove, if only to myself, that I could actually walk away. Inside I was so hot for him. My whole body heated up from just one look, so his words had ignited an inferno. When he'd touched me, I went absolutely liquid.

I took the stairs as quickly as I could without tripping over my uncertain feet. I wanted to look up, but I didn't need to. I could feel his gaze, and he was angry. I had seen the flash of irritation in his eyes. It turned them from that smoky grey to icy blue.

"Did you get what you needed?" Beckett asked when I was back downstairs.

"What do you mean?" I asked breathlessly. Oh no. Had he heard? Had the entire restaurant heard? Did everyone know what just happened?

Beckett gave me an odd look. "Did you get the shots you needed?"

Oh, thank God. "I think so." I was so flustered, so completely off my game. My head was spinning, and all I could think of was *his* proposition—*I want to fuck you. Hard. Long.*

I shuddered from the thought of the pleasure of him inside me.

"How about a few of the kitchen?" Beckett suggested.

"Of course." At that point I would have done anything to get away from *his* gaze. I grabbed more batteries and a lamp and braved one last look at the loft. Stormy Eyes was gone. A part of me was devastated, but the part that valued logic and self-preservation cheered.

*****

"Coffee?" Beckett asked after we'd told Ben and Amanda good-bye and stowed my gear in the Volvo. "I know you want to work on the shots, but you look a little drained."

"Okay," I said.

"That was easy." Beckett slung an arm around me and led me to the next block, where we found a Starbucks, ordered, and plopped into large purple armchairs. "I ordered you a scone," Beckett said immediately. "And don't argue. You need nourishment."

"Okay."

Beckett's eyes widened. "What's with you? You're never this easy."

I laughed. "Apparently, that's not the vibe I was giving off all morning." Over a mocha and a warm scone, I told Beckett about Stormy Eyes. When I got to the part in the loft, Beckett's eyes widened, and he shook his head.

"Shit, Cat! You turned him down? How could you?"

"How could I?" I almost spit out my mocha, not believing that Beckett would question my response. "He's a jerk. He didn't even know my name, and he propositioned me. He said he wanted to fuck me, for God's sake. Who does that?" I took another sip. I'd only managed to nibble the scone. I was starving, but not for food.

"I'll tell you who does that. A guy who goes after exactly what he wants does that."

I couldn't believe that Beckett was on *his* side and thought *I* should have acted differently. He continued. "Do you know who your Stormy Eyes is?"

"An asshole?"

"Well, possibly But he's also William Lambourne. The third."

I blinked. "So?"

"So? William Lambourne is Chicago's most eligible bachelor."

"He's Chicago's most *arrogant* bachelor," I retorted.

"He can afford to be arrogant. He's rich. As in billionaire rich, Cat. Old money. And he owns… everything. Hotels, vineyards, real estate—"

"Restaurants?"

"Of course."

"Does he own Willowgrass?"

Beckett shrugged. "I don't think so, but I wouldn't be surprised if he was one of the investors. That's why I thought he was there. But now that we know he was who you ran into yesterday, I'm beginning to think maybe he was there to see you."

Beckett couldn't possibly be serious. "Me? Oh please, I'm hardly worth going to all that trouble for. No way he was there to see me."

Beckett rolled his eyes. "Hello! Earth to Cat." He took my face in his hands. "Have you looked in a mirror lately? You're gorgeous. All that thick brown hair, those green eyes, and you don't have an inch of fat on you. What are you? A size two?"

I rolled my eyes. "Six, sometimes an eight."

"A curvy, sexy six. Who wouldn't want you?" This was a familiar conversation. Beckett and I had known each other since we were fourteen. He had always been the skinny boy who loved to cook. I was the artsy, insecure girl who hadn't been surprised when he came out before our senior year of high school. We'd always supported one another. I'd been there when his father disowned him because he was gay, and he'd been there after everything happened with Jace.

"I think he's dating Amanda," I said, thinking of Stormy Eyes.

Beckett shook his head. "First of all, William Lambourne doesn't date women. Women are seen with him, but never the same woman too many times. And his taste leans toward women who are beautiful, independent, and socially connected. Besides, Amanda's married."

"What?" I didn't see that one coming. Amanda and Stormy Eyes had looked so familiar at the restaurant, and after the presumptions I'd made, it was hard to believe there wasn't anything between them. "Why would I want to be seen with him? And how do you know all this anyway?"

"I actually read *Chicago Now*, Cat, usually while I'm on the treadmill at the gym. You should too, by the way. And why wouldn't you want to be seen with him? You'd look great together. You need some fun." Beckett put a hand over mine and squeezed. "Let's talk about it, honey. We never talk about it."

Oh no. He wanted to talk about Jace. And about why I was here—what I never wanted to talk to about. Red flag, red flag, red flag! No matter how much I avoided talking about this, it didn't change anything.

I was twenty-five years old and a real anomaly: a widow. I'd been a widow longer than I'd been a wife. Jace and I had been married for only six months before he died. We got married two weeks after I graduated from UC-Santa Cruz, and for a time, I had everything I thought I ever wanted. I was married to my soul mate, I had a great career doing something I loved, and our life together was exciting. And all of it had been taken away in an instant. To say I had been devastated was an understatement. It took forever, but I had finally climbed out of the deep well of misery I'd dwelled in for so long after the accident. I found the balls to leave Santa Cruz and to start the next phase of my life. All good things and Beckett was a huge part of it, and I loved him for it. But that didn't mean I was ready to have fun with any guy, let alone with a dangerously sexy billionaire bachelor.

I resisted, but I felt tears well up in my eyes and squeezed the familiar sting back. I would not cry again. I'd cried all the tears I had. I offered my standard response. "I don't want to talk about it." I was too vulnerable today. All my emotions were on the surface.

"That's fine," Beckett replied and let it go, sort of. "But consider having a little fun. You're entitled to it, Cat. And it's time. William Lambourne is the perfect guy for you. He's a player, and obviously, anything long-term isn't his style. As long as you know what you're getting into, what's the problem? I hear he's fabulous in bed. You should totally tap that, Cat. If the man was bi, I'd be all over him."

I shook my head. "I don't care about his money or his looks. I'm not interested."

"Uh-huh." Beckett took a sip of his coffee. "That's your story, huh?"

"How do you know he's great in bed? Who told you that? *Chicago Now*?"

Beckett looked sheepish and then laughed. "Okay, well, nobody told me that. Shit, Cat, of course, a guy like that is fabulous in bed. How could he not be? I'm trying to entice you. Letting go can be a good thing, you know."

Who was I kidding? I wasn't fooling Beckett, and I sure as hell wasn't fooling myself. My body still ached for Stormy Eyes. My hand still tingled where he'd touched it. My heart still pounded too quickly. I'd never met a man with that kind of magnetism. Not even Jace had affected me that way. And that's why the attraction felt like a betrayal. But Beckett was right. I was only twenty-five. Widow or not, I had to start living again. I didn't want to admit this to Beckett, but when I'd been alone with William Lambourne in the loft, for just a moment, he'd been all I could think about. I'd forgotten about the past, about what I'd done, and that scared the shit out of me.

*****

Beckett tried to talk me into a late lunch, but I told him I needed to get home and edit the pictures. He didn't argue, but when I got home the shots I took at Willowgrass were the farthest thing on my mind. I couldn't stop thinking about William Lambourne, Chicago's most eligible billionaire. I wished I had a few shots of him. I wondered if all his thick hair would look as soft and glossy on film as it did in real life. I wondered if I would have been able to capture his changing eyes or the shadow of his stubble or the easy way he moved.

It was still cold outside, but the sleet hadn't returned, so I whistled to Laird, got his leash, and we headed out. I didn't arrow for the lakeshore, and instead, we walked through the neighborhood. I hoped a little window-shopping would keep my mind occupied, but apparently, there weren't enough boutiques to ward off the allure of William Lambourne.

I couldn't stop thinking about the intensity of his gaze, the way his eyes darkened from blue to grey, and the sound of his voice as it caressed me in the loft. *I want you.*

I closed my eyes against the wave of dizzy arousal that hit me just remembering his words. *I want to fuck you.*

It had been a long time since someone looked at me that way and... I liked it. I liked the feeling of a man wanting me—a man like William Lambourne. It had been a long time since I'd thought of myself as sexy, and he made me feel sexier than I ever had.

For the first time, I thought that maybe, just maybe, I shouldn't have told him no.

THREE

I spent Thursday morning holed up in my condo, processing and editing my photos of Ben Lee's food. I didn't mind being inside. I loved my condo, and even if it didn't feel like home yet, it was cozy and comfortable. The light from the French windows made it bright and cheery, even on winter days. The floors were hardwood, and I'd painted the walls in pretty neutrals to offset the framed photographs I'd hung. The photos were a mix of images I'd captured during my travels—exotic flowers, serene beaches, plumed birds, shadowed trees, and unusual buildings. I had been careful to hang only still photos, nothing with action or motion. Nothing from Santa Cruz. No pictures of Jace. The irony that I was a professional photographer who launched her career taking candid photos of her athlete husband, but didn't display those images, wasn't lost on me. But I hadn't wanted my new home to become a shrine to Jace and to everything I'd lost. I needed the illusion of a clean slate. Maybe I overcompensated by not having *any* pictures of Jace around, but it seemed like a good idea to leave those memories boxed up.

My bedroom was a little smaller than I would have liked, the queen-size bed taking up half the room, but the living room was large and spacious, more than making up for it. There was a great nook near the window where I'd put my desk and my computer, and this was where I did most of my work. The master bedroom was off the living room, so I could jump out of bed and walk fifteen steps to my "office." I liked working in my pajamas, cozy and snug, while outside the living room windows, Chicago was blustery and cold.

There was a second bedroom near the front door, which I intended for guests, but I hadn't had any yet, so I kept my unpacked boxes shoved in the closet, along with my summer wardrobe. The whole place had been renovated, the kitchen most heavily. Minerva told me the former tenants were avid foodies, which explained why they spent so much money on the kitchen. Apparently, they were crushed that they couldn't take the AGA, but it weighed half a ton and moving it out wasn't feasible. The behemoth cooker was there to stay. Too bad I didn't cook. But I did like a bubble bath on occasion, and one day I wanted to enlarge the master bath and make it truly decadent. *That* I could appreciate.

So Thursday I settled in, throwing a fragrant log in the wood-burning fireplace and enjoying the piney smellwhile my eyes feasted on the mouthwatering photos I'd taken. Occasionally, I looked out the large windows to the right of my desk. The day had dawned clear and sunny, and it was still hard for me to comprehend how it could be so bright and still so cold. Of course, we had cold weather in Santa Cruz, but it was damp cold and didn't usually last for months. The Chicago cold was biting and bone-chilling. I learned about windchill here too.

That's when it feels colder than it actually is because of the wind. And it was windy in the Windy City.

The sky looked the same though. In Santa Cruz, a bright blue sky would have called me to the beach. Now I was happy to be bundled up inside. I had to admit, my condo might not have the views our Santa Cruz place did, but it had its perks. One advantage to having a large, renovated kitchen was that the pantry was the perfect size for a darkroom. I'm sure the former owners would have choked if I'd told them my plans for their spacious pantry, but the darkroom had been finished before I had sheets on my bed.

I took a short break from editing. I couldn't help myself, so I typed "William Lambourne" into my Google browser. Pages of links to business articles filled my screen and I could feel my eyes glaze over. I read enough to learn that William was the head of WML Capital Management, which managed investments "in a wide range of asset classes, including private equity, hedge funds, real estate, and entertainment ventures." I wasn't sure what all that meant, but Beckett was obviously right. William Lambourne really did own everything. I clicked over to images, which were my speed, and the first picture that came up made me catch my breath. There he was, in all his stormy-eyed handsomeness, staring back at me. I could have spent all day looking at him on my screen, but I did have work to finish, so I forced my attention to pictures of honey-dripped figs and delicious desserts.

Later that day, I took Laird for a quick walk then drove to Willowgrass to show Ben and Amanda the images I intended to submit to *Chicago Now*. Outside, the street was empty, but when I stepped inside, the place was a hive of activity, and I was momentarily bewildered. Men and women moved purposefully about, shouting orders, and rushing here and there with clipboards, crates of fresh produce, and cases of wine.

"Catherine!"

I looked up to see Amanda waving from the loft dining area. She looked calm and beautiful in winter white cashmere. I waved back and wished I'd worn something cuter than dark-wash jeans, boots, and an oversized sweater with a T-shirt underneath. At least I had a filmy scarf tied around my neck.

"I'll be right down."

I waited, looking around as unobtrusively as possible. I didn't think there was much chance William Lambourne would be there, but that didn't stop me from secretly hoping. Amanda waved me to the bar, and I made my way around decorators, electricians, and stagers. I had a proof sheet printed, as well as the images on my tablet, and as soon as I opened the digital file, Amanda swiped through them. She scanned each photo carefully before she gave a nod and moved on to the next. Finally, she finished and handed the tablet back with a huge smile. "These are fabulous. Perfect! You're a genius!"

"Well, the food was beautiful, and that made my job easy. And please, keep the proof sheet."

Amanda clutched my arm. "Thanks. You should come to the opening party tomorrow night."

I hopped off the barstool. "Oh, you don't have to invite me."

She shook her head, and I could see I was not going to dissuade her. "Beckett is coming, and I want you there, so we can introduce everyone to the fabulous photographer who took these gorgeous shots. Besides, I wouldn't want to disappoint our investors." She winked.

I gave her a perplexed frown.

She leaned into me. "William Lambourne asked about you after the shoot. He was that tall, dark-haired man in the grey suit? You must have noticed him. He seemed quite taken with you."

"Really?" I tried to act nonchalant, but I felt a spark of fiery heat flare in my belly. "I don't even know him."

"How romantic! You have to come to the party and meet him officially then. I'll introduce you myself. It starts at eight." And then she melted into the crowd of workers.

And that's how I ended up standing in front of my closet on Friday night, trying to figure out what to wear to a restaurant opening party—what to wear to see William Lambourne again. I heard my cell ring in the living room and called, "Beckett, will you get that?" Beckett was fetching wine, even though there would be plenty at the opening. I needed fortification beforehand. He knew I wasn't comfortable at big parties, so he'd shown up with a bottle of white in one hand and a bottle of red in the other.

"Sure!" A moment later, I heard him answer, "Well, hello to you too, Jill! How *are* you?"

Ugh. My mother. I was so not in the mood for her flakiness. I could put her off, but it would only prolong the inevitable. And there was no hoping she'd call back at a more opportune time. She always called at the worst times. She had some inborn sense of when I felt insecure and harried.

Beckett's voice grew closer, so I opened my bedroom door and held out my hand. Beckett made a circling sign, indicating my mother was going on and on, and then finally he said, "Oh, Jill, here's Cat. Bye, now. Kisses!"

"Hi, Mom."

Beckett breezed past me and peered into my closet, immediately shoving dresses aside and shaking his head.

"Hi, baby." My mother's voice was too loud and too bright. And too... southern? "How are you?"

"Good. I'm sort of getting ready—"

"Oh, good, good! Catherine, honey, I told you about Bobby Parsons, didn't I?"

I should have known she wouldn't want to hear about me. Why did I even try? "Bobby Parsons? Um, I don't think so."

Beckett held up a red dress I'd bought ages ago. It still had the tags on it. I shook my head and mouthed, *no red.*

"He's the art collector? From Texas?" That explained the fake accent. My mother was like a chameleon, never uncomfortable in any situation. She just changed herself to adapt.

"Still doesn't sound familiar, Mom." I sipped my wine. Between my mother and Beckett, I might need more than one glass.

"Oh, honey, I told you!" She lowered her voice to a whisper. "Remember—he's rich and divorced?" Not surprisingly, this description did not help. *Rich* and *divorced* described every one of my mother's boyfriends.

Beckett pulled out an orange dress and shook it enticingly. I covered the receiver. "No way!" What had I been thinking when I bought that? I'd look like a pumpkin in that thing. "Listen, Mom, I need to wrap this up. Can you tell me why you're calling?"

"Of course." She sounded cold now. I was an expert on my mother's moods, but anyone would have known she was annoyed at my dismissal. "I can see you have more important things to do."

"Mom…" I sipped more wine.

"I'm leaving tomorrow for St. Barts with Bobby. I didn't want you to worry."

I almost choked on the wine. "Not worry? I don't even know this guy! How long will you be gone?"

"Just ten days." She sounded as though she was smiling. She loved nothing better than to shock.

Ten days! How serious was this? I wasn't exactly shocked, but I hadn't seen this coming.

"There's nothing to worry about. I'll email you with the travel details."

"Mom, no. I really don't think this is the best idea."

"Catherine, really. Learn to live a little!"

I rolled my eyes, even though she couldn't see—especially because she couldn't see. Beckett pulled out a beige dress with a black geometric pattern and made a face.

"Have you followed through on your resolution?"

The stupid New Year's resolution. I knew I shouldn't have spent New Year's Eve with my mother. "Mom, that was your resolution for me. Not mine. I don't want to date right now."

Beckett's head snapped up, and he pointed as if to say, *listen to your mother*.

"Don't want to date?" To my mother, the idea was ludicrous. A woman without a man was like a ring without a diamond. "What are you waiting for? You're an intelligent, successful, attractive young woman. It's time you got back out there. Jace—"

"Mom—" I had a good idea what she would say next, and I didn't want to hear it, so I cut her off. "I'm going out tonight, so I really have to go."

"Wait a minute. You're going out tonight? Why didn't you say so?"

"I did say so!"

"Who are you going out with?"

I sighed. "Beckett. We're going to a really hip restaurant opening party. Lots of eligible guys will be there." Including William Lambourne. "And I'll think about going on a date. Soon, okay?"

"Promise me, honey." And the accent was back again. I wanted to remind her she had been born in Southern California, not South Carolina, but I kept my mouth shut.

"Sure."

"Ya'll take care now."

"We will. Bye. Love you." I flopped down on my bed. I looked at Beckett and whined, "Do I have to go? Can't I make popcorn, sit on the couch, and watch a movie instead?"

"You have to go." Beckett pulled me up. "I'm not seeing the perfect outfit in this closet. Tell me you've already chosen it and are waiting to surprise me with the big reveal."

"That's it, exactly." I walked to my closet, thumbed through hanger after hanger of black and pulled out a classic cashmere sweaterdress. It had a high neck and would keep me warm, plus the black would ensure I blended with the crowd.

"Oh, no! I would accuse you of joking, but I know you too well." Beckett shoved the dress back in my closet. "You are not wearing that. That's for traffic court or for a job interview at a cardboard box factory. Totally not appropriate for a sexy, restaurant opening party for the hottest new chef in Chicago. No, no, no."

"I thought *you* were the hottest chef in Chicago."

Beckett grinned. "Flattery will get you everywhere—except into that dress. You need something sexy. Show off that rockin' bod. The billionaire might be there..."

"I really don't care if he is. I have nothing to say to the jerk." I couldn't look at Beckett when I said this because I knew he'd see through me in an instant.

"You haven't even thought about him?"

"Not even once." Bald-faced lie. I hadn't *not* thought about Stormy Eyes for more than five minutes—his voice, his lips, his hard body. How much I would have liked to feel that body pressed against mine again.

I want to fuck you.

Beckett raised his brows. "Your cheeks are pink, Cat. *What* are you thinking about? Rather, *who* are you thinking about?" He held out the red dress.

"No, Beckett. No red. I don't want to scream for attention. I want to blend with the crowd, you know?" But did I? Did I really? It had been a long time since I'd dressed for a man. I'd forgotten how exciting it could be—the sexy lingerie, the flirty outfit, the anticipation of his response. I secretly wanted to wow William Lambourne. I wanted his jaw to drop, and Beckett was right. The black sweaterdress wouldn't do it. Still, I protested. "I'm not interested in William Lambourne's attention," I said and tried to make myself believe it. Lie, lie, lie.

"Honey, you could wear a paper bag, and that man would notice you. You're gorgeous, and it's obvious he wants you. He *told* you he wants you. How more obvious can you get?" Now, he leaned closer and raised his brows conspiratorially. "Why not torment him a little? Make him sorry for his obnoxious come-on at Willowgrass?"

It was the perfect incentive because Beckett knew I had a competitive streak and could be a little vengeful—not in a *Fatal Attraction* kind of way, but in a you-got-me-but-I'll-get-you-back kind of way.

Beckett reached in my closet and pulled out several items, holding them up to form an outfit. "How about this?"

I had to admit that the outfit had potential. "I don't know…" I could feel my lips curving into a smile. I could see what Beckett was going for, and it wasn't bad. It wasn't bad at all.

*****

An hour later, I walked into Willowgrass looking hot. I didn't need anyone to tell me. I knew it. Beckett had impeccable taste, and his styling was always spot-on. Even I couldn't argue with his choice for the evening. I'd slid into the sleek, fitted leather pants I had worn only one time since I bought them, the tissue-thin, metallic silver tank top, and the vintage man's tuxedo jacket like I'd worn the outfit a thousand times. To top it off, I wore black stiletto booties. I never in a million years would have thought to put these pieces together, but when Beckett did it, I looked amazing.

What Beckett didn't know—or maybe he did—was that underneath I was equally sexy. I had on my favorite dove grey La Perla bra with embroidered cups that had the added advantage of pushing my breasts up, giving me notable cleavage. Yes, my girls were really standing out tonight. I had on the tiny matching thong that went with the bra. If Stormy Eyes could only see me in this… not that I cared what he thought. Much.

Willowgrass was crowded and loud and filled with beautiful people. Music reverberated through the space, and the bass blended with the voices of Chicago's hippest as they mingled and celebrated Ben Lee's new venture. Beckett yelled above the roar that he would find me a drink and disappeared into the crowd.

I shifted from one foot to the other, never sure what to do at these events or whom to talk to. Handsome waiters circled with trays of Ben's creations. I recognized all the dishes, and my stomach growled. Now that I wasn't working with the food, and Beckett wasn't spraying it with chemicals to make it shiny, I definitely wanted to taste it again. Then the hair on my arms prickled, and I gave a slight shiver. When I turned, I found William Lambourne standing beside me. He just appeared, seemingly out of nowhere. He gave me a wolfish grin, and his grey eyes were full of… hunger. I couldn't stop my gaze from sliding over him. He looked amazing in a classic, slim black suit. I could tell without seeing the tag that it was expensive. Very expensive. He'd paired it with a blue spread collar shirt and a meridian blue tie that set off his stormy eyes. I made the mistake of looking into his eyes then and caught my breath.

Those gorgeous eyes looked particularly turbulent, so much so that I had trouble catching my breath. I really couldn't remember seeing a man I would have called beautiful, but that's what this man was. He was beautiful. I had the fiercest urge to reach out and caress the plane of his cheek, trail my fingers down his arm, and feel his hard, toned bicep flex and release. Even as I had the thought, he acted.

This happened in about thirty seconds, so to anyone observing it must have looked like I was standing there, staring. "I'm so glad to see you here tonight, Catherine. Why don't you come with me?" He purred this into my ear, and then he kissed me gently on the cheek. It was unexpected and almost sweet, and the gesture turned me on as much as it stunned me. And then I caught his scent. This time I could identify it—a heady mix of smoky whiskey and cinnamon on his breath. I had never smelled something so delicious. I was already slayed, liquid inside, and ready to do whatever he asked.

I felt the pressure of his hand on my lower back, warm and solid, dangerously close to the curve of my ass, and the boom of the bass was drowned by the thrumming of blood in my ears. I didn't resist and was expertly propelled forward through the packed room, the crowds parting as though we were royalty. And maybe that's what William Lambourne was: Chicago royalty.

I caught Beckett's eye as I was escorted to the back of the restaurant. He was holding two drinks, but he set one down and gave me an unabashed thumbs up and a huge smile. I felt my cheeks heat, but I rolled my eyes and kept walking.

William—Stormy Eyes—I didn't know what to call him since we still hadn't been formally introduced—directed me to an open space at the end of the bar. Wonder of wonders, there were two open bar stools. Imagine that. In a place as packed as this, two seats were waiting. I barely had time to climb into my chair before the bartender set two drinks in front of Stormy Eyes. William nodded and slid one drink in front of me. He leaned close, and there was that dizzying scent again. "It's bourbon. Three fingers. Neat. It's meant to be sipped," he murmured, his voice low and velvet soft. "Let it linger in your mouth and heat up, then swallow. You'll feel the warmth right here." He leaned and touched my chest above the valley between my breasts. I jumped. I didn't expect him to touch me there, and even without sipping the bourbon, I could feel the heat building in me. How did he do that? How did he make taking a drink sound so sexual? I warmed just from the sexy timbre of his voice. Part of me wanted to do exactly what he said. Part of me wanted, desperately, to see what would happen next.

Another part of me glared. Another part of me seethed, unable to believe the nerve of this guy. Billionaire or not, no man had the right to drag me through a party, corner me, and then order me to drink something I didn't even order. Brown liquor and I weren't friends, and when I had indulged in the past—okay, admittedly too many shots of Jack Daniel's at a college party probably didn't compare with whatever pricy elixir was in the glass in front of me—it hadn't gone well. I leveled my gaze at him. "I don't know if this is your attempt at an apology, but it sucks." What the hell. I lifted the glass, slammed down the bourbon in one swallow—no point in wasting it—and with my eyes watering, tried to rise from my stool, intent on making this the last of my encounters with Stormy Eyes. I wasn't ready for this or for him.

The pressure of William's hand on my thigh halted me. Firmly, he pushed me into my seat. "I clearly offended you the other day," he said, his fingers spreading. "Believe me when I say, I'm not usually so forward. Catherine."

I could feel the liquor coursing through me, and I looked at his hand, still on my thigh. "Yes, I can see you're the shy, retiring type, Mr. Lambourne."

He laughed, a full, rich sound that reverberated, heating me up more than the bourbon. "I admit, I value directness. Sometimes I'm too direct, but subtlety has never been my style." Another bourbon appeared before me, but I didn't touch it. I couldn't look away from those eyes. "Please, call me William. Or Will, if you like. Mr. Lambourne is a little too formal, don't you think?"

I narrowed my eyes, and he gave me an innocent look.

"I'm glad you're here. I want you to stay." He continued talking. "Catherine, I like you. Very much. I promise, I'm going to be on my best behavior from now on."

How could he possibly think that he liked me when he didn't know me? I was trying to make sense of what he'd said while feeling the effect of the bourbon, and then a voice said from behind us, "I see you've finally met!"

I turned and saw Amanda smiling.

"William Lambourne, this is Catherine Kelly. She's a wonderful photographer. Catherine, this is William Lambourne, and William is..." She hesitated, "Well, William is incorrigible."

"Thank you, Miss Lee," William said, cutting her off before she could say more.

With a grin, Amanda strode away.

"So, is incorrigible a job description?" I asked. "Or do you have another title? I didn't think being bad was an actual profession." I couldn't believe I was bantering like this, as I was more the stunned into silence type, not the witty comeback type.

He sipped his bourbon. "I have titles, but I won't bore you. And Amanda's exaggerating. I'm hardly beyond reform. Anyway, I'm more interested in finding out about you, Catherine." The way he said my name made a lump rise in my throat. His tongue rolled over the word slowly. "I understand you're new to Chicago. What brought you here?"

I couldn't do this. I couldn't play the game, allow myself to think this could go somewhere. So I blurted it out. "Listen, I'm really not interested in whatever it is you have in mind. I should go find my friend." I started to rise from my seat again, but his firm pressure on my thigh increased, and he pushed me down.

"Catherine, you have no idea what I have in mind. If you want to find your friend, alright. But before you do, I'd like to make sure that I see you again."

"Why?" I tried hard to hold to my defenses, but that hot, liquid feeling raged through me as I watched his gaze narrow.

He gave me his knowing look. "We have a connection. You know it, and so do I."

"I don't know anything," I lied.

He leaned forward. "Do you know what I'd do right now if we were alone?"

The idea of being alone with him made me tremble slightly, and I reminded myself to breathe. "I thought you were behaving."

There was that boyish grin again. I really liked that grin. "You have no idea how well I am behaving, Catherine. If we were alone, I'd peel you out of those leather pants. Taking my time. I've been trying to imagine what you're wearing underneath, and it's driving me crazy. I want to strip you down and touch your breasts."

I really couldn't believe I was sitting there listening to him. Even worse, he was making me hot. My nipples hardened with arousal, aching for his touch, and I'm sure he noticed. I had to make a conscious effort not to push my arms against them to ease the tingling.

"You have exquisite breasts. Do you know that?"

I didn't answer. My breasts felt heavy and sensitive from his gaze alone.

"I want my mouth on them. I want to kiss them, suckle them, and roll those hard nipples over my tongue. Would you like that, Catherine? Would you like it if I put my mouth on you?"

I couldn't answer. I didn't have the words. While he spoke, his warm hand made gentle circles on my thigh, the rhythm steady and erotic. I sipped the second bourbon without thinking. I needed something to do, something to wet my parched throat.

"You seem like a man accustomed to getting what you want," I said finally, trying not to think about the stroke of his hand. I could feel the heat from his touch radiating higher and higher, pressing between my legs, making me throb.

"I always get what I want, Catherine. I always get exactly what I want."

"Is that sort of bravado supposed to be sexy? You won't get me." Oh, what was I doing? *Yes, yes, yes* was like a chorus in my head, but I couldn't let this happen, let anything happen. As much as I responded, I wasn't ready.

He shrugged. "I do love a challenge, but I can see you want me. Why don't you just give in?"

I sipped the bourbon again. "It's tempting."

"There's nothing wrong with giving into temptation now and again."

"You're tempting." I couldn't believe I'd said that. I never talked like this.

He reached out and ran a finger down my cheek. "Catherine, you have no idea the ways I could tempt you."

"I don't do one-night stands or the fuck-buddy thing. I don't do *just* sex, William. And I'm not relationship material." Who was I kidding? I didn't *do* anything, and I really didn't know what I might do or even what I wanted to do. Beckett said I should have fun, but I didn't think I could, now that fun was staring me in the face and had told me he wanted to put my nipples in his mouth.

He looked nonplussed. "We can work something out. Think about it, Catherine. I can take care of you and give you what you need. Right now, you're cold. Chicago isn't nearly as warm as Santa Cruz. Let me take you to a warm, wet beach. Say the word, and we can go tonight."

I stared, the haze of arousal and bourbon clearing. "Wait a minute. You know I'm from Santa Cruz?"

"It's not a secret."

I grabbed his hand, halting the maddening circles on my thigh. "What else do you know?"

I saw a flicker of a shield in his eyes now, a grey shadow in the otherwise blue depths. He didn't say anything but kept rubbing my thigh. I moved to push his hand away.

"Do you know where I live?"

He didn't answer.

"What else?" I jumped from the bar stool. "My parents' names? Where I went to school?" Oh, my God. I couldn't believe I'd let this whole thing go this far. What had I been thinking? I wasn't ready for a relationship, and I certainly wasn't ready for a relationship with a man who aroused me more than I cared to admit and frightened me too. If he could find out where I lived and where I was from, what else could he find out?

I wasn't ready. Before he could stop me or touch me, hypnotizing me once again, I jumped from my seat and stalked toward the kitchen. I knew the restaurant layout, and the kitchen was close. I could easily duck out the back door and find a cab. That was Rational Cat thinking. That was the Cat I needed. I could call Beckett from the cab, assure him I was fine, go home, and go to bed.

No more William Lambourne. No more Stormy Eyes.

FOUR

The deafening clatter of plates clinking against one another, the hiss of the stove, and the shouts of the line cooks assaulted my ears as I stepped into the kitchen. It was jumping with waiters queuing to fill their trays with Willowgrass's delicious food, workers washing dishes and stacking dry ones next to the food prep areas, and Ben's sous chef calling out orders as he expedited. It took me a moment to recognize Ben, who was dressed for the party rather than the kitchen tonight. But it was clear he was in charge. He stood to one side, coolly surveying everything, but he didn't see me. It sounded as though demand for Ben's creations had exceeded expectation. The opening was a success, and I was happy for Ben and Amanda.

But I wanted to go home. I wanted to get away from William Lambourne and his stormy eyes, skilled hands, and velvet words. He was affecting my better judgment. I couldn't let that happen.

I wouldn't let it happen.

And I really thought I'd gotten away, but I'd taken only a dozen steps when my skin prickled with awareness. I turned, and *he* was there, standing in the doorway, looking angry and sexy at the same time. I had the urge to run, but I couldn't make my feet move. Instead, I stood rooted in place while William took three large strides

73

across the kitchen to stand before me. Even with the mouthwatering mix of scents from the food cooking, I could smell his unique scent. It made me hungry, but not for comfort food. No, there was nothing comforting about the way he looked at me.

Without a word, he took my arm and pulled me aside. I wouldn't have been able to hear him above the clatter and clink of dishes, but he might have made an effort to speak. A refreshing cold and sudden silence descended, and I had a moment to realize we were in the walk-in cooler before his hot mouth descended. As soon as his lips touched me, I was his.

He didn't ask, he didn't hesitate, he merely took, and I couldn't help but offer myself to him. His lips, his tongue, the way he slanted his mouth over mine, claiming me completely, made my knees weak. I think I moaned or whimpered, but I didn't object. I should have been cold, standing in a freezer in only my jacket and thin tank top. I should have been turned off by the slabs of meat and the stacks of fish surrounding me. Instead, I was burning up, fevered with want. I couldn't get enough of William's mouth, his tongue, his body against mine.

And suddenly, I didn't care if we were in a freezer. I didn't care that he was an arrogant ass with a filthy mouth. I didn't care that I didn't want a relationship right now. All I cared about was the slow burn moving through my body as William kissed me. I hadn't expected his kiss to be ordinary, and I wasn't disappointed. He knew how to tease, nipping at my lips with teeth and tongue, giving me a taste of what I hungered for before pulling back.

I fisted my hands in his hair and pulled him closer, sucking on his tongue, pressing my body against his, feeling his warmth and hardness. I was aware of every inch of his tall, athletic body, especially his hard thighs, which brushed against mine, and the more we kissed, the more I abandoned myself to pure sensation. With a groan, he pushed me against one of the shelves, and I felt the cold metal through the material of my tuxedo jacket. But it didn't penetrate. Nothing penetrated except the heat of William's body and the taste of his mouth. He was bourbon and cinnamon and sex.

Our tongues dueled, vying for dominance, and I felt my control slipping farther and farther. I lost it completely when William turned gentle on me. He cupped my face in his hands, drew back, and then whispered in a dark voice strained with need, "I knew I was right. I knew it would be like this. You should really listen to me, Catherine." Then he kissed me with such skill and such sweetness that if it hadn't been for the below freezing temperature, I would have melted into steam. His lips brushed mine, sending sparks of heat spiraling through me. Warm, delicious tendrils of pleasure infused me from the tips of my fingertips to my toes. My heart thundered, and my hips rhythmically arched forward and pressed into his. I wanted to feel his hand between my thighs. I wanted to feel his fingers probe and press and slide inside me the way his tongue had slid inside my mouth. He flicked his tongue across my lips, and I wanted his tongue on me too.

I moaned. My body betrayed me, and I could no longer control the sounds of pleasure I was making. His tongue stroked mine, filling my mouth, stroking me in a rhythm, a pattern I knew well. I clutched at his lapels, needing more and wanting more. So much more—

"Sorry to interrupt…"

I ripped myself away from William, feeling bereft as soon as we parted. Suddenly, the cold of the freezer washed over me, and I shivered. I darted my gaze to a line cook standing in the doorway and closed my eyes in mortification. The kid couldn't have been older than twenty, and he looked a bit chagrined. William, on the other hand, was all composure. "It's all yours," he said, pulling me out of the freezer.

Suddenly, we were surrounded by sound and fury again, but it was a blur. My head spun as he pulled me through the restaurant, outside, and onto the sidewalk in front. The January night air bit into my skin, and that's what snapped me back to reality. Part of me wanted to slide against William, steal his warmth and heat, but I kept my distance.

This wasn't what I wanted, I reminded myself.

He wasn't what I wanted.

My God, I didn't know him, and I had been making out with him in a freezer in the middle of a party. I wasn't ready. I didn't want a relationship—or whatever this might be—with a man who went through women like I went through camera batteries. I was an emotional wreck, and as much as I'd enjoyed myself in the freezer, I couldn't do this. Okay, maybe I could, but I shouldn't. Time to put a stop to this.

"I can have a car here in less than thirty seconds," William said, pushing me against the wall of the building and into the shadows while nuzzling my neck. "Say the word, Catherine, and we can take this where we both want it to go."

I opened my mouth, but my lips felt bruised and tender. I couldn't speak. He ran his thumb over my bottom lip. His eyes were a liquid grey that told me he was aroused. "You know, you make me do things, think things. Do you even know how fucking hot I am for you?" He reached down and adjusted himself, and even in the darkness, I could see he had an impressive erection. I'd made him that aroused? I'd made him want me that much?

"I can't," I said, but I didn't sound convincing.

"You can," he murmured, his warm breath at my neck. "And you will. This is just the beginning, Catherine. I'm going to have you." His fingers caressed mine, moving in slow, tantalizing circles. "We are going fuck in more ways than you can imagine. And I'm going to show you pleasure you didn't know existed."

Oh, my God—more dirty talk. I shuddered because I liked it when he talked to me like that. I guess I appreciated directness too.

This was not what I wanted, I reminded myself. "I don't even know you," I protested weakly.

"You know me. Your body knows me. You think this kind of reaction happens every day? We're going to happen, Catherine. It's inevitable. Why wait?"

I knew he was right. There was something extraordinary simmering between us, chemistry I'd never felt before, not even with Jace. And with that one thought, all the sadness crashed down.

I shut my eyes tightly. "No." I shook my head, keeping my eyes closed. One look at his intense eyes, and I would lose my resolve. "I can't do this." I pushed away from the wall of the restaurant, stepping toward the curb and raising my hand for a cab.

"Fuck," William cursed behind me. I heard the frustration in his tone, but then he stepped beside me, whistled, and a cab pulled to the curb. He opened the door, and I thought he might climb in beside me, but he shut it as soon as I was in. Instead, he leaned in the window, told the driver my address, and handed him what looked like a hundred.

"I have money," I protested.

He ignored me. "Take her home. Safely." Then he stepped back, shoved his hands in his pockets, and fixed his turbulent gaze on mine. Our eyes locked, the connection unbroken until he faded in the darkness as the cab pulled away.

The ride was blissfully silent and the driver quiet. I didn't want to talk. I didn't want to talk to anyone. My nerves were raw, and my whole body craved release. I was edgy and frustrated, flustered and confused. I'd had to run, though walking away from the sexual magnetism of William Lambourne was one of the most difficult things I'd ever done. I couldn't have stayed. The feelings were too intense, my reaction too raw. He made me forget everything, and I couldn't allow that to happen.

I grabbed my phone from my purse and texted Beckett that I was in a cab on my way home.

Immediately, he texted back. *Alone?*

Yes. Yoga tomorrow?

Hell, yes. I want details.

I shoved the phone back in my purse. Details? I was hot, frustrated, and completely in lust with a man I didn't know. And I'd just told him I couldn't do what he wanted, what we both wanted. I closed my eyes and leaned my head against the seat. I could feel William's hands on my face, taste the bourbon on his tongue, and feel his hard body pushed against mine.

It was going to be a long night.

*****

The next morning I met a bleary-eyed Beckett at our usual Bikram yoga class. Beckett and I were in the back, and we'd just finished our stretches. It was one hundred and five degrees in the room, and we were slicked with sweat. Beckett looked like he'd stayed out too late, and I was glad I'd left the party early. My black mat was beside his grey one as we bent our knees for the Awkward Pose. I was dressed in black Lululemon boogie shorts, a pink and black sports bra, and nothing else.

We shifted into Eagle Pose, and I breathed deeply. I'd always loved yoga. It centered me and made me feel cleansed. Today, I really needed to feel centered. I hadn't slept well last night. Big surprise. My thoughts had kept returning to Mr. Billionaire and the walk-in cooler. Even in this incredible heat, I could still feel the cold air and William's fingers caressing my skin.

"Are you cold, Cat?" Beckett murmured. He was supposed to have his eyes closed. The instructor was saying something about a meadow and deep breathing, and we should have been listening.

"Just thinking about last night."

"Oh, really?" The rest of the class shifted into Standing Head to Knee Pose, and we followed. "The memories are that good, huh?" Beckett wobbled, and I struggled to find my balance.

"So a bourbon, neat, magically appeared after he seated you at the bar?" Beckett said, recapping our discussion before class.

"He didn't exactly seat me. He didn't give me a lot of choice." My leg trembled from the effort it took to hold the position, and I grit my teeth. The instructor would have been so disappointed.

"A man who knows what he wants and goes for it," Beckett said, sliding into a Standing Bow. He was in the zone now. "I like it."

So did I, much to my chagrin. Through the Balancing Stick and the Triangle and the Tree Pose, I filled Beckett in on the rest of the evening, and when I finished he looked thoughtful—not an easy feat in the Toe Stand Pose. "So... would you have gone all the way?"

"Huh?" I was struggling to get my ankle on top of my knee. There. Balance... balance.

"Would you have fucked him in the deep freeze?"

My leg buckled, and I went down on my bottom with a thud. The instructor frowned at me, and Beckett grinned, while managing to look at peace. His blond hair was plastered to his head, and his muscles were standing out from the tension of holding the pose. I wondered what William would look like all hot and sweaty.

"He's right, you know," Beckett said when we were lying on our backs.

"About what?"

"About the chemistry. That kind of attraction doesn't happen every day. Look at me. I've been trying to find it for years. And every time I think I've found Mr. Hot and Heavy, he ends up scorching me."

I reached across our mats and took Beckett's hand. "You're going to find the right guy, Beckett. You just need to stop looking in bars."

"It worked for you!"

"It didn't work for me. I'm not seeing him again."

"Oh, yes, you are! You can't drop him. Not until you fuck him. I have to hear all about how William Lambourne is in bed."

"Beckett!" We were close, but there were some things I couldn't imagine sharing in detail.

"No, seriously, Cat." His expression sobered. "He's the perfect guy for you." Beckett held up a finger. "The chemistry is there." Another finger. "He obviously wants you." Another finger. "And he's a commitment-phobe."

We turned onto our bellies for the Cobra Pose. "He's a commitment-phobe?"

"Do you know what Google is, darling? Search for commitment-phobe, and William Lambourne's picture pops up. Okay, not literally. But that's his thing. He's never with one woman for long. No long-term girlfriends as far I can tell. He loves them and leaves them. He's perfect."

I dropped onto my mat, burying my face in the rubber and latex. "All I found on Google were a bunch of boring business articles. And exactly how is a guy who's a commitment-phobe perfect for me?"

"You need to dig deeper. But more importantly, you need a rebound guy."

I shook my head. "No. I just can't, Beckett."

"Cat," Beckett said, dropping his pose too. "It's okay to get on with your life. You have to move on at some point. It's been three years."

I'd heard all this before, and logically, I knew Beckett was right, but that didn't change the way I felt inside. I didn't want to look at Beckett so I moved into the Locust Pose. "I'm not ready."

"You're ready. Besides, you'll never know if you don't give it a shot. A rebound guy is a good way to test the waters."

"I've never had a rebound guy before."

"You never needed one before. You do now."

"Why?"

Beckett threw his arms back, forming the Full Locust Pose. "For the hot sex! You use Stormy Eyes for all the hot sex you can handle and then move on. No strings, no attachments, just fun." He dropped the pose and sat, his expression serious. "Honey, you need a little fun now and then. Or a lot of fun *now*!"

"I have fun," I said, through the strain of holding the Full Locust.

"You have watch-TV-in-your-pajamas fun, Cat. You need sweaty-roll-around-in-bed- with-chocolate-flavored-lube fun. Seriously, Cat. If you don't get laid, I think you're going to burst into flames."

I laughed, losing what little concentration I had. Beckett wasn't kidding, and I knew he was right. It had been a long time since I'd had sex. Yes, I'd had sex since Jace died, and I didn't want to think about how long ago it had happened or whom it had been with. It had been horrible—truly sick-to-my-stomach, big mistake, what-was-I-thinking horrible. The instructor moved to the back of the room, a subtle warning that we were disruptive, and we finished the workout in silence.

Afterward, I showered and changed, and Beckett and I went our separate ways. The yoga studio was in the Gold Coast neighborhood, and even though it was cold, I decided to walk a bit and window-shop at the trendy, expensive boutiques nearby. After last night, I could use some distraction, and besides, I had nothing waiting at home except the dog. I didn't want to dwell on hot bourbon and cold freezers all day.

But even window-shopping couldn't get my mind off the man with the amazing blue-grey eyes. While William Lambourne was ideal in Beckett's estimation, he was dangerous in mine. On paper, he might be the perfect rebound guy, but I could see myself getting too wrapped up in him. It wasn't his money. I could care less about however many millions he banked, but there was that indefinable *thing* I felt with him. It pulled me in, he pulled me in, and I knew I could lose myself in it and in him.

I stopped to study a pair of black shoes in a window then moved on. I didn't want shoes today.

One glance at the other women at the party last night made it clear that I wasn't the only one he had this effect on. I was nothing special. Men didn't routinely fall all over me. Why, exactly, was William Lambourne pursuing *me*? He was pretty direct about what he wanted to do with me and to me. Just sex, obviously. That might be fine for him, but I wasn't sure I could do that, even if Beckett thought I needed a rebound guy. I'd never considered a no-strings-attached sexual relationship with someone.

I stopped again, this time in front of a lingerie boutique. I knew Beckett and my mother, God love her, wanted me to be happy. But dating wasn't going to make me happy, and sleeping with someone just because the opportunity presented itself wasn't going to make me happy in the long run either. The big issue was that I didn't deserve to be happy. Why should I be happy after what had happened? I'd killed my husband. Yes, it had been an accident—a *horrible* accident, as my mother liked to say with added drama—but it wasn't the kind of thing a lover or a potential boyfriend could look past. It was the ultimate conversation stopper and mood killer. "Hi, I'm Catherine. The widow. I'm twenty-five, and I was driving the car in the accident that killed the one person I loved more than anyone in the world. Do you want to fuck me now?"

I hadn't told anyone since I moved to Chicago. I'd gone back to my maiden name and stopped wearing my wedding ring, so there was no reason for anyone to think I'd ever been married. I'd talked about Jace and the accident in my grief support group, but we'd all shared our baggage in confidence. Beckett knew, of course But since I'd left Santa Cruz, I'd never had to tell anyone new, anyone who didn't already know my secrets.

No, giving in to William Lambourne would stress me out more than make me happy. But I knew what would make me happy, if only briefly. I stepped into the boutique and inhaled the scent of floral sachets and expensive silk.

"Can I help you with anything?" an attractive saleswoman in her mid-forties asked. I could see her studying me, probably thinking *dressed in black, conservative—cotton panties.*

"I want something sexy."

She broke into a grin. "I have just the thing. Size six?"

She was good. "Yes."

"And you look like a thirty-four C."

"Right again."

She nodded and led me to the back, where row after row of gorgeous, sexy lingerie hung on padded and beribboned hangers. I couldn't stop myself from reaching out and stroking the delicate laces, the sheer meshes, and the soft silk. There was nothing like the feel of expensive lingerie against my skin. Except possibly, William Lambourne's body. Shit. I could rationalize why he was bad news all day long, and that still couldn't stop me from thinking about him.

"Any color choice?" the saleswoman asked.

I thought of last night. "Light blue."

In the changing room, I undressed and reached for the matching icy blue bra and ruffled tanga shorts. They weren't my usual style. I preferred thongs, but there was something provocative about the sheerness of the shorts and the way the ruffle teased. I liked the way the bra pushed my breasts up, giving me substantial cleavage. I traced the swell of my breasts with one finger, dipping into the bra. I liked the feel of the silk against my skin and felt my nipple harden against my hand. My nipples had been hard like this for William last night. Given a few more moments in that freezer, and I would have done anything to have William's lips on my breasts. If he could kiss me senseless with that mouth, I could only imagine what that mouth could do to my body.

I leaned back against the dressing room wall. I closed my eyes, and I rolled my nipple between my fingers and squeezed it gently, sliding my other hand down my abdomen and into the shorts. It was easy to imagine my hands were William's. It was William touching me, sliding the shorts over my hips and down my thighs, parting my legs then gently inserting a finger inside. I rocked back and forth as my own finger entered. I felt my slickness and heat radiating from deep within. *I am going to show you pleasure didn't know existed.*

The sound of the bell jingling at the shop's entrance brought me back to my senses. Thank God, because I was—*hello*—masturbating in a dressing room. I was losing my head, and my body craved William in a way I'd never craved anything. I really didn't need more lingerie, but I had to buy the bra and panties now. They reminded me of him, and that was probably a bad sign, but there was no way I was leaving without them.

I paid for the lingerie, unable to make eye contact with the sales clerk, my checking account groaning at the hit, then headed to my car and drove home. I had managed to unearth my vibrator the other day. I think it was time I gave it a workout.

FIVE

As soon as I stepped into my condo, Laird bounded up to me. He was dancing with excitement, and I barely had time to set my shopping bag down before I grabbed his leash and led him out. A brisk walk felt good, and this time I avoided the shops and the lakeshore and walked through the neighborhood. It was a quiet Saturday, and I enjoyed the sound of my boots crunching on frozen ground, Laird's excited panting, and the bleating of car horns along with the occasional siren in the distance. Above me, the sky was remarkably blue and the sun shone. It still threw me when the weather was a contrast. In Santa Cruz, grey fog had meant cold, and blue skies indicated warm weather. I felt like I'd never be warm in Chicago.

I'd changed since I'd arrived in Chicago, too. I was paler now, my hair darker. I'd lost my surfer tan and the blond streaks in my hair. I thought my hair actually looked better without sun and saltwater damage, but I was still getting used to seeing my face without a smattering of freckles and a pair of sunglasses perched perpetually on my nose.

Finally, Laird began to flag—meaning, he stopped running full tilt and just galloped—and we headed toward the groomer's, which was only two blocks from my condo. Today was his monthly appointment for a bath and the extras he loved. I had just handed Laird's leash to the attendant and promised to pick him up in a few hours when my cell buzzed. I answered, tucking it under my chin so I could pull on my scarf and hat as I started walking. My hands were numb because I'd forgotten my gloves. Again!

"Cat?" a man's voice asked.

"Hi, Dad!" I felt my cold cheeks break into a stiff grin. "How are you?"

"I'm good. I've been puttering around all morning, trying to figure out what's missing." That was not new. My father was nothing if not absentminded.

"Your glasses?" I suggested.

"No, Cat. You! It's Saturday. We always had brunch together on Saturday."

I felt a pang of sadness lance through me. "You're right, Dad."

"Did you have brunch with that friend of yours? What's his name again? Bob?"

"Ha ha, Dad. I was with Beckett." My dad had known Beckett for as long as I had and this was a running joke between us. The walk back to my condo was quick, and I was upstairs now. I shrugged off my coat and began pulling at my boots. "No, we went to yoga, but I miss you too. You should come and visit."

"Maybe I'll come when the semester is over." My dad was a professor in the computer science department at UC-Santa Cruz. His whole life was semesters and exams and binary code. I thought sometimes he related better to computers than people. I don't know what he and my mother ever saw in one another. Well, that wasn't entirely true. My mother was beautiful and vivacious. I could see why men were drawn to her, but I don't know what drew her to my father. He was quiet and serious and devoted to his work. He wasn't rich or extravagant. Not surprisingly, they divorced when I was seven.

"Come for a week before the summer session," I said, falling back on my couch from the exertion of removing the winter gear. That was one thing I never had to do in Santa Cruz. "I'll take you to the lake."

"I'd love that, honey. Are you doing okay?"

"Great." I filled him in on the job with Willowgrass—leaving out the bits about William Lambourne—and told him I had an upcoming meeting with the Fresh Market people.

"Sounds like you're doing well. Do you like Chicago?"

"It's cold. But it's growing on me."

"You could always come back." I heard the wistfulness in his voice.

"I wish I could, Dad."

"And why can't you? This is your home, Catherine. I never understood why you felt you had to run away. We could have faced what happened together. It wasn't your fault. People would have come to see that."

"Maybe, Dad, but Santa Cruz without Jace didn't feel right. Everything is new here, and the scenery is different." And colder. "I needed a change."

He sighed. "Alright. Now, when should I come? Let me write this down…"

After I got off the phone, I was still cold. And my thoughts swirled around Stormy Eyes. My body craved him and I felt tense and edgy with pent-up frustration. I decided to warm up with a hot bubble bath and then find my battery-operated friend and orgasm until I couldn't think about William Lambourne or any man for days.

I undressed to a pair of white lace panties and an oversized T-shirt that almost reached my knees. After I threw my hair into a ponytail, I reached for the hot water faucet as a knock sounded on the door. I guessed it was Minerva, since nobody could get upstairs without getting buzzed in through the front door, and I hadn't heard the intercom. I knew she wanted to hear about the party. I'd tell her I'd come down later to chat. I opened the door. "Hi, Min—"

But it wasn't her.

William Lambourne stood outside my door in the hallway, holding a tray of coffee in one hand and an aromatic bakery bag in the other. In the back of my mind, I was aware that I was only half-dressed, that my face was scrubbed clean of makeup, and my hair was up in a messy ponytail, but it was impossible to concentrate when faced with a man like Stormy Eyes. As usual, his eyes were what drew me first. They were clear blue today, like the sky on my walk. I allowed my gaze to wander over the rest of him.

He looked good. Really good. I didn't know if it was the scent coming from the white paper bag in his hand or the sight of William, but my mouth watered. His hair was slightly tousled, and the curls fell around his face luxuriously. I felt the familiar impulse of wanting to run my hands through the thickness. I remembered how soft it had been last night. He hadn't shaved, and the shadow of his beard made him look rugged, even hotter. His lips were curved in a seductive half-smile, but I had to skim over his lips, or else I would have been lost. Instead, I noted his buttery soft leather coat, open to reveal a grey T-shirt under a black V-neck sweater. His jeans were snug, showing off long legs, which I followed down to leather boots.

"Like what you see?" he asked. He was cocky. Who was I kidding? He was beautiful and irresistible.

"How'd you get up here? I didn't hear the buzzer."

"Your neighbor was going out as I was walking up, and she let me in. Guess she thought I looked respectable enough."

Okay, so he had charmed Minerva with his dashing smile. Still, my interrogation continued, and I kept him standing in the hallway. "What's in the bag?"

"Let me in, and I'll show you. I might even let you taste it."

I stood there, hesitating. Echoes of *The Three Little Pigs* whirled in my mind—*little pig, little pig, let me come in.* I understood how those little pigs felt when the big, bad wolf knocked on their door. And if the wolf had arrived with coffee and whatever the hell that bag held that smelled so sinfully divine, then they probably would have saved the wolf the trouble of blowing the house down.

Finally, I opened the door wider and moved back.

He stepped inside without hesitation, catching the door with the toe of his boot and shoving it closed. My condo suddenly felt far too small and warm. I realized I hadn't moved aside, and we were standing close enough to touch. I was wearing just panties and an oversized T-shirt, which I clutched at the bottom, self-consciously pulling it down. If he noticed, he didn't let on.

"I hope you drink coffee."

"Of course, I drink coffee."

"I left it black. I don't know how you like it."

"You seem to know everything else about me."

His smile widened. "There might be a few details I'd like to learn through experience." He leaned closer. "So, Catherine, how do you take your coffee?"

I swallowed. "I prefer lattes." What was I, ten? I was acting like a spoiled brat, but I couldn't help it. My heart was racing as though I'd drunk five espressos, and I felt too warm, even though I wasn't wearing enough clothing.

His grin widened. "You're hard to please, aren't you?" he said playfully, brushing past me and walking into my living room. His arm skimmed my breasts as he moved beside me, and I shivered. I hated to admit it, but I liked his playful side. I liked the boyish grin he'd flashed. It was the same one that had charmed me, against my will, last night.

I turned and saw him moving through my living room, past my desk and toward the kitchen as though he owned the place. It was infuriating. Who breezed into someone else's home like that? But even worse than his nerve was the fact that he looked so good in my condo. He looked like he belonged there.

"Nice place," he said, glancing at the framed photos and the throw pillows on the couches. "It looks like I imagined." He glanced at me. "It looks like you."

I wanted to ask what he meant. What exactly did I look like? But as he moved into the dining nook and then the kitchen, he halted. "Now this is unexpected," he said.

I followed him and watched as he set the bag on my counter then moved closer to the cooker. "An AGA." It was funny to see a grown man felled by my cast-iron kitchen contraption. He caressed it, his touch light and reverent. My body tingled just watching him. "I'm impressed." He glanced around and spotted the huge Sub-Zero refrigerator. "Nice kitchen." His eyes met mine. They were darker now, not quite so light a blue. "Very nice."

The scent coming from the bakery bag drove me insane, and I nodded to it. "What's in the bag?" I asked again.

"You'll love it." He opened the bag and moved it so that I could see inside. I stepped closer and swayed at the aroma of fresh-baked croissants and chocolate assaulting my senses. I closed my eyes and simply inhaled. It smelled so sweet, and I could feel the warmth coming from the bag. I knew the pastry would be gooey from the warm chocolate. I had never been so ravenous.

"It's *pain au chocolat*," he said, his accent impeccable. "It's fresh from the oven, and the chocolate is infused with cardamom. It's delicious—one of my favorites."

My center felt as warm as the pastry, and our gazes met. We stared at one another for a long moment. Inside me, everything went hot and heavy. I was hyperaware of my sensitive nipples pushing against the cotton of the T-shirt, of the lace of my panties on the skin of my hip, of the smooth hardwood under my bare feet. My hands flexed, and I wanted to touch Stormy Eyes, pull that coat and sweater off, and run my fingers over his hard chest. As if reading my mind, he shrugged out of his coat, tossing it on the counter. He gave me a look, begging me to challenge him. I didn't, of course. I wanted to be pissed. I wanted to tell him to go to hell for being presumptuous. I meant what I said last night. I couldn't do this. But now, I was too excited to see what would happen next. I was far more aroused than pissed off. And maybe my anger was fueling the arousal.

"Lattes, you said?" he asked, breaking the spell so I could breathe again. I gulped air and nodded. To my surprise—though why anything this man did should surprise me was a mystery—he turned and opened my refrigerator. He peered inside at the pitiful contents— a Styrofoam container of leftovers, three yogurts, a bottle of decent wine, an apple, and various condiments. No milk.

Suddenly, I felt embarrassed. I hated to cook. I didn't need to stock the fridge. But I was willing to wager everything I owned that William Lambourne's refrigerator was never empty. I was sure he had gallons of everything from skim to buttermilk. I stormed over and slammed the door, an angry retort on my lips. "Look—" I opened my mouth to tell him to get the hell out, but when the refrigerator closed, a gust of cold air washed against my bare legs. My body trembled, and I remembered the way he'd kissed me in the freezer at Willowgrass the night before. I remembered the feel of his body against mine and the taste of the bourbon on his tongue.

I was lost, and everything I was thinking clearly showed on my face. Before I knew what was happening, William pushed me against the fridge, and then his mouth was on mine. I was enfolded in the taste of sweet, baked croissants and warm chocolate. His lips were soft and persuasive, and I couldn't stop from opening to take him in. Our tongues twined, and I wrapped my hands around him, digging my fingers into his thick, rich hair, pulling him closer until he pressed against me. His kisses went from light and playful to deeper and more demanding, and I couldn't think, couldn't breathe.

He pulled away, and I gasped for air, grasped for reason.

"Open your mouth."

My gaze darted to his. His blue eyes were steel grey now. Even as I resisted his order mentally, I felt my lips part, and then sweet warmth exploded in my mouth. I groaned aloud at the taste of the *pain au chocolat*. I had never tasted anything so sensual, so rich, so addictive. I didn't know if it was the food or the kiss, but I was on the verge of ecstasy. My whole body quivered, tensing, ready for more.

William slid another bite of the delicious *pain au chocolat* between my lips, and the second taste was as good as the first. The flaky pastry was moist, the chocolate gooey, and I could feel a dribble at the side of my mouth. I watched William's eyes turn to liquid silver as he bent close and flicked his tongue out. Electricity sparked through me as his tongue teased and his lips nibbled, and then he bent lower, trailing a hot path down my neck. I couldn't believe this was happening. This felt like some sort of dream, and I knew I should end it, but I couldn't do anything but what he wanted. Everywhere his lips touched turned to fire. His arms came around me, his lips returned to my mouth, and I was so lost in his kiss that I barely realized we had slid down the fridge to the floor. Then his lips were back on my mouth, and his hands... his hands were everywhere. He had skilled fingers. Everywhere he touched left me wanting more.

I could feel the cold stainless steel of the refrigerator at my back, and William's hot fingers trailed a path across my thighs. "Your skin is so soft, Catherine," he murmured between kisses. His voice was low and husky. Hearing the need in his tone made me hotter. It thrilled me to think that this man wanted me. It made me feel sexy and powerful, even though I was completely at his mercy.

He slid his hands under my shirt, the pads of his fingers grazing my hips and my belly, and I quivered in response. I gasped in a breath and tried to stifle the sounds in my throat. His touch was gentle and light, and I craved so much more.

"Lift your arms."

"No," I said, suddenly feeling self-conscious and grabbing my T-shirt to hold it in place.

"Lift your arms," he said again, his tone not to be challenged. Part of me was thrilled that he was telling me what to do, what I wanted to do, so I did as he ordered. In a moment my T-shirt was off and tossed over his shoulder. He hissed in a breath as his eyes went impossibly darker. For a few seconds, he just stared at my exposed breasts. With another man, I might have felt like an object, but with William I felt revered.

"You're stunning, Catherine. More than I'd imagined." His voice was filled with awe. "I have to taste you."

My nipples hardened in anticipation, but he didn't make a move to touch me. Instead, he pulled off his sweater and raked a hand through his hair, which was sexy and tousled. Then he reached for the bag of *pain au chocolat* again, dipped a finger inside, and withdrew it covered in chocolate and swiped his finger across one breast and then the other.

The warm chocolate heated my skin, sending spirals of pleasure down to my core. I moaned, loudly, and though I should have been horrified, I wasn't. I squirmed, feeling the need in me rising. William was beside me now, bending forward. He brought his mouth to my skin, licking the chocolate little by little until he reached my nipple. He took me in his mouth, sucking hard and long, until I cried out. My back bowed, forcing my swollen nipple deeper between his hungry lips.

"Patience, Catherine." His breath smelled like chocolate as it feathered over me. "Good things come to those who wait. You don't want dessert before the first course." His gaze met mine. "Or do you?"

I couldn't believe I was letting this happen. I should have been uncomfortable on the hardwood kitchen floor, but nothing except William's touch, his voice, his body mattered. His hands hadn't stopped their torment as he caressed my breasts, teasing my nipples until they were so hard they ached. When he took one then the other in his mouth again, I arched against him. He sucked harder, and I thought I might come then and there.

"Where else should I kiss you?" he asked, more to himself than to me. I was too dazed to answer anyway. No one had ever talked to me like this. No one had ever catered to me so completely, and I couldn't believe how much I liked it, how much I wanted to see what would happen next. I felt William's arm wrap around me, supporting me as he maneuvered my body so that I was flat on my back next to the SubZero, and he was between my legs. Then his lips were on me again, delving lower, brushing against my abdomen, his tongue teasing my belly button. His teeth fastened on the little bow at the waist of my panties. "White lace," he murmured. "I like these. But they're not really needed, are they?" He didn't ask this time, and I didn't resist. In one deft movement, he pulled them down, then off, and tossed them behind us. I was completely naked. Then he parted my thighs. His gaze raked over me, and I whimpered, feeling as though I'd go mad if he didn't keep touching me. I'd never wanted anyone so much. I'd never desired a man like this.

His look, hungry and turbulent, met mine. "Do you want me to make you come?"

I tried to speak, but I couldn't make my mouth work. No one had ever directly asked me. No one had ever made my pleasure paramount or understood my body so well. So I nodded and closed my eyes.

"Look at me, Catherine," he said, as he swiped his finger against my inner thigh and teased my skin with warm chocolate.

Kneeling before me, he bent and kissed the inside of one knee. I convulsed, knowing if I pressed my thighs together, my release would follow. But he held them open, kept me parted while he feasted on my skin, licking it, tasting it, tormenting me until I ached with need. I whimpered, tried to quiet the sound, and whimpered again.

"Don't take your eyes off me. I want to see those beautiful green eyes when you come."

I could feel the smooth floor under my bare back and bottom and his warm hands and mouth on my skin. I kept my eyes open, locked on William as he went to work between my legs. The scent of sweet pastry and chocolate infused the air and my senses, making me hungry for food and for him. When his hot tongue finally lapped at the chocolate on my inner thigh, I jumped. Pleasure shot right to my belly, and I writhed against him. He chuckled low, and his hot breath made my skin pebble. He kissed a trail of fire up my leg until he reached my center. Every one of my nerve endings fired, waiting for the feel of his mouth. He waited, poised just above my clit.

"I love the way you smell," he said, as he inhaled me deeply. "You're lovely here too, Catherine. So pink and lush. So soft."

"Please, please, just..."

He stroked me gently, up and down, and I felt dizzy with need. I should have been embarrassed at the way he was talking, but I loved it, and I was so overwhelmed I couldn't even complete a sentence. I loved how much he wanted me. Even though he was pleasuring me, I could see in his eyes he was as aroused as I was. The grey was so dark and liquid it was almost pewter.

"I wonder if you'll taste as good."

And then he flicked his tongue out, raking it across my swollen clit. I dug my fingers into the floor and bucked, but he held me steady. His mouth was on my sex now, and he swirled his tongue through my folds, stopping to gently spread me apart with his fingers, dipping his tongue inside, then swirling again. The pleasure slammed into me, hard and hot, I thought I would combust. It washed over me in wave after delicious wave, rippling through me. I'd never come so quickly before. I moaned, bit my lip, and arched my back, pressing hard against William's mouth. I was shameless, and I didn't care. Somewhere, in the back of my mind, I realized I was naked on my kitchen floor with a fully dressed man I hardly knew between my legs. Somewhere, in the back of my mind, I realized he'd just licked chocolate off my body, giving me possibly the best orgasm I'd ever felt. But I didn't care. I'd never let go like this before. Never let something like this happen.

I closed my eyes and let the last rolls of pleasure rise and spread through me.

"That's it," William was saying, his voice seductive and reassuring. "You're so beautiful right now, Catherine. I could watch you come all day."

I felt his hands on my mouth, parting my lips, and then he slid another bite of the *pain au chocolat* in my mouth. I barely needed to chew it. It melted, all the warm chocolate sliding down my throat. Then he kissed me, the taste of me on his lips melding with the taste of the bread and chocolate. It was sinful and erotic. I wanted more than anything to cover his body with chocolate. I wanted to lick every inch, slide his cock in my mouth with all the gooey chocolate and taste the two together.

"Have you ever been tested, Catherine?" he murmured into my mouth.

I opened my eyes. "What?"

"Are you on the pill?"

I shook my head, my thoughts jumbled. "I have an IUD." I'd had it inserted when I was with Jace. It didn't need to be removed for another year.

"Have you ever been screened? I have. I'm clean, but I don't fuck women who haven't been screened."

Reason came slowly crawling back, and with it, a little of my dignity. Was I simply going to be one of the women he fucked? Of course, I was. And apparently, he required paperwork before he took a woman to bed. What the hell was I doing here?

"I'm fine," I stuttered. "I'm clean. But I'm not one of your women. And who said anything about fucking?" I put a lot of emphasis on that last word, and it felt raw and harsh coming out of my mouth. I seethed and rose to my elbows, pushing him back. "I didn't ask you to come over. I didn't ask for any of this."

"Well, we have to talk about it. The sooner we get it out of the way, the sooner we can move on to other activities." He was grinning wickedly now.

I sat up and started to scoot back to grab my T-shirt. It was drafty on the kitchen floor. That I was totally naked and William was fully clothed wasn't lost on me. "Maybe you should go. I told you last night, I'm not into the fuck-buddy thing."

William was undeterred.

"Oh, we're not done yet." One of his hands settled on my bare thigh, and I felt my resolve slipping. Who was I kidding? I'd just had the best orgasm of my life. I had no resolve, and I felt myself heating up again.

"I want to keep you safe, Catherine. I want you to know you're safe with me. And now, I know I'm safe with you." His hand moved up my thighs, parting my legs again. "Doesn't it feel better when you know we're safe?" His fingers grazed against my swollen skin, and I moaned.

He turned me on more than I could have anticipated. I said I wanted him to leave, but really I wanted him to stay and keep doing exactly what he was doing. I allowed my head to loll back. His fingers stroked me slowly at first, lightly. I felt my body quiver. There was no way I could come again. Not this quickly. Not after the orgasm I'd just had. But his fingers continued their torment, and I felt my body move to meet his rhythm.

"I love watching you move," he said. "I want to see you come again."

I shook my head. "It's not going to happen." I moaned as his touch became firmer and more insistent. There was no way. I'd never had two orgasms this close together.

"You can." One finger slid into me, and I cried out with pleasure. "You're so wet for me, Catherine. I love how much you want me."

I let my legs fall to the sides, and I opened for him. I didn't know what was wrong with me and why I was acting like this, except that his hand felt so damn good that I didn't want the sensation to end.

"You're so tight, so greedy," he said, sliding a second finger inside, thrusting up, stroking me, then sliding out again. "Has it been a while Catherine? Is that why you're insatiable?"

I didn't want to go there, not now.

Wasn't it enough that he made me insatiable? I'd never acted like this before. He slicked his two fingers over my clit then thrust inside again. I felt my legs falling open wider, felt my nipples hardening, felt the white-hot pleasure rising. I hardly knew this man, and now, I'd not only let him go down on me, I was allowing him to finger fuck me on my kitchen floor. His fingers stroked me again, deep and hard, and then he stroked upward and hit that sensitive place on top. Instantly, I felt my pleasure peak, and I felt the building pressure and tightening again.

"Open your eyes," he said, and I did. "Look at me, baby." I did. "Now, come." I did. Completely. I rode his fingers, convulsing against them and shattering apart. His eyes were so dark they looked almost black as he watched me. I could tell he was aroused. I didn't know why he didn't unbutton his straining jeans and plunge himself into me.

"Now," he said, when I could focus again. "Come for me again."

I laughed, but I probably should have cried. I was weak, completely drained. Instead, I shook my head and uttered protests, which came out sounding like moans of pleasure.

One of his brows rose as though he'd been challenged. "I'll tell you when you're done. You're going to come again, Catherine."

I shook my head. "I can't," I whispered. But I felt his fingers slide over me again, felt my body betraying me. There was no way this was happening. But as William teased me and stroked me, I felt myself warm to him, felt my body tense and pull in. I was so sensitive now that it was almost painful. He slid his fingers inside, thrusting deep and long, and then he bent his head and tongued my clit.

I moaned because it felt good. The pleasure was almost agony, yet I couldn't find the strength to make him stop. The more his tongue raked over me, the more the pleasure built until I was panting with it, pushing myself into his mouth, and coming again.

Six

Oh, my God. My brain was still fuzzy with pleasure, but it was clear enough to realize what William and I had done—or rather, what he had done to me—in my kitchen. Between the hot yoga with Beckett that morning and the mind-blowing, shattering orgasms William had given me in front of my Sub-Zero, my legs were rubbery. I couldn't think about moving, much less about getting off the floor. So I lay there and felt my face flush as I replayed every delicious detail in my mind. I couldn't believe I'd let this happen, but I felt too good to care.

"What are you thinking about, Catherine?" William's velvety voice made my bare skin tingle, and I shivered. He had the sexiest voice.

I opened my eyes. "You."

"Good." His eyes darkened to deep blue, and he held out a hand. I took it and rose unsteadily to my feet. As I stood, I noticed the thick outline of his erection. It was hard to miss. The snug jeans he wore looked ready to burst. There was something flattering about seeing him that aroused because of me. But it was confusing too. Why hadn't he asked for anything in return? Why had he done all of that to me—for me? And how was it possible that I had come so many times? That had never happened. Ever.

My legs were so wobbly he had to support me. This, too, was a first. I'd never been weak after sex. But then I'd never had an experience like the one I'd just had. I could feel William's warmth where I leaned against him and smell the lingering scent of chocolate and spice on his lips. I wanted him to kiss me again, and I didn't understand that either. How could I want more when I already felt better than I ever had after sex?

And, realizing that, I felt a stab of guilt. I had loved Jace wholeheartedly, but he'd never made me feel like this. And that's why sex wasn't everything.

But I couldn't deny there was something between William and me.

"Spread your legs." His voice held a dark promise my body couldn't help but respond to. I would have done anything at this point. I knew he could make me feel what I'd never felt before. He *could* take me to heights of pleasure I hadn't known were possible. I definitely wanted that from him—all that and more. But at the same time, I needed to think, step back and get my head right. Everything was moving so quickly.

And yet, I spread my legs for him, wantonly, feeling my breathing speed up. I wanted him to touch me again, to fill me with his hard length I could see straining for release.

"Now, step." He bent over.

I frowned and looked down. He had my panties in his hand and positioned them at my feet. "But I thought—"

"Step." The tone of his voice didn't allow for argument. I could tell he was someone who rarely, if ever, dealt with dissent. Before I knew what I was doing, I stepped into my panties and allowed him to pull them up my legs.

He didn't move quickly. He pulled them slowly, so that the feel of the white lace was a caress against my bare skin. When he reached my ass, he allowed his fingers to linger, cupping the curve. Finally, my panties were back in place, and he looked me in the eye. "This was all about you, Catherine. I want to see you again. I want to take you out, feed you, take you somewhere you haven't been."

I stared. I could have looked into his eyes forever. They were constantly changing. First blue, then grey, then blue again. I loved that his every emotion seemed to be reflected in those eyes. I already knew he wasn't going to be the kind of man who spoke about his feelings. I'd have to learn to read his eyes.

And why was I thinking about the future anyway? This was about now. And right now, it appeared we were through. "You don't want anything in return?" I must have sounded incredulous because he gave me a brief, amused smile. I loved it when he smiled. It was sexy as hell.

He handed me my T-shirt, and I slipped it on as he was talking. "Like I said, I was disappointed when you left last night. I worried about you."

Did I miss something? Did he say that earlier? Maybe he said it while I was coming on his hand when I couldn't hear anything except my heart pounding in my ears. This man, who owned most of Chicago, and possibly several small countries, had worried. About *me*.

"But I see you're fine. More than fine now, I hope. Maybe you're not so hard to please after all…" He smiled again, and this time it was his devilish, sexy grin that practically made me melt. Everything inside me fired up again from that one grin. Did he know how sexy he was? Did he know the effect he had?

I was reeling, feeling surreal. I kept glancing at my kitchen floor, willing myself to believe I'd allowed this man I hardly knew to do all of that to me a few moments ago. I still didn't understand how he could have made me feel like this when we barely knew one another. He had an intuitive sense of what pleased me.

"I obviously interrupted you this afternoon," he continued, "and it's too late for coffee." He gestured to the cups he'd brought, which I imagined were cold by now. My gaze settled on the *pain au chocolat*, and even though I could still taste it on my lips, my mouth watered again. I wanted to see what he would taste like covered in that rich, spicy chocolate. And then I was horrified by the thought. I had said I wasn't relationship material, and I meant it. I didn't want this to go any farther.

Or did I?

"Tell me I can take you out."

I blinked. "I… William, I told you—"

"I'd like to see you tonight." His eyes were a steely blue. It was his negotiation look. I had a feeling he lost few negotiations.

"Tonight?" I stammered.

"I know it's short notice, but I'd like you with me, Catherine."

My belly clenched. I hadn't been on a first date in years, but I still remembered it was bad form to ask a girl out the day of. But how could I refuse him? I didn't want to refuse him. I wanted to be with him too, if only to see where this would lead. My core throbbed, and I had a good idea where it would lead. There was no point in fighting it now. I liked that direction.

"It's a formal event at the Art Institute. I'd get out of it, but I'm expected. Say you'll go."

"I'll go," I heard myself say. I would have agreed to go to a drive-thru and eat burgers and fries, but there was no way I could refuse. "I love the Art Institute."

"I know."

How could he know? And that made me wonder what else he knew about me.

"I'll pick you up at seven." He lifted the *pain au chocolat* from the counter. "I'm leaving this here for you." His eyes caressed my lips in a way that made me hungry—but not for food.

"It's better warm. Heat it for a few minutes in the warming oven." He gestured to the AGA. I wasn't aware it had a warming oven. The whole machine was a mystery. I didn't understand why ovens had to be complicated.

"I barely use that thing." I rolled my eyes. A high-maintenance stove. Who would have thought? "I'll microwave it."

"No." William took my hand firmly. "You won't." He pulled me over to the AGA and nimbly opened one of the compartments, as though it were as simple as a child's play kitchen. "Put it in here for five minutes."

I leaned closer. "Where do I turn the warming oven on?"

William rolled his eyes, clearly exasperated. "Catherine, an AGA is never cold. It's always hot. Always burning. It's always turned on."

I caught my breath and flicked my gaze to his. His eyes were dark again, and I could feel my skin heating and my nipples puckering at the arousal I saw reflected. "I know the feeling." The comeback girl had reappeared.

He laughed. "Good. I intend to keep it that way. I want you burning for me, Catherine. I want you to want me as much as I want you."

I didn't really think it was possible to want him more than I already did.

He kept talking, which was surprising. "I want to fill all your desires, starting with your desire for food." He tugged my wrist, bringing me closer to his heat. "And someone has to teach you how to use your cooker."

I felt a shot of heat pierce me, and my knees wobbled. Only a man as sexy as William Lambourne could make using a cast-iron stove sound erotic. He lowered his mouth to mine, kissing me deeply, taking possession, and making me hunger for so much more. My breath quickened, and I dragged a hand through his soft curls. Slowly, he took my hand, lowered it to my side, and broke the kiss. "I'll see you tonight." His eyes, an indigo blue, were filled with promise.

And then he grabbed his sweater and his coat and walked away, cutting through my small dining area. I stood next to the ridiculous oven and listened as his boots clicked authoritatively on my wood floors, the sound muffled when he reached the rug in the living room, then a faint click when he opened my door and closed it again.

*****

The rest of the afternoon flew by in a blur. I was alternately nervous and giddy with excitement. I hadn't been on a date, and this was no ordinary date—as though anything I did with William Lambourne would be ordinary.

I still had time before I had to pick up Laird from the groomers, so I popped over to a spa I walked past sometimes and asked if they could fit me in for a manicure and pedicure. Then I luxuriated in the pampering, feeling pretty and girly again with my nails polished and buffed. Laird looked good after his grooming, and he was excited to see me. I felt bad that he'd be on his own tonight and took him to the park to play fetch. It was cold, but by Chicago standards, it was a perfect day to be outdoors. I was bundled up in a hat, scarf, and coat, and the sun was out. Laird yipped happily, and I couldn't wipe the smile from my face.

Despite the fun playing with Laird, I couldn't keep my thoughts off tonight and what had happened in my kitchen. I was confused about my reaction to William, uncertain I'd made the right decision in agreeing to go, but I wasn't panicking. Nothing refreshed and calmed me like being outside in the fresh air.

Finally, Laird plopped down at my feet, tongue lolling out of his mouth, and I slipped on his leash and headed to the condo. As we walked back, my phone vibrated, and I dug it out of my pocket.

It was a text from William. *Did you eat more?*

I could hear his voice in the words, and I shivered.

I paused and texted back. *Yes, I heated it in the AGA too.*

It had been impossible not to think of him. The *pain au chocolat* had been delicious warmed up as he'd promised. I was going to forever associate William Lambourne and his talented tongue with the lingering taste of spiced chocolate.

I'm sending you a package.

I blinked at the text, a little surprised and then excited at the novelty. What could William be sending me? *What is it?* I texted back.

I stared at my words, waiting for his reply. He could afford anything, so there was no way I could guess what it could be.

A cup of coffee? A new car?

You'll see.

I had to laugh. Had I really believed he'd tell me? Laird and I arrived home a few minutes later and headed upstairs. I barely had Laird's leash off, and I was unwrapping my scarf when my intercom buzzed. "Hello?" I answered.

"I have a delivery for Catherine Kelly."

"Come on up," I responded and buzzed to let him in.

A few moments later, I opened my door to an older gentleman, probably late fifties, with a military bearing. He wore a black suit and stood at attention. He wasn't much taller than me but had more brawn and muscle. He was distinguished, with his clipped silver hair. I glanced at the oversized shopping bag, containing what appeared to be a large rectangular box. "Can I help you?" My heart pounded, and I imagined all sorts of horrific scenarios.

"Hello, Miss Kelly."

I half expected him to salute—or pull out a gun and shoot me.

"I'm George Graham. I work for Mr. Lambourne."

I relaxed slightly and gave Laird a reassuring pat.

So that was the package William was sending.

"Mr. Lambourne asked that I deliver this. May I come in and place it for you?" His gaze drifted toward Laird, who wagged his tail.

I didn't really need a box "placed," but before I could refuse, George Graham moved into my condo, marching toward the living room.

"Um, okay." What else could I say? He was already inside.

"Where should I place it?"

I faltered. I had never been good at this. I searched the living room. "Why don't you... um, put it on the coffee table?"

"Very good, Miss Kelly. I am to remind you that Mr. Lambourne will see you this evening at seven."

"Thanks." I followed him and watched as he delicately set the bag with the box on my table, centering it just so. "What's in it?" I asked, releasing Laird's collar. He bounded into the kitchen where his food and water waited.

"I'm afraid I cannot answer that, Miss Kelly. Please do be ready promptly at seven."

It was a little annoying that William thought I needed someone to remind me of a date we'd made only a few hours ago, but I tried not to let my irritation show.

"It was a pleasure to meet you, Miss Kelly," George said, giving me a smile and stepping back from the table. "Enjoy the rest of your afternoon."

And then he walked away, striding through my living room as though it were his own. I locked the door after him then stood there. How weird was that? I felt like I was an undercover operative for the CIA. In which case, I'd better see what was in my special delivery. I was giddy with anticipation. I pulled the large box out of the bag and removed the lid. And then my cell rang. William already? But when I glanced at the screen I saw it was Beckett. Perfect.

I answered and hit speaker. "Hey, Beckett."

"Hey, yourself. You sound like your day improved."

I grinned, fingering the delicate tissue paper inside the box. "You have no idea." I filled him in on the events of the day, editing very little—I decided I might as well give him full disclosure—and he *oohed* and *aahed* at just the right times.

After I related the kitchen floor scene, he interrupted. "And he didn't want anything in return? Are you making this up?"

I laughed. "In fact, he asked me out on a date tonight. We're going to an event at The Art Institute."

"Formal?"

"Uh-huh."

"Damn. I wish I could come over and help you get ready, but I have a thing tonight. I can't get out of it."

"I'll be fine." I was beginning to panic a little now. I had been counting on recruiting Beckett's help. Now I'd have to get ready by myself. "I'll be fine," I repeated for my own benefit. "I got a mani and a pedi and everything. And guess what happened on the way home?"

"I would have never guessed oral sex on your kitchen floor, which, by the way, I will never look at the same way again. You'll have to tell me."

"William texted me he was having a package delivered, and when I got home, this butler commando guy delivered it."

"Oh, my God! What was in it? Diamonds? Keys to a Mercedes?"

I rolled my eyes. "I don't know. I pulled off the lid but haven't looked inside yet."

"Cat! Open it! Hurry!"

"Okay, okay!" But I was laughing so hard I had to take a deep breath.

"It's like Christmas all over again," Beckett said, and I could hear the anticipation in his voice. "What do you see? What does the box look like?"

"Um, it's a white box, large, deep, and rectangular. It was in a shopping bag without any writing on it. I pulled the top off and inside is thin, white tissue paper."

"The good stuff."

"There's good tissue paper?"

"Just open it already! You're killing me!"

I started laughing again, but I pulled the folds of the paper away, revealing something red. I reached out to touch it and felt the soft silk slide through my fingers. "It's red and silk," I told Beckett.

"What is it?"

"Hold on." I lifted the gift from the box and stood, allowing the long silk dress to cascade to the floor. "Oh, Beckett." I sighed. No one had ever given me surprise gifts, and no one had ever given me something like *this*.

"What is it?"

I couldn't begin to describe it. It was too beautiful. The dress was deep red with a plunging neckline accented by intricate beading. There was no way that could have been done by machine. It must have been hand-sewn, and that meant the gown was ridiculously expensive. "It's a dress, Beckett. A formal one for tonight." I described it, hardly doing it justice, and finally, I took a picture and texted it to him. Had William picked this out? If so, his taste was exquisite.

When Beckett received the picture, he sighed. "It's going to look fabulous. Wait. Is it your size?"

I checked the label. "Yes. Exactly. Is that creepy?"

"Maybe a little."

I carefully draped the gown over the couch and caught a glimpse of something else in the box. "Beckett, there's more." I couldn't believe this. This kind of stuff just didn't happen to me.

"More? Tell me!"

I reached into the box, moved the tissue aside, and pulled out a red and black lace bra and thong set. I knew this set. I had it on my if-I-win-the-lottery wish list. It was incredibly expensive and stunningly gorgeous. And the red and the black were scorching. Really sexy. I'd been coveting it ever since I first laid eyes on it. I checked the label and was stunned that, again, the set was my size.

"Beckett, you're not going to believe this. You know that bra and thong set I showed you?"

"Cat, you show me dozens. You're obsessed."

"It was red and black lace and seriously expensive."

"Oh, right. I remember. Do *not* tell me he sent it to you."

"The exact one—my size. And there's more."

"I can't take it! What else?"

I couldn't take it either. Why was William sending me all this? He was spoiling the wrong girl. He might have correctly guessed my bra size, but he didn't know me at all. I pulled out another lacy item. "Beckett, there's a matching garter belt. It's gorgeous." I reached back into the treasure box. "And black silk stockings. Beckett, you have to feel them. They're weightless and impossibly fine."

"This is so hot. He obviously knows what he likes. Your tastes mesh."

Except I didn't like to wear red, and it felt totally weird to receive lingerie from a guy I barely knew. I should send it back. How could I possibly accept this? And then I gasped because I saw shoes. "Shoes!"

"Cat, I seriously hate you right now. Describe already."

"Black pumps. Really sexy and…" I hissed in a breath when I saw the red soles. "Beckett, these are Christian Louboutins." I flipped them over and stared at the signature on the inside.

"Those have got to run like nine hundred dollars."

"I know, and they're my size and everything." I slipped them on and admired the way they looked. "They're gorgeous." I stared at the dress, the lingerie, and the shoes. It was all exquisite, chosen by a man with impeccable taste. And it was too much for any woman on a first date, and definitely too much for someone like me.

"Cat, I'm happy for you. You totally deserve this," Beckett said as though reading my thoughts. "I need a picture after you get dressed." Beckett continued squealing in delight, but I had to sit on the couch. I was overwhelmed. How did William have time to shop for all this? And how did he know my sizes? Not just my dress size—my bra size and my shoe size. I peered around my condo half afraid I'd spot a spy camera.

I slipped the shoes off and started to place them back in the box when I spotted two smaller boxes. "Beckett," I interrupted. "There's more."

"Shut *up*!"

My heart was pounding now. This was crazy and exciting. I wanted it to stop, but it felt like Christmas to me too. "Two smaller boxes. I'm opening the first one." I pulled the lid off. "It's a crystal vial with amber liquid."

"A decanter?"

"It's small, like the size of perfume."

"What's the label?"

"There isn't one."

I pulled the delicate stopper out and inhaled deeply as the most amazing scent wafted to my nose. "Oh, my God, Beckett. It smells so good." I dabbed a little on my wrist and couldn't stop sniffing it. "It's delicious."

William really knew how to pull out all the stops. Perfume, shoes, lingerie. It was too much. And it wasn't over.

"I'm almost afraid to open this last one," I told Beckett. "It's small and leather. It looks expensive. Really elegant."

"Jewelry?" Beckett asked, his voice breathless.

I flipped open the box and stared at a bracelet. My jaw dropped. "Holy shit. It's a bracelet," I whispered.

"Jewelry! I knew it!"

"But, Beckett, you have to see it. It can't be real. There's no way this is real."

He blew out a breath. "Cat, William Lambourne is a billionaire. *Billionaire*. It's real."

"Then it's too much. You should see it. It's a silver cuff, about three inches wide." I stared at it. This was crazy. He couldn't be giving this to me. He didn't even know me. First, oral sex on my kitchen floor—now expensive gifts? Everything was moving so fast. I couldn't recover from one shock before I received another.

"Nice."

"It's covered—I mean covered—in diamonds. Beckett, it's breathtaking." My hand shook just holding it. It sparkled like nothing

I'd ever imagined. I wanted to slip it on my wrist, but I didn't think I'd ever take it off again. I never dreamed I'd ever wear something this stunning. I wasn't poor by any standards, but this was totally out of my league. It was beyond my wildest dreams. "Okay, I'm sending you another picture." I quickly snapped a photo of the bracelet and texted it to Beckett. Then I placed the bracelet into its box reverently and lifted a small white card on heavy monogrammed stock.

The monogram was *WML*.

I didn't even know his middle name. He was giving me a diamond bracelet, and I couldn't even answer a basic question about him. "There's a card," I told Beckett.

"Ooh, read it!"

"*I can still taste you, Catherine. And I am hungry for more. See you tonight. W.*"

"That is so fucking *hot*," Beckett crowed. "I mean, Cat, I'm fanning myself here."

"Yeah." I stared at the bracelet and the gown and the shoes and the perfume and shook my head.

"Oh my God, Cat. The bracelet is amazing. I wish I didn't have plans tonight."

"I don't need help." But my voice wavered. I was feeling really insecure now. This was a lot of attention. What did William expect in return? How could I possibly measure up to his expectations? Suddenly, my confidence wavered.

"With all those gorgeous things, you can't go wrong," Beckett said. "This is your Cinderella moment. I only wish I could be your lady-in-waiting."

I laughed, but the uneasy feeling didn't lift. Maybe this date wasn't a good idea. The gifts were spectacular, but they were too much. I voiced my concern to Beckett, and he scoffed. "Too much? Cat, you're worth all that and more. You cannot back out, or you'll regret it for the rest of your life. Besides, you said this afternoon was amazing."

That was true. The *pain au chocolat*, William's kisses, his hands, his mouth on me, his tongue inside me—all that had been incredible. I'd wanted more. And I had agreed to go on the date, knowing that William wanted more. But this… this was a full-press seduction, and I wasn't sure I could handle it. Thinking with my sex drive was getting me into deep trouble.

"I don't know, Beckett. It feels too fast. And it's creepy, right? How does he know my sizes, my preferences?"

"It's romantic!"

"It feels like an invasion of privacy. I didn't even know this guy a few days ago. He was a stormy-eyed stranger I met on the street. And now, he's buying me shoes and jewelry?" Granted, that stranger totally rocked my world this afternoon. I didn't know I could feel that way—*three* times—but what did I really know about William M. Lambourne? He was rich and handsome and had good taste in jewelry?

"Cat, don't over-think it," Beckett warned. "I can hear you over-thinking it."

"It's not over-thinking to be weirded out when a guy asks you on a date and then acts like you're a doll for him to dress up. This is my first official date in years, and it's weird!"

"Cat, this guy sees how special you are. Why shouldn't he show it?"

"With a diamond bracelet?"

"He's a billionaire! To William Lambourne, a hundred thousand dollars is pocket change."

"I doubt that."

"Cat, when you picked up the phone, you sounded happy. This guy makes you happy. Or at least he made you happy in your kitchen. Please go."

I did feel kind of happy, actually. Beckett was right about that. And I couldn't deny that whatever was happening between William and me was something extraordinary. But it felt so much like a whirlwind that I didn't have time to think or to analyze. I hadn't felt like this in so long—maybe I'd never felt like this. I could only imagine what actually doing it with William would be like. Even after three shattering climaxes on my kitchen floor, I was still aching and I still wanted him. But what if he was building me up into some sort of ideal I'd only tear down when I had to tell him the truth? These gifts were beautiful, but they weren't for me. They were for some other woman—one who hadn't killed her husband.

And yet, I'd agreed to go. William would only show up and talk me into going anyway. I had no willpower when it came to him.

"Okay," I said with a sigh. "I'll go."

"Yes!" Beckett yelled.

"I can't let him get away. Not yet." Not before I'd sampled all that he had to offer.

"The sex is going to be fabulous."

I laughed. Beckett could always read my mind. "How do you know?"

"Rebound sex always is. You should definitely have some. Multiple times!"

"Well, there is that New Year's resolution. I don't want to disappoint my mother."

"Exactly. Cat, just have fun. Don't *think* so much."

"Okay, I'll go. On my terms, Beckett."

SEVEN

It seemed to take an eternity to get ready. I was so nervous my hands shook as I tried to style my hair and put makeup on. I second-guessed every decision and wished Beckett had been free to come over. I needed serious help.

When I got out of bed this morning, I had no idea I'd be going on a date tonight, let alone attending a formal event. I felt mentally unprepared. What was I going to talk about? First dates were awkward enough without having been naked together. Well, when at least one of you had already been totally naked. Did we gloss over this afternoon, or was sex expected now? And that was the big stuff! There were tons of little things. Did he come up to get me? Did I wait for him to open the car door? What were the rules? Had they changed? Was there an Internet site I could reference? And then, suddenly, it was five to seven, and I was out of time to panic or obsess.

There was a tap on my door at seven o'clock exactly. Punctuality was obviously one of William's hang-ups—definitely not one of mine. I was late for pretty much everything. Sometimes, I tried to trick myself by setting all my clocks ahead, but that only worked for so long before I adjusted.

I took a deep breath and steeled myself for the night ahead. I needed to be cool and composed in the face of William's stormy eyes and staggering hotness. Every time I made any decision about him, once in his presence, I couldn't think about anything but how incredibly sexy he was. All my resolutions flew out the door.

I smoothed my dress, praying he would not see how nervous I was, and opened the door. My breath whooshed out. He looked every bit as good as I expected and more. My lungs tightened, and I felt my legs turn to mush. How could any man be that gorgeous? And I was never the kind of girl who could resist a man in a tux. William looked dashing in his perfectly cut and classically elegant black tuxedo. The coat accentuated the breadth of his shoulders and the slimness of his waist. His hair was swept back from his forehead and artfully styled, his stormy eyes fixed on me. I wanted to drag him inside, rip off the tux, and forget about the date.

Fortunately, I couldn't do anything but stare at the god in my doorway. His blue eyes raked hungrily over me from top to bottom. And then, for a moment, I caught a flicker of disappointment. It was gone instantly, and I might have thought I imagined it. He opened his mouth. My heart seemed to falter. I'd made the wrong choice. He wasn't happy. "Is everything okay?" I asked quietly.

He shook his head and swallowed. "You look gorgeous, Catherine. I can hardly speak. I'm overwhelmed."

The warmth of his voice made me flush, but I knew he wasn't seeing what he wanted. I wasn't wearing the red gown he'd sent. I couldn't. It wasn't my style—too attention-grabbing, too loud. And anyway, I barely knew him and I wasn't about to let him make wardrobe choices for me. So I'd gone with my own selection for the evening, which was none too shabby. I thought the ensemble I'd put together was elegant and chic, if more minimalist than maybe William would have liked. I wore a sleek, figure-hugging, black wool jersey dress with a back that dipped low. Very low. The dress draped artfully to the floor, and the sleeves were long and billowing. The dress hugged my curves, and I felt sexy, but still like me.

I hadn't completely disregarded William's gifts. I couldn't wear a bra because of the back, but I was wearing the tiny red and black lace thong. I loved the garter belt and stockings, but the dress was clingy, and the belt would have showed, so I opted for my own thigh-high black stockings with lace on the top band. And hopefully, William had noticed I was wearing the shoes, the bracelet, and the perfume.

I'd piled my hair in an artfully messy bun and applied soft, shimmery makeup. Except for my lips. I'd chosen a deep matte red color, drawing attention to my mouth and making it, with the exception of that fabulous bracelet, my best accessory. I saw William's gaze return to my lips over and over, and I couldn't help but feel relieved, knowing my choice was having the desired effect.

"You're beautiful," he said. "You take my breath away."

"Thank you." I tried not to fidget, but I was waiting for him to say something about the red dress. "I know this isn't what you sent me, but..." On a whim, I turned, showing him the deep plunge in the back. He drew in an audible breath of appreciation, and I felt my pulse kick up. It felt good to be looked at with admiration, though I could feel my cheeks flush with embarrassment and self-consciousness.

I turned to find William staring at me hotly. His stormy eyes were virtual tempests of desire, and I went liquid inside looking at him look at me. No wonder he was so successful. With one look I was ready to do whatever he wanted. Again.

His desire was palpable, and I worried we wouldn't make it to the event. His eyes lingered on my mouth, and I could all but feel his need to kiss me. Or maybe, it was *my* need to be kissed. I wanted his mouth on me. I wanted his hands on me. I wanted to feel his body pressed against mine.

"You're lovely, Catherine," he said, finally breaking the silence. "Sexy. Black suits you, and no one would dare mistake you for a grieving widow in that dress. It's a killer."

My blood chilled. I actually felt my body cool. My stomach clenched, and I felt nauseated. William was still talking, but all I saw was his mouth moving. All I could hear was blood rushing in my ears. Did he know? Had William found out about Jace? I hadn't told him anything. I hadn't told anybody. The only people in Chicago who knew were Beckett and the people in my support group. Beckett would never have said anything to William.

Had he checked up on me? Had he done research, like he might do for a company he wanted to buy? Maybe that's what I was to William—an acquisition. He thought I was an easy purchase because I was vulnerable. And that was how I felt—like I'd been ripped open, all my secrets exposed.

I was also confused. If William had checked on me, why would he bring it up? Why even mention it? It would have been easy to pretend he didn't know. If he knew, he would never have sent me these exquisite gifts. There was no way he could have known. It had been an offhanded comment, and I was overreacting.

"Catherine?"

I blinked and realized William had stopped talking. It took me a moment to notice the sparkle in his stormy eyes and the wicked grin on his sensual mouth.

"I'm sorry. What did you say?"

He leaned close so that his mouth brushed my ear. "I said, maybe what you're mourning is my mouth between your legs, my tongue teasing you until you can't take it anymore, and you coming hard against my lips. Like you did this afternoon."

I took a shuddering breath, hot all over again. William didn't know. There was no way he would have phrased his sex talk like that if he knew. As I'd suspected, it was a poor choice of words, and my reaction would make him wonder, if I wasn't careful. My own neurosis was getting the better of me.

"Maybe we better go before we end up staying in," I said. Turning, I grabbed my wrap and my evening clutch from the side table in the small entry area and stepped out.

Downstairs, a handsome man with café au lait skin and a shaved head opened the door to my building. He was in his thirties and dressed like he'd stepped out of a stylish version of *Men in Black*. An earpiece that coiled to the back of his neck and disappeared beneath his shirt collar accessorized a dark suit and tie. Like George Graham, who had come to my door earlier, this man had a military bearing. I wouldn't have been surprised if he had a gun concealed under his coat or beneath his pant leg. I supposed that a man as wealthy as William needed security, but I couldn't imagine William not handling himself. He moved with tightly coiled power and control. From my brief explorations through his clothing during our encounter on my kitchen floor earlier today—had that only been a few hours ago?—I knew there wasn't an ounce of flab on him. His chest, arms, and abs had felt hard and muscled under my fingertips.

The driver pressed his hand to his ear, listening to a message, and then opened the door of the black SUV he guarded. Long and black with tinted windows, it gleamed in the light from the street lamps. "Good evening, Miss Kelly. My name is Anthony."

"Hi, Anthony." I looked at William and raised a brow. "Don't tell me your code name is POTUS."

He smiled, and even though I loved the intense looks filled with desire he flashed me, I liked his casual, fun side too. "Not yet."

I laughed and then realized perhaps he was serious. Anthony held out his hand and assisted me up the step and into the interior of the luxury SUV. I sank into the plush leather seat, which was wonderfully warm and cozy. I could get used to this. William followed, seating himself beside me. Anthony closed the door, and I noticed the SUV had a privacy window. It was closed, so William and I were alone.

I heard the clink of ice and watched as William pulled a bottle from the bucket where it had been chilling. "Champagne?" He raised his brows in a smoldering look that set my heart racing.

"Yes, please." It was exactly what I needed to relax and retrieve the sense of anticipation and excitement I'd been feeling before William's poorly worded comment. He lifted a flute and poured the bubbling liquid into it. I studied the bottle, interested in the brand billionaires chose, and saw familiar initials: *WML*.

"What label is that?" I asked as he handed me the flute and poured another for himself. He sipped his champagne and watched. His look was scorching. He was scorching. Half of me wondered what I was doing with a man this gorgeous. The other half was way too turned on to think.

"My label."

"You have a winery?" I shook my head. Of course, he had a winery. Was there anything he didn't have?

"I do, and it's one of my recent acquisitions." His eyes shown as he spoke, and I could tell this was a subject close to his heart. "I've always enjoyed wine, and I thought I might see if I was any good at being a vintner."

"So you take an active role in the process?"

"Yes." He rested his flute in the car's built-in glass holder. "I take an active role in most ventures." He reached for me, putting his arm around me, dragging me closer. The heat from his body infused me, and I felt a magnetic pull that made me want to get closer. It felt good to be in his arms, good to be pressed against him, and even better when he nuzzled my neck. I closed my eyes and shivered with pleasure. His soft lips were like a drug on the sensitive flesh of my nape.

"You smell amazing, Catherine," he murmured against my neck. "I couldn't resist." He looked at me, his expression almost apologetic. "What were we talking about?"

My mind went blank for a moment. "Oh, um, your ventures?"

"God, no wonder my mind wandered. I'll bore you to tears. I'm glad you agreed to come with me tonight."

"Me, too." And I meant it. It felt right to be held, comforting to have his hand trail up and down my arm. I felt like I was in a cocoon of warmth and safety. "How did you know I liked the Art Institute?"

"A guess," he said, running a hand lightly over my hair. "You're an artist, and it's a fabulous museum. It's one of my favorite places in Chicago."

"Really?" I was truly surprised. It seemed this man continually surprised me.

"Absolutely. I grew up in Chicago, and my mother took me and my brother to the Art Institute when we were young. She'd call it a cultural day, and we'd sleep in late and play hooky from school." There was that boyish grin again. I could feel the excitement he must have felt as a kid on those special days.

"We'd take the L to the museum, which was always fun—you know boys and trains—and wander around for hours. Then, when we were ready to collapse, we'd have lunch somewhere and talk and eat delicious food."

"It sounds wonderful," I said.

"It was. And now, you're part of that memory too." He looked at me for a long moment, seeming to drink in the sight of me, and then his mouth touched mine in a slow, soft kiss. His arms tightened on my body, pulling me closer, holding me tighter. He was warm and solid. I could feel his strength, but his kiss was soft and sweet. And then his lips parted, the kiss deepened, and his mouth melded with mine. His hands stroked my hair, my cheek, and my throat as he moved his mouth over mine.

He slid one hand down my arm, my belly, and then my thigh. I trembled in anticipation as his mouth kept up its gentle torture. He kissed me softly and deeply, even as his hands stroked up and down my body with reverence. He explored me, worshipped me, and made me feel as though I was the most beautiful woman he'd ever seen. I knew it couldn't be true, but I didn't care. His skilled hands had me hot and wet, and when he palmed my braless breast through my dress, I couldn't stop a quiet moan. My nipples were painfully hard for him, and he rubbed them through the jersey material, easing the ache, and ratcheting it up too.

"Did you do that on purpose?" he growled, his fingers pinching one nipple lightly then rubbing it to soothe the sting. I shifted on my seat, barely able to keep my hips from wriggling. I wanted him. I was more excited by these soft caresses than I'd been after hours of foreplay. He had a way of arousing me to fever pitch quickly and mercilessly.

"Do what on purpose?" I answered, vaguely aware he had asked me a question.

"Your lips. That color. I can't stop thinking…" He broke off, and I heard a buzzing sound. "Damn it," he muttered and shifted to reach for his pocket. When he saw the number on his cell, he withdrew, setting me away slightly.

My head swam. One moment I'd been in his arms, warm and aroused, and now, I was pushed to the other side of the SUV.

"Lambourne," he said into the phone then listened.

I watched, waiting for him to give me an apologetic look or whisper he would be just a moment, but as the call went on, I could see that wasn't going to happen. And anyway, the mood was broken. I took out my mirror and repaired my lipstick, taking my time.

"That won't be necessary," William said into the phone. He leaned farther away, turning so I couldn't hear his words. An icy anger settled in the pit of my stomach. I might not have dated for a while, but I knew it was bad manners to take a call in the middle of kissing someone. I knew it was rude to have a lengthy conversation and ignore your date. Even if my mood hadn't soured, I could feel the coolness oozing from William. Whatever the person on the other end was saying, it was not good news. William was royally pissed.

"Fine," he barked finally. "Do that. I expect updates." He slid the phone in his pocket, and I waited for him to turn back to me.

He didn't. Instead, he stared moodily out the window, not speaking or looking at me.

"Is everything okay?" I asked after a long moment of silence.

"Fine," he said.

I frowned. What was going on? Had I done something wrong? "William—?" I began.

"Get your wrap," he snapped. "We're here."

EIGHT

Stung by William's harsh tone, I fumbled for my wrap, and when I found it, I wound it protectively around my shoulders. I looked at him, expecting an apology or an explanation, but he acted as though he'd forgotten I was in the car. From his look, it was clear his thoughts were miles away.

The SUV slowed, and I peered out. We were in a line of limos and luxury cars heading toward the Art Institute. I recognized the façade of the new modern wing, though I'd never entered this way. I'd been to the Art Institute several times since moving to Chicago and had always entered from Michigan Avenue, between the iconic lions that guarded the main entrance. But I liked this view of the museum. The clean lines and boxy shape were eye-catching but didn't detract from what the real treasures were—the art inside.

It was dark, and the museum was lit up, the soft bright lights spilling onto the street and illuminating the well-dressed crowd inside. My belly fluttered with anticipation and unease. Was William going to ignore me all night? Surely he was going to snap out of this sudden morose mood. This was not my scene, but I was willing to be open-minded and sample William's world.

The SUV slid to a smooth stop, and Anthony appeared to open the door. William exited first, perfunctorily holding his hand out. I took it and stepped down, looking at the impressive building and shivering without the heated seats to keep me warm. I started for the entrance then almost jumped when William took my hand and pulled it to his lips. With a smile, he kissed my knuckles. It wasn't the apology I'd expected, but it was better than nothing. He drew back slightly, noting I was wearing the diamond cuff.

"It suits you," he said with a smile.

"I should have thanked you."

"Seeing it on your wrist is thanks enough." He tugged my arm. "Come on. I hate these events, but at least one part of the evening won't be painful. The food should be amazing."

We joined the queue of formally dressed men and women and made our way into the building. William took my wrap and checked it then led me into Griffin Court, a long rectangular open space with windows to showcase the stars and blond wood on the floors. On either side were rooms filled with art. Women in formal gowns and men in tuxedos meandered and mingled, while waiters moved through the crowd with champagne and hors d'oeuvres. I could see that I was out of place here. The crowd was older, and judging by the jewels on the women, very wealthy.

I turned to William. "I never asked what this event is for." The man beside me was once again the stranger I'd glimpsed after the phone call. The relaxed manner he'd shown when he kissed my hand was gone, replaced by a stern façade. The smiles he'd lavished earlier had vanished, and his expression was severe and hard. Even his stormy eyes looked cold and intense. "William?"

He flicked a glance at me, as though he didn't even know me. As though he was looking at a stranger. "I beg your pardon. Did you say something?" Even his voice was different, formal and flat.

"I asked about the purpose of the event."

"Fundraiser," he said shortly and looked away.

If he'd slapped me in the face, he couldn't have been crueler. Where was the warm, sexy man from my kitchen this morning and the SUV moments ago? Once again, I wondered if I'd I done something wrong. Why was he shutting me out?

A waiter passed, and William took two glasses of champagne from a tray, handed me one, and then put his hand on the small of my back. His palm was warm and his pressure gentle as he urged me forward. His touch reminded me of his hands on me in the SUV. I glanced back, wondering if he was thinking of our kisses on the drive over, but he wasn't looking at me. What had I done?

Suddenly, an older man and his much younger trophy wife were standing in front of us.

"Lambourne!" the man said, shaking William's hand. "Good to see you. I recognized some of your pieces."

Confused, I glanced at William for an explanation. *His* pieces? Was he an artist?

"Good to see you, Martin. And you, Sheila."

The blond gave him a huge smile, then reached out and stroked his arm. "I was hoping you'd be here."

I raised my brows at her flirtation. I imagined it was commonplace for a gorgeous man like William.

"And who is this beautiful woman on your arm tonight?" Martin asked. I felt William's fingers tighten and release on my back. He hesitated, but it was long enough to make me wonder if he didn't want to introduce me.

"Martin and Sheila Warwick, this is Catherine Kelly."

"Lovely to meet you, Catherine," Martin said, taking my hand warmly. William stiffened as our hands met. "May I say you look lovely tonight?"

"Thank you."

"Hello," Sheila said, looking away without interest.

Martin's gaze shifted to William. "How are things going with the Taggert people? Any movement on the term sheet?"

What ensued was a lengthy discussion on conversion rates, liquidation preferences, and anti-dilution adjustments. I was no idiot, but I couldn't follow the conversation, and neither William nor Martin included me. Sheila drifted away immediately, but I didn't know my role. Was I supposed to stay and listen? Attempt to contribute? Stand beside William and look pretty? His hand stayed firmly on my back, but he didn't look at me or acknowledge me.

Finally, Martin had the answers he wanted and moved away, enveloped by the growing crowd. I estimated over two hundred people were in attendance, and I wondered if there would be a dinner, or if the black-tie event would consist of champagne and mingling.

William had mentioned great food, but I had yet to taste the hors d'oeuvres.

When Martin Warwick moved away, I took the opportunity to engage William again. "Mr. Warwick mentioned recognizing your pieces," I said, though William wasn't looking at me. Instead, he moved me down the hallway and deeper into the crowd. He nodded to people as we walked, and I saw blatant envy on the faces of many women. I could hardly blame them. William, even this new William, was hot. If I'd had my eye on him, and a woman I'd never seen showed up on his arm, I'd shoot daggers too.

That thought pacified me a little. After all, William was mine for the evening. He might be virtually ignoring me, but I was the one he had asked to accompany him.

"Warwick talks too much," William said abruptly. I wasn't certain what he meant, and then I remembered I'd asked about his pieces.

"Is it something you don't want to talk about?" I asked, trying to understand what I was doing wrong to earn this reaction.

"It's fine. Warwick is referring to pieces from my personal collection. I have them on loan to the museum."

My jaw dropped. I could now add art collector to his billionaire endeavors.

A steady stream of people approached us for the next half hour. The men talked business, as did some of the women. Other women all but openly propositioned him. I tried to appear interested. I attempted to follow the conversations. Once, I even interjected a comment, but that only earned a long silence from the man speaking to William and an annoyed look from William himself. Finally, that group moved away, with a promise to chat at dinner, and I said, "I think I'll go look at some of the art."

"No."

I blinked at William in confusion. "Excuse me?"

"I need you with me."

I shook my head but had no chance to reply before a woman and two men appeared, eager to shake William's hand. I began to move away, and William grabbed my hand, holding it tightly, keeping me by his side. It was ridiculous. I'd been standing next to him for the better part of an hour, completely ignored, and now that I wanted to walk around, he suddenly needed me. I'd never felt so bewildered by a man's behavior. One moment I was flush with his warmth and passion, and the next I was frozen out. This was supposed to be an enjoyable night, not a mind-fuck. I thought a date with William would be fun and exciting, but now, I wondered if this whole thing had been a mistake.

I began to wonder if I should have come at all. Jace never would have treated me like this. Jace would have been as bored as I was. We'd have sneaked off and got drunk. But William wasn't Jace.

I pulled away from William and his tedious business conversation. When he reached for me, I said in a low voice, "You're busy, and I understand. I'll be fine."

He looked as though he wanted to argue, but he could hardly do so in front of his colleagues.

I gave him a reassuring smile. "I'll see you when dinner is served." I moved away, and William finally allowed it, but I felt his gaze as I wandered through the crowd. I stopped to admire the art, but I couldn't help my gaze drifting back to William. I watched him speak and gesture. He seemed to be someone else, not the man who had kissed me in the freezer at Willowgrass, or brought me *pain au chocolat*, or tongued me until I screamed in ecstasy on my kitchen floor. The man across the room was cold, distant, and hard. I didn't like him much. In fact, I was pretty pissed. I thought about just walking out.

Instead, I snagged another glass of champagne—my third or fourth, I couldn't remember—and moved into an adjacent room housing an exhibit of modern photography. I recognized the artist and smiled as I studied the familiar pieces. These were some of my favorites, and seeing them up close was inspiring. I studied the angles and the lighting, the choice of subject and the choice of film. Two women entered, chatting, and I was so caught up in my admiration, I didn't take any notice. But when one mentioned William, I couldn't help but listen.

"William Lambourne looks even better in person than in *Forbes*. I wouldn't mind taking him home." She was a slim brunette in winter white.

I moved along the wall, keeping to myself, but listening with a small smile. Either they didn't know I was his date or hadn't seen me. I didn't mind the girl talk. As far as I was concerned, they were welcome to Stormy Eyes and his mercurial moods. I couldn't wait for this night to end.

"The pieces on loan aren't the only reason he's here," the other woman, dressed in an embellished navy sheath, added. "His company underwrote some major acquisitions in the modern wing. He'll have the best table tonight."

I slipped out as their conversation went on. I didn't really want to hear more about William Lambourne and his many acquisitions. I was feeling like one of them now. I moved through a group of women in blinding jewels and stepped into another room adjacent to Griffin Court. This room wasn't filled with photography, but I could admire the art nonetheless. Each time I visited the Art Institute, I saw something new and fascinating. The museum's collection really was world class. I thought about seeing if the rest of the museum was open. I would have liked to see more photography, but dinner would be served soon. So I moved into the main hall and took another flute of champagne. It was going down far too easily, making me more than a little insecure.

Had I misread William in the SUV? He'd seemed happy I was with him. Maybe he was pissed that I hadn't worn the gown he sent, but he'd seemed pretty turned on by this one. It was annoying how much I second-guessed myself. I could be insecure all on my own, thank you very much, William Lambourne.

And then I spotted a familiar face. It broke into a smile, and Ben Lee, the head chef from Willowgrass, strutted over and enveloped me in a big hug. I couldn't help but laugh.

"Catherine, it's great to see you!" Ben leaned back and gave me a quick once-over. "You look great."

"Thank you. You clean up pretty well yourself."

"Thanks. I didn't expect to see you here."

"I didn't know I'd be here. I'm William Lambourne's date."

Ben's eyebrows shot up. "Really." Ben gave me another once-over, this time scrutinizing me closely. He met my eyes with a knowing smile. "He's moving really fast with you."

I frowned. What did that mean? Did he move slower with other women? Was everyone here tonight looking at me and wondering how long I'd be on William's arm before he tossed me aside for the next notch on his bedpost?

I took a deep breath and forced myself to get a grip. Who cared what everyone else was thinking. And maybe Ben meant something different than the way I'd interpreted his comment.

"Oh, Catherine! Do not move." Ben flagged a waiter and waved him over. Across the room, I caught a pair of stormy eyes watching. William looked more than a little irritated. I could tell he didn't like that I was talking to Ben. Too bad. I finally had someone to mingle with. He couldn't ditch me at a party and then be annoyed when I found a friend.

"You have to try this," Ben said, taking one of the artfully arranged hors d'oeuvres from the tray.

"What is it?"

"It's a caviar and smoked salmon blini with crème fraiche. It's going to melt in your mouth."

"Did you make it?"

"No, Emil LeClerc did. I trained under him in France, and he's doing all the food tonight. He's why I'm here."

"Lucky you."

"Actually, the thanks goes to your date. William is an investor in Chef LeClerc's New York restaurant. Not that I blame Lambourne. Emil is a genius. Open your mouth. You won't be disappointed."

I opened my mouth, and Ben popped the blini inside. I closed my lips and my eyes and savored the taste. The caviar burst in my mouth with a salty pop followed by the smoky flavor of the salmon and the rich creaminess of the crème fraiche. It was delicious, the flavors perfectly balanced.

I opened my eyes and found myself looking into William's stormy ones. They were blazing with lightning as he glared. "Catherine, I've been missing you."

I'd had too much champagne and replied, "It didn't look that way to me, and I ran into Ben. I'm starving, and he took pity and found me a blini."

Ben held his hand out. "Good to see you again, William."

William did not take Ben's hand. "I'm here now, and I'll be the one to take care of Catherine."

Ben looked a little stunned, then took a step back. "No problem. Catherine, I should find my date. See you around." And he was gone.

I rounded on William. "What the hell was that?"

"I could ask you the same." He still glared, obviously pissed, but at this point, I really didn't care.

"Whatever," I said, waving a hand. I was tired of trying to figure William out, and our date had turned into a major disappointment. I wanted it to be over.

Unfortunately, that was the moment we were called to dinner.

We walked upstairs to the Millennium Park Room, which was airy with a high ceiling and a spectacular view of the surrounding park, twinkling with lights tonight. I counted more than twenty tables of ten seats each and the room was far from cramped. William led me to our numbered table, and we searched for our place cards. I realized we weren't sitting together. Earlier tonight I would have been disappointed. Now, I wished Ben and his date were seated at the table. At least I'd have someone to talk to.

William escorted me to my seat and pulled the chair out. As I sat, he leaned down, and his breath feathered my ear. "That's the last time you'll open your mouth to another man," he said, his voice husky and seductive. I couldn't stop the tremor of pleasure that raced through me at his sexy tone. "From now on, I'm the only man who feeds you." My skin where his breath touched it fired in response, and I squirmed in my seat. His closeness and his voice turned me on, but I didn't appreciate his warning. Who the hell did he think he was? Did other women tolerate this sort of behavior? Why did he think he could get away with the constant shifting from cold to hot and back again?

I thought the night couldn't get worse, and then I saw William's dinner companions. On one side sat a twenty-something, attractive blond who greeted him as though they were old friends or lovers. I suspected the latter. On William's right was a petite older woman, cougar written all over her and obviously a socialite. She wore a low-cut strapless gown and a necklace of diamonds that showcased her remarkable cleavage and her latest face-lift. As the first course arrived, I watched the socialite exercise her flirting skills. She did everything but hop in William's lap to get his attention. Her hand was rooted firmly on his arm, and she had him chatting and smiling. It was a polite smile, but more than I'd garnered all night.

Meanwhile, the man on my left was engaged with his companion, and the woman on my right was busy texting. So I took solace in my wine. It was good wine. The champagne had been good as well, so at least the night had that going for it.

The courses arrived, one after another. They were small and artful, and if the blini Ben fed me earlier was any indication, delicious. But watching William and the socialite killed my appetite. I took a few bites to be polite, but nothing appealed to me except the wine. Between brief, polite exchanges with the guests on either side of me, I sipped my wine and watched William.

I would have preferred not to watch, but I found myself stealing glances. I couldn't help but notice how his hands looked when he held his flatware. He had large hands, but I happened to know they were anything but clumsy. Watching him maneuver his fork and knife was like watching an artist paint. William held them delicately, balancing them elegantly between the proscribed fingers. I watched his hands manipulate the utensils and thought about how he manipulated my body with those same fingers. And then he placed a piece of beef tenderloin in his mouth. He had a sexy mouth. His lips were full and sensual, and I knew they could tease and excite. His mouth closed on his fork, and he took his time to appreciate the morsel. I watched him chew and couldn't banish the image of his mouth on my breast and between my legs.

I really should have looked away, but William was not an easy man to ignore. I kept looking back, noting his chiseled jaw, the way a lock of hair had fallen over his forehead, and of course, those stormy eyes, trained alternately on the blond or the socialite. Never on me.

He was incredibly sexy. I didn't want to be drawn to him, but I couldn't help it. He was a walking sex god. And that thought made me want another swig of wine. And another.

Finally, dessert was served, and I felt like rubbing my hands together in glee. I wasn't about to turn down dessert. I'd tasted Ben's desserts, and I wagered Emil LeClerc's would be just as delicious. But even as slabs of decadent cake arrived on small plates—the server said it was chocolate cherry with rum ganache—I noticed that the other guests were leaving the table and drifting toward the dance floor. I didn't get it. The dessert looked absolutely delicious. Why would they leave it untouched?

And then I remembered where I was. Of course, these calorie counters didn't eat dessert. Nary a chocolate-covered carb ever passed their lips. What was I thinking?

The orchestra began to play, and the audience applauded. The musicians were playing old standards, which I loved. Really, if I'd been here with anyone else I would have been enchanted. The setting was lovely, the music was perfect, and the food was delicious. But all I could think about was how much I wanted to leave. I was bored and disgusted. Maybe the way William was treating me was the norm. Maybe it was exactly what any woman who dated William Lambourne—notorious commitment-phobe and billionaire playboy—signed on for. But I wasn't having fun, and I'd foolishly expected more.

I'd taken a chance, stepped out of my comfort zone, accepted a date I wasn't quite ready for, and now I was hating every moment of it. I wanted to just go with it, but I couldn't. Besides, I told myself, it was better to nip this thing in the bud sooner rather than later. My kitchen, the nuzzling in the SUV—it was all too much, way too soon. I'd tell William good-bye and call it a night, but first I had to find the ladies' room. I'd drunk too much wine and champagne, and it was catching up with me.

I grabbed my clutch and began to rise, but William was behind me, pulling out my chair. I must have looked startled because he took my elbow to steady me and pulled me close. "We need to dance," he growled.

I pulled my arm away. "I don't think so. I'm going home." I stepped back, planning my escape. Better just do it now. "Thank you for...an interesting evening," I began, "but—"

Ignoring my protests, William artfully captured my arm again and pulled me close, steering me onto the dance floor. The man obviously didn't take no for an answer. I could tell by the set of his jaw there was no point in resisting, so I resigned myself to one dance. Maybe it would help my buzz from the wine would wear off.

The orchestra struck up Cole Porter's "Night and Day," and I smiled. My dad always loved Frank Sinatra, and I'd probably heard Ol' Blue Eyes sing this song a thousand times.

"You're smiling," William said. "Does that mean you'll stay?"

"It means I like the music. My father used to play this song."

"He has good taste." William turned me expertly. "I always wanted to sing like Sinatra, but I can't carry a tune."

"You mean you have flaws?"

He arched a brow. "One or two."

It seemed appropriate that this song played for my dance with William. He was just a little too intense and jealous, and "Night and Day," was the perfect anthem for obsession.

Even as I had the thought, William pulled me flush against him. His warm hand on my bare back sent electric currents rippling through me. It annoyed me that he could do this. His touch alone could turn me on. He moved with me—he was a great dancer, so I added that to his many talents—and my nipples hardened as our bodies rubbed together. I didn't want to want him, but my body had a mind of its own. He pressed his pelvis into my belly, and I felt him stirring. He wanted me. It was gratifying but confusing as hell. Why had he ignored me all night?

"I love that I can do that to you, Catherine," he whispered in my ear, his breath hot. "I love that I can make your nipples instantly hard."

Pleasure spiraled through me. *Oh, shit*, I thought as my head spun from the wine. I could feel my body reacting to his closeness and the sultry sound of his voice.

"I've been thinking about your mouth all night. Those red lips. I imagined you kneeling in front of me, your lips sucking me, and your perfect tits rubbing against me."

No.

I didn't want to get hot and bothered again, but I couldn't seem to stop it. We swayed elegantly to the music, and I'm sure no one watching could have guessed all the dirty things he whispered in my ear. I thought about breaking away, but he held me possessively, his fingers drumming and caressing the bared skin of my lower back. His hand was so low that if he dipped it another fraction of an inch, he'd be able to touch the lace of my thong. I took a shaky breath and realized I wanted him to touch me there. I wanted him to do so much more.

"Every man here wants you, Catherine," he said. "It's those scarlet lips and your damn fuckable mouth."

I wanted to argue, but between the music and the wine and William's hard body against mine, I couldn't think. I was thankful the music was loud enough that no one could hear his words. They were purred for me alone. Against my better judgment, I closed my eyes against the dizziness I felt and reveled in the feel of William's arms around me. If I hadn't drank so much, if I'd eaten something, I could have made witty comebacks. I could have put him in his place. But all

I could do was to keep dancing and resist the urge to ask him to take me right then and there.

"I want to fuck your mouth, Catherine. I want to see my cock between your red lips."

Yes. I wanted that too. I was already wet for him. If he'd pulled me off the dance floor and into a private room, I would have sucked him off without protest. He could make me do anything he liked.

"I moved your place card," he said, bringing my attention back to the dance and the fundraiser. "The speeches will start in a few minutes, and I want you sitting next to me. No more taunting me from across the table."

I pulled back and looked up at him. "Can you do that? Just move the place cards?" If he could simply pick up a place card and move it at will, then why hadn't he done it earlier? Why had he made me sit across the table from him? A punishment? Or was it because he wanted to keep me at a distance? Or maybe he wanted to get close to someone else. The blond came to mind, but I didn't voice my thoughts.

"I paid twenty-five thousand dollars a plate for that table," he growled in my ear. "I can do whatever the fuck I want."

I did the quick math in my head. Twenty-five thousand a plate meant the table alone cost a quarter of a million dollars. How many of these did he go to in a week, a month, a year? I couldn't fathom that kind of money or that kind of power. It turned me on. This man who could have everything wanted me.

The song ended, and we were near the edge of the dance floor. Before he could lead me into another dance or take my hand and escort me to the table, yet another business-type vying for his attention approached him. William gave me a frown, but I put my hand on his arm. "I have to find the ladies' room. I'll see you at the table."

He nodded, and while the music started again, I watched as hot, sexy William Lambourne walked toward a group of powerful men, where he would probably hold court.

I took an uneasy breath and headed for the restrooms. I wasn't leaving after all. Maybe the night would turn out okay. Maybe we'd just gotten off to a bad start.

I'd barely made it off the dance floor when the blond seated beside William at dinner sidled up next to me. "Hello, Catherine," she said over the music.

"I'm sorry. Have we met?"

"No." The tone in her voice indicated that not only had we not met, I was fortunate to be meeting her then. "I'm Lara Kendall." She said her name as though I should have heard of her. She was definitely the ice-princess type—the kind who probably grew up with every privilege and advantage and dedicated herself to volunteering, shopping, lunching, and exercising. I disliked her immediately and wondered what her connection to William could be. Was she a former lover? A current lover? A man would have to be dead not to be attracted to her. She was tiny, one of those size zeroes, but curvy in the right places. She was a classic beauty with porcelain skin, large blue eyes, and that corn silk blond hair most women could get only from a bottle. I felt huge and drab beside her. My freckles, so perfect for the beaches of California, felt ugly and common. And though I was a size six, she was so slim that I felt fat and bloated.

I took a deep breath and decided to get through this quickly. "I'm Catherine Kelly, but you seem to know that already."

"So you're here with William." Her gaze flicked to the other end of the room. He was ensconced in—if the looks on the men's faces were an indication—a serious conversation. "How long have you been together?" Lara asked.

I laughed. I didn't know if we *were* together. "Not long." Feeling self-conscious standing beside the Ice Princess, I tucked a stray tendril of hair that had come loose from my bun behind my ear. Great. I hadn't checked my hair or makeup all night. I probably looked a mess.

Before I could lower my hand, Lara grabbed my wrist. "What a lovely bracelet." But her voice and the look on her face didn't match her words. She gripped my wrist tightly, twisting my arm to get a better look. The angle was uncomfortable, as awkward as having this woman I didn't even know touching me.

"It was a gift," I said, trying to gently pull my arm back. Lara didn't let go.

She smirked. "I'm sure it was. William does love to spoil his women."

I must have jerked in surprise at her words because she tightened her hold.

"If I had to guess, I'd say this was platinum, about ten carats." She looked directly into my face. "Wow. You must have extraordinary skills." Her gaze settled on my lips, and suddenly, they felt overly done, too heavily rouged. She smirked, and I yanked my arm away, stunned by the cutting comments that rolled off her tongue with her smile.

"Excuse me," I said coldly. "I need to find the ladies' room."

"Oh, good idea," Lara said. Then she leaned close and fake-whispered loudly, her smile still plastered on her face, "You have a bit of lipstick on your teeth. Nice to meet you. And have a good night." Then she turned and strutted away.

My head reeled, and I stood dumbfounded, seemingly rooted in place. The band finished the song they'd been playing with a flourish and launched into another of my father's favorites, "The Lady is a Tramp."

I shook my head as the singer sang about a woman too hungry to wait for dinner and arriving unfashionably early for the theater. That was why the lady was a tramp.

How fitting, I thought, because that was exactly how I felt. Like a tramp.

I scanned the room and found the group of men William had been chatting with, but he was nowhere to be found. As the band sang about the woman who wouldn't dish the dirt with the rest of the broads, I pulled off the platinum and diamond cuff bracelet, walked to the empty table, and set it beside William's place card. As promised, my card was beside his, but I wouldn't be joining him. I left the dining room, hurried down the steps to the empty Griffin Court, and stopped to get my wrap at the coat check.

I walked into the frigid night. Hailing a cab was easy in my formal wear, and I told the driver to take me home to Lincoln Park. Then I sat back, closed my eyes, and fought the sting of tears.

NINE

I woke on Sunday morning with a headache and an empty stomach. I'd turned off my phone when I got in the cab, and when I checked the time I saw I had a slew of voice mails and texts. With a sigh, I scrolled through the texts, deleting all messages from William.

Where are you, Catherine? Are you okay? Just call me. I'm worried.

I figured the voice mails were the same and deleted them without listening. There were a few messages from Beckett, starting at one in the morning.

Are you home yet? How was it?

The latest voice mail was from eight this morning. "Cat!" Beckett's voice made me smile. "You naughty girl. Too busy to text me back last night? I want to hear *all* about those bad things you did. Call me ASAP. I want the full postmortem on your fairy-tale date with Chicago's hottest bachelor. Call me!"

I let the phone drop on the bed and pulled my pillow over my head, stifling an angry scream. I couldn't deal with the phone messages or the texts. I didn't want to think about the disaster that was my first date in years. I didn't understand how it had gone wrong. It started off so well.

When I thought about the ride in the SUV, my insides fluttered and melted. Even though I was mad as hell, I couldn't deny the chemistry between us. William had more sex appeal, more animal magnetism, than any man I'd ever met. Just thinking about him could make me hot and flushed. My body tingled, and my thoughts turned to the many ways he could make me come. I had the urge to reach down and touch myself, but I resisted. Under the desire, I also felt used. Was I just another in a long line of women William Lambourne plied with gifts, bedded, and then checked off his list?

I was confused, and my visceral reaction wasn't helping. How could I properly analyze everything happening between us when every time I was with him, my body just reacted? What did I feel? What did I want to feel?

At the moment, all I wanted was to get past this ridiculous screw-up and move on. I shouldn't have listened to my mother and Beckett. I rushed into this, thinking I could be fun and spontaneous. I thought I'd have great rebound sex—thank God, I hadn't actually slept with him—and not give the matter another thought. But that wasn't me. William Lambourne and his scene weren't me. I was out of my league, and I shouldn't have agreed to go on a date with a known commitment-phobe and billionaire playboy. If you play with fire...

And I'd definitely been burned—in the freezer, on the kitchen floor, inside the SUV. What the fuck, Cat? I chided myself. That kind of behavior might suit my mother, but it wasn't me. I didn't know what I had been thinking. Was I crazed with lust? Had I hit my head and taken leave of my senses?

I rolled over and stared at the weak sunlight streaming through the slats in my blinds. And what was with William last night? He'd been charming at Willowgrass and engaging in my kitchen. He'd seemed open and relaxed in the SUV. All that charm and warmth had quickly been replaced by asshole and jealousy issues that, to me, were definite hard stops. I'd expected to attend an event with the adorable, surprising guy who'd shown up on my doorstep with fresh-baked pastries. Instead, I got Jekyll and Hyde. The guy I'd been attracted to in my kitchen was nowhere to be seen on my first date in… I did the math… seven years. What a way to start over.

With a whine, Laird poked his head in my bedroom door and climbed on my bed. He thought I had been in bed long enough and wanted breakfast and a little exercise. Poor guy. I didn't blame him. He'd been the same way on those lazy Sunday mornings when Jace and I had lolled in bed, reading the paper, sipping coffee, and making love. Tears sprang to my eyes. I would have given anything to get those comfortable mornings back. I didn't want to date an asshole billionaire, no matter how many diamond bracelets he gave me, or designer dresses he sent. I'd had everything I wanted, and now, it was gone. Nothing I could do or say or think was going to change that.

Laird whined again and put his nose next to mine. I patted his head, giving him the doggy love he craved. I could tell that, despite the sunshine outside, today was one of my dark days. I wanted to open my inner black box of hurt and wallow there for a while. I needed to feel something other than used and confused. There was nothing I wanted more than to curl up under the covers and indulge in my feelings of self-pity, but I couldn't stay in my condo. I couldn't risk William dropping by uninvited. He'd done that yesterday—and look how it had turned out. I obviously had no willpower to resist when it came to him. I had to get out and away.

I thought about calling Beckett, heading to his place, but I wasn't ready to deal with him either. I didn't want to rehash the horrible evening. There would be time for that later. I grabbed my phone and texted Beckett.

Hunkering down. My code for a self-pity day. He would understand and know I didn't want to be bothered.

He'd get the idea that the date had been less than the fairy tale I'd expected. I'd call him tomorrow, and we could dissect the evening over drinks or coffee.

"Let's get out of here, Laird," I said. His ears perked up at the sound of his name paired with the word *out*. I grabbed a quick shower, dressed in my customary weekend outfit—comfortable jeans, a blue, long-sleeve silk T-shirt, layered with a warm sweater, and boots. I pulled my hair into a sleek ponytail and dabbed on pale pink lip gloss. Then I found my beloved Leica and my camera bag, checked my supplies, and called for Laird. He raced down the stairs, and I wasn't far behind. I stashed my equipment in my Volvo and climbed in after Laird. A day out of the city was exactly what I needed.

It was another bright, frigid day, but I was warm enough with the heat in my SUV, along with my layers plus my coat and gloves. I'd forgotten my gloves again but found a spare pair in my camera bag. Chicago, for all its advantages, was a big city. The noise and the crowds got to me at times. I missed the quiet and the peace that was Northern California. I decided it was a good day for a drive and headed to the most scenic route I could think of: Sheridan Road. I drove along the North Shore for miles, the blue of the lake barely visible between the impressive houses that got grander and grander as I drove. It was a nice change from the city skyline and bumper-to-bumper traffic.

Laird sat happily beside me, peering out or resting his head on his paws. I had Muse on my stereo, and Laird gave me curious glances when I sang along. The music reminded me of Jace, which fueled my pity party. God, I missed him. We listened to this band all the time. I remembered laughing with him and arguing and making up. I was lucky to find a great guy like him, and after the date last night, it felt like I'd never have that kind of connection again. It didn't seem fair that there were many people who didn't appreciate what they had. I'd known how lucky I was to have Jace. I loved him unselfishly. It wasn't that I thought the whole universe was against me, but there were days when it seemed so.

I sang about dying together and love lasting forever and kept driving. After an hour, I was ready to stretch my legs. Lake Forest was ahead, and I figured that was a good place to stop.

As I drove past the grand estates built by Chicago's most illustrious families, the families with buildings and stores named after them, I looked for a beach where Laird could run, and I could walk and think. I spotted a lovely area and pulled off the road. Laird bounded out immediately, but I paused to grab my camera bag. Laird wanted to run, and I followed him at a leisurely pace. It was cold, far colder than I liked, but the chill cleared my brain. While Laird frolicked, I snapped pictures of the lake. It was frozen near the shore, and the thin layer of ice sparkled and shone in the sun.

I caught veiled glimpses of mansions perched along the lakeshore. I knew from browsing the real estate pages that these houses were enormous. It was difficult to believe people lived there. They looked like museums or English country estates. I supposed this was where Chicago's royalty lived, and I wondered if one of the houses belonged to William. Perhaps the one I'd passed earlier with the stone façade? Or maybe that one with the brick?

I snapped picture after picture of patterns in the sand and cracks in the ice on the lake with my Leica. It was a fabulous camera and a pleasure to use. I took shots of the woods and the trees or the dead leaves under the thin layer of snow on the ground.

Laird and I walked, stopping frequently so I could take another picture. Photography had always centered me, and this day was no exception. I felt like I was regaining my senses. Out here in the quiet and the cold, the fiasco with William seemed far away. I felt as though I could look at the situation more objectively. What had happened to make me go so fast and so far with a man who was totally unsuitable for me? And why hadn't I seen the signs earlier?

Was I just desperate to find someone to fill Jace's place? Lonely? I admitted I was, but I hadn't been looking. William sought me out, and I tried to rebuff him. I was far from desperate. I studied the barren trees and the frozen lake and thought about Santa Cruz. I missed the green there. I missed not having to dress in layers, and being alternately cold and then too hot. I missed my friends and my dad. I'd needed a fresh start, and Chicago had been good—until William had stepped into my life and wreaked havoc.

The problem, I decided, was that I was more cut out for love than lust. I'd thought I could do casual with William. I thought I could have fun, and look how that turned out. I wasn't the right woman for him. He needed someone who didn't have expectations or want commitments. He needed someone who wanted his wealth and power more than anything else—someone like Lara Kendall from the event last night. I wasn't that woman. Sure, I liked money as much as the next person, but I didn't need it. And I wasn't willing to sacrifice myself for it.

So there it was. I would end things with William. I would tell him I didn't do casual, and I was only interested in finding someone I could fall in love with and who could fall in love with me. And maybe, that meant I ended up alone. Maybe what Jace and I had was a once-in-a-lifetime thing. Maybe no one else would ever fall in love with me. Maybe I wasn't that lovable, or maybe I was too damaged to love someone in return. If that was the case, did I deserve to be loved?

I wasn't a bad person. I'd made mistakes like everyone, but I thought that underneath it all, I was a good person. I wallowed and I wallowed and my thoughts ran around in circles and didn't always make much sense, and I took nonstop photos with my Leica.

There was something about seeing the world through the lens of a camera. I could control my camera. I could focus it on what I wanted to see. And what I saw was beautiful. There wasn't snow perched precariously on tree branches in Santa Cruz, there weren't dog footprints encased in white, there weren't ice crystals sparkling in the sun. This world was beautiful.

William Lambourne and I had that much in common. A man who collected art, who chose a heady fragrance and a gorgeous gown and bracelet for gifts, loved beauty as much as I did.

And the more I thought about William, the more my body reacted, heating and tingling from the remembrance of his touch. It happened every time I thought about him. He stirred me up. There was something undeniable between us. And I could have sworn there was more to William than I'd seen. There was something deeper, hidden deep within that I could fall in love with. He wasn't the man at the event last night. That man was a mask for the real William, a man who, for reasons unknown, felt it necessary to hide this real self behind unassailable walls. Maybe there was a woman who could breach those walls. Maybe William didn't want them breached. In either case, I wasn't the right woman.

That decision made, I whistled for Laird and loaded the SUV. It was late afternoon, and I was ready to go home. I didn't listen to music on the way back. Laird snored softly beside me, and I told myself over and over that I would say no to any more propositions from William Lambourne. I would push him out of my life for good.

I arrived at my condo around six, and I was exhausted. It was already dark, making it seem later than it really was. The cold air had deflated me, and I was ready for a long, hot bath, my pajamas, and mindless TV. I unloaded the SUV quickly with Laird at my side. We headed upstairs, and I paused to fish my keys out of my bag and unlock the door. When I swung it open, an amazing aroma wafted around me, causing my mouth to water, and making me realize I was ravenous. I hadn't eaten all day.

The lights in the condo were on, and I heard music playing. Both had been off when I left. And then Laird raced inside, barking like crazy. What was going on? I was uneasy, but curious. What kind of burglar turned on lights and cooked dinner?

Dropping my bags at the door, I walked in and arrowed for the kitchen. I stepped inside and halted because *he* was there.

TEN

I stumbled to a shocked halt and stared at William Lambourne. He seemed to have gotten sexier overnight. He stood barefoot in my kitchen, wearing a tight black T-shirt and jeans. A dish towel was tucked into his waistband as an impromptu apron. Beside him, pots were bubbling away on the AGA. Laird was going nuts, barking. He had William cornered by the fridge. And William, for his part, looked adorable. I didn't know if it was the apron or the bare feet or the smudge of flour on one cheek. I wanted to be angry, but it was difficult when greeted by a sight this cute.

"Laird," I said over the noise. "Laird, down! Down, boy."

"Attack dog?" William asked, unconcerned that he might soon be eaten.

"Something like that. Laird!"

Laird ignored me, so I grabbed his collar and dragged him to the guest room.

"Sorry about that," I said when I got back. "He's harmless." I narrowed my eyes. William's adorableness had distracted me from the fact that he was here uninvited. And I was royally pissed for the way he'd behaved the night before. "What are you doing here? And how exactly did you get into my condo?"

166

William walked toward me with casual confidence and kissed me on the cheek. "Nice to see you too." He stroked my arm. "I'm making you dinner." Up and down. His fingers caressed my arm lightly. Up then down. "Bucatini with my special Bolognese sauce. It's simple but filling. And delicious, I have to say. I brought you flowers too," he said, pointing to a beautiful arrangement of yellow tulips sitting on the counter.

I stood dumbstruck as my cheek burned where his lips touched it, and my stomach did flip-flops with every stroke of his fingers. *No, no, no.* This was not happening again. I wasn't going to allow it to happen.

And I was changing my locks.

William's hand slid up my arm again.

Tonight.

"I asked how you got in here," I said.

William turned back to the AGA, seemingly at home in my kitchen. With his bare feet and that apron, he looked like he belonged here more than I ever had. "Minerva Himmler let me in," he said.

"Why?" I thrust my hands on my hips. "What line did you feed her? That's your thing, isn't it? Charming your way to getting what you want from women. Offering expensive gifts when it doesn't work."

I expected my harsh words to have an effect, but he went about stirring pots and adding a dash of this and that as though I hadn't spoken, and that pissed me off even more.

"I told her we're dating. How could she turn away a man with an armful of groceries who'd come to cook?"

"Obviously, I'll have a talk with her. Minerva should know better than to let a strange man into my condo. And you need to learn a lesson about boundaries. You can't just come into my house because you want to. I didn't invite you. I don't want you here."

He wore a shaky grin, and I could tell he knew he was on tenuous ground. He struggled to keep his composure. "You get a little line right there when you're angry." He pointed his spoon at my forehead. "It's quite charming."

Oh, I'd show him charming. "I suppose you've seen me angry often enough to recognize the signs."

He shrugged. "And Mrs. Himmler and I said hello when I was here yesterday morning." He glanced at me over his shoulder. "Remember yesterday morning?"

My breath caught at the look in his eyes, but I pushed my desire down and allowed my ire to rise. "Actually, I do remember yesterday—all of it—and I'm really angry with you. I'm not even sure I like you. Yesterday was when you took me on our first date and ditched me."

"Actually, Catherine, it was you who left." His grey eyes turned stormy, and his voice took on a serious tone. "And without saying good-bye. I'm not used to my dates walking out, and since you didn't have the courtesy to respond to my texts or messages, I needed to make sure you were okay. And…"

"And nothing! I don't know what your typical dates put up with, but I'm not a doormat. You can't kiss me one minute and ignore me the next. I felt out of place, insecure, and nervous last night, and you did nothing to make me feel comfortable. You barely spoke to me. You weren't even nice to me."

I saw realization in his eyes. Clearly, he was not used to being spoken to like this, and he didn't see last night the same way I did. Until now.

"William, that was the worst date I have ever been on. I've never been treated so rudely, and I'd really like you to leave."

He stared. "I…"

I raised my brows and waited in seething silence.

"I'm not sure what to say. I had no idea you felt that way." He was stiff now, not the confident, casual man I was used to seeing. And, if I was not mistaken, there was panic in his eyes.

"You might apologize."

"Of course. Let me make it up to you."

I shook my head. "I really want you to go." It didn't escape my notice that he hadn't apologized.

"Catherine." He moved toward me, his expression one of desperation. "I'm not good at this." He reached for my hands clumsily then released them to rake a hand through his hair. I could tell he was shaken. "I admit I don't have much experience with this, and obviously, I'm fucking up. But I'm willing to try. If you'll give me another chance." He gestured to the AGA. "I made all of this for you. As a peace offering." He gave me a hopeful look, and my anger dissolved. It was incredibly difficult to resist his earnestness, but I could not allow my resolution to push William Lambourne out of my life to weaken. I'd made up my mind. William Lambourne was out.

"Catherine, I didn't mean to intrude. But I wanted to see you. I couldn't stop thinking about you all day."

I clenched my fists. This was the thing I hated about him already. He knew what to say to weaken my resolve. "I'm certain Lara Kendall would have been happy to take your mind off me."

His eyes narrowed in confusion. "What does Lara Kendall have to do with anything?"

"We had an interesting chat last night after you and I danced."

"Oh, shit. So that's why you left. Catherine—"

I held my hand up, keeping him at a distance. "Lara seemed to know you quite well, and she was fascinated by my bracelet. She said that I must have extraordinary skills to warrant a gift like that."

"Catherine…"

"I told you. I have no interest in being another one of your women, another convenient lay you keep at a distance with expensive trinkets."

His eyes turned ice-blue. "No! How could you think that's what I want?"

"What am I supposed to think when your friend calls me a whore to my face?"

"Lara is not a friend. She's nothing to me. She knows nothing."

"You seemed pretty chummy at dinner."

William raked a hand through his hair again. "It's... complicated."

"Really? That's what you're going to go with?"

"That's the truth." He pinned me with his gaze, and his eyes were wild and stormy and sincere. He stepped closer. "Catherine, believe me when I say I want to be with you. Only you. There's something about you—about us together. I know you've felt it." He took another step closer, and I wanted to back away, but I couldn't. "There's an energy between us, and it's electric. It's unlike anything I've felt before."

I knew what he meant because I could feel it too. I felt it right then, the closer he moved toward me. Could I believe this, or was it another charming line? And if it was true, that was worse. I wasn't ready.

"I have never felt this way with anyone," he murmured. "If you believe nothing else, believe that. You have this effect on me..." The hand went through the hair again. God, I would never be able to resist him. "In the back of the SUV—" His gaze met mine, intense and filled with desire. My own desire flared seeing it in his eyes, remembering the feel of his hands and his mouth on me.

"The way I feel when I'm with you, Catherine. I didn't expect that. I'm not used to it, and I fucked up. I thought everyone at the gala would see how hot I was for you. I needed some distance. Look, I can't apologize for what Lara said, but I can apologize for how I behaved last night, and for tonight. I am sorry, Catherine. I never want to hurt you. "

He removed my dish towel from his waist, folded it neatly, and placed it on the counter. "I really don't enjoy those kinds of events, but they're necessary. They're business. It's not your scene, and it's not mine either. I threw you to the wolves last night and I'm sorry. But that's not who I am." He grabbed his sweater from the back of a chair and pulled it over his head. "The sauce is ready, and the water's boiling."

I could smell the aroma of the Bolognese. It was making my mouth water.

"Put the pasta in for five minutes. It's fresh and doesn't need to cook longer." He slid his coat on and shoved his feet into his boots. "There's bread in the warming drawer and salad in the fridge. I opened a bottle of red. I think you'll like it."

I blinked, trying to take everything in. I couldn't process. I was stunned by William's apology, and by his honesty. Did I really make him feel something he'd never felt before? I felt that way, but was his response as off the charts as mine?

And this dinner—I didn't know what to think. I *couldn't* think with him so near. And then, I realized he was leaving. "I don't understand. You made this amazing meal, and you're not staying?"

"It's for you, Catherine. I'm not forcing myself into your life. Eat, enjoy, and maybe we can talk later this week. I'll give you time to think about what I said. I meant every word." And then he kissed me. I didn't see it coming, and I certainly didn't expect it to be the kind of kiss that made me melt inside. His lips were soft, and his mouth lingered on mine, making me hungry for more. He tasted like garlic and red wine, and I was ravenous for him.

"Call me," he said. He caressed my cheek, looking into my eyes. I couldn't breathe when he looked at me like that. And I didn't remember ever seeing his eyes so serene. There was none of the turbulence from the night before. His eyes were beautiful, a silver grey.

I sighed, thinking that I could stare at him forever. "Okay."

And then he was gone.

"Shit," I muttered. "Shit, shit, shit." What had happened to my resolve? Where were my good intentions? They flew out the door as soon as I spotted William. And that wasn't the William from last night. That was charming, delectable William. How could he be two totally different people in the space of twenty-four hours? And what kind of guy came over, made spaghetti—not just spaghetti, but bucatini with Bolognese from scratch—and then left? My world was spinning.

First things first. I had to eat. I was starving, and the smell was amazing. Even I, who did not possess a culinary bone in my body, could boil pasta. I threw it in, let Laird out of the guest room, and poured myself a glass of wine.

Finally, I sat down and sampled my meal. "Oh, my God," I said to Laird. "This is unbelievable." The pasta was so tender, and the sauce was rich and thick and flavorful. I couldn't get enough. I tried the bread and closed my eyes in ecstasy. It was obviously freshly baked, buttery and crusty and to die for. I ate and ate until I was finally sated. It was so good, I gave Laird a taste. He didn't appreciate it quite as much as I did, but that didn't stop him from begging for seconds.

By my second glass of wine, I was ready to run through the date again. Maybe I'd judged William unfairly. Maybe I hadn't given him enough of a chance. Maybe I'd been a little drunk. He was making an effort at the end of the night, and I left. I could hardly blame him for what someone else said. He didn't tell Lara Kendall to approach me.

But that didn't mean I'd forgotten everything I'd decided this afternoon. I wasn't a person who did casual. And I wasn't certain I was ready to jump into anything else, especially something as intense as what William and I had.

And that's what it all came down to. There was something undeniable between us. Even now, I felt the black cloud that had been hanging over me all day lifting. Maybe it was the food or the wine. Maybe it was seeing William in my kitchen again, maybe it was his apology, but I felt happy again. Content.

So maybe, I *should* give him another chance. Maybe it wasn't going to be a casual rebound thing. William's words had taken my breath away. Maybe I could put my heart out there, and he would reciprocate…

My phone buzzed, and I checked the caller ID and smiled.

"I couldn't wait," William said in his sexy, velvet voice. "I wanted to hear your voice. Am I forgiven?"

He really wanted to know. A man like William Lambourne wanted my forgiveness. I found it endearing. I wanted to hug him.

"Yes," I said. "The dinner was amazing. And I accept your apology. I wish..." I hesitated, uncertain if I should say what I was thinking.

"You wish? What do you wish, Catherine?"

"I wish I could thank you in person."

There was a pause. Maybe I overstepped? I could feel nervous tension creeping into my shoulders.

"Then why don't you?" His voice was deep and sensual, and I exhaled a shaky breath.

"I've finished my second glass of the excellent red wine you left. I'm now in no condition to drive. I don't even know where you live. Do you realize that?"

"Look out your window."

He lived outside my window? I stood and moved to my front window and peered down on the street. Parked outside was the black SUV from last night. Anthony was standing in the cold, waiting patiently.

I gasped. "Have you been down there this entire time?"

"No, I'm home. But I sent Anthony..." His voice trailed off.

"Because...?"

There was another long pause before he answered. "Why do you think? I do believe in hope, Catherine."

He didn't need to ask, and what he wanted was perfectly clear. What I wanted became clear too. I wanted him. "Give me ten minutes."

*****

It was more like an hour by the time I climbed into the warm and cozy backseat of the SUV. I'd told Anthony to leave the privacy screen down. I peered out the window, trying to figure out where we were going. It was downtown somewhere. "Anthony?"

"Yes, Miss Kelly?"

"Where are we headed?"

"Mr. Lambourne's penthouse is at State and Walton, Miss Kelly."

I knew where that was, and I knew it was one of the priciest addresses in Chicago. Oh, my. I took a deep breath and glanced at the outfit I'd changed into. I'd taken a quick shower and put on a red bustier and matching red thong. The bustier was stretch satin with underwire cups embellished with pleats and jacquard lace that put my breasts on full display. I remembered how turned on William had been by my breasts, and I wanted that same effect tonight.

I'd pulled a lightweight, wraparound sweater over the bustier, skinny jeans, and my black stiletto booties. Beckett would have more than approved. Instead of my pea coat, I threw on my vintage, black leather motorcycle jacket. I wanted William to see a different side of me. I wanted him to know I was as into him as he was into me. And I wanted him to see a woman who was more than ready for hot, mind-blowing sex. I was giddy with anticipation, ready to do whatever William asked. I knew that whatever we did, it would feel amazing. He hadn't yet touched me without turning me on. I was ready to feel him inside me, ready to take the next step.

"This is it, Miss Kelly," Anthony said.

We pulled up to an imposing building, and I knew we had arrived. My pulse kicked, knowing William was nearby. The drive was circular and made of cobblestones. Anthony drove around a fountain and manicured shrubbery before stopping in front of an impressive door. The city was freezing, but this place had green bushes and flowing water in the fountain. The building was lit with warm, inviting lamps, highlighting the white stone exterior. I might have gaped longer, but Anthony opened my door and offered his hand.

I stepped from the SUV, and a uniformed doorman greeted me. "Good evening, Miss Kelly. Right this way please. Mr. Lambourne is expecting you." He led me from the main elevators to a private elevator and pressed a code, causing the doors to slide open silently. "This will take you directly to Mr. Lambourne's residence. Have a good evening, Miss Kelly."

"Thank you." The doors slid closed, and I turned around. As elevators went, this one was posh. It was rich wood and gold accents. The embellished metalwork around the mirrors and the frosted glass gave it an air of elegance. I watched the numbers on the elevator as it took me silently to the fifty-sixth floor. It came to a smooth stop, and my heart pounded painfully in my chest.

Breathe, Cat. Breathe.

The doors slid open, and William stood there looking good enough to eat. He wore his jeans and little else. I stared at his chest, stunned by the gorgeous physique. This was a man who worked out regularly. His chest was defined and toned with a smattering of dark hair, his abs hard and chiseled. I wanted to run my fingers and my tongue all over that chest and feel his muscles bunch beneath me. My gaze tracked down to the waistband of his jeans. I saw a thin line of hair—a glory trail that led to what I am sure was his amazing cock. His jeans hung off his hips in that way I loved, highlighting his sexy V muscle. If I'd conjured a man from pure fantasy, he wouldn't have looked better than William. The man was scorching.

I looked into his eyes and pulled in a labored breath at the hungry expression I got in return. He looked predatory and famished. There was something incredibly arousing about being his meal for the night.

My gaze flicked behind him, and I gasped. I had forgotten to look at the penthouse, but it was every bit as stunning as William. It was huge, ridiculously spacious, and behind William were windows twenty feet high that showcased the glittering lights of the city and the black expanse of the lake in the distance.

I couldn't keep my eyes off William for long, and I drank him in again. My core was throbbing. I licked my lips, finding my voice to say hello, but he didn't wait. He took two steps and swept me into his arms, my legs dangling. The heat of his chest warmed me as his mouth came down over mine, kissing me deeply and passionately, claiming me completely. He took my mouth without apology, without any hint of the gentleness he'd shown earlier. This was raw and carnal. I could feel his need as his tongue swept inside my mouth, and I twined my tongue with his, mating with him in the most primitive way. Our tongues slid and licked and tasted. I took his deeper into my mouth, sucking lightly until he groaned.

He broke the kiss for a moment and set me down. He put his hand under my chin and tilted my head back, so I was looking directly into his eyes. "I thought maybe you had changed your mind. That was the longest ten minutes ever."

I laughed, and part of me thrilled that I'd kept him waiting. "A girl needs time to get ready, you know," I replied.

Our eyes were still locked, and I could see his need smoldering. "Are you sure about this, Catherine?" he asked gently.

I didn't know where any of this was going to go, but I knew I absolutely wanted to be here and I was ready. "Yes," I said, unable to contain my smile.

William grinned in relief and said, "Good. I can't wait to get you naked." He picked me up again and carried me into the master bedroom, and then his hot mouth was on me again, blocking out any thought but that of what he was doing to me.

At some point, my feet were on the floor, but I clung to William for support. My head spun, and I was on fire. I needed him more than I'd ever needed anything. I couldn't get enough of his mouth and his kisses. I ran my hands over his hard, sculpted back around to his sleek abs and back up through his thick hair. The more I touched him, the more I needed to touch him. His skin was so warm, so alive. His hands were all over me, sliding my jacket off and moving my hair off my neck so he could kiss the tender flesh behind my ear. I shivered and moaned in response, feeling myself grow wet.

"I have to have you, Catherine," William's voice was throaty in my ear.

"Yes," I all but begged. "Yes."

He pulled off my sweater and groaned when he saw the bustier. "What you do to me, Catherine. You have no idea." But I wanted to find out.

His hands slid over the lace and down to the waist of my jeans. He unbuttoned them and pushed them over my hips then removed my shoes. It was erotic, watching him perform that task. Such a small thing, but it turned me on. My jeans pooled on the floor, and he lifted me again and laid me on his bed.

For a moment, he stared at me. The look in his eyes was so filled with need I all but squirmed with my desire for him. I reached for him, but he shook his head. "I want to look at you. God, you are so fucking beautiful." His gaze met mine. "I'm going to make you come so hard, Catherine. I'm going to make you scream my name."

I was ready to come just from the way he was looking at me, and then he bent and kissed me, kneeling on the bed and pushing my legs open. His hands were everywhere, tracing hot, delicious tingles of pleasure wherever he touched. "Your skin is so soft," he murmured into my shoulder. "It's like silk." His deft fingers unclasped my bustier, freeing my breasts to his hot gaze and his hotter mouth. He tongued my nipples, sucking and rolling them until I arched into him, impatient with need and mewling with desire. His mouth could make me feel a thousand sensations from sharp pain to gentle soothing to a raging need for an orgasm I could already tell would be explosive.

His lips left my breasts, and I made a cry of distress. I could barely stand not having his mouth on me, but he was kissing his way down my belly now. "You smell so good, Catherine.'" He slid a hand under my thong and peeled it off. I rose to my elbows and watched— I knew he liked it when I watched—as he trailed his hands to the apex of my thighs. "You're pink and perfect here too. I love how wet you are." His fingers teased between the folds of my sex, and I felt this thick thumbs spread me open, baring me completely. He knew I was watching, and he gave me a wickedly sexy look before I felt his tongue on me. He took his time and explored every inch of me with his mouth, laving my folds and circling my opening until he plunged inside me, gentle at first then more demanding. He licked me with long, perfect strokes. I writhed with pleasure now, my hips lifting to his demanding mouth. Sensing my need, I felt his hot tongue on my throbbing clit. He sucked on it, and then I released in powerful waves, shattering and feeling the pleasure surge through me. I fell back, breathless, letting the sensation wash over me.

Then in an instant, William's mouth was on mine, his lips crushing and slippery from my arousal. I was writhing beneath him, ready for him to take me when he whispered in my ear, "Catherine, do you want me to use a condom? I can, but I'm clean. I already told you."

"No, we're fine," I managed to say, my voice breathy with desire. "I'm ok. Please, please, I can't wait…"

"Good," he groaned in my ear. "I want to feel every part of you." His body covered mine, and he braced himself above me. I was naked, but he still wore his jeans. I reached between us and unbuttoned him, pushing them down, freeing his cock, and then William did the rest, kicking them to floor. This was the first time William had been naked with me, and I couldn't resist exploring him. My hand dipped between us. He was big, and I circled his hard shaft, feeling its thickness. William groaned, "Fuck that feels good, but I need to be inside you. Now. You're ready for me."

And then William was over me, pushing my legs farther apart, pressing at my entrance. He thrust into me in one long stroke, and I moaned from the new onslaught of pleasure. He was so thick and hard, and I winced—it had been so long since I'd been filled so completely.

"You are so wet, Catherine, so tight. I can feel your greedy muscles clenching around me, taking me in." He thrust harder, and I dug my fingers into his back as my pleasure mounted. "I want to make you come like you've never come before. I can already feel how hot you are for me. You feel so good around my cock." He growled in my ear as his body took mine, stroking in and out until I didn't think I could take more. But I knew I would. I wanted more, and he gave it to me. Just as I adjusted to his rhythm, he changed it, swirling his hips with a skill that left me in awe. He was pressing just the right place inside me, and I moaned, paralyzed with pleasure as my body tingled with a thousand new sensations.

"I can feel how hungry you are for me, Catherine. I want my cum inside you."

"Yes. *Please*."

I was arching against him, pressing my hips up and into his as he pumped into me. Then he pulled back, and I felt his fingers on my clit, circling my sensitive bud. I couldn't hold back, even if I'd wanted to, and another blinding orgasm slammed into me. "William!" I screamed his name.

"No control with you, Catherine," he ground out through clenched teeth. I felt him swell and thrust deep, and then his hot release filled me. My own climax still pulsed, and I felt my walls clutching him as he came.

Holy.

Holy.

Shit.

ELEVEN

I woke feeling sore, but pleasantly so. I stretched, and my muscles protested. I'd used muscles I hadn't known I possessed last night. I opened my eyes and reached for William, but the bed was empty and cold. Frowning, I rolled over and grabbed my jacket from the floor. I tugged my cell out of the pocket and squinted at the screen. It was barely seven o'clock. It was also Monday. I supposed billionaire moguls might have to be at work by seven on Mondays, but after the night we'd shared, he could have texted. I had two texts—one from Beckett and one from my mother.

I ignored both and sat, dangling my legs over the side of the bed. The floor was bare of carpet, and it looked cold. What I really wanted was to snuggle under the covers and go back to sleep. I'd gotten little sleep. The first time had only been a warm-up for William. The man had stamina and endurance. I think at one point I asked if he took medication, and he laughed and gave me another orgasm. I lost count after three or four. I blushed, remembering all the ways he'd had me—we'd had each other—last night. I think he knew my body as well as I did, and it was a strange feeling. Only Jace had been that close to me.

I hadn't wanted to give William so much of myself, but he had a way of surprising me. One moment he'd be aggressive and possessive, ordering me to come, and the next moment he was tender and gentle, coaxing me, moving so slowly I ended up ordering *him* to make me come. William had skills that I could hardly fathom. It was obvious he'd been with a lot of women. But, strangely, he hadn't made me feel like one of many. With him, I felt I was the only woman he'd ever touched. He seemed enraptured by my body and my reactions to all he did. It was as though he thought only of me—what I would like, what I wanted and needed.

It was a heady feeling, being treated like that by a powerful man. It was dizzying to be treated that way by any man, and I knew I could get used to it. I could so easily fall in love with William Lambourne.

I had to be careful. I mean, I hardly knew him.

And then I realized I was alone in his penthouse. I didn't want to go back to sleep. I wanted to explore every inch. I'd been so wrapped up in William I hadn't done more than ogle the penthouse before falling into William's arms.

Now, I had time to really look. The bedroom was decorated in a sleek, modern minimalist style. Everything was white and grey and light wood. No pictures hung on the walls. No books sat on the nightstands—nothing personal anywhere in the room. The rumpled sheets were grey, and the coverlet was off-white. On each natural wood nightstand stood a metal lamp with a large white, bulb-shaped shade. A white modern chair was off to one side, and on the other, white curtains spanned the wall. I rose, wrapped myself in a sheet, and walked to the windows. The floor was not cold, as I'd expected. It must have been heated. I stood in front of the curtains and pulled them open. I'm certain there was some sort of remote that opened and closed them, but I didn't know where it was.

Sunlight streamed into the room, highlighting its starkness, while outside I had a view of downtown Chicago. The sun was just rising, the city lights still twinkled weakly, and the frozen lake sparkled in the distance. The whole wall was floor to ceiling windows, and the view was breathtaking.

I heard what sounded like a door open and close, so I headed back to bed. Just as I sat down, William walked in, carrying two smoothies. He wore shorts and a T-shirt and looked as though he'd been working out. I would have thought we'd had enough of a workout last night. He smiled when he saw me and held out one of the drinks. "Good morning, beautiful."

I loved it when he smiled. He didn't do it often, but when he did, it made me catch my breath. *He* was the beautiful one. And he was bringing me breakfast. I didn't see how it could get any better.

William sat on the edge of the bed and gave me a slow, lingering kiss—the kind of kiss that made my toes curl. Before it could go farther, he pulled back and caressed my cheek softly, reverently. "The best way to start my day is with you in my bed." He looked directly into my eyes, and his gaze penetrated. I knew he meant every word.

"Last night was amazing," I breathed.

"I agree. I'd like to start every morning like this." He set his smoothie on the nightstand. "I want to see you as much as possible, Catherine. In and out of bed." He grinned.

His grin was infectious, and I laughed, but my laugh hid my uneasiness. I wasn't ready for how fast this was moving. Where was the legendary commitment-phobe?

"We just met." I said. "Let's not get ahead of ourselves." I would have climbed out of bed and ended the conversation there, but he touched my cheek again.

"I've been thinking about a million ways to make you come since you dropped your camera bag in front of Willowgrass last week, Catherine."

"I think you made a good start last night," I said playfully, hoping to lighten the conversation.

A lump had caught in my throat. Had he really been thinking about me as much as I'd thought about him this past week? His eyes, a molten grey this morning, burned into me, and I could feel myself panic. This was moving so quickly.

"I'm serious. I want to see more of you, Catherine. Only you. I'm not interested in any other woman, and you said you weren't seeing anyone else. We can be exclusive. Starting right now, we are exclusive."

"Wait, wait, wait!" I'd never been ordered to be exclusive, and I wasn't certain I liked it. And then a part of me liked it more than I wanted to admit.

"Is there someone else?" His eyes had turned stormy again.

"No. I'm not seeing anyone else, but I told you at Willowgrass, I'm not relationship material. The sex last night was great." It had been way more than great. I definitely wanted more time in William Lambourne's bed, and I knew I'd told myself I wasn't a casual kind of person, but that didn't mean I wanted to define everything so quickly. Why couldn't we just see where things went? "A relationship is a lot more than sex."

"You can't fight what's between us," he said calmly. "I know you feel it, Catherine. It's electric. I don't want it to end. I want more of you. And you should know I always get what I want."

My body flushed with warmth at his words. I'd always been an independent woman, but something about the way he took charge was a major turn-on. He knew what he wanted and didn't waver. Amazingly, what he wanted was *me*. I could see what that would entail. He'd had me driven here last night, brought me breakfast, and before we'd had that awful date, he'd sent me that dress and the lingerie and the bracelet…

This was a man who knew how to take care of a woman, and I could get used to being taken care of like this. One of the hardest things about losing Jace was having to do everything on my own, make all the decisions, take care of all the problems that arose from broken air conditioners to flat tires. William would make those stresses go away.

But for how long? I couldn't help but wonder if this was a pattern. After all, he did have that commitment-phobe reputation. "What about the Lara Kendalls of the world, William?" I said, thinking about the women who'd glared with envy when we'd been at the Art Institute. "I'm sure there are legions of tall, leggy blonds scattered all over the city who sat where I'm sitting now. I don't know what I'm up against." I thought of Jace. "And neither do you."

"I'm not innocent, Catherine," William said, his gaze unwavering. Nothing I said made a dent in his confidence. "I can't change my past, but you are the only woman who has ever been in this bed. That's what you're up against."

I shook my head. I couldn't believe what he was saying. He'd never brought another woman to his bed? My belly did a slow roll, and I trembled.

"It's different with you." He caressed my cheek, calming me. "You're different. I want to keep feeling the way I feel when we're together. It's addictive. I don't want it to stop." The way he looked at me with those hard blue eyes told me this was non-negotiable. It would not stop. Then his gaze softened, and I saw, for an instant, another side of him. A side I could love.

"This is unchartered territory. I've never done this before." His vulnerability made me come undone. Behind his eyes was much more to this man. At that moment, I wanted to wrap him in my arms and never let go. "I'll never get enough of you, Catherine."

My head was spinning. It was all too much. "You don't even know me. And nothing has changed since Friday."

"*Everything* has changed. I've tasted enough to know I want you. Only you. They'll be no one else—for either of us. No other men, Catherine. That's an absolute for me."

And that commanding tone was back. It both irked me and made me hot. I could see I wasn't going to win this battle—but did I really want to? "Well, I *absolutely* can't see you tonight. I already have plans."

He smiled, that cocky smile that made my heart trip. "I'll give you tonight, but I won't be able to stay away for long." His hand trailed over my bare shoulder. "And you'll be hungry for me sooner than you think."

His touch, the velvet in his voice—I wanted him again. Which was ridiculous. I was still sore from the night before. But I could feel myself giving in to him. I was exasperated with myself for being so weak and exasperated with him for…well, for being William M. Lambourne. "This is crazy, William. I haven't agreed to anything. Like I said, we hardly know each other. I don't even know your middle name."

He stood and pulled his T-shirt over his head. My mouth went dry as I saw his hard, defined abs in the sunlight. He slid his shorts off and started for the bathroom. I stared unashamedly at his toned ass. When he looked over his shoulder, he said, "It's Maddox."

I made myself take a deep breath. I couldn't believe a man like William *Maddox* Lambourne wanted me. He was so gorgeous, and I'd had him all to myself last night. He was right. I wanted more. I wasn't certain what I'd agreed to this morning, but I absolutely felt the charge between us. It was undeniable and addictive.

And it scared the hell out of me.

William emerged from the shower, looking and smelling fantastic. I watched from the bed as he finished dressing in a black custom-cut suit. I loved a man in a suit. That was one thing Jace had never worn, except to our wedding. William looked right in a suit. He looked as though he belonged in that world. And as I watched him slide his jacket on, I wanted nothing more than to take it off him again. He grinned, as though reading my thoughts. "I hate to leave, but I have a meeting I can't reschedule."

"I'll get dressed and out of your way."

"No." He shook his head. "Stay as long as you want. Cook will make you whatever you like for breakfast."

I blinked. There was staff here? Had they been here all night or just arrived this morning?

"And George will take you home or wherever you want to go. If you change your mind about tonight, just stay." He crossed to the bed and gave me a long kiss. "I'd love to come home to this... to you." And he was gone.

The offer was tempting, but I had meetings I couldn't reschedule as well. I'd lazed around enough and made myself get up. I felt odd knowing there was staff here, but they obviously had orders to leave me in peace. I decided to shower and snoop a little. William was such an enigma. I was hungry for any little bit of information about him. I padded to the bathroom, which was huge, similar to the bedroom, decorated in whites and greys. Large fluffy, white towels hung on chrome towel racks. A double vanity in the same natural wood as his bedroom had been placed along one wall. It had white, square basin sinks and stark, rectangular mirrors above. Between them, where in my bathroom a pile of toiletries would have cluttered the space, was a white figure of a shell. There was no evidence William had just been here. No towels on the floor. No water on the vanity. No toothbrush lying about. I turned and studied the huge sunken tub and the walk-in shower behind glass doors. It had a shower with half a dozen heads and a bench where two people could sit. It was empty of shampoos, body washes, and washcloths.

Did William really live here? I opened one of the medicine cabinets, and there was the evidence I'd sought. His toiletries were in perfect order, but at least I had proof that he actually had a toothbrush, toothpaste, and razor. There was a bottle of cologne, sans label. I sprayed a bit on my wrists and closed my eyes when the scent wafted to my nose. This was definitely William's. The scent made me think of sex.

I took a quick shower, playing with the controls, so I sampled all the showerheads and their settings. And then, wrapped in a towel, I left a wet trail across the heated bathroom floor to William's closet.

If I'd envied the bedroom and the bathroom, it was nothing compared to what I felt when I walked into the closet. It was enormous—the size of a small studio apartment. Everything was wood and built-ins and soft lighting and flattering mirrors. Racks and racks of shoes lined up perfectly. Glass doors showcased suits and shirts and trousers hanging in perfect order and arranged by color. There was storage above, hidden by drapes, and a rolling ladder so that it was easily accessible. In the center was an island filled with drawers. It made a comfortable space to toss change or a watch, but it was clear of clutter. I could not imagine how one man—one person—could have so many clothes. I opened one of the drawers. I had to tap it, and it slid open slowly and soundlessly. Cashmere sweaters were folded perfectly inside. I ran my hand over them, feeling their softness. I lifted one and put it to my nose. It smelled clean, but there was a hint of William there.

I walked around the island and saw the first piece of clutter—the diamond cuff I'd returned the night of our date at the Art Institute. It sat in a decorative marble bowl on the island, glittering softly in the warm light. Here, too, were several sleek picture frames. I peered at the photos—a man who looked like an older version of William, a beautiful woman who clearly adored the man, and two boys. One was William. I would have recognized those eyes anywhere. And the other must have been his older brother. There was definitely a family resemblance. William looked about ten or eleven, and the other boy was closer to thirteen or fourteen.

The family was beautiful. They could have been models posing for a frame ad. Another picture was of an older William with another man, woman, and three girls. There was still a family resemblance, but I did not think these were William's parents. And William must have been about fourteen. He looked different in this picture. There was no smile, and his eyes were haunted. He looked lost, and for a moment, I thought of the brief glimpse of vulnerability I'd seen this morning in the man.

I heard a sound and decided I to get dressed and head home. I couldn't snoop with the staff lurking, and poor Laird probably needed to go out.

I dressed in my clothes from the night before and headed out. After declining an offer of coffee and breakfast from the cook, I had George drive me home.

I wished Anthony had been on duty this morning. George stood rigidly and never smiled. As soon as I was in the back of the SUV, he said, "Where to, Miss Kelly?"

"Home, please. I guess you know where that is. " I repeated my address anyway.

"Very good." The words were innocuous, but I got the feeling he thought I should have gone home hours ago, or perhaps, never left my condo in the first place. The car was silent, and then George said, "Are you working today, Miss Kelly?"

"Yes. I have a meeting this afternoon."

"And what is it you do again?"

"I'm a photographer."

"Freelance?" His tone was clipped and polite, but somehow, I suspected he didn't think this was a profession. I made good money, at least by my standards—not that my income was any of George's business.

Then it struck me. Did he think I was after William's money? Did he have some objection to photographers? Maybe he thought I was a secret paparazzo. And did I even care what George thought?

"You haven't been in Chicago long, have you, Miss Kelly?"

I didn't know George well, but I understood his type. He knew exactly how long I'd been in Chicago—probably to the hour and minute. He was protective of William, I got that, but I felt as though he saw me as a threat.

"How exactly did you and Mr. Lambourne meet, Miss Kelly?"

"You know what, George? I think that would be a good question to ask Mr. Lambourne," I said.

That shut him up. He wasn't going to ask William anything. That wasn't his place. And I didn't want to put up with the third degree. I should have called a cab.

I finally arrived home and was happy to jump out of William's SUV. The remainder of the drive had been made in strained silence, until I said, "thank you" and got out. I jogged up the stairs and unlocked my door.

After being in William's world, my own condo looked so normal, so average, but I was glad to be home. I took Laird for a brisk walk then sat down to work. I had a meeting with the Fresh Market people downtown today. They'd loved my photos of the kebabs and wanted more. Since meeting William, I could see the appeal of food as sex. There had been a trend toward food porn in commercial photography these past few years, and since no one was better at staging food sexually than Beckett, I'd brought him in to work with me on the Fresh Market campaign. Besides, I owed him big time for all the work he'd gotten me.

Beckett!

I grabbed my phone and read his text then quickly replied that I'd be happy to meet him for a pre-meeting lunch at a casual bistro we both liked. I hurried to change and get ready. All the while my thoughts were on William and the talk we'd had this morning. The more I mulled everything over, the angrier I became. Not at William—he was just being himself—but at *myself*. I'd promised myself on Sunday that I would end it with him. And now, I was in deeper than ever.

As soon as I walked into the restaurant, Beckett could see something was wrong. He gave me a hug, and said, "You look great." It was meant to cheer me up, and it did. I was wearing a slim black skirt, black tights, black boots, and a black-and-white print blouse with a vintage green Chanel jacket. It was my best "business" outfit and I wanted to look good for the Fresh Market people. Of course, I also had my coat, scarf, and hat. I'd forgotten my gloves as usual.

We ordered at the counter. This bistro had great sandwiches, all local, organic ingredients, but I wasn't hungry. We sat by the window, and before I could take a sip of my water, Beckett said, "Alright Cat, what's up?"

I launched into a detailed description of the date with William, my thought process, the decisions I'd made on Sunday, and coming home to find William in my kitchen making bucatini. Beckett was always a good listener, and as I talked, I felt lighter. It was good to open up to someone.

When I was done, I sat back, and Beckett whistled. "This would make a great movie," he said. "It's got the whole *Cinderella/Pretty Woman* thing going for it."

I laughed. "Beckett, be serious. I'm more confused than ever. Commitment-phobe William thinks we're in a relationship now, and I don't know what I think." I sipped my water again and pushed my sandwich around on the plate.

"Why are you thinking so much?"

I rolled my eyes. "I can get that kind of advice from William."

Beckett shrugged. "Then maybe you should listen. Really, Cat, step back and look at this objectively. It's romantic. A fairy tale!"

"I thought you said to look at it objectively."

"Okay, *objectively*, you had great sex with a hot man."

"It was better than great."

"*Amazing*, mind-blowing sex with a drop-dead gorgeous billionaire—I hate your guts, by the way. So what's the harm in that? You don't have to marry him. Just fuck his brains out."

I laughed again. It felt so good to talk things over with Beckett. "But I'm not the kind of person who does casual. And this doesn't feel romantic. It feels confusing."

"Because you're thinking too much. You married Jace, but that was a different time in your life. Maybe the new Cat should live in the moment and see what happens."

I shook my head, and Beckett reached across the table and took my hand.

"Cat, Jace would want you to be happy. You've been closed off for so long. I think William is good for you. You're finally opening up. You're stepping out of the little cocoon you've built."

"I just don't know if this is what I want."

"You don't want the fairy tale? Girl, everyone wants the fairy tale. But seriously, you can't deny yourself forever. You're twenty-five, not eighty. Act twenty-five. Have fun."

"Eventually, the fun has to end, and where is this going? William is so serious about everything."

"That's his deal. You don't have to marry him. You don't even have to love him. Honey, enjoy the perks!"

"Really, Cat," Beckett continued, eating the last of his sandwich. I had barely touched mine. "Every girl, and some guys, I know would love to be in your shoes. You're Julia-fucking-Roberts in *Pretty Woman*. But prettier, of course. You are William Maddox Lambourne's *girlfriend*."

Julia Roberts in *Pretty Woman*. The comparison resonated. And the real question remained—was I the princess or the whore?

*****

I'd taken the L into the Loop because parking near the Fresh Market office was expensive. Plus, I'd scored a great spot Sunday evening and was now reluctant to move my Volvo. Beckett always took the L or a cab, so we walked from the restaurant. My cheeks were burning from the cold by the time we stepped inside. Beckett and I were a few minutes early, and we were met by the assistant art director, who showed us into the conference room.

"I'm Alec Carr," he said as he led us back. "I'm excited to be working with you. I saw what you did with the kebabs. It was genius."

"Thanks." I ducked my head, always unsure how to respond to compliments.

"We're excited to have you on board too, Mr. Altieri."

Beckett waved a hand as we entered the glass-walled conference room. "You can call me Beckett."

Alec smiled. "And you can call me Alec. Seriously, I'm a big fan of your work."

I glanced at Beckett and raised my brows. There was definitely something going on here. Alec was cute in a Justin Timberlake way. He had light brown hair, a great body, and black-rimmed glasses that made him look funky and fun. He was the perfect compliment for Beckett's blond hair and blue eyes.

"I love what Fresh Market is doing," Beckett said as we took seats around a rectangular table. "Sex sells, Alec, and when you put food and sex together, the combination is explosive."

"I agree completely," Alec said. "And that's why I didn't hesitate when Catherine insisted we bring you on board. There's no one better at staging food as sex than you."

"I'm sure you're equally good at what you do, Alec."

Alec grinned. "I have a few hidden talents."

"I have no doubt."

I hid my smile. It was cute to see Beckett flirting with Alec.

Two executives I'd met before entered, and everything turned to business. We discussed different campaigns and listened as they outlined their ideas. Then Beckett and I made suggestions and offered advice. I felt like the meeting was going well. The executives were excited, and Alec couldn't stop smiling. And then, with about fifteen minutes left, Beckett's phone buzzed. He checked the text and scowled.

"Everything okay?" Alec asked.

"Great," Beckett said and returned to our discussion of strawberries. I could tell everything wasn't great. Something was wrong.

We wrapped the meeting up and Alec showed us out. "Call me if you have any questions," he told us. "I'm available," he said with a suggestive look at Beckett.

We stepped outside, and I nudged Beckett. "I think Alec has a thing for you. You should call him."

"Maybe I will. He's cute."

"He's *really* cute."

"Cat, I need to show you something." He pulled his phone out. There was something in his voice that made me tense. "I got this during the meeting."

I took the phone and studied the link for a Google alert for William Lambourne. Huh. I should have set up a Google alert for him. I hadn't thought about it. I opened the link and scanned the first lines of a society column article about the Art Institute event on Saturday night. The writer mentioned some of the more prominent attendees, including "benefactor William Lambourne, who attended with a mystery brunette."

"This is so weird," I told Beckett. I was a *mystery brunette* in a society column. Life couldn't get much stranger.

"Keep scrolling," Beckett said.

"There's more?"

I scrolled down and took a step back. The picture showed William dancing, but it wasn't with me. I recognized Lara Kendall immediately. I scoured my brain for the sequence of events and knew this dance had been after I'd left. William hadn't danced with anyone but me while I was there. I scrolled farther and read the caption.

Is Chicago's favorite couple once again an item?

"Oh, my God." I pushed the phone back at Beckett. I couldn't stand to see it anymore. How could I have bought William's bullshit this morning? He was all talk about exclusivity, but I probably hadn't been gone five minutes Saturday evening before he was dancing with that bitch.

"I have to go," I told Beckett.

"Cat, I'll walk with you."

"It's out of your way, and I'm fine." I doubled back and gave him a hug. "I'll call you later."

We split, and I headed for the L. I wanted to be home right now. I was such an idiot. Had I really believed William when he'd said Lara was nothing to him? Had I really trusted him when he'd claimed no other woman had slept in his bed? Clearly, he wasn't being completely straight with me—about his relationship with Lara, or who had really slept in his bed.

Chicago's favorite couple! I was so pissed I nearly ran into a woman who'd slowed to pick up a package she'd dropped. I walked at a punishing pace, eager to be alone. Maybe I'd Google him again myself and see what I turned up.

My phone dinged, and I looked at the screen, expecting a text from Beckett. I stopped dead. It was from William.

Can't stop thinking about you. Thinking of a dozen ways to make you scream my name.

"Asshole," I muttered and shoved the phone in my pocket. I kept walking. The wind whipped my hair against my cheek until it stung and the smell of exhaust burned my nose and eyes. I heard my ringtone, and swearing, I fished my phone out again. William was calling. I almost shoved the phone back in my pocket, but at the last second, I answered.

"I'm thinking about you," he said, his voice low and seductive.

"I can't talk now," I said.

"Is something wrong?"

"I'll call you later." Like, maybe never.

There was a long silence, and then, "Where are you?"

"I'm downtown. I had a meeting at Fresh Market."

"Where are you now?"

"Um…" I looked around. "State and Wacker, by the river. Why?"

"That's not far from my office. Come over."

I didn't want to see him, talk to him, or know he existed. I wanted to forget this enormous mistake. "Another time. I need to get home."

"Catherine, I need to see you."

"Well, you're just going to have to learn to live with disappointment, like the rest of the world."

"What the hell does that mean?

I didn't answer, which obviously wasn't the response William wanted.

"Catherine, I'm sending someone to get you. I'll have you carried up, if necessary."

Jerk. "Don't bother." I hit End, stuffed the phone in my coat and kept walking. The L wasn't much farther. I kept my head down, my face out of the wind, and walked resolutely. Then, as I was crossing the Michigan Avenue Bridge, something made me look up. William stood at the other end of the bridge. I stopped dead in my tracks and stared. His overcoat was unbuttoned, and it flapped in the wind. His face was flushed with cold, and he wore a steely expression. My breath caught in my throat. He was devastating. If he hadn't been glaring, I would have thought he was waiting for someone else—an impossibly gorgeous goddess.

When I didn't continue walking, he strode up to me and grabbed my hand. "You never have gloves," he said and slapped a pair of black cashmere gloves into my hand. Stunned, I pulled them on. How did he know I always forgot my gloves? And what did it mean that he'd thought to bring me a pair?

"Come with me," William ordered. "We need to talk."

That broke the spell. He might be impossibly handsome, but he was annoying as hell. How did he get here? How did he know where I was? And who did he think he was, dragging me off as though I was a naughty child?

I was too stunned and angry to do more than stumble along behind him. He navigated the pedestrian traffic, and I didn't resist. But I was planning the throwdown to end all throwdowns. He would be sorry he'd fucked with Catherine Kelly. We'd walked a few blocks and arrived before an impressive skyscraper. There were many in Chicago, but this was one of the tallest, jutting into the sky like a victorious fist, its windows gleaming in the late afternoon sun.

We entered a warm lobby, and I looked up. The lobby was open for several stories, and glass elevators soared upward. Trees and a waterfall, even the sounds of birds surrounded me, and I wondered if I'd accidentally stepped through the wardrobe into Narnia. I wanted to look around, but William tugged me to one side and pressed a key card against the panel for a private elevator. It slid open, and he guided me inside.

This elevator was not glass. It was all chrome and sleek lines. William inserted his card in another slot and pressed the button that read Executive Floor, and the doors closed. The elevator whooshed upward. I stumbled to catch my balance, but William caught my arm to steady me. At least I thought he would steady me.

Instead, he pushed me against the cool chrome wall and kissed me. How dare he? Did he think this was going to work? That this would make everything alright? I didn't want to kiss him back, and I tried to push him away. He grabbed my wrists, imprisoning them above my head. His mouth slanted over mine hungrily, urging me to take back. "No," I moaned.

"Yes." He kissed me again, his tongue twining with mine, his persuasive lips coaxing the reaction he wanted from me. I felt a surge of excitement. My breasts were heavy and tender, my mouth bruised. My body wanted this—wanted him. I locked my fingers with his and kissed him back, nipping his lips, sucking his tongue, pressing myself against his arousal.

"No!" I tore my mouth away and pushed hard. I needed to stay in control. This time he released me, but something potent and charged remained between us. I could feel the current drawing us together, and it was difficult to fight. "How did you know where I'd be? Are you Batman or something?" I asked breathlessly, my heart thundering in my chest.

The corner of his mouth twitched, but he didn't smile. "You said you were at State and Wacker, heading to the L. That meant one of two directions. I got lucky." He shrugged. "Now, tell me what's going on." He stood with his legs braced apart, so close that if either of us moved a fraction of an inch we'd touch. He looked down at me, his eyes stormy with desire and anger.

The elevator slowed, slid to a stop, and chimed softly. The doors slid open to reveal an opulent reception area with an elegant sign that read WML Capital Management, LLC. Everything was cream and beige and brown, muted colors that soothed and bespoke luxury. Soft music floated over me as William tugged me by the hand from the elevator. The office was quiet, and the few men and women I saw spoke in hushed voices or hurried by, looking busy and important. I got a couple curious glances. I wondered how many women William had dragged through his office.

We walked toward two large glass doors, and an attractive woman in her mid-thirties looked up and smiled expectantly. I saw her eyes flick over me, but her smile held. She rose. "Good afternoon, Mr. Lambourne. Would you like your messages?" Her gaze followed him.

"Not right now, Parker. And hold my calls. I don't want to be disturbed."

We breezed past her through another door, and William keyed a code into the panel that locked it behind us. I turned and took in the enormous office. I didn't want to think about what the rent must run every month. Of course, William could afford it, and I bet that he owned the building, so he could give himself a discount. The office was huge, and like his penthouse, it was mostly windows. One side overlooked the city. Unlike the warm lobby, this office was stark and modern. William's desk was glass, bare of anything, even a computer. His chairs were black leather. There was a sitting area with a settee and coffee table, and black accents added contrast to the otherwise clean white room. It was one of the most minimalist rooms I'd ever seen, except for William's bedroom.

"This is…" I tried to think how to describe it. Austere? Cold? "Large."

I turned and saw William slip off his overcoat. I'd watched him don it this morning, and now, he slung it over a chair, the clutter uncharacteristic in this room. William himself looked out of character. His hair was windblown from meeting me outside, though I'd seen him run his hand through it a time or two when I was exasperating him, and I suspected that might have contributed to the disarray. His cheeks were flushed from the cold, he wasn't wearing his suit coat, and his shirtsleeves were rolled to the elbows. His tie was loosened at his neck. He looked almost casual, almost normal.

Which made it easier for me to be mad. "I don't like being dragged here. I don't want to see you right now."

"But I want to see you." He circled me, wolfish in the way he watched me. He walked across the room and opened a panel in the wall that concealed a small refrigerator. "Do you want a coffee? I can have Parker make you a latte. I have water—still and sparkling. You need to eat too. I have fruit here, but I can get you whatever you want."

"Will you stop it? I'm not hungry. And I don't want a latte. No, thank you. I told you—I don't want to be here. I don't want to talk to you right now. I need to go."

"Catherine, I don't understand. Tell me what's going on."

I blurted it out. "I saw the photo of you and Lara Kendall at the Art Institute."

I watched his face closely, looking for any sign of guilt, but he looked bewildered. "What photo?"

"I don't know what paper it was in. Beckett got it in a Google alert. The society pages speculated that Chicago's favorite couple might be back together."

William blew out a breath. "So that's what this is about."

I put my hands on my hips. Obviously, he thought I was overreacting, and that made me angrier. "Yeah, that's what this is about. Sorry to bother you. Now, can I go?"

"I told you already. There's nothing between Lara and me."

"Sure. That's how it looked in the photo. You were dancing with her after I left. Did you wonder where I'd gone before you pulled her into your arms?"

"Catherine, don't be ridiculous."

"Oh, so now I'm ridiculous!" I could hear my voice getting louder. I was losing it.

"You're the one pictured with your ex-girlfriend."

"She wasn't my girlfriend. Our relationship wasn't important. You can't believe everything you read. If you're going to be with me, you have to learn that right away."

"So you can dance with any woman you want, talk to any woman, and if I find out later, I shouldn't believe everything I read? Is that about right?"

"Catherine, I told you. I don't want anyone but you. You have to trust me."

"You don't trust me! Just an hour before you got cozy with Lara Kendall for the cameras, you were in Ben Lee's face because he was talking to me."

"That's different."

"Yes, it is! Ben and I worked together, and we've never been involved. Oh, and Ben didn't call you a whore."

William gritted his teeth and then surprised me by pulling me into his arms. "Catherine, I swear, Lara is nothing. You're all I think about. All I want. I can't stop thinking about you, wanting you. You're in my office, and you've been in my bed. I want only you."

"But—"

He crushed my protest with his mouth. I wanted to fight him. I really did. I knew I should because the more involved we became the more I would open myself up and the more vulnerable I would become to being hurt. And I didn't know if I could stand any more pain in my life. And then there was that part of me that felt disloyal to Jace. I tried to cling to that part, but it dissolved in the wake of William's punishing kisses. I couldn't resist his mouth. When he kissed me, every part of me came alive.

He angled my jaw up, and his mouth moved to my neck. "I've been thinking about your skin," he said, his breath hot against my throat.

His hands tugged my jacket off, gliding under my blouse, cupping my breasts. He touched me through the thin, lacy fabric of my bra, and I moaned. We were moving backward, and finally, my back was against the wall of glass.

"You have the softest skin, Catherine. You're so delicate. I don't want to hurt you," he growled. His hands massaged my breasts, making me pant. His touch sent spirals of pleasure through me, and the heat and throbbing between my legs built. I pushed against him to ease the pressure.

Me, delicate? I almost laughed. "You're not going to hurt me. Sometimes I like it a little rough, you know." It came out sounding like a challenge.

"Oh, do you?" His voice was dangerous, and I was instantly wet. "Then I'm going to take you fast and hard, Catherine. Right here, right now."

I made a pathetic attempt to push him away, but I wanted him as much as he wanted me. I could feel him throbbing against my belly. He was hot and thick and hard. He grabbed my waist and spun me around. I had a view of dusk falling on Chicago from the river all the way to the lake. In the background, I saw our reflection as he lifted my skirt and tugged my tights and then my panties down. He pushed me against the windows, and I splayed my hands to keep myself steady. He kicked my legs apart, and then his hand was there.

"You're so wet," he said, his voice husky. "Tell me you want me." His fingers dipped into my slickness then circled my clit. I could feel my orgasm building.

"I want you." The wanton voice that came out didn't sound like mine. I was so turned on.

And then his fingers were gone, and I felt the head of his penis between my legs. He rubbed it against my clit.

"You want to come, don't you? You're like an inferno, and I can feel you throbbing."

He stroked me, teasing and tantalizing me until I cried out, fisting my hands against the window.

"Yes. Make me come."

He thrust deep inside me. I bucked against him then surrendered to the first stabs of pleasure. He fucked me fast and hard, our bodies slapping together as he filled me again and again. I came violently, crying out and clenching him. He showed no mercy and kept thrusting, his strokes possessive. "You're mine, Catherine. Mine," he growled into my ear, and my pleasure built again. I could feel him tensing, knew he was about to come, but he controlled it, waiting for me. "Come for me, Catherine."

In an instant, I was over the edge, and then he let go, crying out as he came hot and hard.

TWELVE

I rested my warm forehead against the cool glass and stared at the view of the city. I couldn't believe we'd just had sex in his office. His admin was right outside the door. We were plastered half naked against a bank of windows overlooking downtown Chicago. Anyone could have seen what we were doing if they had a pair of binoculars.

I felt William move away and wondered if he was as mortified as I. Gently, he turned me around, cupped my face in his hands, and kissed me. It was the sweetest kiss I'd ever received. Then he leaned down and pulled my panties and my tights up. "There's a washroom through that door," he said, indicating a door behind his desk. "You can freshen up."

"Thank you."

The washroom was as luxurious as the rest of the office with a walk-in, glass-doored shower, heated towel racks, a flat screen TV, two phones, and an assortment of shampoos and soaps behind glass cabinet doors. I made myself presentable, then stepped out to find William sitting, hands in his hair. He rose as soon as I stepped out. "I should go," I said, avoiding his eyes.

"Come home with me. Let me make you dinner." He walked over and reached for me. "Let me pamper you, pleasure you." As he spoke, he stroked my cheek with his thumb.

"I can't. I…" I glanced at the frosted door. "Do you think anyone heard?" I shook my head. "I cannot believe we did that."

"It's soundproof, but do you want me to ask Parker?"

"William!" I didn't think I could be more embarrassed.

"I'm kidding. This was a first. I've never done that here. And I don't know how I'll be able to get any work done now…" His voice trailed off as he looked at my telltale handprints all over the wall of windows across from his desk.

"Really?"

His thumb continued to stroke my cheek. "I told you, Catherine. This is new for me. I don't want to let you go. Come home with me. Please?"

It was tempting—to be pampered and pleasured and fed a dinner that would surely be delicious—but I couldn't. "I have other plans," I said. He scowled and looked disappointed, and I took his hand, giving it a squeeze. "I promise I won't be dancing with anyone. That's probably more than you can promise."

"Catherine…" He gave me a warning look, but I saw amusement in his eyes too.

"I'll see you later this week."

He sighed. "Tomorrow," he corrected. "I'm taking you out — somewhere we'll both enjoy."

Even if I'd had plans for Tuesday night, which I didn't, I couldn't see putting William off again.

"Fine. I'll see you tomorrow then." I gathered my coat and scarf and the gloves William had given me and bundled up. "I'd better go."

"Anthony will drive you home."

"That's not necessary."

"Yes. It is." He had crossed to his desk while I dressed, and now he was seated there. His finger swiped across the surface. I leaned over and noticed he had some kind of computer screen projected onto the surface. Or perhaps the surface was the device itself, like a large tablet. In any case, he was back in work mode. His expression was serious and focused.

"I'll see you tomorrow then."

He looked up, and his gaze followed me as I crossed to the door. For a split second, I wondered how I would open it, then the light on the panel flashed green, and the door unlocked. I looked over my shoulder at William. He was absorbed in his work again.

I stepped out of his office, and Parker—I didn't know whether Parker was her first or last name—looked up from her tablet.

"Here goes the walk of shame," I muttered to myself. "Bye," I said to Parker, trying not to look as though I'd just had hot sex with her boss in the next room while she sat here and worked.

"Have a good evening, Miss Kelly."

"Thanks."

It was almost five o'clock, but the activity in William's office hadn't slowed. The people surrounding the lobby looked as busy as ever. A few looked up to smile, but I walked resolutely toward the elevator. William had used a key card to activate it, but it slid open. Anthony was inside, and he nodded. "Miss Kelly, I'll drive you home."

"Thanks, Anthony." I stepped into the elevator. "And it's Cat."

He frowned. "I'm sorry?"

"My name. You can call me Cat." We might as well become friends if he was going to drive me around.

He smiled. "I will, Miss Kel—Cat."

Anthony drove me in a dark sedan without a privacy window, which was fine, though I wondered where the SUV was. We chatted about favorite restaurants and argued over the best pizza—he was firmly for Gino's East, while I was a fan of Lou Malnati's. We agreed Kuma's Corner had the best burgers in town. But mostly, I sat quietly and watched as he navigated through traffic and construction.

It had been a strange day. I'd started by arguing with William that we were not in a relationship. I didn't know what I wanted, but it was not a relationship. I couldn't do that yet. I wasn't ready to forget Jace and our life together. But I'd ended the day having wild sex in William's office.

So maybe, we were having a relationship? And maybe, I should take Beckett's advice and not over-think it.

*****

At home, I spent time with Laird then showered and changed clothes before hopping in my Volvo and driving to a neighborhood restaurant. It was quiet, not usually crowded, which was the main requisite for these dinners. When I arrived, Allison McIntyre and Dana Sullivan were already seated.

"I hope you didn't wait long," I said, hugging both.

"We just got here," Allison told me. While I shrugged off my coat and scarf, Allison and Dana continued their conversation about a movie they'd seen. I listened and took the opportunity to study my friends and note how they were doing.

I'd met Allison and Dana in a grieving spouses support group I'd joined when I moved to Chicago. After meetings, we three would stay and chat, and our chats evolved into dinners. We didn't have much in common, other than the deaths of our husbands. Allison was in her late thirties and had two young kids. Her husband had died three years ago of cancer. Dana was in her early fifties and also had two children, but they were grown and on their own. Her husband had died of a heart attack five years ago. Dana still went to meetings, but Allison and I no longer attended.

The waiter came to take our orders. We had a routine. We ordered salads and then split the most decadent dessert. When the waiter left, Allison rested on her elbows and said, "So, what's up with you, Cat? You look happy."

"I do?" I could feel the smile on my face. I realized I'd wanted to talk about William and this new... whatever it was. "I mean, I am. I met someone."

Dana's eyes widened in surprise, and Allison grabbed my hand and squeezed. "That's great! Who? Tell us all about him!"

I told them how William and I had met and how he'd cooked for me and taken me out. "He's really gorgeous," I said with a smile.

"And obviously, pretty good in bed to have you smiling like that," Allison said.

"In bed, in the kitchen, in the back of his car…"

"Whoa!" Allison fanned her face. "I'll just live vicariously through you."

I didn't reveal his name or details about what he did, but it was fun to talk about William like any girl would gush about her new boyfriend.

"Have you told him about Jace?" Dana asked. She'd acted excited, but I could tell she wasn't quite as thrilled for me as Allison. Dana had been a widow for five years and still wore black in mourning. Her widowhood was like a badge she'd sewn on. She had told us on more than one occasion that she would never find anyone else. No one could ever replace her Frank.

I sighed. "No, I haven't told him about Jace yet."

"Why?" Allison asked.

"I hate the initial conversation. You know, when you say your husband died, and you get the look of pity? I don't want that. I mean, why go there if we're just having fun?"

"It sounds like it might be getting serious," Dana said.

"It is."

"And you still haven't told him?"

"I don't know how he'll react," I said. I could be honest with these women. They had experienced the same feelings at one time. "I don't want him to see me differently or to pity me. And I don't want him to feel as though he has to compete with a dead guy."

"That's his issue, not yours," Allison said.

"Unless you're not ready to move on," Dana pointed out.

Dana had read my mind. "That's just it," I said. "I don't know if I'm ready. A part of me is scared that if I move on, I'll lose the memories I have of Jace and our life together. Those memories mean everything."

"Why should that change?" Allison asked. "Your relationship with this guy, even if you married him, will be different than the one you had with Jace. There's room in your heart to treasure what you had with Jace and love a new man."

"I'm sure Jace would want you to find someone else," Dana said.

I wasn't so sure. I couldn't imagine Jace with anyone else. "Would he? It feels like a betrayal of what we had. Of our marriage."

"No," Allison said firmly. "It's not a betrayal to love someone else. Jace is gone, honey. He's not coming back, but you're still here. You're young and single. You should enjoy the whirlwind and have fun."

"I doubt we're going to fall in love," I told Allison, "but I understand what you're saying."

"I'm sure Jace would be happy for you," Dana said.

I frowned. "Would Jace be happy for me? If he were alive, he'd be jealous as hell and hurt. And he wouldn't like that I've already slept with William. I made him wait seven dates."

Allison laughed. "You were a lot younger then."

"You have a point," Dana added. "Things are moving fast with you and this new guy. Have you had time to think it through?"

Our dessert arrived, and we moved to other topics. I hadn't eaten much of my salad and didn't do more than taste the dessert. Dana was right. I really hadn't thought this through—or at least, every time I did think about it and made a decision, I completely disregarded it the next time I saw William. And I felt as though I was keeping something from William—keeping *someone* who had been and still was the most important person in my life from him. It made Jace seem less important if I didn't tell William about him. But how could I know if this thing with William—this relationship—was going anywhere, if I wasn't honest about my past? I wanted him to be honest about Lara Kendall. I had to come clean too.

One thing was certain. As little as I liked the idea, I had to tell William about Jace.

*****

The next day I worked from home on the ideas Alec had proposed at the Fresh Market meeting, brainstorming and imagining possibilities at this fun stage. It was almost eleven when I got the first text from William.

Have you eaten anything?

I smiled. He was always taking care of me. I texted back: *I've had two lattes.*

I sat at my computer and opened my email. There was a follow-up message from Alec, summarizing our discussion, and my dad had forwarded a funny picture.

My phone dinged again.

I'm going to feed you tonight, but I want to do it slowly. Eat something, so you're not ravenous.

My belly fluttered. *I'm always ravenous for you.*

I scrolled though my inbox while I waited for his reply. I saw an email from Beckett with links about William and WML Capital Management. I'd read the first few articles. They were from business journals and raved about William's innovative leadership and driving ambition. He wasn't afraid to take risks. I could have told them that.

Below those articles were older ones, and I moved to click on one as my phone dinged again.

Catherine, you're making me hard.

I smiled. *What are we going to do about that?*

The reply came instantly. *I'll show you tonight. I'll pick you up at seven. We'll go somewhere casual.*

Casual with William probably didn't mean yoga pants, a hoodie, and fluffy socks, what I was wearing at the moment. I'd have to build time into my afternoon to shower and change. That was the only problem with working from home. I got used to lounging in my sweats and showering at about three in the afternoon.

I'm looking forward to it. And then, because it was almost lunchtime, I went to the kitchen and popped a frozen meal in my microwave. While I waited for it to cook, I clicked on the next link in the email. And promptly, forgot all about food.

Prominent Chicago Businessman and Family Missing, Presumed Dead

Alaskan officials confirmed that the private plane carrying business tycoon William Lambourne II, 46, his wife Mary Alice (Gibson), 41, and son Wyatt, 14, did not reach its destination in the remote fishing village of Anvik, Alaska, on Tuesday. Lambourne is the CEO of WML Capital Management, an investment firm. Sources state the Lambournes were in Alaska on a planned fishing holiday. Their younger son, William, 11, was not on the aircraft. No representatives for the Lambourne family were available for comment. Alaskan search and rescue teams are combing the last reported location of the bush plane, a DeHavilland DCH-3T, looking for signs of wreckage or an emergency landing. Airplane crashes are not uncommon in Alaska and are often the result of wind gusts, ice, and sudden dangerous weather. This is the fifty-seventh plane reported missing in the state this year.

I felt sick to my stomach, and my heart ached for the little boy whose world came crashing down. No wonder he was so guarded. How could he trust anything or anyone again when everything had been taken from him in an instant?

I wondered how William felt about having his life made so public. I knew what sudden, unexpected death felt like, and I knew what it felt like to have your personal tragedies exploited by the media. Jace's death was covered widely in the surfing world, especially online. I couldn't imagine how an eleven-year-old boy could deal with it while going through such pain and loss.

I clicked on the next article, also from the mid-1990s. Despite an exhaustive search, no wreckage from the plane was recovered. William's family was presumed dead. An article published several years later, a piece in a business journal on up-and-coming young professionals mentioned William's business acumen and referred to his tragic past. Sole custody and guardianship of William had been given to his aunt, his mother's sister, and his uncle—Abigail and Charles Smith. I thought back to the pictures I'd seen in his closet. The three girls must have been William's cousins—Lauren, Zoe, and Sarah. They'd lived in Lake Forest, but references indicated that William had trouble adjusting initially. Not that I could blame him. Still, the fact that he had a picture of his adopted family in his closet made me think he had loved them.

There was one last link, and I clicked on it. The article talked about William not taking full ownership of his company until he turned thirty, which was nine months away. Certain divisions had been held in trust, but he was the sole heir to everything. And from what I could gather, the holdings for WML Capital Management were vast, all but unimaginable. I was dating one of the richest men in America. I clicked on the next page, and my eyes widened.

In perhaps the most telling display of Lambourne's tenacity and determination, he deferred acceptance to Northwestern University to spend a year in Alaska, searching for evidence relating to the disappearance nearly a decade earlier of a bush plane his family had hired to transport them to a remote fishing village. Sources close to the family revealed that Lambourne had the investigation of the crash reopened, employed every resource available, and spent millions of

dollars in an effort to find answers or locate his missing family.
Though extensive efforts were made to locate the plane and recover
any wreckage, Lambourne found nothing.

I felt his grief when I read that. I knew how determined and single-minded he could be. He would not have given up until he'd exhausted every avenue. And I understood, too, the hope he must have felt that there had been some mistake, that his family was still alive. After the accident that killed Jace, I had those feelings. I wanted it to be a bad dream. I wanted it to be a mistake. But I'd had to identify Jace's body, fly from Hawaii to California with him, and I'd known there was no mistake. I buried Jace, but William never had that closure.

I didn't know if reading the articles helped me understand William better, but he didn't feel like a closed book anymore. And I understood why he was hesitant to share his life. I was willing to bet he no more wanted the piteous looks he'd received when he mentioned his family's plane crash than I wanted those I received when I mentioned Jace's death.

My phone rang, startling me, and I picked it up, expecting William. It was my mother. "Hi, Mom? Are you still in St. Barts?"

"Hi, baby. No, I came home early." The Texas accent was gone, and she sounded like my mother again. "It wasn't working out with Bob."

"The art collector?"

"Ha! That's what he said he was, but the man knew less about art than I do. I'm so tired of the dating scene. It's impossible to get past a person's mask."

"Yeah. I know what you mean."

"Do you? Have you made good on your resolution and gone on a date?" Now she sounded motherly.

"Actually, I did."

"Well, who was the lucky guy? Tell me about it."

I could see her pushing back in her chair, propping her feet up, and settling down to listen to all the details. But I wasn't ready to introduce William to my mother quite yet. "Just a guy I met here. We've gone out a few times. In fact, we have a date tonight."

"Sounds serious."

"Serious?" I chewed my lip. "It's complicated."

"Oh, honey. I know you're still grieving for Jace, but this doesn't have to be complicated if you don't let it be. It's about honesty. Be honest with your feelings and with him. If you two are meant for one another, the problems will work themselves out."

I didn't subscribe to that rose-colored glasses philosophy, but my mother was right that I did make things more complicated than they needed to be. Look at her. She'd met a guy, followed her heart, and went to St. Barts with him. When it wasn't working out, she didn't question it or analyze it, she came home. There was something to be said for simplicity.

Maybe part of the reason things were so complicated with William was because I was keeping so much of my past a secret. I really needed to tell him about Jace.

✱✱✱✱✱

I knew William would be punctual, so I was ready at quarter to seven. I'd chosen jeans dyed the color of eggplant, black boots, and a cowl-necked black sweater. Underneath, I wore a sheer black bra with Chantilly lace arranged strategically over nude tulle. I'd paired it with matching nude and black Chantilly lace panties. I was a little nervous about telling William about Jace, but it didn't have to be the first conversation of the night. We could go out, have fun, and I'd tell him at the end of the evening. That way, if he wanted an out, he had one.

William knocked on my door at precisely seven. "Laird, sit," I ordered then opened the door. When I saw him, my heart thudded. He looked good in jeans, a fitted sweater, and a black leather jacket. "You look good enough to eat," I said.

He grinned. "So do you. I hope you're hungry."

I was. I hadn't known how hungry I was until he mentioned food. I'd forgotten the microwave meal. It was still sitting in the microwave. I wrapped a dressy cashmere scarf around my neck and donned a long wool coat. As soon as I stepped outside my door, I realized I'd forgotten the new gloves William had given me.

"Here," he said, holding an identical pair.

I took them, frowning. "Thanks. How many pairs did you buy, or should I ask?"

"Don't ask." He put his arm around me, and we walked downstairs. It felt good to be with him, comfortable and easy. And I actually forgot my worries about Jace for a while. William was relaxed and smiling, his good mood infectious.

Anthony drove us to a wine-tasting at a funky new place in River North. The wine was great, and so were the appetizers. I knew I'd have to take Beckett. He would have loved it there, especially when the band started to play. They were a mix between alternative and classic rock. They played a few covers and their own stuff, too. By the end of the set, William and I were singing along to the songs we recognized.

"I think I found something you don't do well," I told him, leaning over so I could be heard.

"What's that?" he said smiling.

"Singing. You're awful."

He laughed. I mean, he really laughed. It was such a surprise to see him let loose. I couldn't speak for several seconds.

"I told you I can't carry a tune," he said. "I chose choir as my elective in middle school, and at the end of the semester, the director recommended I try art. So I did, though I'm no artist." He took my hand. "Not like you. But I did gain an appreciation for which I am grateful."

"And I'm sure 'moody artist' was more appealing to the girls than choirboy."

"True," he conceded. "But before I changed classes, I did learn the entire score of *Cats*. How many men can say that?"

I laughed. "I'm glad it wasn't a complete waste of time."

He pulled my hand to his lips and kissed my fingers. "Nothing is ever a waste of time. Every experience is a lesson, even your failures."

"Mr. Lambourne? I'm sorry to interrupt."

We'd been staring into one another's eyes, and I'd almost forgotten that we were in public. William was seriously hot, and perhaps the interruption was a good distraction, because I was having rather warm feelings toward him.

William pulled his gaze away, and we glanced at the man in the chef's uniform. "I'm John Levin, the head chef. I want to thank you for coming by tonight." He held out a bottle of wine and a box.

"What's this?" William asked.

"My favorite wine and an assortment of pastries. If you enjoy them, I'd love to hear from you."

"Of course. Thank you." William shook his hand, and the man returned to the kitchen.

"Does that happen often?"

William shrugged. "I invest in restaurants. As you know, I also have a winery. I'm sure he hopes I'll love it and invest in him."

"It's a tough job, but I suppose someone has to be the test subject for wines and desserts."

He grinned. "My job has its perks." He stood. "Why don't we take our wine and pastries to my place? I'd like to sample these in private."

I stood and took his hand. "Great idea, but let's go to my place tonight."

On the ride home, William and I didn't unclasp hands. We didn't want to stop touching one another, and I knew I would have to bring up Jace right away if I wanted to say something before our clothes came off.

We walked into my apartment, and William took me into his arms and kissed me. I was immediately lost in his touch, his mouth, his warm body. He pulled away, gently, and said, "I'll open the wine."

We were in my condo, but he didn't hesitate in the kitchen, finding the corkscrew and opening the wine. It was a red, so he let it breathe while he arranged the pastries on a plate. They looked delicious. I lit candles in the living room and curled up on my couch, smiling when he brought me a glass of wine and the pastries. I sipped the wine. "This is good."

"I agree. Here, try this." He held out a square of what looked like tiramisu, and I opened my mouth, allowing him to feed me. The dessert was sweet and delicious.

"This is delicious too," I murmured.

"You're delicious." He leaned over and nuzzled my neck. I shivered in anticipation. His hand on my knee made lazy circles, and I really wanted him to keep going. But if we had sex, we wouldn't talk, and I needed to talk.

I hated ending a perfect night with a discussion of my former husband, but I would hate myself in the morning if I avoided the topic. "William," I said, between kisses. "Stop."

He looked at me, his expression confused. "What's wrong?"

"Nothing. I mean—you've done nothing wrong. I have to tell you something…"

THIRTEEN

William sat back, his expression curious but guarded. "What is it?" He took my hand. "You can tell me anything, Catherine." I saw the flicker of fear in his eyes. Before I might have thought it annoyance, but now, I knew better. A man who had his world shattered in an instant does not like surprises. And so, I would be succinct.

I took a deep breath. "It's about my last relationship." I took another breath. "It was serious. Very serious." William stared intensely, his eyes locked on me, and I couldn't hold his gaze. So I looked down and blurted it out. "I was married, William."

Silence. After what seemed like an eternity, I looked up, and William's brows were drawn, his eyes ice-blue. He was obviously carefully considering how to respond.

"*Was*. You're not married now, right?" He spoke slowly, methodically.

"I'm not, but it's a bit more complicated." I hedged. I knew I was hedging.

"What's complicated? Is your ex moving to Chicago or something? Is this going to be an issue?" He pulled his hand from mine.

"My husband died. William, I'm a widow." I never thought I could shock William Lambourne, but clearly, I just had. As I watched him closely, there was a split second flicker, and then it was gone. I'd seen it, and I knew no matter what he said or did now, I was suddenly different in his eyes. I waited for William to speak, but he was quiet. The romantic mood, the easiness between us, was gone.

"I'm sorry for your loss," he said finally.

If only I had a dime for every time someone had said that to me.

"How did he die?"

"It was a car accident. We were in Hawaii and had been at a party. I was driving. A car came out of nowhere, and he was killed instantly."

William squeezed my hand. I appreciated the gesture.

"Had you been married long?"

"Only six months, but we'd been together since freshman year of college. We got married after I graduated."

Another awkward silence. I felt like I had dropped a lead weight, and we were trying to figure out how to maneuver around it. I wished I had kept my mouth shut. This was uncomfortable. William had finally opened up, and now, I'd shut everything down.

"Do you want to talk about it?" he asked.

"Not really." I hoped that we could move on and regain the relaxed vibe from earlier in the night.

"How long has it been?" William asked. "Am I the first person you've been with since?"

"A little over three years, and…no." I'd considered that William might ask me that question, and there were two ways I could answer. I could leave my answer at no and stay on my careful path of avoidance, or I could take a chance and put myself out there. I swallowed. "But you're the first person I've been interested in."

I expected William to be thrilled at this revelation. After all, he'd told me over and over how different I was and how he wanted to be only with me. Instead of showing happiness and relief, he released my hand and rose. I watched as he ran a hand through his hair then paced back and forth. "William?"

He turned to face me abruptly. "So you'd still be with him then? If he hadn't died?" He sounded petulant.

"Of course I would. Jace was the love of my life."

His eyes turned stormy.

"I didn't say this because I want to bring up old relationships. I want to be honest, and I needed to tell you." I rose. "I thought you would understand after all you've been through."

I could see the mask descend as his features went carefully neutral. His eyes turned colder and harder, devoid of warmth, like we were back at the Art Institute. He didn't speak. He looked at me, and the silence grew. I raced to fill it, make it less uncomfortable.

"I know about your parents and your brother." I crossed to him. "I'm sorry for *your* loss. I can't imagine how hard it was, and you were so young…" I tried to put my arms around him, but he moved away. His look was stern, unyielding. We might have been negotiating a business deal, rather than talking about the deaths of our loved ones, although I was the only one talking.

"I need a glass of water," he said, voice flat. "Would you like one?"

"No."

He was already walking to my kitchen.

I stood alone in the living room, wondering what the hell had happened. I hadn't expected this to go well, but in my worst imaginings, I didn't see William acting pouty. He'd seemed annoyed that my marriage had been happy. I was prepared for William to return from the kitchen with some excuse for leaving. I'd crossed an invisible line, and he probably couldn't wait to get away. To his credit, William came back with a glass of water and sat on the couch. I raised a brow. Perhaps he was going to stay?

He leaned forward and surveyed the assortment of pastries. "I read Chef Levin's cheesecake is delicious. Come and try it." He lifted it and held it out.

Reluctantly, I sat beside him and opened my mouth obediently. I wasn't going to refuse cheesecake. It was delicious. Then William poured us more wine, and we regained some of the ground we'd lost with my revelation. By the time we'd finished the second glass of wine, he was nuzzling my neck again.

He stood and pulled me to my feet. "Let's go to bed."

I didn't argue as he led me to my bedroom, undressed me, and sat me on the bed. He kissed me, touched me, did everything right, but it was different. Before it had been explosive. He hadn't led me to the bedroom—he'd carried me. The sex was still hot. He made me come with his mouth twice before he entered me and thrust until I came again. But something was off.

We didn't talk when it was over, and I think he was dozing when I turned to him again. Sunday night he'd been insatiable. I didn't think men could perform over and over like that. Now, I wanted to see how much he wanted me. Did he still find me tempting or was once enough? I kissed his chest, and he moaned approvingly. I saw his sex stir and grow hard, and that turned me on. It didn't hurt that his chest was the kind a girl usually only saw in firefighter calendars. I worked my way down his body until I fastened my mouth on his erect member. He grabbed my hair and guided my head, showing me what he liked. "That's right. Suck me hard, Catherine. Make me come."

I looked up. "Oh, I will, but not like this."

He raised a brow, and I straddled him.

"I like this view," he said, taking my breasts in his hands and massaging my nipples until I panted. I took his cock and rubbed it against my clit until I was wet. Then I inserted the head into my sex and clenched around him.

He groaned. "You're torturing me."

"I think it's only fair. You've teased and tortured me plenty."

I slid him out and then back in, taking another half inch. In and out, in again, until finally, he filled me. It was so deep like this. I was impaled on his long, thick erection, and I moved my body up and down his glorious length, taking all of it. His hand came between us and massaged my clit, causing me to moan in pleasure. He was fully embedded now, and I could feel my orgasm mounting as I rode him.

He grabbed my hips, steadying me and thrusting. "It's too much," I said breathlessly, even as I opened myself to take him again.

"You can take me," he answered, thrusting again and filling me. He pulsed inside, his huge cock swelling. And then, I felt his hot release, and I convulsed and shuddered. I would have fallen to the side from the strength of my orgasm if he hadn't held my hips steady as he came. I arched back, and he touched my clit again, shattering me.

Finally, I grabbed him. "Enough." We collapsed together, sated and exhausted. I dozed and tried not to think about what it was that was off between us. The sex had been excellent. Better than excellent, but…

I fell asleep with William spooning me. His arms were warm and tight around me. I felt safe and happy, but when I woke, I was alone.

I sat and pushed my hair out of my eyes. "William?" No answer. The bed sheets where he'd lay were cold. I checked the nightstand and then wandered into the living room, where I'd left my phone. No note, no text, no message.

He was gone.

*****

"I knew it," I muttered to myself. "I knew something was off." Still, he couldn't say good-bye? He walked away? Maybe it was for the best. I wasn't ready for this anyway, but that didn't stop me from being royally pissed.

I was holding my phone, and I decided I wasn't letting him off easily.

Not even a good-bye? I texted. I waited and stared at the screen.

Didn't want to wake you.

I waited. Was that all? No flirtation? No sexy comment?

Another message popped up. *I'll be in touch later.*

I stared at the phone then threw it down in anger.

I'd opened up. I'd made myself vulnerable, and this was the payment I received. But really, what could I expect? I was a twenty-five-year-old widow, and that was too much baggage—probably for most men.

Maybe William's family history made it harder.

Maybe being with me reminded him of the family he'd lost.

Maybe he was an asshole who'd totally dumped me.

Everything I'd feared had come true. Before I started sobbing I grabbed my phone again and called Beckett. It was early, but he'd understand. The phone rang three times before he answered. "Hey, Cat." He sounded sleepy but not angry.

"Hey." My voice cracked, and I could almost see him awaken and sit.

"What's wrong? Are you okay?"

"Yeah. It's just—I really need to talk to someone."

"I'll be there in half an hour."

"Thanks." I felt guilty about making him run over so I could dump on him, but I felt better when I remembered we had to discuss the Fresh Market account anyway. It wouldn't be a total dumpfest.

I threw on sweats and took Laird outside for a quick walk then showered and dressed in leggings and a long sweater. As I pulled my damp hair into a ponytail, Beckett called. I buzzed him up and opened the door to the smell of coffee. He held out the tray. "You sounded like you needed this."

"Thanks." I took a cup and sipped, knowing Beckett had doctored it to my preferences.

"I don't suppose you have anything to eat," he said, walking inside and giving Laird a pat on the head.

"Actually, I do." We sat at the table, eating the profiteroles and cream puffs in the bakery box William and I had brought home. They were delicious, but I hardly tasted them. Beckett raved about how good they were for five minutes then leaned forward.

"Now, tell me what's wrong."

I told him everything, how William and I had a great date, how we'd come back to my place, how I'd got up the nerve to tell William about Jace.

"Did he run?" Beckett asked without preamble.

"No, he slept over part of the night. He was gone when I woke up."

"That explains the early morning phone call."

"Sorry." I stared into my coffee.

"I'm glad you called. You took a big step last night. I'm proud of you."

"Yeah. It worked out great."

"You don't know how it's going to work out." He rooted in the bakery box. "Do you want this tart?"

I waved my hand, indicating permission.

"Cat, you can't change your life. You loved Jace. He loved you. And he died. You are still alive, and you can't stop living because Jace isn't here. I've told you before, and I'll say it again, it's okay to fall in love. Maybe this guy isn't the one."

"You think?"

"But…" He held up a finger. "But maybe he is. Give him a chance. If he really cares about you, your past won't matter."

"I know you're right." And that was why I'd called Beckett. He always knew what to say. "Since you're here, we might as well discuss Fresh Market."

We went over the meeting and our ideas, comparing notes. We had a couple great shots in mind. I told Beckett he could contact Alec with the questions. I could see he was looking for a reason to speak with the cute assistant art director. "So what are you up to the rest of the day?" Beckett asked.

I shrugged. "Work, I guess."

"How about I come over tonight and make you dinner? I scored some beautiful organic duck breasts last night, and I've got this great recipe for a mushroom truffle polenta that I want to try."

"Glad you're so excited about breasts." I couldn't help it and cracked up.

"Ha ha, Cat."

"Okay, sorry. It sounds fabulous. I'll get some wine."

"Perfect. I'll be here at six to start cooking." He gave me a kiss on the cheek and left.

I ambled around and worked for a few hours, feeling sorry for myself, and then I remembered the film I'd taken on my Leica on Sunday. I pulled the camera out, changed into ratty old clothes stained with developer fluid and smelling of stop bath. I threw an apron over everything, pulled my ponytail into a messy bun, and headed into my darkroom.

I didn't need the darkroom for work. Just about everything I did in that arena was digital. Yet there was something amazing and inspiring about seeing an image develop before my eyes. That feeling of creating with my own hands made me cling to the old art form of developing my own prints. And for me, working with my hands, coaxing the image onto the paper, rinsing the chemicals, and watching them dry was cathartic. It took my mind off whatever was bothering me. I'd done a lot of work in my darkroom in Santa Cruz right after Jace had died.

I didn't even hear the knock on the door at first. And when I did, I swore, pulled my gloves off, and slid behind the black drape before opening the door to my pantry. I glanced at the clock, worried it might already be six, and I hadn't picked up wine for dinner. But I had plenty of time.

I pulled the door open and stared in wonder at William. He was wearing a slim-fitted, blue pinstripe suit, and he looked dashing, like he was born to wear it. I, on the other hand, was a mess.

He raked his eyes over me and gave me a bemused smile. "In the middle of something?"

"Yes, as a matter of fact."

"I came directly from the office. I wanted to see you, but I did pick this up." He held a small brown shopping bag with handles.

"What's in the bag?" He never showed up empty-handed.

"Catherine, are you making me stand in the hallway?"

I swung the door open. "Fine. Come in."

He did, and I closed the door behind him. He set the mysterious bag on the small hall table. I already knew what would happen. There was no way our relationship could work and he was here to end it with me. Last night I'd laid it out—my heavy, depressing stuff. And he'd bolted. That was exactly why I'd waited to say anything. It was why I didn't talk about it with anyone, why I hadn't pursued other relationships. It was too much to deal with. I mean, I'd been a widow at twenty-two. That wasn't fun or sexy.

"I know why you're here." I began before he could. "I know this is never going to work between us. It's been good to know you, William."

I waited for him to say something, to turn back toward the door or protest weakly, but he simply stared, his eyes a stormy grey. "What the *fuck* are you talking about?"

"I'm making it easy. We can't see each other anymore. It's been fun, but it's over. I'm fine with that."

William crossed his arms over his chest. "Catherine, you're not getting away from me that easily. We belong together. You're mine. Nothing can change that."

I wanted to believe him, but I couldn't help but think he hadn't got it yet. "You're wrong. What I told you last night changes everything. I was someone else's first, William. There's a part of me that belongs to him. Always. That's never going to change."

William was quiet for a long moment. With his arms crossed over his chest and his expression stern, he looked like a warrior king contemplating his next battle. Finally, I saw the flicker of a decision in his eyes. I closed my own, knowing this was good-bye, willing it not to hurt.

"And I never want those circumstances of your life to change, Catherine," he said quietly. I opened my eyes.

"It was what brought you to me." He took my cold hands in his warm ones. "It kills me that you've lived through something like that." His voice hitched, and I knew he meant every word. He ached for me as only someone who had his heart broken could. He swallowed, regained his composure, and I watched as the broken little boy he'd buried was supplanted by the controlled man he'd become. "But here, now, it doesn't matter. It's in the past and you have a future ahead. I'm your future." He squeezed my hands.

Unbidden, the sting of tears burned my eyes. I felt the wetness on my cheeks and swiped it away. "I saw the way you looked at me after I told you. And it was different between us last night. I could feel it. I know you felt it too."

He sighed. "I could have handled the situation better." That was as close to an apology as I was likely to get. He raked a hand through his hair. "But Catherine, you have to cut me slack. I had no idea."

The tears were still flowing, and I knew my nose would start running. Then I'd look really great. "I thought you'd understand because of your parents… I thought—" I broke off when the warmth in his eyes turned to ice. He stood deathly still, and the room went silent. From the corner of my eye, I saw Laird, sleeping on his doggie bed by the window, raise his head at the sudden tension.

"I do understand, Catherine." His voice was hard and level. He was fighting the return of the vulnerable boy. There was no emotion in his tone whatsoever. "I don't talk about my parents or my brother. Ever."

Okay. I could respect that, but it meant another facet of William Lambourne that would remain a mystery. "You weren't here this morning," I said.

William's posture relaxed. "Is that what this is about? You woke up alone?" He took my hands again and pulled me close. "I hit the gym at four-thirty every morning. I didn't want to wake you, though it was tempting with your warm, naked body pressed against mine."

I frowned. "I thought—"

"That's the problem. You think too much." He put his arms around me and pulled me close, kissing me twice. "I told you before, you need to trust us. This is new to me too. I've never done this before, and I don't do sleepovers."

I blinked. Now, I was the one taken off-guard. He'd never spent the night with a woman before me?

"But I'm willing to try…for you."

I snuggled into him. It felt good to be in his arms again. "Thank you."

"So," he said after a moment. "Is this a fashion statement, or are you working?"

I laughed. I'd forgotten about the apron and the ratty clothes. I must have looked like a street urchin with my red nose, my stained clothes, and my hair a rat's nest on top of my head.

"I'll show you." I took his hand and led him to the pantry, but not before he grabbed the bag off the table. "This needs to go in the fridge."

"What is it?" I asked.

"Dark milk chocolate ice cream and a pint of fresh strawberries. I thought we might try cold chocolate this time. We've already done melted." His eyes twinkled mischievously, and I knew he was thinking about the *pain au chocolate* and our first time on my kitchen floor. "First I want to see what you're working on."

He was familiar with my kitchen and must have known I'd turned the pantry into a darkroom. I doubted he approved, but it wasn't like I needed it to store food. Outside the door, I said, "Wait until I close the door before you move the curtain."

We squeezed inside, and I closed the door then pulled him into my workspace. It was small, but I didn't need a large area. Since I was working with black-and-white film, I had a red safelight on, which illuminated the various developing trays, my Beseler enlarger, and the small sink and rinsing tub I'd installed. William headed for the drying racks, where I'd been using tongs to transfer prints from the rinsing tub. I'd taken so many shots on Sunday that I'd hung some on a clothesline.

William put his hands behind his back and studied them. "Where were these taken?" he asked.

"North Shore—Lake Forest."

He smiled. "Looked familiar." He examined them individually, taking his time and really looking. "I love them."

I hadn't realized I was holding my breath, waiting for his approval, until that moment.

"You captured the starkness of winter." He gestured to a shot of a bare tree, its branches jutting to the sky like a skeleton. "This one, in particular, is spectacular. You have an amazing eye." He looked at me, and I saw frank appreciation in his eyes. "Have you always worked with still life?"

"No," I said. "I started as a sports photographer. I took pictures of surfers. I was somewhat well-known." I ducked my head. I was seriously understating my fame.

"You used to surf?"

I glanced up. William frowned in the concerned way I recognized. "I've surfed all my life, practically since I could walk."

"Isn't that dangerous?" he asked, his frown deepening.

"That's part of the thrill," I said with a grin.

He made a noncommittal sound, and I could tell I'd thrown him. He thought he'd known me, but he didn't know everything. He didn't know reckless, wild Cat Ryder.

"These are a far cry from surf photos," he said, looking at the shots of Lake Forest again. "You must have been feeling really down when you took these."

"It was a difficult day. Taking the photos helped me work it out."

"From now on," he said, pulling me into his arms, "*I'll* help you work it out."

I wanted to believe him. I wanted, desperately, for that to be true. William still studied the prints. "What kind of camera did you use?"

I reached for my Leica. "This one. It's a vintage Leica M3."

He took the camera, turned it over and examined it. "Impressive. Classics can't be improved upon." He lifted it, aimed it at me, and shot a couple pictures. I laughed at the novelty of in front of the camera. "Beautiful," he said as I stuck out my tongue. "Now, the two of us." He leaned beside me, held the camera up, and took one of us. "This is a nice camera."

"Jace gave it to me." I tensed when I said it, and the room grew quiet. William put a finger under my chin and notched my head up.

"It's okay, Catherine. You can talk about him. He was part of your life. You don't have to hide your life from me."

The relief I felt was amazing, as though a huge boulder had been removed from my shoulders. He really was okay with me being a widow. It wasn't his words but the look in his eyes that let me know he meant every word. I wanted to tell him he didn't need to hide his life either, and that included talking about his brother and his parents. But I didn't want the spoil the moment.

"It was a wedding present," I said as he handed the camera back.

"He knew you well."

"Yes." I remembered the first time I'd held the camera. Jace and I were still in our wedding clothes. We were slightly drunk and had stumbled, kissing and laughing, into our honeymoon suite. And then Jace had produced a small, badly wrapped gift. It was the Leica.

I looked at William, so different from Jace. Jace had been compact and athletic, a true California boy with a surfer tan, an easy smile, sun-bleached blond hair, and clear blue eyes. William was tall and dark. He wasn't tan, but his complexion was naturally bronze. He had thick curly hair and stormy eyes I loved. It wasn't just looks where the men differed. Their personalities were opposite as well. Jace had been fun-loving, open, reckless, and lazy when it came to anything other than surfing. William… well, I was still figuring William out.

I lifted my Leica, thinking it might reveal his secrets. I snapped a picture, then another. William didn't pose for the camera. He watched me, and as he watched me, his expression and his eyes changed.

Finally, he took the camera from my hands, set it on a small worktable, and held my face in his hands. His lips brushed mine, teasing me before he pressed his mouth sweetly to mine. I sighed into his mouth as our lips slid together, and our tongues met in a lazy roll. He nipped at my lips, and I sucked his tongue, our kiss growing hotter and passionate. His arms came around me, holding me close, stroking me.

We broke from the kiss, and his hands stripped me of the apron and pushed me against the wall. A few trays and tongs I wasn't using clattered to the floor, but we ignored them. I slid my hands under William's suit coat, pushing it off his shoulders, eager to get under his shirt, to feel his skin against mine. He was eager too. He had his hands under my shirt, tracing my sides and brushing tantalizing strokes over my breasts and hardening nipples. I fumbled with his tie, and he paused to rip it off then unbuttoned his shirt. I closed my mouth on his warm, hard chest, raking my fingers down the skin, now tinged with red from the lamp, until I reached his leather belt and the button of his trousers. His erection strained against the expensive wool, and I ran my hand over him.

"What you do to me," he murmured.

"Let me do more," I said, wanting to show him how much I cared. "Let me pleasure you." Without waiting for his answer, I ran my hand along that length of his hardness, and through the fabric, I felt him pulse beneath my touch. His reaction emboldened me. I wrapped my hand around him, squeezing gently, and he hissed in a breath.

"What are you doing to me?"

I smiled. "What would you like me to do?"

He shook his head as though resigned, but he wore a wicked smile. "That's a difficult question to answer when my cock is in your hand. The possibilities are endless."

I stroked him again, slowly, teasing him, building the need I recognized. He closed his eyes briefly. "God, woman, you're killing me."

I smiled. That was how I always felt with him, and it was the feeling I wanted to duplicate. I noticed he didn't resist.

"Would you like it if I put my mouth on you, William?" I said, my voice deep and sexy.

He'd said the same to me at Willowgrass, and by the way his eyes widened for a moment, I knew he remembered.

"Would you like that, William? Do you want my lips wrapped around you?"

Desire flared hot in his eyes. I had thought they were stormy before, but now, they were raging.

"That's exactly what I want, Catherine."

I took him by the shoulder and changed places, pushing him against the wall of shelves. My hands shook as I danced my fingers up his thighs to release the button of his trousers, and then I pulled the zipper down. It took little to free him. Seeing his hard, erect penis jutting from between his legs gave me a moment's pause. He was gorgeous, veined and imperial. I slid my hand over the velvet tip and down the thick, impressive length. I pulled my hand back up and down again, watching his face. He gave nothing away, his gaze locked on mine. His skin was hot like molten steel, and I liked how his erection jumped when I wrapped my hand around his tip and squeezed lightly.

Keeping my gaze locked with his, I fell to my knees, bent, and touched my tongue to the head. His eyes widened when I swirled my tongue around him. He was burning. His skin was sleek. I forced myself to go slow. I wanted to lick every inch, find the sensitive spots and exploit them. I licked my way to the root and back up, taking the head into my mouth and sucking.

"Catherine." William's hands clenched, and he clutched the shelves behind him. I smiled and sucked again, then ran my tongue up and down, teasing him, making him anticipate release. I fluttered my tongue over him then took him in my mouth again. He groaned, and I moved faster, fisting my hand around his shaft and sliding my hand in tandem with my mouth.

The more I slid him in and out of my mouth, the more aroused I became. My nipples were ultrasensitive as they pushed against the fabric of my sweatshirt, and my sex was wet and swollen with need. I pushed my own need aside and sucked him, alternately greedy and gentle then punishing.

I reached down to cup his balls, feeling their heaviness. His fingers dug into the metal shelves, and I knew he was exerting tremendous control. I wanted to see him lose control. I looked at him, allowing him to see my desire as I slid him in and out of my mouth.

"You're killing me," he said again, and this time his voice sounded strained. I looked down and saw the bead of pre-cum on his tip. With a finger, I slicked it off and tasted him. Then I licked and teased and took him as far as I could. He gave a slight moan, and I felt him pulse and tighten and then his release filled my mouth and slid down my throat, sweet and thick.

Finally, he exhaled and stared intently. "I think you might ruin me, Catherine," he said, and I couldn't tell if it was a compliment or a curse. I still knelt between his legs, and he slid to the floor beside me and pulled me into his lap.

"Did you like it?" I asked.

"*Like* is an understatement," he murmured, stroking my hair.

"Stay for dinner." I didn't want him to go yet. I didn't want to lose the closeness we'd regained.

"Are you cooking?" I heard the amusement in his voice.

"No, Beckett is."

He was silent for a moment. "Alright. I'll get the wine."

We dressed, and he left to get the wine while I cleaned up. Poor Laird needed a walk, but before I put his leash on, I texted Beckett.

William is joining us for dinner. Hope that's okay.

Beckett texted me back a happy face. I'm sure he thought I was insane. One moment I cried about the man, and the next I'd invited him to dinner.

I took Laird for a quick walk, then showered, and brushed on makeup. This was a casual dinner, so I decided on grey wool trousers, a black tank top, and a sweater wrap. I wore my diamond studs, dried my hair, and walked into the living room when Beckett arrived, his arms full of shopping bags. William arrived shortly thereafter with the wine, and we opened it and chatted while Beckett cooked. He and William discussed acidulated water, charcuterie, and the Brix scale. At one point, as we were eating Beckett's duck breasts and polenta— which were excellent—the conversation turned to barding. I asked if it had anything to do with Shakespeare and received two amused looks.

I listened after that. I didn't mind being left out of the conversation. I liked hearing the two talk so amiably. The wine was excellent. It was William's label, of course. As Beckett was getting ready to go, William offered to send him a case of his WML label— reds or whites, Beckett's choice. That won Beckett over.

I walked Beckett out, and when I returned I could hear William speaking low. I peeked into the kitchen and saw he was on the phone. He saw me and held up a finger, waving it around to indicate he was wrapping up.

I wandered into the living room and turned on the TV. Wednesday was a good evening for TV, and I snuggled into the couch with Laird. A while later, William joined me. He seemed in no hurry to leave, so I figured he was staying the night. He was trying.

Sometime before the news, I dozed off and had a vague memory of William carrying me to bed and undressing me. Then he snuggled next to me, and I was out. I dreamed I was on the beach in California, the sand and the surf caressing me. They slid over my body with long strokes, cupping my breasts and teasing between my legs. I moaned, coming awake to the feel of William's hands and mouth. He kissed me and slid over me, his warm body, heavy and solid. I was half asleep and unsure whether I was dreaming or awake. My body simply reacted, arching into his, opening for him as he touched and licked. I came with a sigh the first time. It was sweet and gentle, and then he was inside me, moving slowly. Our bodies moved together as if in a dream. Everything was tender and easy. We came together, and I snuggled back into him, closing my eyes.

"Catherine, I have to go." He untangled himself and rose.

I was sated and sleepy, but I managed to murmur, "Will I see you later?"

It was dark, but I could hear him dressing.

"Not today. I'll be in meetings all day."

I burrowed under the covers. "I'll come to your office…" I smiled. "I'll wear a skirt."

"Very tempting, but I'll be in London."

I sat and pushed the hair out of my eyes. "What?"

He had his shirt and trousers on, his jacket slung over an arm. "I'm heading to O'Hare now. The jet is waiting. Go back to sleep. I'll see you tomorrow night." And he was gone.

I heard the door open and close, and I lay down, trying to go back to sleep. My thoughts turned over and over. What kind of relationship was this? Just when I thought we were becoming close, he jets to London and doesn't even tell me. I was beginning to wonder if I was ever going to really know him.

FOURTEEN

Thursday I mulled over William's need for secrecy and mystery while I caught up on business. As I answered emails from potential clients and followed up with Fresh Market, I wondered if William realized how evasive he was. Maybe he was so used to keeping to himself, he didn't think of sharing the details of his life. Maybe he didn't realize going to another country, crossing an ocean, was something that should be mentioned to one's girlfriend. And maybe, he didn't want a real girlfriend. That would mean allowing someone to get close, and I understood why, after the death of his family, he avoided close relationships.

My thoughts were going round and round, so I decided to work on my expense spreadsheet. Accounting always put me in a stupor, and today was no different. I could thank William that I'd be ready with my taxes in April.

Later, I went for a run by the lake, and the cold cleared my head. After a shower, I ordered Chinese and popped in a DVD. I picked at the food and watched the movie. It was a romantic comedy, and everything worked out too easily for the characters. No one's husband had died. No one had a mysterious boyfriend who jetted to another continent without mentioning it. No one lived unhappily ever after watching lame movies and eating bad Chinese.

On Friday, I was finishing up interior shots of a commercial property for a brochure when I got a text from William.

Dinner. My place. Eight.

I tried to ignore how much it sounded like an order. He was coming home. He wanted to see me. *Sounds delicious.*

It will be.

What should I wear? I sent back, happy to see his teasing side I liked so much.

As little as possible.

That night I dressed in a simple black and beige wrap-dress and the red and black lingerie William had sent for our first date. The dress was easy to get out of and didn't cling, so I could wear garters and stockings. I slipped on the Louboutin heels. They matched the underwear, and I could imagine William's look if I stripped and stood in my heels and lingerie. And I thought it was fun to pair the expensive lingerie with my reasonably priced dress, which I'd gotten on sale after Thanksgiving.

I'd asked Allison to keep Laird overnight, figuring I wouldn't be home until morning. She'd agreed and said her kids would love a dog to play with, so he could stay as long as I wanted. I thought about packing a toothbrush and other toiletries, but I didn't want to presume. And besides, bringing some of my things over felt very relationship-y.

Anthony buzzed me at seven-thirty, but I wasn't ready for another fifteen minutes. I put on my coat and my gloves—I was so proud I'd remembered—and headed down.

"Good evening, Miss Cat."

"Miss Cat?" I said as I slid into the back of the SUV.

"A compromise."

"I like it." We pulled away from my condo, and I leaned forward. "Did William have a good trip to London?"

"I think so. I haven't seen him."

"You didn't pick him up from the airport?"

"I couldn't. His flight arrived about an hour and a half ago. He has another driver."

I considered this. "So William is just getting home?"

"I believe he arrived about forty-five minutes ago, Miss Cat."

I mentally lowered my expectations. William was probably exhausted. Maybe we'd order takeout and watch a movie.

But when I stepped into William's penthouse, the scents of sautéing garlic teased my nose. My stomach rumbled, and I followed the smell into William's kitchen. I'd seen his kitchen briefly when I'd stayed over. It had the signature William Lambourne style. Minimalist and stark, the appliances were stainless steel and top-notch. I'd been in enough kitchens to recognize designer names—Liebherr, Viking, Miele. The cabinets were sleek and white and the counters made of stone I couldn't identify. There were no ceramic roosters on the counter, no magnets on the refrigerator, no signs that read *William's Kitchen*, or plaques with cartoonish chefs riding bicycles. It could have been a display kitchen, except now I saw William in it, and I understood this place was his.

He looked over his shoulder when I walked in and smiled. He was wearing his suit, but he'd removed the jacket and rolled up his sleeves. His grey and black striped tie was loosened and flipped over his shoulder, the top button of his shirt undone. He'd been standing at the counter, chopping something, and he looked like he belonged. He'd looked more relaxed than I'd ever seen him. He was at home here.

"Hi," I said with a smile.

"Hi." He walked toward me and took me in his arms. His kiss was long and lingering and absolutely delicious.

"Mmm," I said when we broke apart. "What's for dinner?"

"Soon enough," he promised. "I'll take your coat."

I turned so he could help me and looked around. "No staff tonight?"

"I wanted the place to myself. I wanted to cook for you."

He indicated a leather stool at the counter where he was working on chopping tomatoes. I pulled myself onto the seat and crossed my legs, allowing the dress to fall open and show a little leg. Now that I saw him, I realized how much I'd missed him. "William, you must be exhausted. You don't have to cook."

"It relaxes me," he said. "And I like to cook."

"Then at least let me help you."

He gave me a bemused look and slid a cutting board and several onions toward me. "Do you know how to chop onions?"

"Of course."

He handed me a large knife, and I looked at the knife and then at the onions. "You just start chopping, right?"

He moved behind me and placed his hand over mine on the knife. He leaned down, his warm chest rubbing my back. "First trim the ends." He guided my hand as I sliced off first one end of the yellow onion then the other. The fragrant smell filled the room and stung my eyes slightly. "Now, cut it lengthwise." He propped the onion on a flat end, his hand warm and sure over mine as I cut it in half. "Take one half at a time and lay it flat. Slice crosswise through the onion." His hand moved over mine, showing me the correct motions. I tried to concentrate, but I could feel his muscles under his shirt and smell his cologne. It felt so good to touch him again.

"Stack the sections and flip them sideways," he was saying. His hand caressed mine as he positioned the sections. "That's it." His breath feathered my ear, and I gulped in air as though I was drowning. "Then cut downward, moving lengthwise toward your fingers. Be careful of your fingers."

"I will."

"Good." He moved away, and I instantly wanted him back again. I ached to have him beside me, touching me again. "Keep going," he said with a smile. He knew the effect he had on me.

I continued slicing, trying to concentrate on the task before me. Beside me, William moved confidently, sprinkling some of this, mixing that, slicing something else, opening and closing his oven door—not an AGA, I noted.

"How was your day?" he asked, not breaking stride.

"Fine. I had a shoot." I had to look up from my slicing to answer. "I did the usual. How was London?"

"Busy."

I peered at the pan he prepared to place in the oven. "Is that all you're going to say? Busy?"

He shrugged, opening the oven door again and popping the pan in. "It was business. I don't think it would interest you."

"Everything about you interests me, William."

He smiled, and the warmth in his look made me flush.

"What are we having for dinner?"

"I thought we'd start with oysters."

I made a face. "Yuck. I'll skip that one."

"I don't think so. Have you had them before?"

"I grew up next to the ocean. Of course, I've had them before. They're slimy. Not my favorite."

He laughed. "That's because you tasted with your eyes. Not your mouth." He trailed his hand over my eyes and down to my lips. I bit his finger playfully.

"I'm pretty sure I tasted them with my mouth."

"Let's do an experiment. Close your eyes."

"Okay." I closed them.

"Now, open your mouth."

I opened my mouth, and my eyes as well.

He frowned. "Open only your mouth."

"What are you going to feed me?"

"Trust me, Catherine. Close your eyes."

I sighed and closed my eyes again. I could hear him moving, hear the hiss of the pan on the stove, the sound of the refrigerator as it kicked on. I jumped when William's warm finger skated over my lips. "Open," he murmured.

I obeyed.

"Open more."

I felt something hard and cold touch my lips. I touched my tongue to the edge and realized it was a large spoon. It was chilled, and my lips tingled and burned as the cold touched them. Then William tipped the spoon, and it was like the ocean exploded in my mouth. It was smooth and creamy, and a dash of heat and spice caressed my tongue. It was a chilled mousse, but it wasn't sweet. And it was vaguely familiar. "Can I open my eyes?"

"Yes."

He was looking at me, one brow cocked. "That was our *amuse-bouche*."

"That's foodie for first course," I translated. "Really good. I'd eat it for the second course too."

He grinned. "Close enough. What was it?"

"I don't know. Something I've eaten before. Some sort of mousse, but it had a kick."

"That was the cayenne pepper. Any other ingredients you could identify?"

"Maybe cream?"

William crossed to the refrigerator and brought out two small plates, each with a pale pink mousse. "Salmon mousse made with fresh Scottish salmon. I brought the fish back on the jet," he said.

"Salmon? Really? I'm surprised. And you brought fish on your jet?" Just saying it made me laugh.

"One of the many perks of having my own plane, Catherine." William's eyes twinkled. "But let's not lose focus. This proves my point. You eat too much with your eyes. I can fix that." He looked around then grabbed the knot of his silver and grey striped tie and loosened it, pulling it off. He walked toward me, and I smiled. I had a feeling I knew what he had in mind. He wrapped the tie around my eyes and knotted it in place at the back of my head. "Can you see?" he asked.

I moved my head from left to right. The world was grey. "No."

"Good. Don't move. You don't want to fall off the bar stool."

"Okay." I sat still, listening to the sounds of him preparing something. "Now what are you making?"

"Listen, smell, taste." Something warm but hard touched my lips. It wasn't a spoon this time, but something uneven and ridged. "Open your mouth," William said, his low voice close and tantalizing. "Take this in, savor the taste, then swallow. No chewing."

I tensed. "William."

"Trust me."

I opened my mouth and something warm and salty glided over my tongue. It was more sweet than savory but quite frothy and laced with a zing. I swallowed the small morsel of meat and opened my mouth again.

"You liked that, did you?" William asked.

"It was different."

He chuckled. "I doubt Warm Oysters with Champagne Sabayon has ever received so menial a compliment as *different*."

"I can't believe that was an oyster. It was delicious."

"Now try this." I felt something cold and firm against my lips. He tapped the food lightly against my upper lip, holding it below my nose for a moment so that I could smell it. It smelled a little tangy. I heard the slice of a knife, and he said, "Stick out your tongue."

I did and he touched the…was it a fruit? A vegetable? I was uncertain, but he tapped it against my tongue lightly, then he rolled it over the tip and slid it inside my mouth. "Cherry tomato," I said. "Very good."

"And this?"

I stuck out my tongue again and felt something cold and hard caress it. The texture was ridged, and I couldn't taste anything definitive. He rolled the edge over my lips, tracing them, then skated down my chin and my neck, to the V in my wrap-dress. I showed a bit of cleavage, and apparently, that fact hadn't escaped William's notice. My skin broke out in gooseflesh as the coolness of the food skated over it, followed by the warm caress of William's fingers.

"Open, but do not bite," he said.

I opened my mouth, and something cylindrical slid inside. It was warm from my skin, and I thought it might be a carrot or a zucchini stick. William slid it out then gently pushed it in.

When he pulled it out again, I said, "We could try this with something other than zucchini."

"Tempting." He slid the zucchini into my mouth again. "Now bite."

I did, and it wasn't zucchini at all. "Squash?" I asked. "No, wait. Carrot."

"You're getting good at this."

I felt his warm hand on my knee as he lifted it, uncrossing my legs. My breath hitched as I strained to sense what he was doing. He spread my legs and stepped between them. I felt the material of my dress slide up my thighs. He groaned softly. "You're wearing the garters. Do you know what that does to me?"

"Probably the same as having your hands on my thighs does to me."

He ran his palms along my stockings. "I am going to fuck you so hard later."

"Why not now?"

"Patience." His hands slid up again, parting my dress farther, until my panties were exposed. "Nice," he murmured. "I pictured you in this when I bought it, but you look even better."

My sex ached at his warmth, and I felt my own skin heat in response. I wanted to slide closer. His hands lifted, and I prayed he would touch me again.

"This will be a little cold, but I think it necessary to cleanse the palate."

I nodded, unable to speak. Suddenly, something icy trailed up my bare leg. I jumped slightly from surprise, but the contrast between my flushed skin and the ice caused my body to come alive. My core throbbed as the ice slid closer and closer to my hips. Drips of water slid down my stockings, and as he moved closer to my sex, down my bare skin, tickling and tantalizing. I shifted, my body eager for release—eager for his touch.

Then the sensation was gone, and I sat forward. I heard a rustling, and I listened intently. Was he undressing? *Please, God, yes.* But another sliver of ice skated down my collarbone and rested for a moment. I felt a drop of cold water slide into my cleavage. William drew in a long breath then slid the ice past my lips. It was refreshing, and I rolled it in my mouth, sucking until it melted.

"Open," he said.

This time I didn't hesitate. I felt a small spoon slide into my mouth with something sweet and spicy as William pressed his body against my sex. The pressure where I needed it paired with the creamy, smooth, and decadent taste exploding in my mouth had my pulse racing and my breaths coming in short pants. I moaned and opened my mouth again.

"More?" William asked.

"Please." It came out more as a plea than a request. He knew what I wanted. My nipples were hard, my sex wet, and my body primed.

Again, he slid the spoon into my mouth, and this time he pressed what felt like a hand between my legs as the custard slid over my tongue. "Yes."

"You're wet for me, Catherine."

"Yes. Please." I pushed against him, but he withdrew his hand. I almost cried out.

"Do you know what you have in your mouth?"

"Custard? It's delicious. More?" Anything to make him touch me again.

"Vanilla bean with cinnamon, cardamom, and Caribbean chocolate—all aphrodisiacs. I want you ready tonight. I want your senses heightened."

"I'm ready."

"I'll decide that. Open your mouth."

I opened and felt the edge of a glass touch my lips. I stuck my tongue out as he tilted it and felt bubbles burst on my flesh. Champagne. My tiny sample had shown me it was dry but sweet. He tipped the flute farther, and the champagne flowed into my mouth. I wasn't prepared for the volume, and a little spilled onto my chin and my chest. I moved to wipe it away, but William grasped my wrist and pressed his lips to my chin. He kissed a path down my neck, following the rivulets of champagne, until he nuzzled between my breasts. I felt him open the top of my dress and knew that except for where the dress tied at my waist, I was clad only in lingerie.

"That bra does amazing things for your tits," he murmured, fondling them. "And they're already amazing." His hand brushed an aching nipple, and my body convulsed with pleasure. He could have made me come so easily.

"Don't stop."

"Do you like the champagne?"

"Yes."

He cupped my breasts, his thumbs rubbing my tender nipples. "I wonder what your skin would taste like dribbled in champagne."

"Please find out."

"I intend to, Catherine." His hands moved away, and I reached for him.

"But I want to feed you before I fuck you." He pulled my dress closed over my breasts and moved out from between my legs, swishing the fabric against the garters and stockings. I felt his hand on the knot of the blindfold. "And I don't intend to waste all this food."

I blinked as he removed his tie from my eyes. He still stood in front of me, cool and composed. I, on the other hand, was painfully aroused. I didn't care about the food whatsoever. I wanted William's hands on me—his mouth, his body.

I might not know William well, but I did know he liked to be in control. He wanted to wait, and if I tried to push, my efforts would be gently rebuffed.

He walked to the stove and returned with a plate of scallops artfully arranged on a puree and set it between us. The onion I'd been cutting was gone, and no sign of my work remained. He took the stool beside me. His knee brushed mine, and I closed my eyes against that small touch. I felt as though an electric current had zinged through me.

"I thought we'd eat here. No reason to sit in the dining room."

"This is nice." And it was—close, intimate.

He'd adjusted the lighting when I was blindfolded, and now the kitchen was warmer, less stark and white. "We've had our first course. These are seared scallops, with a puree of winter squash."

I looked for a fork or any flatware, but the only silverware was in front of William. "Don't I get to eat?"

"I'll feed you," he said, lifting a scallop onto his fork and offering it. I felt silly, being fed like a child, but when our gazes met as the scallop slid onto my tongue, my body reacted with a throbbing pull. I was dizzy with arousal. I watched him eat, watched him savor, chewing slowly, his eyes on mine. I imagined his lips on my body, tasting me, savoring me, making me come.

"Catherine," he said gently. "Your eyes are an emerald forest. Aren't you hungry?"

"Not for food."

"Did you think about me while I was away?" He placed another scallop in my mouth.

"Every moment," I said after I swallowed.

"Did you touch yourself?"

I flushed from embarrassment and from desire. "No. But I'm aching for you, William. How long do I have to wait?"

Instead of answering, he removed the scallops and brought over two small silver bowls filled with yellow sorbet. I reached for mine, but he caught my wrist. I pulled my hand back and waited until he fed me. The tangy lemon exploded on my tongue, heightening my senses. He'd taken food and sex and intertwined them tonight. I would have to wait for him to feed me, and I would have to wait for him to pleasure me. He was in control, and I marveled at how much I loved being cared for like this. He brought out steaks next, and they were cooked perfectly, so deliciously tender and juicy. I tasted the subtle seasonings and the smoky flavor of the marinade. I could barely make a hamburger, and he'd managed to sear scallops, puree squash, and cook perfect steaks. The portions were small, and William fed me three or four bites of every dish, keeping me hungry, and whetting my appetite. He did not limit my wine. Between every bite, he lifted my glass to my lips. We'd had a white with the scallops, and he poured an excellent Malbec to go with the steaks.

I was slightly buzzed when he finally brought out the cheese plate. I recognized the bleu and the Brie, but the others were unfamiliar. Then my eyes widened.

Beside the cheese was a small wooden box with a white bow. "What's this?"

"I couldn't go to London and not return with a gift."

I looked at him. "You were hardly there for a day, and you don't need to give me gifts. This dinner is a gift."

He lifted the box, opened my hand, and placed it inside. "I like to give you gifts. And this is one I know you need."

I untied the bow and opened the box. Nestled on the ivory interior was a slim silver and black watch. "It's lovely," I said. I pulled it out, and William helped me fasten it. "You know I already have a watch."

"This is a Patek Philippe."

I'd seen that name on the box and had no idea what it meant. "I suppose you can't get that at Walgreens."

William closed his hand over the watch. "I want you to wear it always. Now, you'll have no excuse for being late."

I laughed, but I hadn't realized my habit of being a couple minutes behind schedule bothered him.

"It's lovely, William. Thank you."

"You're very welcome. And now, are you ready for dessert?" he asked.

"Always. More custard?"

"I have something else waiting."

FIFTEEN

He took my hand and led me to the bedroom. The lighting here was soft and romantic. A sheer drape had been drawn across the windows, giving us a muted view of the twinkling city lights. On the nightstand was a silver bucket with the neck of a champagne bottle peeking out. William crossed to it, popped the cork, and poured two flutes. He held one to my lips, and I sipped. This one was quite sweet. He set the flutes aside and reached for the tie on my dress. "I've been wanting to undress you all night." The dress opened, and he slid it off my shoulders. I stood before him in my heels and my red and black lace garters, stockings, thong, and bra.

"Do you like them?" I asked when he didn't speak.

"I'm wondering how I got so lucky," he said. "I don't deserve you."

I blinked. "*You* lucky? Have you taken a look in the mirror?" I unfastened his shirt, button by button. I spread it over his chest, undid his cuff links, and then slid the shirt off his muscled arms. "I'm the lucky one."

He grinned. "You like what you see?"

"I'll tell you in a moment." I reached for his trousers, but I could already see he was hard. I unfastened them and reached inside, taking his hot cock in my hand. "Oh, yes. I like this." While I fondled him, he unfastened my bra so that it slid to the floor. My breasts tingled as I felt his searing gaze slide over them.

"Lay on the bed."

I bent to remove my shoes, but he stopped me. "Leave them on along with the garters and thong."

I did as he asked and watched as he removed his clothing. His cock jutted out proudly, and my sex ached to feel it. My hands wanted to touch his chest, the muscles of his thighs, his corded forearms. He removed a small silver bowl from the wine bucket, and I arched on my elbows to see what was inside.

"You're killing me," he said. "That position is erotic as hell, but I have another in mind." He produced the silver and grey striped tie he'd used for my blindfold. I hadn't realized he brought it. I could go for being blindfolded again. He stood over me. "Put your hands above your head."

I arched a brow. "Why?" This wasn't what I expected.

"Catherine…" His tone held a warning. He didn't want to be challenged.

Slowly, I complied, lying back and raising my arms over my head. He bent over me and secured my wrists together with the tie. I could smell his scent and inhaled deeply as he knotted the silk. It wasn't uncomfortable, but it was tight enough that I couldn't get it off on my own.

He drew back, and his gaze raked over me. I wanted to wriggle from the intensity and the tingle of arousal. Being at his mercy, under his control, thrilled me. He could do whatever he wanted now. I was his.

He removed what looked like a grape from the silver bowl. "Let me show you." He sat beside me and showed me the grape. It was dark red and frosted with ice. He brought it to my mouth and rubbed it over my lips. The grape was frozen, and my mouth buzzed in response. He slid it inside, and I slid it back out, playing with it on my tongue. William watched, his eyes dark and deep.

He reached for another grape as I bit into the ripe fruit and felt the fresh juice slide down my throat. I opened my mouth again, but this one he skated over the slopes of my breasts. I jumped then moaned as he brushed it over a sensitive nipple. The cold made my skin pucker and harden. He traced a path along my stomach to my navel and then leaned down and lapped the frozen fruit off my skin. His warm mouth on my belly caused heat to rush between my thighs. I parted them slightly, wanting his hand there. He removed another grape and rubbed it over my other nipple. I moaned when he lowered his mouth, covering the cold grape with his hot tongue and licking my skin. He sucked my aching nipple, his hands sliding down my body and unfastening the garters. Then he moved down the bed and unrolled my stockings, gliding them down my legs, removing my shoes, and then replacing them.

"I'm going to fuck you with the shoes on," he said.

He took another grape and slid it to the ruffle of my thong. He closed his mouth over the grape and the lacy silk and drew the thong down with his teeth. I lifted my hips as his mouth caressed me, but the ache only grew. I was panting, hot all over, my need building. I knew if I clamped my legs together hard I would come.

Instinctively, I began to close them, but he caught my knee with his hand and opened my legs, spreading them. He reached for another grape, held it between his lips, and ran the cold skin of the grape down my body until he reached my sex. His mouth paused at my clit, and the cold grape rubbed against that most sensitive spot. And then the grape was gone, replaced by William's warm tongue. I came immediately, waves of ecstasy throbbing through me. I had a vague sense of William moving, and then he was between my legs again.

I let out a little scream when chilled champagne flowed at the apex of my thighs. "Your sheets!"

"I told you I want to taste champagne on your skin." He licked the champagne off, dipping first his finger in the flute then inside me. His tongue followed until I was bucking against him, begging for another release. "Not yet," he said, watching me, enjoying seeing me so hot and not able to touch him since my wrists were tied. He licked me again, spreading my folds with his fingers. Slick with arousal and champagne, I felt his fingers inch down until he pressed one finger gently around my anus.

"William!" I tried to close my legs to resist his unexpected touch, but he wouldn't allow it.

"I'm going to have you here at some point, Catherine. I'm going to claim every inch of you. There's no part I won't own. You're mine."

I moaned as he slid his fingers over me and then dipped his tongue to my clit again. I didn't want to admit it, but I was more turned on. I'd never had anal sex. I'd never wanted to, but I knew sex with William—any kind of sex—would be amazing.

William pressed champagne-cooled fingers against me then breathed warm air and laved me, and I came again. His tongue lashed me, and I begged him to stop.

"More, Catherine." My body responded, and as I shattered, he slammed into me, heightening my climax so that it went on and on, rising with each thrust. He drove into me, and when he came he called out my name. I felt his hot release burst inside me then trickle down my champagne-cooled legs, and we lay in sated exhaustion.

William reached and pulled the tie off my wrists, freeing my hands. We held each other, caressing one another's skin, murmuring, and then William's hand closed on my breast. I felt him stir again. He was all but insatiable. I lost count of how many times he had me. At one point he licked champagne from my navel, and I repaid the favor, though I licked him a little lower. His cock tasted fabulous coated in champagne, and his cum was all that much sweeter as it slid down my throat.

Finally, when neither of us could move, William stripped the bed of the champagne-soaked sheets and ran a bath. We were a sweet, sticky mess. I watched as he filled the bath with deliciously scented bubbles and turned on the jets. I stepped into the sunken tub, sliding into warm, soapy water to my chin. The froth reminded me of the champagne we'd licked off each other's bodies.

"This is fabulous," I said. He settled behind me, and I laid my head on his shoulder. "Thank you."

"For what?" he murmured into my hair.

"A perfect evening. I've never been tied up. It was intense. You should go to London more often."

William chuckled. "I thought you'd like it. And I will, go to London more, if you come with me."

"Only if I get to meet Kate Middleton."

"That could probably be arranged."

I laughed and then wondered if perhaps he wasn't joking. "Is it strange," I asked him, "to have everything you want? You buy me gifts all the time, but what am I supposed to get you for Valentine's Day or for your birthday or Christmas? You have everything."

"Not quite everything. All I want is you." He put his hands on my shoulders and pressed his thumbs into the base of my skull and massaged in small, strong circles. It felt divine.

"That may be all you get."

"I like that you're thinking about the future."

"I'm still not certain I'm relationship material."

He kissed my temple. "Catherine, you are definitely relationship material."

The bubbles were all but gone, and my fingers were prunes by the time we climbed from the bathtub. I felt full and sated and ready for sleep. While I dried off and brushed my teeth with a new toothbrush William produced, he went to make the bed with clean sheets. I tried to finger comb my hair into something that looked less like I'd been through a windstorm. I was about to join William in the bedroom when I heard the low murmur of his voice.

Curious, I grabbed my new watch and padded into the bedroom. William stood at the windows, arms crossed over his robe, phone to his ear. The bed was half-made, so he'd been interrupted by the call. I reached into the pocket of my robe and drew out the watch. It was one in the morning. Who was calling at that hour, and why had he taken the call?

He turned and saw me then showed me his back without acknowledging me. His voice remained low, barely above a whisper. What the hell? Did being a billionaire mean that you were *always* available? These late phone calls were ridiculous.

I went to the bed and finished pulling the fitted sheet over the mattress then fanned the flat sheet over the bed and tucked it under. Finally, I pulled the comforter on and climbed into bed. Alone. I kept my robe on, glaring at William.

Finally, he ended the call and crossed to me. "I'm sorry. Business."

"Business at one in the morning?"

"It's not the middle of the night in other parts of the world. I wouldn't have taken it if it wasn't important."

He was right. I was overreacting. He probably had more on his work plate in one day than I dealt with in three years. I would have to get used to sharing him with other priorities. We snuggled, and I laid my head on his chest. For the first time in as long as I could remember,

I felt safe. I felt right. I felt thoroughly taken care of. I fell asleep, listening to the sound of William's heart beating.

*****

I woke alone. I stretched and snuggled under the covers, waiting for William to return from the bathroom. After five minutes, I sat and said, "William?"

No answer.

I was sleeping alone in William's bed. Again.

I climbed out, lifted his shirt from the floor, and put it on, rolling up the sleeves and buttoning the middle buttons. I checked the bathroom and closet, didn't find him, and wandered into the kitchen.

He sat at the counter, reading the paper. He was dressed in workout clothes, his hair damp. He looked delicious.

At that moment, he looked up, and his gaze raked me from head to toe. "I need to have more of those shirts made. You look sexy as hell in it."

"Thanks. I woke alone and wondered where you were. Don't you sleep?"

"I'm an early riser, and I like to work out."

"You just got back from London. You couldn't sleep in one Saturday morning?"

He shrugged. "I don't need much sleep. Three or four hours, and I'm good. I've been like this since I was a kid."

I gaped at him. "Are you serious? That can't be healthy." What kid can get by on four hours of sleep a night? Then it hit me: a kid who lost his family. My heart ached for him. Had he been plagued by nightmares? Haunted by survivor's guilt?

"Do I seem to lack energy?" he asked.

I had to admit he didn't. And he seemed healthy too. Very healthy. Still, three or four hours was not sustainable. "Is it insomnia?" I asked. I'd dealt with a bout after Jace died. "I know some techniques—"

"Catherine, I don't need sleep like most people. I'm an early riser, and that's not going to change. Let's talk about what we're doing today. I thought we could go out for brunch. I know a fabulous restaurant. It's a bit of a drive, but it might be fun to get out of the city for a few hours—"

"Wait a minute," I protested. "That sounds great, but I can't run off with you. My friend Allison and her kids are watching Laird. I have to make sure he can stay for the day. She might have other plans."

"Call her."

I looked around for my purse and spotted it on the counter where I'd set it the night before. I dug my cell out and frowned at the screen. "It's dead. Do you have a charger?"

He held out his hand and looked at my phone. "Not for this model."

Which was a nice way of saying my phone was old.

"I'll get you a new one. In the meantime, there's a phone in my study. You can use it."

I wondered why he didn't offer to let me use his cell, but I didn't argue. He pointed in the direction of the study, and I wandered that way, examining the modern furnishings and the eclectic art on the walls. Everything was carefully placed. Nothing was crooked or stained or looked as though it had ever been used. With the high ceilings and the wall of windows, it felt more like a museum than a home.

After stumbling on the laundry room—which had a state of the art washer and dryer—I finally found the study. It was dark and masculine, with rows of books on shelves behind a mahogany desk that looked as though it had been used. It was clean and tidy, but it did have papers, pens, and assorted folders in neat piles. On one corner were a laptop and a tablet. On the other was the house phone. I sat in William's leather chair, behind his desk, and took a moment to pretend I was the Great and Powerful Oz. I'd order everyone to sleep in on Saturdays and give a two-day notice in advance of overseas trips.

With a smile, I rose and reached for the phone. My smile froze as I spotted a name on the tab of a file folder.

Jenny Hill.

That was odd. It couldn't be the same Jenny Hill I knew. It was a common name, but something made me grasp the folder anyway. I knew this was none of my business. I knew I shouldn't snoop, but I couldn't stop myself. I flipped the folder open and stared at Jenny. She and I weren't friends, but we were working photographers in Chicago and knew one another professionally. In the folder lay half a dozen photos of her, from casual shots taken as she left Starbucks or her apartment, to a shot I recognized as the one she used for business cards and her website. Beneath the photos—a typed report, single-spaced and at least fifty pages. Jenny's name was at the top and below that I read Personal Profile. I flipped through it, noting headings like Profession, Family, Past Relationships.

What the hell was this?

I kept flipping and spotted bank records going back seven years, credit checks, a detailed medical history, pictures of her family. I flipped faster. There were transcripts of conversations she'd held and information on past boyfriends.

This was a dossier. It looked like the kind of file the FBI or CIA would compile. Why would William have this? I laid the report aside and found an itinerary. I scanned it and realized it was for the evening I'd first met William at Willowgrass. It detailed when she was expected to arrive that afternoon, as well as her commitments at Willowgrass in the following days. It was the same itinerary I had followed when I'd taken over for Jenny that morning.

My heart beat fast as I found the last section in the folder. This report recommended discussion topics, tips on what Jenny liked and didn't like, along with suggestions for the number and length of dates. Another sheet made recommendations as far as when to exit the relationship.

Apparently, after eight dates, Jenny would likely get emotional. The report even recommended a parting gift. I fell back into William's chair and stared at the blurring information. This was a dating profile. It was the kind of package I imagined a dating service would send clients, but it was way more detailed than any service would provide. This dossier contained really personal information about Jenny. I mean, the number of yeast infections she'd had over the past five years was specified! This was information beyond normal for a prospective dating partner. Not only that, all financial information had to be protected by law. The health records too. No way was this dossier legal.

So William had planned to date Jenny. That was why he was at Willowgrass that day. That was why he came on strongly in the loft. He'd thought I was Jenny. The tip sheet mentioned Jenny liked strong come-ons. But he hadn't met her, and even though there were tons of pictures—Jenny and I didn't resemble one another—he still went after her... me. If he did this much research on someone he had not even met, then what information must he have on me? I scanned the top of the desk. Where the hell was my dossier?

My head spun as my thoughts came fast and furious. He made dossiers on the women he dated. How fucked up was that? I'd told him all about Jace, but had he known already? Was his reaction an act? Was this whole "relationship" a manipulated lie? Had he been following recommendations for me on every date? What was his exit strategy?

The door opened, and William poked his head in. "Did..."

He must have seen something in my face because his gaze fell to the desk. He noticed the pictures and the scattered papers then stepped inside the office and closed the door.

I waited for him to speak, but he didn't say anything.

Finally, I swallowed. "This is all just a big lie, isn't it?" I asked, sweeping my arm to encompass both of us. I shook my head. "I'm such an idiot. I told you *everything* about me. I told you I killed my husband. I told you I was the one responsible for his death. And I *agonized* over it. But you knew it all already, didn't you? You knew I'd had a drink and that I was at fault."

He didn't speak, didn't react.

"You knew, didn't you?" I shouted, standing. "Where's my file? I know you have one on me." I scattered Jenny's papers on the floor then pulled out file after file stacked on his desk. None were dossiers as far as I could tell. I dumped them all on the floor, but he didn't flinch at the mess I made of his perfect little world. I wanted to make a mess of his world, like he'd bulldozed mine.

"That night we met, you were going to meet Jenny. You were planning to date her. Since she wasn't there, did you decide to take the next best thing? But then I'm not really your type, am I?"

He folded his arms over his chest, his expression unreadable but not apologetic, and not ashamed. I pulled a picture of Jenny from the pile of papers. "I'm not tall or blond or model-y. I'm not like Jenny Hill or Lara Kendall or any of the other women I saw you standing beside in photos from charity events. So what are you doing? Am I an experiment? Is this a manipulation? A game?" Tears stung my eyes, and I willed them away.

"I told you," he said softly. "It's different with you."

"How? Because I'm not blond? Because you didn't have the dossier on me before we met?"

"I've never felt this way. I've broken my rules with you. You're different, Catherine. Our relationship is different."

"Relationship?" I swiped at the stupid tears that were falling despite my best attempts to hold them in. "This isn't a relationship. Relationships require honesty and openness. You're not honest. You're not open. This is it. I'm done."

His look was steely, his eyes stormy.

"I can't be with someone who isn't honest. You call this a relationship, but you haven't shared anything deep or personal. I'd accepted it because I know." I sniffed and used the sleeve of his shirt to wipe my tears. "I *know*. It's really hard to talk about loss. It brings it all back. It makes you vulnerable. You talk about trust!" I was screaming, and he was calm, completely unaffected. I don't think he gave a shit what I was saying, but I couldn't stop. I was furious and devastated. "You talk about trust, but you don't trust me enough to talk to me. I thought, maybe over time, you'd trust me, and you'd open up. But..." I pointed to Jenny's file. "That was stupid because our *relationship* was never going to last long anyway. You would have ended it before it got messy or complicated. God, you must have had a good laugh at me." My heart was breaking. The ache in my chest cut through me, making it almost impossible to breathe. I was sobbing now, my body shaking with the effort it took to control the sobs. I put my hands palms down on his desk and forced myself to take a deep breath. I'd done this after Jace died, learned to collect myself, calm myself.

When I looked up, I'd staunched the tears. "I have to leave. And I don't *ever* want to see you again." I ran past him, cutting through the cold house to his bedroom. I found my dress on the floor and gathered it in my arms.

I heard William come in behind me. "Get out of my way." I headed for the closet, but he grabbed my arm, spun me around. He pulled me hard against him and kissed me. "No!" I pushed back, slamming my fists against his chest, struggling to free myself. But he was strong, and he held me.

"It's not like that with you, Catherine," he said, breaking the kiss. "It's never been like that with you. You've consumed me, can't you see that?" He raked a hand through his hair, and I, too shocked by what I saw in his eyes, forgot to escape. He was terrified of my leaving, and he was desperate. The lonely little boy inside him feared his world would collapse again. "You've stolen my soul." He shook me. "Yes, the dossier routine is fucked up. I'm fucked up. It's what I do—or did—but never with you." He stared into my eyes. "*Never* with you."

I swayed, so exhausted and confused that I wanted to be anywhere else—with anyone else. I didn't know what to believe. I didn't know what was real and what was a fabrication, what was true and what was part of an elaborate plan.

I shook my head. "I don't believe you," I said calmly, stepping from his embrace and turning my back. I shed his shirt and pulled my dress on, cinching it tightly. "I don't want to see you anymore." I found my coat and threw it over my arm, stuffed my feet into the shoes. I would have left them like I was leaving the lingerie. I didn't want any part of him, but I couldn't go out in the freezing cold without shoes.

I pulled my coat on and closed it around me protectively. "Stay away from me." I strode past him into the living room and pressed the button for the elevator. When it arrived, I stepped inside, rode down, and walked out of the building, telling the doorman I needed a cab.

William didn't come after me.

I stood in the cold morning alone, watching my breath frost the air, hot tears sliding down my frozen cheeks.

SIXTEEN

I didn't wait for the cab. I couldn't stand there, crying in front of the doorman. I didn't think William would come after me, but the longer I stood in front of his building, the more I worried he might. And the more I worried I wouldn't be able to resist him. So I walked off, heading for the L. Since it was Saturday morning, the train was pretty empty, and no one looked at my tear-stained face and bare legs in high heels for too long. I stared out the windows and watched the cold, grey city as it blurred by.

When I got home I was grateful neither Minerva nor Hans was around. I didn't want to answer questions. I didn't want to speak. I was, quite simply, exhausted. My condo was lonely. I'd dropped Laird at Allison's yesterday afternoon, and now, I regretted doing so. Laird was used to my tears and my sadness. Whenever I cried over Jace's death, he stayed by me, chin on paws, sad look in his eyes. But I didn't even have the comfort of my dog this morning.

I could still smell William around me—in my hair, on my skin, on my clothes. I stripped and headed into my tiny, decidedly not luxurious bathroom. I ran a hot shower and stood under the scalding spray for what seemed like hours. Once I was in the shower, I cried in earnest. Huge, wracking sobs shook my shoulders, and I fell to my knees and let the water pound my back. I cried until I was little more than a drenched ball of despair, and then I crawled out of the shower, dried off, and pulled on my oldest pair of sweatpants and a ripped T-shirt. My sheets were clean and inviting, and I climbed under the covers, making myself into a little cocoon. The tears started again, and I let them fall.

I hated William. I hated myself. I hated stupid Jenny Hill for breaking her wrist the day before William and I met. And I wanted William back. That was the pathetic truth. My body already missed his touch. And I missed the way he laughed and smiled in those rare unguarded moments. I wallowed, and I wept with abandon. I wanted to purge myself of William and all the memories flooding me.

Finally, my throat was parched, and I padded to the kitchen for a glass of water. I trudged back to my room with a pint of ice cream and a spoon. There was little rocky road ice cream couldn't fix. I took a bite then set it aside. I couldn't bear to eat. Even the thought of food reminded me of William.

Everything reminded me of William.

How could last night have been so perfect and this morning so awful? I'd been charmed when he'd given me that simple yet elegant watch. He seemed to always know what I needed and what I liked. I realized I'd left the watch at his penthouse—the new one as well as my regular watch. Panic gripped my chest, and I ran to where I'd dropped my keys and coat when I'd walked in. I dug through the pile but no phone.

Shit!

That damn phone was the reason I was in his study in the first place. If I'd charged it before I left, I wouldn't have needed to borrow William's phone, and I wouldn't have discovered the dossier. I couldn't decide if that was fate or my forgetfulness paying off for once. In any case, I wasn't going back to get my phone. I didn't want to see William again, and especially, not in my current condition. I was actually relieved I had no way to contact the outside world. I didn't want to talk to anyone. Not even Beckett. I wanted to be alone with my shame and my self-loathing.

Why hadn't I seen the real William sooner? Or maybe I'd seen him and didn't want to accept what I saw. The one thing I knew was that we were totally and completely over. He was fucked up enough that he kept detailed dossiers on his "women." It was even more disgusting that he dated that way—with exit strategies and pages of research guiding his topics of conversation. It was a calculated plan to get laid quickly and easily without messy emotions or commitment.

And I had fallen for it. I'd fallen for the whole dog and pony show. I'd thought I was opening myself up and taking a big step when I revealed to William that I was a widow. But he'd known all along. He was a good actor. I had to give him props. He had acted surprised and taken off-guard. But now, I knew the truth.

Even this morning, when I had stupidly blurted out my part in Jace's death, when I had revealed my deepest secret, it was no secret at all. He knew all along that I was the one driving the car when Jace had been killed, and that I had alcohol in my system when I was behind the wheel.

Jace.

Fresh tears welled in my eyes. All the guilt and the horror and the sickening events of that night rushed back. My stomach heaved, and I almost lost the few bites of ice cream I'd managed to swallow.

If I could go back and do it over again...

If I had called a cab... If I had taken another road... If we'd left five minutes earlier or five minutes later... If I hadn't accepted that beer...

But there were no do-overs in life. You got one chance, and if you fucked it up, you lived the rest of your life with the awful consequences. And I would live the rest of my life with the knowledge that I was the one who killed Jace. Not directly. I hadn't held a gun to his temple, but I'd been driving the car.

I shouldn't have been driving. I never should have climbed behind the wheel. I saw myself do it a thousand times in my memory. I dreamed about it over and over. Each time, I tried to call out, to stop myself, to change the inevitable. I'd had one beer. One. I wasn't drunk. I wasn't even tipsy, but there had been alcohol in my system. Had it impaired my judgment or slowed my reflexes? If I'd been stone cold sober would I have reacted more quickly...differently? The pickup truck had come out of nowhere. The road had been dark and empty. Jace and I had the music loud, and we were laughing and talking. We'd been so happy. We'd thought our love was invincible.

And then, in an instant, it was gone. Everything I loved, everything that mattered to me—gone. My husband, my career, my life.

I told myself there was nothing served by replaying it in my mind. I'd been over it thousands of times, but it was like a movie loop I couldn't turn off. It repeated and repeated.

I saw myself telling Jace I was tired and wanted to go. He'd been drinking and laughing with his friends. He wanted to stay at the party and have another. "This is Hawaii, babe. No rules here. No schedules." The bonfire on the beach cast eerie shadows, and the light from the fire flickered over his bare chest, where his shirt was unbuttoned. He wore a shark's tooth necklace. It was cliché for a surfer, but he wore it anyway. His father had given it to him when Jace won his first surfing competition. He said it brought him luck.

"Jace, I've got film to edit tomorrow, and we've had a long day." I'd reached out, fingered the shark's tooth, and slid my hand down his chest. "Let's go back to the hotel and go to bed."

"Bed?" He'd grinned, and his teeth had looked so white against his bronze skin. "Cat, why didn't you say so before?"

He'd said his good-byes to his friends. Neither of us knew it was the last good-bye. I couldn't remember what we'd talked about in the car. Maybe we'd talked about Dax—how every time we saw him he was with a different girl. Maybe we'd chatted about Slater or Kai and their latest moves and how Jace could beat them at the Whalebone Classic in Australia the next month. And then, there'd been the bright lights and the sound of someone—me—screaming. The screech of brakes. The unearthly crunch of metal. The silence.

The police had done a thorough investigation. I wasn't at fault. The truck's driver had been drunk. Really drunk. He had several DUIs and had been driving on the wrong side of the road at high speed. We'd come around that blind corner and never had a chance. But oh, how I wished I hadn't swerved. The passenger side, where Jace was sitting, had been hit head-on. Jace and the other driver had been killed instantly. I'd gone to the hospital with minor injuries.

I knew Jace was dead at the scene. When his parents arrived from San Francisco the next day, his mother had stood over my hospital bed, pointed at me, and said, "You killed my son. It should have been you who died."

In the following months, I'd wished it had been me. Jace's family blamed me, many of his friends blamed me, and I had to change my phone number and my email address because Jace's fans wouldn't stop harassing me. It didn't matter that the other driver was given ninety-five percent of the blame. Jace was dead. I was alive, tormented by that five percent. I had alcohol in my system. My license had been expired. I shouldn't have been driving.

My mom and dad stood by me. They tried to comfort me, but they couldn't understand how much it hurt to be vilified by those who had mattered so much, by those whose support I needed. Most of Jace's friends barely spoke to me at the funeral. His parents had nothing but hate-filled words. And his brother…

I wouldn't think about Jace's brother.

I truly wished I'd been the one to die.

Sometimes, I still felt that way, even though Chicago was a long way from Santa Cruz, away from the memories and the people who hurt me. I'd needed a fresh start. I'd needed a place where I could feel anonymous, where no one had heard of Jace Ryder or the ASP World Tour or a young, stupid girl named Cat Ryder.

Here, I was Catherine Kelly. Here, I could forget, for a little while, how my life had been perfect, and how I'd ruined everything.

It seemed bad decisions weren't solely the domain of Cat Ryder. Catherine Kelly had been the one stupid enough to start a relationship with William Lambourne. It was no one's fault but my own. I'd been warned he was a commitment-phobe. Had I really expected him to be honest? Did I have a right to be outraged and hurt that he was playing me the entire relationship? That what I had thought was something special between two people was carefully orchestrated with the end in mind?

Or maybe, what really pissed me off was that I was his second choice. It had seemed like a fairy tale—destiny had brought us together. Really, it was just a patch of ice. If Jenny hadn't slipped, William would be seeing *her* now. If Jenny had called another photographer—Jessica Willis or Tiana Jackson—William would be seeing one of them now. I was nothing special. I was just in the right place at the right time.

It made me angry, but it didn't hurt me. What hurt was that he'd known my secrets from the beginning. And still, he'd let me confide in him. He'd even had the gall to act shocked and surprised. All the while he'd gone on and on about breaking rules—what rule? His blond rule? He hadn't shared himself with me. Every time I'd asked about his family, he'd shut me down. He hadn't even shared anything innocuous—his schooling, his work, his past relationships. I knew almost nothing about him, while he knew everything about me.

And still, I'd held on, clinging to the little he did reveal, hoping he might open up. Hoping we had a future. Our "relationship" had been a farce—secrets, lies, and sex. That's all it had ever been. Just sex. No intimacy. No love. No commitment. An easy fuck. That's what I was.

Not anymore. It was over.

And the decision made me cry harder. I buried my head in my pillow, closing my eyes against the images that refused to fade— bright headlights, the scream of metal, the smell of *pain au chocolat*, William's blindfold over my eyes, the feel of frozen grapes and William's warm mouth on my body, the taste of William's skin.

I pulled another pillow over my head and cried until I fell asleep.

*****

I woke the next morning and felt like someone had hit me with a camera stand. I stumbled out of bed and stared in the bathroom mirror at my puffy eyes and my red nose. I could feel pressure at the front of my skull, and my throat was scratchy. I was coming down with a cold. Perfect. My life couldn't get any better.

I had to pick up Laird, so I took a quick shower and pulled on old clothes. By the time I was ready to walk out, my nose was running, and I'd sneezed half a dozen times. I opened my door and almost stepped on the padded yellow envelope in front of it. My chest clenched, and my hand shook when I lifted it. It was from William. I knew it was from William.

I ripped the envelope open and slid my phone into my hand. No watch fell out, so I shook the package again. A slip of heavy, cream-colored paper floated to the floor. I lifted it and stared at the initials, WML.

You're better off without me. I'll never forget the taste of you.

I had to press my hand to the wall to keep from falling to my knees. It was over. It was really over. I'd known this, but William's message confirmed it. A small part of me had hoped he wouldn't let me walk away. He'd come after me and tell me it was a big mistake. He'd explain everything, and like a fairy tale, it would turn out to be a big misunderstanding.

But now, I held the end of my fantasy in my hand. William wasn't coming after me. I hadn't misunderstood. I straightened and told myself he was right. I *was* better off without him. Then why was I so miserable?

Weary to the bone, I climbed into my Volvo and drove to Allison's. Laird was excited to see me, but after the kids had hugged him good-bye, she pulled me aside. "What's wrong, Catherine? You look like you've been crying."

"I'm getting a cold," I told her, not making eye contact. I couldn't tell her about William. Not then. Not after we'd had dinner the other night, and I'd gushed about my new relationship. "I need to go back to bed."

"Can I get you anything?"

"No, I'm fine. And you've done enough. Thank you for watching Laird."

She frowned. "The kids adore him. I'm pretty sure they wore him out. He's welcome anytime."

"Thanks again." I was backing up, trying to escape before I burst into tears again. "Bye!"

"Bye. Call if you need anything, Catherine."

"Okay."

By the time I got home, I wished I'd taken Allison up on the offer of medicine. I felt even worse. I'm sure the crying didn't help. I collapsed on the couch and closed my eyes then my phone buzzed. I didn't look at the caller ID.

"Hello?"

"Cat? Is that you?"

"Beckett." Relief spiraled through me. "Yes. I have a cold. And... and..." I couldn't get the words out. I sobbed again, and Beckett told me to calm down and explain. I couldn't calm down. My mind chanted *It's over. It's really over*.

"I'm coming over," Beckett announced.

"You don't have to do that." But I was glad. I felt awful—in body and soul.

"I'll be there in twenty minutes." And he was. Beckett had a key, so it seemed like one moment we were on the phone and the next he was standing over me. "Cat, you're burning up," he said, pressing his hand to my forehead the way my dad did when I was a kid. "Have you taken anything?"

"It's over, Beckett," I said, tears streaming down my cheeks. "With William."

"Oh, Cat. What happened?"

I tried to tell him, but I was crying so much I didn't make sense.

Finally, in the middle of my blubbering, Beckett said, "Do not move. I'm going to the store for supplies." Laird took Beckett's place on the couch, and I must have dozed.

When I woke, Beckett held a small plastic cup of cold medicine to my lips. I drank it along with the tea he'd made and promptly began crying again.

"Cat, you need to sleep. Come on."

It was a monumental effort to drag my weary, pain-filled body to bed, but I did it with Beckett's help. "I'm worried about you," he said after tucking me in. "I'm going to hang here awhile. Make sure your fever doesn't spike."

"No, Beckett," I groaned. "You've done enough."

"Oh, this isn't as selfless as it seems, honey. I'm using your AGA to try out a few recipes. Now go to sleep."

I slept a dreamless sleep, half awake at times, but too groggy to get out of bed. When I woke, it was dark, and I wondered if Beckett had finally gone home. My clock read almost seven, and I groaned. I'd slept the entire day.

I rose and stumbled into the living room, shielding my eyes against the bright lamplight. I heard Beckett in the kitchen and followed my nose. Something smelled delicious, and my empty stomach rumbled. My mouth was watering by the time I spotted Beckett. He was washing pots and pans and looked up when I entered. "You look like hell," he said.

"I feel like hell," I rasped. On the stove, soup bubbled, the aroma irresistible. It was a rich broth, and even my stuffed nose detected the scent of herbs. "Beckett, I can't believe you made me soup."

"I didn't." He gestured to a cooling rack filled with cupcakes ready to be frosted. "I made the cupcakes. William brought over the soup."

"What?" Just the mention of William made my heart beat faster, and pain lanced through my chest.

"I answered your cell while you were passed out. Your friend Allison called and then William. He was pissed when I wouldn't put you on, so I told him you were sick and asleep. Ninety minutes later he showed up with soup."

I blinked. "William was here? Why didn't you wake me?"

"Cat, you were out. William said he couldn't stay. He handed me the soup and said to tell you he hopes you feel better soon."

I stared at Beckett. William had been here. He'd brought me soup.

"Are you sure he knows it's over?" Beckett asked.

"I don't know what to think." I was still confused by William and by my own reaction. One part of me was thrilled he had been so close, another part was still furious. No way were we ever getting back together. Not after what I'd seen in his study. But I couldn't help wondering—if I could have smelled anything, would I have picked up his scent? Would my body have known he was here, even if my mind rejected him?

"So," Beckett said, indicating the soup. "We're not letting this go to waste, are we?" He pulled two soup mugs from my cabinet. "I mean, we can still hate the guy, even if we eat his soup."

"Oh, we're eating the soup," I confirmed.

We sat at my dining table, and Beckett had three bowls while I managed to put away two. It was delicious. I wasn't big on soup—felt like I was drinking my meal—but I could have eaten this for the rest of my life.

"Either I was starving, or that was the best soup I've ever eaten," I told Beckett.

"It was the best soup *I've* ever eaten. I need to find out where he got it."

"I'm sure he made it," I said, sitting back contentedly. "He's a great cook."

"Is there anything the man doesn't do?" Beckett asked.

"He doesn't do normal."

Beckett leaned over and gave me a hug. "He's a great gift-giver. Remember that bracelet?"

"Beckett, I didn't tell you about the watch. I forgot it at his penthouse, but it was beautiful." I described it, and Beckett pulled out his phone as I talked.

"A Patek Philippe?" he asked. "Like this one?" He turned the screen toward me.

"Exactly."

"Cat, that's a sixty-thousand-dollar watch."

"You know what, Beckett? It could be a million-dollar watch, and I wouldn't care. I can't be with someone like him."

"You're too good for him, Cat, but I do wish you'd kept the watch." He ruffled my hair. "I'm going to walk Laird and then head home. Do you need anything else?"

"You've already done too much."

"Nothing is too much for you. Take more medicine, and I'll call you in the morning."

I did. Beckett took Laird for a quick walk, and I drifted into another cold medicine coma.

I woke to the sound of Laird's snoring and my ring tone. Figuring it was Beckett making sure I was alive, I answered. Rather, I croaked. My throat was raw and raspy.

"Catherine?"

It was William. I shot up, my head spinning.

"Catherine, how are you feeling?"

I was miserable, but I took a deep breath and held it together. "I'm okay. Thanks for the soup. It helped."

"Is Beckett still there?"

"No." I closed my eyes, picturing William. I could see his wavy hair, making me want to curl my fingers in it. His long, aristocratic fingers held the phone. His stormy eyes narrowed as I spoke. I swallowed and clenched my hands.

"You sound awful. Are you eating?"

"I'm not hungry." I paused for a coughing fit, and I fumbled for my cold medicine—time for another dose.

"Catherine, I'm coming over."

"No, you're not. I just need another dose of medicine."

"Have you seen a doctor?" He sounded a bit frantic.

"It's just a cold."

"Beckett said you had a high fever. I'll take you to the hospital."

"What? No."

"It won't hurt to have a doctor look at you. What meds are you taking? Have you checked your temperature?"

"William…"

"Are you drinking enough? You can easily get dehydrated."

"William, stop, okay? Just stop." Silence. I would not start crying. I knew he was trying to take care of me, and that was sweet, but there was another side to him. "Thanks for the soup and for your concern, but I don't want to see you."

"I'll send George to check on you then."

"No. I don't want you or your people to check on me. I'm not your concern anymore, and I can take care of myself. I can't be with you, William. I can't be with someone who isn't honest. There are too many secrets. And even if I could get past that, I can't get past the cruelty."

"Catherine—"

"The way you deal with people, with relationships. *Exit strategies. Dossiers.* I can't be with you."

"You're right."

I was? It didn't feel right. It felt like the hardest thing I'd ever had to say.

"You're better off without me. You should stay away."

I really didn't know what to say in response. Was this reverse psychology, or was he serious? I didn't know, and I didn't care. I couldn't allow myself to be drawn into William's seductive, bewildering world again. "I have to go."

"Get well soon."

"Thanks." I hung up and threw the phone down. New tears spilled over my cheeks, and I buried my face in the pillow. Laird moaned and nuzzled me with his nose. I hugged him and sobbed. Everything inside felt bruised and tender. The weight of the breakup coupled with the miserable cold pressed down until I felt crushed. I curled back up into a ball and sobbed.

SEVENTEEN

By Wednesday I finally felt better. I still wasn't back to normal, but I was out of bed, and my head didn't feel as heavy as a pumpkin. Yesterday I'd worried I wouldn't be up for the Fresh Market shoot. This morning I thought I would be okay. When I'd looked in the mirror, my face hadn't been red or blotchy for the first time in five days. My Saturday morning break-up with William felt far away— dreamlike. The last couple days had given me perspective.

One benefit of being my own boss was that I could work when I wanted and how I wanted. No one cared if I worked in my pajamas or put in barely an hour in the morning, a couple hours in the afternoon, and several more in the evening as long as the work got done. I'd dragged my tired ass in front of my computer yesterday to work on the ad campaign for Fresh Market. We were shooting spring foods for the Fresh for Spring ads. Beckett and I were styling and shooting cherries and asparagus. If we nailed these two, Fresh Market might ask us to do the rest of the Fresh for Spring line—foods like apricots, oranges, and my favorite, strawberries. But we had to sex up the cherries. The asparagus I felt good about. Beckett and I had a lot of ideas for making the asparagus look phallic and yummy. The cherries were a little harder, and I still hoped inspiration would strike.

I checked my phone while I dressed for the shoot. William had texted me a few times since our last conversation on Monday, but I hadn't replied. He hadn't called me again, and the texts had petered out. I was checking my cell because I wanted him to call. A part of me still missed him, still felt incredibly sad, still wanted him back. There was a deep ache inside where he was missing. I hadn't realized I'd been touched so deeply by our relationship, and I knew the wound would take time to heal.

It was healing already. I was keeping it together. I might be sad, but I knew I could get through today and the shoot. It would be a grueling day, but I looked forward to the distraction of hard work.

Another aspect of the Fresh Market shoot I looked forward to was the chance to work in the studio. I'd done so much shooting in the wild that working under controlled conditions was a dream come true. Plus, I'd be working with Beckett, and he was the best food stylist in the city. I knew the food would look amazing.

Alec Carr met me in the foyer of the studio Fresh Market had booked for the morning. These studios were in demand and ridiculously expensive. Alec had generously asked Beckett and me how long we needed. We'd said four hours and understood it was a testament to Fresh Market's commitment to my work that they'd agreed without argument. The shoot was costing them a small fortune.

"Beckett is already here and hard at work," Alec told me. "He's choosing the heroes now." The hero was what we called the food we'd shoot that day. Beckett and the Fresh Market people had been searching for the best cherries and asparagus they could find. This wasn't easy in the middle of January.

Alec led me to the studio, and with a nod at Beckett, I set up. A lot of food photographers had assistants do this, but I was a control freak about my work. I wanted to do it myself. The Fresh Market people had already prepared the studio. On a table, light screens, light boxes, and the cardboard stand-ins for the food were ready. State-of-the art computers were on another table behind where I'd shoot, so we'd see the photos immediately.

Beckett was off to the side, hunched over a mound of cherries. He gave me an appraising look, saw I was feeling better, and went back to work. I set my bag down and got my equipment out. For the shoot, I'd use a digital mounted on a tripod. I had several lenses, including a close-up lens I'd used often. The great advantage of my tripod was that it allowed me to move the camera three hundred sixty degrees. I could shoot above the food or from any side angle. Versatility would be the key today if I wanted to get the perfect shot.

As soon as I jumped into the work, I forgot the lingering aches and stuffiness from my cold. This kind of shoot was grueling, and I'd be drained tonight. But I really enjoyed it, and I knew I was good. Excellence was its own reward, though the money was pretty substantial for both Beckett and me.

Once I was ready, I took a few shots of the cardboard cutout to test the lighting and the angle. Beckett came over and studied the images on the computer, and we conferred about minor tweaks. We decided to shoot the asparagus first because I had a clear idea of the shots—sexy and phallic. Beckett blanched the chosen asparagus to brighten its color. He positioned it, and I nodded my approval and took a few shots. "Let's add moisture on the tip," I said. "Just a little."

"Ooh!" Beckett said. "Now you're getting naughty. Pre-cum shot, Cat?"

I blushed and ducked my head. "Just going for a fresh, spring look, Beckett."

"Uh-huh." Beckett styled the asparagus and then stepped back. I focused and took shot after shot, but I could hear Beckett and Alec chatting as they watched me work.

"Those are some impressive stalks," Alec commented. I could hear the teasing tone.

"Oh, I always prefer the thick stalks. You?" Beckett answered.

"I like mine long and hard."

I rolled my eyes and chuckled at their innuendo.

"Cat, we're talking about asparagus," Beckett said, pretending to be offended. "Get your mind out of the gutter."

"Sorry. A few more shots, and I'll need you to prep the cherries."

"Got it. I have a new idea for those. Interested?"

I glanced at Beckett, intrigued. "Sure."

Alec, Beckett, and I studied the asparagus shots on the computer, made a few tweaks, and I took a couple more shots. Then I got a break while Beckett prepared the cherries. I rolled my shoulders and craned my neck then wandered over to see what Beckett was up to.

As soon as I saw what he'd done, I gasped.

"You don't like it." His face fell, and he sounded devastated.

"I like it. It's very fresh." I smiled at Alec, but inside my stomach tightened into knots. Beckett had styled the cherries to look frozen. He'd used a cellulose mixture on the edges of the cherries, similar to what one might use to flock a Christmas tree, giving the fruit a chilled look. He'd sprayed them with water, cornstarch, and whatever secret ingredients he had to create a magic potion that made the cherries glisten. The effect was of refreshingly cold, mouthwatering cherries that would feel wonderfully cool when popped into one's mouth.

Or slid down one's body.

The cherries reminded me of my last night with William and the inventive way he'd used the frozen grapes. I didn't know if I could shoot these cherries without my hand shaking and tears clouding my vision.

"Oh, I love that!" Alec said. He'd come over while I recovered from my shock.

Beckett winked. "I thought you might." Beckett glanced at me. "Want to give it a try?"

"Of course."

Alec wandered back to the corner of the room he and Beckett had been sharing, and Beckett leaned close so he couldn't be heard. "You okay? You look a little pale."

"I'm fine," I said. "Alec loves it, and that's all I need."

I began shooting, focusing the camera, looking for the perfect angle. Beckett came over a few times to reposition or spray the cherries, but after awhile he let me work. I could hear Beckett and Alec's banter, and it was clear something was developing between them. I tried to shut them out and think exclusively about work, but images of William assaulted my mind. William's hand on my breast. His mouth on my belly. His firm body as it rose over mine.

I blinked my eyes to keep tears from forming.

Finally, the shoot was done. While I'd been working, several Fresh Market execs had come into the studio to study my picks for the asparagus shots. I shook hands and went through the shots of the cherries, picking those I thought were best.

Beckett rushed around, trying to preserve the food in case more shots were needed, but it was a losing battle. Fortunately, the execs loved several shots and approved them on the spot. Everyone relaxed, and I started to break the equipment down.

"Can I help with anything?" Alec asked.

I smiled. I'd never known a corporate art director—even an assistant one—to offer to help. He was a nice guy. "I've got it, but thanks."

"Beckett and I were talking about the Major League Chef's Ball," he said as I worked. "Have you been to one?"

"Is that the event where the best chefs are pitted against baseball players?"

"Exactly. It's at the Chicago Hilton, and Chicago's best twenty-five chefs and mixologists compete against guest chefs from

Chicago's favorite teams. Not only baseball. Football and basketball too."

"Sounds fun." I disassembled my tripod.

"It's the best event of the year. Not too stuffy, tons of great food and drinks, super fun atmosphere—dancing and a DJ. It's to raise money for Chicago's charities. Fresh Market is a major sponsor this year, and I'm heading the event."

"When is it?" I asked absently, thinking about William and only half listening.

"Tomorrow night. I'd love for you and Beckett to come. It would be great exposure. We could introduce you to new clients."

"Umm..."

"I can have two tickets waiting at the door. Just say the word."

"Oh, Alec, I don't know." If I'd been paying attention I would have seen where he was going and cut him off before it got to this point. I wasn't up to going out yet, much less being a third wheel with Beckett and Alec. Plus, this was a huge foodie event. It was definitely William Lambourne territory. I didn't want to risk running into him. Not yet. It was too soon after our breakup.

"Cat! You have to say yes." Beckett sidled up beside me. "Think about it. Delicious food, hot baseball players. How can you say no?"

"William might be there."

Beckett waved his hand, dismissing my concern. "Chicago is a big place. William Lambourne can't be everywhere. And this would be good for your career and mine."

Still, I hesitated.

"Look, Cat. If you don't come willingly, I'm going to drag you. This is the opportunity of a lifetime!"

I looked at Beckett and saw the plea in his eyes. He needed me to go, and I owed him big time. He'd had my back over and over, and if this was good for his career, I owed him this much. I smiled. "No dragging necessary. I'm in."

*****

The next morning I woke feeling good. I was stiff and fatigued from the photo shoot the day before, but over my cold. And the photos for Fresh Market weren't due for a few days, so I could take a break from work. Laird hopped on the bed, his leash in his mouth, and I laughed. "Okay, boy, I can take a hint."

The sun was out, and the day was perfect for a run along the lake. Laird and I headed out, but about ten minutes into the run, I wished we hadn't gone so far. Arctic air and the chill beside the lake had taken me off-guard. I'd remembered my hat but not my gloves. Big surprise. My hands were numb, aching from the bitter cold. On the way home, I stopped to get coffee and warm my frozen fingers. Suddenly hungry, I realized I had nothing but yogurt at home. There was an organic market on the next block, so I walked over and picked up groceries.

More accustomed to shopping for lingerie than fruits and vegetables, I collected a shopping basket and picked out whatever looked fresh. I was in a hurry because Laird was tied up outside. Everything went well until I reached the grapes. It was hard not to think of William when I saw them, but I pushed him out of my mind, selected some, and kept shopping.

I could do this.

*****

The next night I shared a cab with Beckett to the Hilton for the ball. Alec was meeting us there, and Beckett was a bundle of nerves. He must have asked three times if the suit he'd chosen looked good.

"Beckett, it's an Armani. You can't go wrong." I wasn't used to Beckett acting insecure. He was usually confident about fashion and style.

"Do I look like I'm trying too hard?"

"No. You're rocking that suit. You look great. Alec won't be able to concentrate on work once he sees you."

Beckett gave me one of his signature grins. "Thanks, Cat. What about these shoes?"

And we started all over again. I didn't mind Beckett's incessant chattering and worrying because it distracted me from thoughts of William. I had dressed carefully in a fitted, black sequined, V-neck dress, by a designer my mom loved. I liked the dress because it was both fun and flirty. It showed off my cleavage, and even though I didn't want to see William tonight, if I did, I wanted to look good.

We finally arrived, and I'd been so busy worrying about seeing William and listening to Beckett, I hadn't paid attention to where we were. Once we walked into the hotel, I put my arm on Beckett's sleeve to stop and gawk. The hotel was gorgeous, the mammoth entrance ornamented by plush rugs and soaring columns. Soft lighting gave the place grace and elegance as did the gold medallions and molding on the ceilings and the paintings in muted colors. I wished I'd brought my Leica and knew I'd have to come back to shoot this place. I turned three hundred sixty degrees, seeing different angles in my mind, before Beckett took my arm. "You haven't ever been here?"

"No."

"Just wait. You'll love the Grand Ballroom."

He was right. The ballroom was huge, lit by ten crystal chandeliers that glinted on the ornate plasterwork. A mezzanine overlooked the space, and ruffled drapes added elegance. Tonight that elegance had been juxtaposed with funky lighting, thumping music, and the best-dressed, most beautiful people I'd ever seen. The energy was high. Sumptuous scents tantalized, gourmet concoctions sizzled, the DJ blasted my favorite songs, and celebrity athletes mingled with those of us considerably less coordinated.

Alec spotted us quickly and made sure we had drinks and samples of the culinary offerings. He introduced us to Fresh Market execs we hadn't met, those not involved with the art department. I tried to make conversation, but it was difficult with the loud music and my worries about running into William. I kept telling myself to stop thinking about him. The place was packed. There was no way I would see him, even if he were here.

Alec made sure our plates were always full. He knew the best offerings from each chef and bartender. Everything was delicious, and after a few drinks, Beckett dragged me toward the dance floor. I tried to say no, but he was such a good dancer, I finally gave in. We danced to several songs, and then Alec joined us, and I said I had to go to the restroom. I didn't want to get in Beckett's way.

Once I was off the floor, I watched them and smiled. Alec couldn't keep his eyes off Beckett, and the look on Beckett's face told me he was flirting big time.

I walked around and stopped to watch one chef cook. It took me a moment to realize the chef was Ben Lee. When he took a break, I leaned over to say hi, and he gave me a warm hug. "Catherine! What a great surprise! Where's your boyfriend? I don't want to get in trouble." He held his hands up to indicate he wasn't touching me.

"He's not my boyfriend anymore, so you're safe. What are you making?" I asked to change the subject.

"It's a new take on grilled cheese. Try it."

I ate Ben's yummy dish and then wandered away, looking for other delicious offerings. I would gain five pounds by the end of the night, but I'd probably lost that much from being sick and depressed about the breakup.

"You're Catherine Kelly, right?" someone asked.

"Right," I said, turning. It was a Fresh Market exec. I remembered that he was a VIP. He was young with blondish brown hair and hazel eyes, and he had a nice smile.

"I was impressed with your work on the kebabs. I'm glad you were chosen for the Fresh for Spring campaign."

"Thanks," I said. "I'm glad too. I'm sorry. I forgot your name."

"Mark Sanders. Are you from Chicago?"

"Actually, I'm a transplant from California."

His eyes widened. "Whoa. How are you liking the winters?"

"They've taken some getting used to." I smiled.

"Can I get you a drink?"

I shook my head. "I'd better not have another. I have work in the morning."

"Then how about a dance?"

I hesitated. Why not? I deserved a little fun. "Sure."

Mark led me to the dance floor and took my hand. He was a good dancer and had an infectious smile. I couldn't stop smiling either, until a movement in the mezzanine caused me to glance up.

My gaze roamed over the railings and the curtained alcoves until I saw *him*. I froze and stared. He was dressed in a dark suit with a slate grey tie. His eyes were as grey as the tie and stormier than I had ever seen them. His hair was brushed back from his forehead, drawing attention to his strong jaw, which looked clenched with tension.

"Catherine?" Mark asked. "Are you okay?"

I glanced at him then back at the mezzanine. No one was there. Had I imagined William standing there?

"Catherine?"

"Sorry, Mark. I'm fine." I fumbled. My heart raced, and I couldn't breathe. I had to get out of there. "I'm a little tired. I think I'm going to call it a night."

I knew I was being rude, but I walked off the dance floor. I steadied myself on a tabletop and stared at the mezzanine again. Had

I really just imagined seeing William? Maybe I'd had too much to drink.

I found Beckett and Alec and told them I was heading home. Beckett tried to convince me to stay, but I didn't want to risk seeing William if he hadn't been a figment of my imagination. I fled to the lobby, my heels clicking on the marble as I made my escape.

"Cat Ryder? Is that you?"

My heart jumped into my throat, and I skidded to a stop. A tingle of unease skittered up my back, making my hair stand on end. Slowly, I turned and glanced around the all but empty lobby.

"It *is* you!" A compact man with a shaved head and a two-day growth of beard waved and strode up to me. He was dressed in a gray suit and tie, but I could easily picture him in a wet suit and sunglasses. "I can't believe you're here!"

"Ryan," I heard myself say. "What are you doing here?" The room tilted, and I felt as though I was walking through a dreamworld. It seemed like I'd known Ryan Lewis in another life. He gave me a hug, but my arms refused to embrace him. I stood stiff while he greeted me as though everything was normal. As though I was still Cat Ryder. He didn't know I hadn't been that girl for three years.

"I could ask you the same!" he said, stepping back. "Listen, I heard about Jace." His expression grew solemn, and he reached out and rubbed my arm. "I'm so sorry. You got a raw deal, Cat."

I nodded, a lump forming in my throat. I couldn't speak. I had to concentrate on blinking back the tears.

"What are you doing now? I'm still with *Sports Illustrated*. This isn't quite as fun as the surfing scene, but I'm moving up in the world. Are you working tonight?" He looked at my clutch, seeming to wonder where my camera might be hiding.

"No." I shook my head. "I'm not doing sports photography any longer."

His eyes widened. "Why the hell not? Cat, you were really good. One of the best—and I know the best."

My breath hitched, and I swiped at my cheek, where a rogue tear had broken loose.

"Let me give you my card." He reached into his breast pocket and withdrew a business card. I took it mechanically. "Call me if you want to get back in the game."

"Thanks," I murmured, beginning to walk away.

"Cat." He grabbed my elbow. "It really is good to see you again. Call me. We could have lunch and—"

A shadow appeared in the corner of my eye, and Ryan was shoved back. "Get your hands off her."

I gasped and stared at William. His eyes were icy blue, his face flushed with anger. He turned to me, his eyes softening. "Is he bothering you, Catherine? I'll take care of this."

I shook my head, my senses reeling. Was this really happening? I'd never felt so torn between my past and my present. Was I Cat Ryder or Catherine Kelly?

"Cat, what the hell?" Ryan said. "Call the guard dog off."

"Sorry," I said to Ryan, but my gaze stayed riveted on William. My body swayed toward his, and I felt myself reacting to his closeness. He was gorgeous with those stormy eyes and that protective stance. I still wanted him.

"I'm sorry," I said again and fled.

EIGHTEEN

I had several meetings with prospective clients the next day and shopping to do. I hoped Fresh Market would call and ask me to shoot more for their spring campaign, so I justified the purchase of a new lens, a couple memory cards, and an upgrade for my editing software. Despite the fact I'd managed to cross tasks off my to-do list, I hadn't distracted myself from thoughts of William.

Or of Jace.

Seeing Ryan again had brought back old memories and emotions, and once at home, I found myself standing outside my darkroom. I hadn't been inside since William and I were in there together, when I showed him my pictures. I missed William, but I was proud of myself too. I'd taken a huge step in my life. Seeing Ryan brought me back to everything I'd had before—and everything I'd lost. I wasn't the shell of a person I'd been after Jace's death. I was making a new life for myself.

My relationship with William hadn't worked out, but that didn't mean it wasn't going to work out with someone else. That I'd let William get close was a huge step. I'd let myself *feel*, and that was major too. For the first time since Jace's death, I thought there was a possibility I could be happy again. I could envision myself with someone besides Jace. For three years, I'd lived in the past, but now, I could look forward.

Happiness without Jace was possible. I would never forget him. I would always love him, but I could move on with my life. Amazingly, I'd come to these realizations in the last two weeks, over what really amounted to just a few days.

In that instant I knew exactly what I had to do. Seeing Ryan made me appreciate how far I'd come. I was finally ready. I stepped into the darkroom and searched among the dozens of boxes on the shelf until I found a roll of undeveloped film.

This was *the* roll.

I held it in my shaking hand and tried to breathe. This was the last roll of photos I'd taken of Jace. These were shot on Oahu's fabled North Shore the afternoon of the accident that claimed his life. Little did I know these were the last photos I would take as Cat Ryder, fearless surf photographer and wife of the most promising new surfer on the pro circuit. This roll symbolized everything I had thought my life would be. It was everything I wanted. Once Jace was dead, once my life veered wildly off course, I hadn't wanted to see that roll of smashed dreams. I'd almost thrown it away a half dozen times, but something always stopped me. And now, I knew why. I'd been saving it for this moment. I needed to confront those images now. I needed to confront my past as Cat Ryder.

I prepared my supplies and soaked the paper in the developer. As I watched, images slowly took shape. The clear, gorgeous blue water of Hawaii was the first thing I saw. These initial pictures were of the waves breaking and the ripcurl. I remember I'd been out on my long board, past the break point, with my heavy waterproof photo gear strapped on. The lens port I'd used on the water housing was gigantic. I loved the bubble effect it created because it allowed me to capture what was happening above and below the surface. These weren't shots you got on land. You had to be in the surf, riding the waves with the guys. I had angled myself so I looked down the barrel to get the deep pocket shots.

The next pictures were of Jace. He was paddling out on his board, his smile as wide as his paddle. And he was looking directly at me. I stared at images of Jace as he waited for the perfect set or went duck-diving when waves broke in front of him. I had shots of Jace catching a wave and pictures of him deep in the tube as a wave curled above. More pictures—roundhouse cutbacks, aerials, Jace hitting the lip—Jace doing a backside bottom turn, a roundhouse cutback, and a carving frontside 360.

My breath whooshed out. I'd forgotten how good he was. He had so much talent. More pictures of him clawing toward the horizon as a set rolled down the reef, pictures of Jace and our friends, waiting on the shoulder, paddling to catch a wave, dropping in. I laughed when I saw the first of the shots where Jace wiped out. The swells that day were wicked, and even after Jace traded in his six-foot board for a seven-foot, he was still tossed around like human flotsam.

Finally, I saw the photos I was really looking for. These were the ones I'd taken back on the beach. Jace laughing and goofing around. He and his buddies were posing for the camera, pushing one another, making muscles. Then there were a few of Jace watching the surfers in the wild waves. He looked serious, contemplative, and focused. I remembered how I loved that look. It made my heart ache to see it again.

Tears streamed down my face as each image emerged in the developer bath. I missed Jace so much. There was a huge hole in my life where he should have been—where he'd never be again. He was beautiful, so full of life. And then I crushed my hand to my mouth because I'd forgotten this last photo. I'd probably taken it to finish the roll. It was an image of the two of us together as I'd held the camera and snapped a picture. I sobbed openly when I saw how young we were. Our faces were pink from the sun, and there was so much love in our eyes as we grinned at one another.

It hurt to look at the two of us. I missed him so much. "Jace," I whispered to the photo. I couldn't speak the words, but I was so sorry. Sorry I was driving, sorry I'd had a beer before we left, sorry I pushed him to leave before he was ready, sorry I didn't see the beat-up, red pickup truck barreling toward us before it was too late.

Sorry I never said good-bye or *I love you* one last time.

I pressed a finger to the image in the bath. "I love you," I whispered. "I love you, Jace."

The image blurred as my tears fell and mixed with the developer bath. I took a deep, shuddering breath and *finally* let go.

I was ready.

Using my tongs, I grasped the picture of Jace and me. I smiled through my tears at the way our heads tipped easily toward each other.

Marveled at our clear eyes and sun-kissed skin. We looked so happy and so young. And we were. We were all of that and more.

This was the picture I wanted to remember. This was the one I'd frame and treasure.

I hung the photo to dry and set the tongs down, almost knocking another roll of film off the table. I lifted it and realized it was the final roll I'd taken on my walk in Lake Forest that afternoon two weekends ago. It seemed like another lifetime—someone else's life.

I hadn't used all the exposures, and when I'd showed William my darkroom, I'd playfully snapped the remaining few of him with my Leica. I took a deep breath and submerged these in the developer bath. I watched as an image of William and his stormy eyes materialized. In the image, he was playful. I smiled, thinking back. I'd been laughing so hard as William and I goofed around. I'd been happy and content. I'd felt safe, relaxed, and…loved.

Oh, shit. Loved! I took a sharp breath. What the hell had I done? Was William right all along? Had I been fighting him and my future? And if he was my future, had I walked away from him and all we could be together?

I heard a buzz and jumped from the unexpected sound. With a frown, I left the darkroom, rubbing my hands on my jeans. Laird was standing by the door, and I pressed the intercom button. "Yes?"

"Miss Kelly, it's George Graham."

I blinked. What the hell did he want?

"May I come up?"

"I…" I sighed. Better get this over now. I pushed the buzzer and opened the door. A moment later, George crested the stairs. Once again, he was wearing a black suit and looked as though he'd come directly from his desk at the FBI. "Come in," I said, indicating my living room. "I only have a minute."

"I'll be brief." He stepped inside, standing stiff and formal, posture rigid. "I must speak with you. This is the only way."

"Did William send you?" I patted Laird on the head, staying near the door. We weren't sitting for this. He could speak and leave.

"No. If Mr. Lambourne knew I was here, I would lose my job. You hold my livelihood in your hands."

"Why would you come against William's wishes?"

For the first time, the man looked human. A flicker of emotion crossed his features. "You need to know the truth. Mr. Lambourne told me you discovered the dossier I created on Jenny Hill."

My eyes widened. "So that was your work?"

"I make one for every woman Mr. Lambourne sees."

"Including me."

"No." He took a step forward. "That's why I came. I never made one for you. Mr. Lambourne told you the truth. I suggested doing so. In fact, I all but insisted. Mr. Lambourne refused. That's the first time he's ever done so."

"What exactly is your job, Mr. Graham? Head snooper?"

I saw the ghost of a smile on his lips. "I'm head of personal security for Mr. Lambourne. I've protected him for years. He's a wealthy man—the perfect target for abduction, violent crime by an anticapitalism group, or exploitation by a certain kind of woman. I make sure no one who hasn't been vetted gets close to Mr. Lambourne. I generally select dates for him. I—"

"Wait a moment. You're like his pimp?"

Anger flashed in his eyes. "I search for women who are Mr. Lambourne's type, those who would make suitable companions. Whether the lady chooses to date him is her decision. You cannot expect a man like William Lambourne to meet women on the Internet or troll bars, and it is frequently necessary for him to take a date to an event."

"And yet, he managed to meet me without your help."

"Yes."

I couldn't help but note that George looked none too happy.

"You were—are—different. I've never seen him act like he's acted with you. And now…" He trailed off and shook his head. "Mr. Lambourne has been miserable the last few days without you. I've never seen him like this, and I've known him a very long time. I worked for his father and I've known Mr. Lambourne since he was a young man. I know you doubt your relationship with Mr. Lambourne, but I came to tell you it's genuine, Miss Kelly. He's never lied to you and what Mr. Lambourne feels for you is genuine."

I swallowed, a lump rising in my throat. Did the man have any idea how much I wanted to hear this? Was this another of William's manipulations? "Why are you telling me this?"

"Honestly, Miss Kelly, I don't know. I suppose I think of Mr. Lambourne as my responsibility. I don't like to see him like this. I could think of no option but to speak with you personally."

I sighed. I didn't want to believe George Graham. I didn't want to know William was miserable without me, that his feelings hadn't been a fabrication. That he never ordered a dossier on me. I had gotten past the worst of the pain, and I couldn't imagine going through a breakup again if we got back together.

"I know you have severed all ties with Mr. Lambourne," George said, "but if you reconsider, you will find Mr. Lambourne at a benefit dinner tonight for the new cancer wing at Chicago Hospital. Mr. Lambourne endowed the new wing."

"Of course, he did," I muttered. "And what's a million or two?"

He held out an envelope, and I hesitated before taking it.

"This is a ticket to the event. Perhaps you will attend. I promise it will be worth your time if you care to see the real William Lambourne." He pulled his black leather gloves from his coat pocket. "And it was twenty million, actually. Good afternoon, Miss Kelly."

He opened my door and disappeared down the steps. I stood in my empty living room for a full minute before looking at Laird, who yawned. I gave Laird a hug and pulled the ticket from the envelope. The event was at The Peninsula Hotel, and the ticket stated it was black tie.

I dug my phone out of my purse and called Beckett. "Hey!" he answered. "You left too early last night. You missed all the fun."

I smiled. "Did you go home with Alec?"

"What kind of guy do you think I am?"

"The easy kind?"

"You know me so well. All we shared was a kiss. It was nice. Didn't you have a good time?"

"Yes, but then I saw William, and it freaked me out."

"Cat, it was your imagination."

"No, it wasn't." I told Beckett about running into Ryan Lewis.

"Oh, Cat, I didn't even think. Of course, *Sports Illustrated* would cover the event."

"You couldn't know they'd send someone I know, and that's actually not why I called. Something weird happened." I told him about my conversation with George Graham. "I don't think I should go, Beckett. It's not like William apologized. So what if he's miserable? He said himself I was better off without him."

"Bullshit, Cat. You don't believe that. The man is pining over you and—hello—you have been pining over him. This is your chance. It's so romantic, like Harry and Sally on New Year's Eve."

"Except he's not Billy Crystal, and I'm not Meg Ryan. And it's not New Year's Eve."

"Cat, I see you running into the hotel, looking frantically for William, spotting him across the room…" He sighed.

I forgot what a hopeless romantic Beckett could be.

"It's a black-tie event, Beckett. William and I don't have a good history at high-end charity functions."

"Don't go then." He sounded petulant. "Give up. This might be your last chance at finding true love again. What if William is *The One*? And you won't go to one event?"

"Yeah, an event that William's creepy CIA guy gave me a ticket to."

"The man risked everything for true love! How can you be so hard-hearted?"

I laughed. Beckett could be so over the top. "Okay, Beckett. When you put it that way, how can I refuse?"

"So you'll go?"

"I have to."

*****

Beckett was right. Not about the Harry and Sally thing, but about my chance for finding true love again. I did love William.

I sat in the back of a cab, dressed in the fabulous red gown William had sent for our first date. Strangely enough, I felt comfortable in it. I didn't mind the red like I thought I would. That didn't mean I wasn't nervous and as skittish as a rabbit.

I couldn't believe *I*—Catherine Kelly Ryder—was doing something so outrageous. I finally knew. I wanted William Lambourne. It was more than attraction, more than great sex. I *loved* him.

William was right when he said there was something undeniable between us. I couldn't deny it anymore. I had no idea how William would respond when he saw me, but I didn't care. I had to try. I had to take my chances.

I *needed* to see him.

The bottom floors of The Peninsula Hotel housed retail shops, so it took me a few moments to reach the hotel. When I did, I found the place, as expected, superb. I was so anxious to see William that I barely noticed the luxury. The concierge informed me the event was in the Grand Ballroom, and I made my way there as quickly as possible. I showed my ticket and entered, but as soon as I did, I realized I was late. The guests were seated at their tables, listening attentively to the speaker on the platform. The voice sounded familiar, and I gaped when I realized William stood behind the podium at the front.

I hadn't known he would be speaking. This was a rare chance to watch him unnoticed. I stood quietly inside the door, listening to William's address. "I could stand here and tell you that cancer research is vitally important," he said. "That as a nation, as a world, we are called to support this research in every way we can. I could tell you the statistics, the different forms of cancer, the number of people who die from it every year, the cost to our nation and our world. But none of that would mean much unless you had a personal connection. I suspect many of you, like me, do have a personal connection."

I was impressed so far. William was a compelling speaker, and I was all but leaning forward, listening.

"When my aunt, a woman who is like a mother to me, was diagnosed with cancer two years ago, there were few places that offered cutting-edge treatments for a cancer like hers. I could send her to Houston. I could send her to New York or Baltimore. Here we are in Chicago, the country's third largest city, and we had nothing to rival MD Anderson or Sloan-Kettering. It stunned me. I hadn't realized how vital cutting-edge cancer treatment centers were or that my own city was lacking. But then, none of us do—until we're touched by cancer personally.

"Unfortunately, many of you have been or will be touched by cancer in your lives. You or a loved one will be diagnosed, and I am pleased to say that in the Lambourne Cancer Wing at Chicago Hospital, the most cutting-edge cancer research and treatment options will be offered to patients. Chicago is a world-class city, and it's only fitting that we offer the latest and the best. And so, on behalf of the Lambourne family, I am pleased to be part of something that will save the lives of so many…"

William was not done speaking, but applause exploded. I clapped too. I had never seen him speak so earnestly, so passionately. He rarely spoke of anything personal, but this was close to his heart. He paused, as if to control his emotion, before going on.

William waited for the applause to die down, glancing about the room. As he did, his gaze landed on me. Our eyes locked, and even though I wanted to look away, I couldn't. The pull I felt when he looked at me was too strong.

Finally, William cleared his throat and spoke again. "Proton therapy, smart drugs, treatments aimed at new genes and cancer pathways—these are but a few treatments the Lambourne Cancer Wing will offer patients." He went on, speaking about immune systems and targeting cancer cells, but I couldn't concentrate. All I could see were his stormy eyes, focused directly on me. And though he must have looked down at his notes or out at the audience, I felt as though he were speaking to me alone.

The speech ended, and the applause rose. The audience did too, giving William a standing ovation. William looked relaxed and easy as he left the podium, shaking hands, smiling, looking like a politician. He was in his element, no doubt.

And there was something else I did not doubt. He was headed straight for me.

My heart raced, and my hands shook as he neared me. I couldn't move. My feet seemed to be rooted to the floor. I couldn't stop staring at this glorious man who had been, briefly, mine.

He finally reached the edge of the room and held out his hand. My arm felt like lead as I lifted it. Electricity jumped between us when he embraced my hand in his large warm one, his grey eyes riveted on me. I could hardly breathe, hardly think.

"Catherine, how are you feeling?" he asked, as though we were alone, rather than surrounded by a dozen people.

"Better. I'm well."

His hand tightened on mine. "Good. I've been worried about you. I'm glad you're here. I wasn't expecting you, or…do you have a seat?" He looked around seemingly lost.

"I do actually. Your speech was wonderful. I was really moved."

"Thank you. I'm overwhelmed by the response." He was speaking formally, but his eyes searched my face for some clue as to where we stood. "You look beautiful," he said, his gaze dipping to take in my dress. "Red suits you." He was nervous. It was sweet that he was as nervous as I. He was trying so hard to maintain his public façade, and I hurried to reassure him.

"This may not be the right time, but I was hoping we could talk at some point. I have some things to tell you. The first is that I'm sorry."

This time I squeezed his hand. His eyes widened, and I could see the shock. He had not been expecting this.

"Secondly, I've missed you."

His hand tightened.

There was a third thing. I wanted to tell him I loved him, but this was not the place. "There's more, but I'll save it. Maybe you could buy me a drink?"

His whole body relaxed. "Catherine."

It was so good to hear him say my name, to see him look at me with those beautiful eyes. How had I survived one day without him? He put his arm around me, pressing me tightly to his side, and led me toward the bar. The crowd parted as we made our way through the ballroom. And then I saw her.

A tall blond turned toward us, stared in surprise, then spun and arrowed for William.

My heart thudded into my belly. It was another of William's blonds. Another Lara Kendall. What backhanded insult would this one give me? Or…oh, God! What if she was his date? He spotted her too, and I slowed.

"William, if this is a bad time, we can talk tomorrow. I don't want to cause problems. I can leave—"

"No!" His grip on me tightened so that it was almost painful. "I'm not ever letting you go again."

"William," the blond approached, still smiling. She held out her hand. "Hi, I'm Lauren, William's cousin. And you must be Catherine."

His cousin. I laughed with relief. She was his cousin!

"Yes. How did you...?"

She waved a hand. "Oh, I've heard all about you. I'm thrilled I finally get to meet you." She held a hand up conspiratorially. "I wasn't sure you really existed. William, she has to meet the rest of the family. You don't mind, do you? I know my parents are dying to meet you."

"Um..." Meet his family? I glanced at William. He looked... resigned. "I'd love to."

We followed Lauren to one of the front tables, where several people stood chatting. I recognized the older man and woman from the photograph in William's closet.

"Mom, look who I have! Catherine Kelly," Lauren gushed. "Catherine, these are my parents, Abigail and Charles Smith."

As though in a dream, I shook their hands. "Nice to meet you."

"And this," Lauren continued, obviously the social director of the group, "is my sister Sarah, who's in from D.C. Oh, and this is my husband Zach."

"Catherine," William's aunt said, "I didn't realize you would be here, or I would have seated you at our table."

"It was a last-minute decision," I said.

"It doesn't look last minute," Sarah commented. "I love your dress. William's choice?"

"Sarah," William chided. He'd barely spoken, and I could feel his impatience and energy. I could tell he wanted to be alone with me. I wanted that too. Desperately.

I laughed. "How did you know?"

"Oh, William always did have the best fashion sense of any of us," Lauren said. "For a while there, we thought he might be gay."

"And that would have been fine," Abigail said. "We wanted him to be happy, to find someone he cared about." She reached out and took my hand. "And now, he has!"

"And next you're going to pull out the embarrassing childhood photos," William remarked. "It might be a good time to excuse myself." He stepped away, and from the corner of my eye I saw him approach a hotel exec, speaking quietly.

I continued the conversation with his family. I was thoroughly charmed—his outgoing cousins, his doting aunt, his indulgent uncle. It was clear William's family loved him deeply, and they were very, very proud of him. It was such a different picture of him, such an intimate piece of him, when, previously I'd seen none.

William returned and tolerated a few teasing comments before saying, "I'm sorry to cut this short, but Catherine and I have to be somewhere."

"Then we'll get together again soon," his aunt remarked.

"I'd love to. It was wonderful to meet you."

As soon as I stepped away, William grabbed my hand.

"Come with me."

Even if I'd wanted to refuse, I had no choice. He had my hand firmly grasped in his. We headed toward the elevators, waited with several people for one to arrive, and then stepped inside. We didn't speak, didn't look at one another, and I didn't see which floor William pushed, but we were heading into the hotel. My pulse sped up, racing as I thought about being alone with him. My body thrummed at his nearness, and the way he stroked the inside of my wrist with his thumb made me very warm.

Finally, we reached the sixteenth floor and exited. William still held my hand, and we walked quickly down the hallway. We stopped, and he pulled a keycard from his pocket and opened the door to a suite. I stepped inside the lighted room, while William put the *Do Not Disturb* sign on the door. It clicked closed, and I heard the lock.

I turned, and William pulled me hard against him.

NINETEEN

It felt good to be in his arms again. I couldn't believe how much I'd missed him—his smell, his body, his mouth—definitely his mouth. It crushed mine with a searing kiss that left me breathless and weak in the knees. I kissed him back, tangling my tongue with his, nipping at his lips, sighing into his mouth. He groaned, a deep-throated sound that made my belly flutter. His hand on my back tightened, pulling me against him where I felt his hardness.

He was ready for me, and my body screamed for him. I didn't realize the depth of my need for him until I was in his arms.

He pushed me against the door, his mouth hot and needy, his kisses deep and drugging. His mouth made everything inside of me go molten. I pushed wantonly against him, mewling my desire.

"I've missed the taste of you," he said, his mouth delving to my ear to murmur in a low, husky whisper.

I'd missed the taste of him too—champagne and mint and something indefinably William Lambourne. It was erotic as hell. His hands slid down my back, and I pressed my aching breasts against his chest. Every part of me was heavy with need, and the demanding stroke of his hands made me crazy.

"Catherine, I can't believe you're actually here." He nipped at my shoulder then soothed the delicious sting with his lips. "I was going insane without you. When I saw you standing at the back of the room in that red dress..." His hands tightened on my waist and cupped my bottom, pulling me harder against him. What I felt between us left no question as to his opinion of the dress.

"You're beautiful," he whispered, and I heard the awe in his voice. Closing his eyes, he leaned his forehead against mine. "Catherine, I know you want to talk, and we can talk all night, if that's what you want. If that's what you need. But right now, I need to be inside you. I need to take you to bed and make love to you. Please tell me we can talk later." His mouth was on mine again, his tongue sweeping inside, stroking me, filling me, showing me what he wanted to do with his body. "Let me take you to bed."

"Yes," I murmured.

In a moment, he swept me into his arms. I laughed, dizzy and charmed by his impatience and the romance of this impetuousness. He carried me across the suite, kicking the door of the bedroom open. He was breathing hard and his skin was hot. His stormy eyes raged with need, and I wanted nothing more than to feel that need stroking me, filling me, and bringing me to new heights of pleasure. The depth of his need for me thrilled me, and it frightened me as well. William had so much untamed passion. He was raw and wild and savage. The sweetness of his carrying me to bed meant more to me because of the restraint he showed. This wasn't simply about him. William always thought of me first.

I'd had mere glimpses of the suite—images of soft light, sumptuous materials, and elegant décor. William set me down, and I looked around, getting my bearings. The bed was huge, covered with fluffed pillows. The duvet was thick and snowy white. The brocade divan and small mahogany table matched the antique armoire that probably housed the mini bar and the TV.

William watched me with those tempestuous, passion-filled eyes. The way he looked at me made me feel as though I were a rare jewel or artistic masterpiece, rather than plain Cat Kelly.

"Turn around," he breathed.

With a nervous laugh, I turned, showing him my backside. I looked over my shoulder, gave a teasing look, and spun back. I had a feeling the plunging neckline was the real reason he'd bought me this dress, though the way the material hugged my curves was pretty sexy too.

"You like it?" I asked.

"You look stunning—better than I envisioned." He crossed to me, and I tensed in anticipation. I wanted him. He said I looked stunning, but he was the one with the impossibly good looks. In his tuxedo, with his hair tousled and his eyes glittering with passion, he was every woman's fantasy.

His nimble fingers found the zipper and slid it down with a cool hiss. Instead of tearing it off and ravishing me, William sat on the bed.

"What's wrong?" I asked, uncertain.

He sat back, his eyes glistening with hunger and admiration. "Take the dress off, Catherine." His voice was a low, sexy purr, and his gaze never left mine.

I looked down, turned aside slightly, and began to disrobe.

"Look at me," he ordered. My gaze snapped to his face. His eyes burned with desire. He was hot for me, and I could tell that when I looked at him, I made him hotter. "Now, take off your dress."

Caught in that searing gaze, my body throbbing with need, I allowed the dress to slide slowly off my shoulders over my body, until it pooled on the floor. William's gaze darkened, and his breath hitched. I waited for him to tell me what to do next. Something about surrendering to his control aroused me even more. And he was beyond aroused. The tent of his erection in his trousers looked painful. He obviously had some fantasy about me in this dress, and I was going to fulfill it tonight. That excited me too—the thought of William fantasizing about me.

I stepped out of the dress and stood in my black lace bra, panties, garter, stockings, and high-heeled shoes. I could feel the sweep of my long hair on the bare skin of my back and imagined it was William's fingertips.

"Take off your bra," William said.

I reached to do his bidding.

"Slowly," he stressed.

The bra had a front clasp, and I unfastened it, tugging it off inch by inch until my heavy breasts were freed. William hissed in an audible breath, and my nipples instantly peaked and hardened.

Knowing the effect I was having, I allowed the silk and lace to fall to the floor, then cupped my tingling breasts and massaged them gently. William's gaze was riveted to my every movement.

"That's right," he growled. "Your tits are beautiful—perfect."

I ran my fingers across my erect nipples, feeling my body respond with zings of pleasure.

"Your nipples are so swollen," William murmured. "I love how pink they are, how hard, and those desperate noises of pleasure you make when I feast on them. You'll be making those sounds soon, Catherine."

I rubbed my nipples, imagining it was his hands that touched me, his mouth.

"Are you wet for me, Catherine?"

I felt a wave of heat flush my cheeks, but I nodded.

"Let me see," he said. "Take off your panties. Slowly."

I did as I was told, sliding the scrap of lace over my hips, taking my time to unfasten and refasten the garter belt then allowing my damp panties to fall to the floor. I kicked them off and stood before him in only my garter belt, stockings, and heels. I was so wet, so hot. I could barely stop myself from reaching between my legs. He was fucking me with his eyes, and I knew the smallest pressure would make me come.

"You're so beautiful," he breathed.

He stood, shrugged off his tuxedo jacket, and loosened his tie. I wanted to touch him and leaned forward. "Stay right where you are," he ordered. "Let me look at you."

He took his time, removing his cuff links and setting them on the nightstand with two clicks. His gaze never left mine, sliding over my body, caressing it, making love to it. He opened the top three studs from his shirt, making a V at the neck. I watched as that tantalizing glimpse of his flesh was revealed. The ache deep in my belly grew, and I could feel dampness on the inside of my thighs. He rolled up his shirtsleeves, revealing corded forearms, then he stepped before me and fell to his knees. My sex was right in front of him, and he inhaled deeply, burying himself in me. "I love your scent," he murmured against my sensitive flesh. I trembled with need. "I cannot wait to taste you, get you ready for me."

My legs were shaky and wobbly. His nearness, the feel of his hot breath, made me mad with desire. I needed him to touch me, taste me.

He leaned forward with tortuous slowness, his hot breath making me sway. His tongue darted out, licking my cleft and making me shudder. He spread my folds, put his hand on my backside, and pulled me toward his hungry mouth. I was lost in sensation. He teased and licked, his tongue swirling until I panted. Then he pulled back, only to taste me again, sucking me. I jumped when his finger slid into me. "You're so wet, Catherine." His finger slid out, replaced by the fullness of two fingers. All the time his mouth worked me. "Does it feel good, Catherine?"

I could only moan my response.

"Do you like my mouth on you?"

I could barely speak, but I nodded. His fingers slid in and out, making me buck and press hard against his mouth. I needed to come. I'd never needed anything more. "Please, William. I can't hold back."

"Don't worry. I have you. Just breathe."

I snatched in short bursts of air as his hands and his mouth stroked and massaged and manipulated me to new heights of pleasure. I couldn't take it anymore. I was going to explode. "Do you want to come, Catherine?"

"Yes, *yes*!"

"Come for me."

I shattered completely, crying out. His mouth on my plumped bud sucked until it became an exquisite torture. Spasms rocked me and my walls gripped and stroked his fingers.

"Yes," he murmured. "You're so tight, Catherine. I can't wait to feel you clamp down on my cock when I make you come again."

I was shaking all over, the orgasm pulsing through me. My knees were weak, and my body would have crumpled if William hadn't supported me. It was the most intense orgasm I'd ever had, and standing in only my garter, with William kneeling before me, one of the most erotic.

Finally, he looked at me and smiled. "Beautiful, Catherine. Perfect. Good girl."

He took my hand and led me to the bed, pushed me down, then bent to remove my shoes. His hands unfastened my stockings, rolled them down, and then unhooked the garter. I was naked, lying before him, when he stood and began to undress.

My breathing hitched as he shed his shirt. I loved his body—the flat, rock-hard abs, the sculpted chest. He watched me watch him, dragging his trousers over his hips. My gaze followed the path down, over his V muscle, to his jutting manhood. It was large and hard for me. I wanted to take it in my mouth, lick its delicious dark red head. William leaned over me, his skin sliding against mine. He kissed me deeply, and I tasted myself on his lips and his tongue. His body rubbed mine as he took my mouth, and I sighed when he moved down my body, nuzzling my breasts and suckling my nipples.

I felt my need building again. I arched against him, wriggling impatiently. His hand caressed my body, moving between us until he cupped my sex.

"You're wet for me again, aren't you, Catherine?"

"Yes. I need you."

"You're plump and hot. Are you ready for me?"

"Yes. Please."

He eased in slowly, when I wanted fast and hard. He must have felt my impatience, because he stilled my rising hips.

"I don't want to hurt you, and you're going to take all of me, Catherine. I'm going to fill you." He opened me, sliding inside me, his swollen cock stretching me until I was impossibly full.

"In all the way," he growled in my ear then pumped once. I moaned, and he kissed my neck, moving in a steady rhythm. "You feel so good. I can't get enough of your tight body. I'm going to come so hard inside you."

The pressure built as he took, his cock thrusting into me with unwavering control. "William," I breathed.

"You fit me like a glove. I feel those little flutters. You're getting ready to come again." He moved, a slight adjustment, and I gripped the bed covers with my fingers, trying to hold on. He hit my g-spot, and the pleasure was blindingly intense. I couldn't hold back. Ecstasy spiraled, consumed me, until a shattering orgasm ripped through me. I felt William reach his peak, felt him swell and explode, but he didn't stop. He pumped, and I continued to come as the ripples went on and on, to extraordinary heights.

I'd never felt anything so powerful or so intense. I felt the sting of tears burn my eyes. I was moved, my emotions shattered, my core laid bare.

William was still inside me, his weight on me as he lay spent and exhausted. He raised his head, touched my wet cheeks, and his expression went from satisfied to concerned. "Oh, baby, why the tears? Did I hurt you? Was I too rough?" He ran a hand through his hair. "I lost control for a moment. You do things to me, Catherine, things that I can't explain."

I laughed through the tears that William wiped away with his thumb. He looked into my eyes, his expression tender. "I'm fine. I don't know why I'm crying. It's just… I feel… it's so much…" I knew I loved him now. I wanted to tell him, but I was feeling too emotional.

William wrapped me in his arms, holding me, kissing me, shushing me. "I know. I feel it too. I'm right here and not going anywhere."

It was what I needed to hear. I hadn't known how much I needed to hear those words. And then his mouth captured mine, took my sobs with his lips, and turned them into sweet kisses. His hands were on my body, caressing me, worshipping me, delving between my legs to stroke my swollen folds and tender nub. I was beyond sated, but my body could not help but respond. Waves of pleasure built deep within my core, rising until I ached with need again. I felt him harden within me, that glorious member making me stretch and pulse. This time was slow and tender, as he moved with deliberate sweetness. I didn't think it was possible to come again, but William's gentleness slayed me. I came again—twice—then fell into a satisfied sleep, safe in William's arms.

I woke, momentarily disoriented, and glanced at the clock on the nightstand. It was after one, and I was alone in bed. Panic sliced through me, fear that William had left, that I had misunderstood or imagined our encounter. Then I heard the low rumble of a male voice in the living area of the suite.

I sat up, and my stomach rumbled. I was completely ravenous. I rose and stumbled to the bathroom. I splashed water on my face and glanced in the mirror. My skin was pink and flushed, my eyes a bright green. My hair was an absolute mess, but I looked and felt like a well-pleasured woman. I unhooked the robe from the back of the door, pulled it on, and tied it at my waist. I padded back to the bedroom, opened the door adjoining the living area, and walked in. I spotted William immediately.

Shirtless and in black boxer briefs, his back was to me, but I could see he was on his cell. He paced, running his free hand through his hair, which told me he was agitated. I couldn't hear what he said, only the tone made it sound like he was finished with the call. How long had he been out of bed and on the phone?

Suddenly, he turned, and his gaze caught mine. He said something curt and ended the call. He crossed to me and took me in his arms. "Did I wake you?"

"No."

He stepped back, and I had a clear glimpse of his face. His distracted look indicated he was thinking about the call.

"Is everything alright?" I asked.

His strong arms might have been around me a moment ago, but his eyes were a deep stormy grey, and he looked like he was miles away. For once, *he* needed *me*. I wrapped my arms around him and laid my head against his bare, muscled chest. He was tense, but as I held him, the tension ebbed away. I wanted to ask whom he had been speaking to on the phone, but I didn't. I had a feeling he wouldn't tell me. I just got him back, and I didn't want to argue.

William squeezed me. "Everything will be fine, Catherine. Don't worry about anything."

I almost laughed. I was supposed to be comforting him!

"My aunt would like you to come for dinner. Is that okay?"

"Of course. Was that her on the phone?"

He laughed, a throaty laugh that I loved.

Finally, I had my William back. "No, that wasn't her at this hour. She sent a text about thirty seconds after we left the event."

I smiled at her eagerness, but his answers didn't stop me from noticing that he hadn't offered information about his call. My stomach rumbled loudly, and William's eyes widened. "Someone needs food. I'm hungry too. I'll order something."

"William, it's after one in the morning. The kitchen is closed."

He laughed and gave me a quick kiss. "Twenty-four-hour room service, darling. I'll be right back."

He crossed to the hotel phone, spoke quietly then turned back. "The food will be here in fifteen minutes. Can you wait that long, starving girl?"

"Of course. I'm fine."

He walked to the table in the living room, grabbed two bottles of water, and rifled through a large hospitality basket I hadn't noticed. It was filled with assorted treats—crackers, cookies, fruit. He grabbed a jar of elegantly packaged gourmet jelly beans and patted the couch. "Come sit with me."

When I sat down, he pulled me into his lap. "William!" I said when I almost fell over. He laughed, tickled me, and then kissed me. He was rarely this playful, and I couldn't help but giggle. He opened the jar of candy and popped one into my mouth. "It's good," I said. "Root beer, I think."

"Sorry. I hate root beer. Why do they make jelly bean flavors that taste like soft drinks or mixed drinks? I like the classics."

I searched the jar until I found a yellow one. "Not me. I like to mix it up. If you combine this yellow, this white, and this red, it tastes like a banana split." I popped them, one by one, into his mouth and laughed at the disgusted look he gave me.

"It doesn't taste like banana split. Here. This is my favorite." He fed me a purple bean.

I shook my head. "Grape candy never tastes like grapes. I don't like it."

"Good. It's my favorite. Now I don't have to share." He ate another one.

"I bet you like the black ones too."

"They're the best. My cousin Lauren likes them, and we always fought over who got the last one."

"I never had a brother or sister. That's why I'm so bad at sharing."

"I'm lucky that way," he said. I raised my brows. I wouldn't have called his circumstances *lucky*. "I know what you're thinking, but I was lucky. My aunt and uncle loved me and treated me like one of their own. I was fortunate to have family when I lost my mom and dad and Wyatt."

I held my breath, willing William to continue. He never spoke of his family, and now I feared if I blinked, he would stop.

"I always had a brother," he said, feeding me a red bean and taking a white. "It took me awhile to get used to having sisters. That's what Lauren, Zoe, and Sarah are to me. They talked all the time, and there was all the…" He gestured to indicate piles. "All the stuff in the bathroom—hair stuff and face stuff and nail stuff. After a few years, I could host a tea party, with the best of them and I knew every line to *Cinderella*. You can test me."

I laughed. I couldn't picture the William I knew watching a movie about a princess.

"They became your family," I said.

"Yes. They are my family."

We both reached for a pink bean. "Uh-oh," he said. "We might have to share the pink."

"I can't believe you, a gourmand—an epicurean—likes jelly beans."

He laughed and stole the pink, popping it into his mouth. "As you know, Catherine, my tastes are many." He kissed me, and he tasted like strawberry sugar.

Now, I thought. *Now is the time to tell him I love him.* A quick knock sounded on the door, and William put me on the couch and rose to answer. I sighed, telling myself there would be time later. He'd surprised me again, ordering burgers and fries. It was the perfect late-night dinner, but I had expected something elegant. I watched as he dug into his burger and slathered his fries with ketchup. He might be eating common food, but he still savored each bite.

After I'd taken enough bites to satisfy my rumbling belly, I said, "So what is it with you and food? I didn't think you'd have time to cook with everything else you do."

"I've always liked to cook," he said.

"Really?" I was surprised.

"It's a family trait. My mother was an accomplished cook and my first teacher. I spent hours in the kitchen with her. It was our special time. And then cooking is something my aunt and I have in common. She loves to cook too, and I learned a lot from her."

"My mom never cooked," I said, but only because he looked at me as though he expected me to say something. I was afraid to speak for fear I'd ruin the moment. William had really opened up tonight.

"It's becoming a lost art, but I always enjoyed working with my hands. Making things. I like to make things. And food, well, it's one of life's greatest pleasures." He tucked an errant stand of my hair behind my ear. "You, Catherine, are another of my life's great pleasures."

"William..." I toyed with my French fries.

"It's true. Look at you. So beautiful."

"I'm a mess."

He caught my chin, forced me to look into his eyes. "No, you look sleep-mussed, well-pleasured, and sexy as hell. Have I told you how happy I am that you're here?"

"In more than one way."

"Your being here tonight took me by surprise. It was unexpected. You've made me very happy."

"I'm happy too." I twined my fingers with his. "I hated being apart from you."

"I couldn't sleep. Couldn't concentrate. Couldn't stop thinking about you."

"Really?" Had he missed me that much? It was difficult to imagine this controlled man thrown by anything, much less me. "I was in pain, Catherine. It was almost unbearable without you."

"I felt the same," I whispered.

"And then, when Beckett said you were sick, I went crazy with worry. I needed to see you, make certain you were taken care of, but I couldn't."

"You brought me soup and returned my cell phone."

"It took everything not to push past Beckett when I brought the soup. I wanted to see you."

"I didn't want to see you. Your note with my cell phone broke my heart."

"Catherine. No."

"How could you say I'd be better off without you?"

He shook his head. "I fucked up, Catherine. I wish you hadn't seen the file on Jenny Hill. It was careless to leave that information sitting out. You weren't meant to see it. I swear I've never had a file on you." His eyes were intense, and I couldn't have looked away had I wanted to. "I knew everything I needed to know the instant you bumped into me and dropped your camera bag. It's always been genuine between us, right from the start."

My mind was reeling. This was the conversation I'd had with him over and over in my mind, but now, it was real. Of course, I realized he wasn't explaining why he needed his "women" prescreened, though my secret meeting with George provided me with explanations. I suspected—no, more than suspected—I *knew* there were more reasons than William's security. A dossier like the one on Jenny Hill went past what was necessary for security. There were more reasons for those dossiers William had made... deeply personal reasons, I suspected.

But now was not the time to press for those answers. Now, we were starting over, and this time we were getting to know one another. Besides, in my heart, I did trust him. He was telling the truth. And I could wait for the answers I wanted. "I know you never had a file on me. I believe you. But what could you have known from our first meeting? Other than I can be clumsy?" I lifted my burger, poised to take another bite.

"I knew everything about you, Catherine. I knew you were beautiful. You had green eyes, gorgeous hair, and flawless skin. You smelled great, and you had a smile that dazzled."

I still held the burger, unable to taste it. Had William really thought all this about me?

"What else?"

He thought for a moment. "You were artistic, organized, modest."

"Modest?"

"You blushed when I looked at you and averted your eyes. You were gracious, charming, and...that jolt of electricity when our hands touched. Tell me you felt it too."

"I felt it."

"As soon as we touched, I wanted you. I wanted to feed you, pleasure you, and take care of you. I'd never had that response to a woman—an instant response. From that moment on, I needed you."

I stared, my burger all but forgotten. He thought all of those things about me. *Me*. Just from our first, momentary meeting. It stunned me, but I remembered my response to him too. How I'd been intrigued by his stormy eyes, and I'd wanted him to touch me again.

"I knew you weren't Jenny Hill, Catherine. There was no mix up. When I went to Willowgrass that first night, I asked Ben. And then I made sure I was there for your shoot the next day. I wanted only you."

I shook my head, trying to comprehend it all. "So you didn't know anything else about me? You really didn't know about Jace...or the accident?" I whispered the last. I hated to bring Jace up right now, but I had to know. Otherwise, I would always wonder.

He took my burger and set it on the plate, then clasped my hand. "Catherine, I had no idea."

I took a deep breath, ignoring the way it hitched. I had one more question, the one I'd been dreading. There was no going back now. "William, are you sure you wouldn't be better without *me*? Are you sure I'm not a liability?"

He looked as though I'd slapped him. "Catherine, don't... None of that matters now. Let me rephrase that. I know how deeply it matters, and I understand. The past is the past. It kills me that you've had to go through this. I know how hard it is. And I know what it's like to feel guilty for surviving." He clenched my hand tightly, and I knew this was more than he'd ever said to any other person. "You have survived. And you're not alone, Catherine. I'll protect you. "

I wanted to feel comforted. I wanted to fall into William's embrace and be protected, but I couldn't. "You don't understand. People *blame* me for Jace's death. It doesn't matter that I wasn't charged with anything. They still hold me responsible. *Me.* Jace's parents, his friends, his fans. It's why I moved to Chicago. They *hate* me. Just because I got away doesn't mean they've moved on. I don't want to drag you into this. It could get ugly. You're a public person, William. It won't take much digging before—"

"Damn it, Catherine," he said, interrupting me. "I refuse to let this ruin us before we've started. Trust me. I'll take care of you. I know what I need to know. We'll be fine."

The hotel phone rang, and William rose to answer it. "Yes, everything is fine." *Room service,* he mouthed and listened again.

He thought he knew everything he needed, but he didn't know the most important part. "You don't know that I love you..." I whispered so that he couldn't hear.

"Checking that the food was to our liking," he said as he hung up. "Do you like it?"

I smiled. "It's perfect." I polished off the rest of the juicy burger, my salty fries, and a few jelly beans for good measure.

Finally, we walked, hand in hand, back to bed. It was after two, and I was exhausted. I felt happy and safe. It had been so long since

I'd felt both. In bed, William wrapped his arms around me, and I fell into a deep, comforting sleep.

TWENTY

I woke, squinting at the rays of bright sunshine streaming through gaps in the hotel draperies. I tried to turn my body away, but a heavy weight pressed on my chest. Shocked, I realized it was William's arm. He had it slung across me, and he was still asleep beside me. I'd never seen him sleep, and since he was on his stomach, I couldn't get a good view from this angle, but his breathing was deep and regular. I craned my neck to see the clock and could hardly believe it was eight-thirty. We had slept in together! This was the first time I'd wakened with him beside me.

The opportunity was too good to pass up, and I angled my head to catch a glimpse of his face. His mouth was soft and pliant, his cheeks darkened with stubble and slack. He looked relaxed, more relaxed than I'd seen him when he was awake. He was impossibly handsome, youthful, and untroubled. I enjoyed seeing him like this. It made me feel closer to him.

I gently extricated myself from his embrace and climbed out of bed. He stirred but didn't wake. Clearly, he was breaking yet another of his mysterious "rules." He'd slept for six and a half hours and hadn't risen before me. We were definitely starting over!

I smiled then headed to the bathroom. I peed, washed my face, and found a brush for my hair and teeth among the complimentary toiletries. When I felt refreshed, I tiptoed into the living room and found my purse. The remains of our meal were still on the table, and I remembered our conversation. I found my cell and saw I had a bunch of texts from Beckett. He'd slept over at my condo, ostensibly to take care of Laird and be there in case I came home in tears, but I knew Beckett wanted to bake in my AGA. When I hadn't returned after an hour, he'd invited Alec over to watch a movie.

That was good news. I was happy Beckett and Alec had gotten closer. The last text from Beckett mentioned hot yoga. I felt like I'd been doing hot yoga all night, so I texted back that I wasn't going to make it and explained.

Best night of my life. Call you when I get home. Thanks for hanging with the hound. XO.

I sneaked back into bed, the sheets warm from William's body. I thought I'd gotten away with my field trip, but he rolled over. He was awake and frowning. "I thought you left me. I don't like to wake up alone."

I raised a brow. "It doesn't feel so good, does it?" I responded, feeling saucy.

"Point taken, Catherine." William had a wicked grin and pulled me closer then rolled on top and pinned me to the bed. "I always begin my days early. Are you going to start getting up with me at four-thirty?"

"No way. But if we're making this work, I do need to know where you are. And when you leave. That means waking me and giving me a proper good-bye. It also means no jetting to another continent without telling me."

William grinned, his eyes full of mischief. He ducked his head and kissed my neck, teasing the skin near my earlobe then growling. "Any more demands? I like it when you're fired up."

"William, I'm serious. If you want me to trust you, to trust us, I have to know that you're in this relationship with me and that you'll tell me stuff. That's what a relationship is—two people talking to each other and sharing."

He looked at me. "Catherine, I want to share everything. If that's what it's going to take, ask me anything." He was back to kissing my neck, and I felt his morning hardness press against my leg. It would be easy to give into temptation and let the issue drop, but I couldn't. It was too important.

"You said I could ask you anything. I want to know who was on the phone last night."

His body went still, and he ceased nuzzling. He rose on his elbows and looked me straight in the eye. "George."

I waited, but when he didn't go on, I realized he wasn't elaborating. "George? At one in the morning?"

"We've had a security issue," he said, his voice clipped. I imagined this was what he sounded like when involved in business negotiations. "George is taking care of it. That's what he does. He's good at his job, but it's important to be kept up-to-speed on what's happening. Even if that means phone calls in the middle of the night."

A ball of concern formed in the pit of my stomach. I sometimes forgot how rich and powerful William was and how dangerous his position could be. "Should I be worried?"

"No, Catherine. You definitely should not be worried. More questions?" His eyes flashed stormy grey.

I was trying his patience, but who knew when I'd get another chance? "What's the story with you and Lara Kendall?"

William groaned and lowered his head. "Seriously Catherine? Can't you feel this?" He pushed his rock-hard erection against me. "You make me so damn hard. All I want is to bury myself in you. Only you, Catherine. Lara Kendall means nothing. We went out a few times. She's a social-climbing dilettante who went to school with one of my cousins. We were never serious. If you keep making me talk about her, *this* is going away. I guarantee it." He moved his hips, pressing his hard-on against me.

I felt my body respond, but I wasn't ready to give in. It was fun keeping William at bay, seeing his impatience. "Did you sleep with her?"

"*No*. I did not." He tickled me playfully, but I could see he didn't enjoy the question. His expression was serious, his tone authoritative. "That's enough." He nipped my shoulder. "No more talking. No more questions." His mouth trailed to my breasts. "I need to be inside you. Now."

I was more than ready, and when he entered me, I forgot every other question—everything but William and me and our own little world.

*****

We spent most of the morning in bed. It was wonderful not having to be anywhere or talk to anyone—to just exist in our cocoon. Wrapped up in one another, we enjoyed being back together. The day was full of possibilities.

I finally managed to crawl out of bed and take a shower.

A few minutes later, as I lathered my body with shower gel, the shower door opened, and William joined me. "Now this is a lovely sight," he said.

I laughed. "You've seen me naked for the last twelve hours."

"That's how I like you best." He was hard again, and I was truly amazed. The man had admirable stamina. He kissed me, sliding his wet hands up my soapy back and over my slick breasts.

"I want this to be slow," he said, "but I need you now."

"Fast is good," I said, breathlessly. "I want you inside me."

He groaned again, and he lifted me and pushed me against the wall. I wrapped my legs around him, feeling his hardness pressed intimately against me. He rocked against me, once, twice, and my desire was so great I had to bite my lip to keep from begging. His mouth captured mine, his hands cupping my face, touching me as though he couldn't believe I was there. I rubbed my slick hands over his shoulders, feeling the combination of muscle and sinew beneath my fingertips. I caught our reflection in the bathroom mirror and marveled at my flushed face and his strong, powerful back and legs.

His mouth curved over my jaw, and his lips skated over the sensitive flesh of my neck. The gruff sound of need he made when his lips reached my breasts made me wet. His mouth worked on me, sucking, laving, teasing until I was panting and close to coming.

"Not yet."

"What happened to fast and hard? I want you, William." I rocked against him to prove my point, and his hands tightened on my breasts then slid to my thighs. I shivered and rubbed my hands down his chest. All those 4:00 a.m. workouts had paid off. I ran my fingers over the ridges of muscle and saw his control waver momentarily. The hot water from the shower warmed us and made our bodies slide against one another.

In the mirror, I could see my hands skate down the sleek, bronze skin of his back. His hands on my thighs tightened and slid upward. He stroked me, slowly working his way up until he brushed my sex.

I moaned as his fingers slid into me. I clenched around him as he thrust hard then pulled back and circled my clit. I could feel the first stirrings of my orgasm building.

"You want it, don't you?" he said against my ear. His fingers slid inside me again. "Go ahead. Come."

I did. I arched hard, pressing myself against his fingers as he slammed them into me until I cried out and shattered.

"My turn." He adjusted the way he held me, and in the mirror I saw the muscles of his ass flex as he pushed against me. I throbbed, and I made a mewling sound. His hand cupped me again then moved away until I could feel him hot and hard, resting against me. He rubbed the tip of his cock on my sex, and I almost came again. "Patience," he demanded. "I'll make the wait worth it."

Slowly, he filled me until I was impaled and blinded with pleasure. He rocked me against the wall, and I whimpered.

"More?" he asked.

"Yes. Please."

He slid in and out, filling me so completely I didn't think I could take it. I watched his buttocks flex in the mirror as he thrust inside. I felt him swell as he all but lifted me with a final thrust. His hand came between us, his finger pressing against my clit, and I exploded again as I felt him come. He called out, pushing me against the wall.

Finally, he lowered his head, resting his forehead on my shoulder. "Catherine." It was a plea and a prayer.

The water had turned lukewarm, but neither of us had the energy to turn the knob toward hot for several minutes. We adjusted the temperature, rinsed off, and stepped from the shower. I should have been exhausted after so little sleep and so much sex, but I felt energized. I wrapped the robe around me and dried my hair, and when I emerged, William was standing beside the bed, dressed in dark pants and a sweater. I opened my mouth to ask where his clothes had come from, but then I saw the divan. He had an outfit laid out, and his eyes were on my face, gauging my reaction.

I smiled and lifted the lovely green cashmere wrap-dress. Along with it were cable-knit tights, buttery soft riding boots, a charcoal cashmere coat with fur trim…and, of course, gloves. He had not forgotten the lingerie. In a small box filled with tissue paper were a matching ivory lace bra and panties.

"William," I breathed. "Thank you. This is so thoughtful."

"Do you like it?" he asked.

"I love it."

I did have reservations. None of this was what I would have picked for myself, but he had been right about the red gown. I would give this a chance. And, not surprisingly, once I was dressed, I felt comfortable, as though I'd had this outfit for years. I studied myself in the dresser mirror and smiled. I looked sophisticated and elegant.

I didn't know how he managed to choose the right style and do it without seeing me in the clothes. He really did have exceptional fashion sense.

"You look beautiful, Catherine," he said, when he saw me. "Breakfast?"

While I'd dressed, he'd ordered room service. I was, once again, ravenous.

When we finished eating, he asked, "Are you ready to go?"

"Yes."

We would return to my apartment to check on Laird, but after that we had no specific plans. These were the kind of days I loved—

days where anything was possible. We took the elevator down, holding hands, and there was a black Range Rover waiting at the valet station. I waited for Anthony to emerge, but William opened the door for me and then climbed in the driver's side. This was a first. I'd never seen him drive. I suspected he did it well, like everything else.

We pulled out of the hotel and drove up Lake Shore Drive, heading north. William held my hand in a casual way.

As I looked at the frozen lake, I knew today I would tell him my feelings. I had to find the right moment. I could spot blue open water past the icy shore. There wasn't snow on the ground, but it was bitterly cold. The weather app on my phone read twenty-one. It was too cold to spend much time outdoors, and there were more clouds than sun, and the temperature was not predicted to warm. We'd already spent much of the day inside.

"What would you like to do, Catherine?"

I leaned my head on the seat rest and looked at him. "How do you usually entertain your girlfriends?" I spoke mostly in jest, but William didn't smile.

"I told you—I don't have girlfriends. But I now have *a* girlfriend." He looked at me with a smile. "What you would like to do, *girlfriend*?"

I laughed. "Well, *boyfriend*, it's your job to come up with ideas. If you don't have any, I might think of something. Do you feel like a drive?"

"Where do you want to go?"

"There's an exhibit I've been dying to see."

"At the MCA?"

"No, in Milwaukee."

He nodded. "That's a good idea. It's a great museum. And I know a perfect place to hit for an early dinner. You'll love it." He squeezed my hand and laughed. "We're going to Wisconsin."

I laughed as well. The trip was unexpected and impulsive. I loved it.

A little while later William parked on the street across from my condo. We walked over, hand in hand, and I spotted Hans and Minerva as we entered the vestibule.

"Catherine, dear! Hello!" Minerva called.

"Hi." I turned to William, gesturing. "Hans and Minerva Himmler, this is William Lambourne."

"It's lovely to see you again," Minerva said, giving William a kiss on the cheek. I could tell the gesture surprised him. Hans shook William's hand and said something about having heard all about him.

"You've set the bar high for us men," Hans said with a smile.

"And why not!" Minerva said. She gave me a knowing smile. "Any man who would cook you a meal is one worth holding on to. Don't let this one go, Catherine. Especially because he's so good-looking." She winked.

I laughed and gave Minerva a warm hug. As we embraced, Minerva whispered, "I'm so glad to see you happy."

It felt good to *be* happy.

William and I headed upstairs, and I unlocked my door. Laird wagged his tail and jumped with excitement, calming when I gave the order, then exposed his belly for rubbing. He eyed William warily, but that was a step up from his response to people he didn't know well. That response involved barking incessantly and cornering my guest.

"Beckett?" I called. No answer, so I headed into the kitchen. There was the evidence of Beckett's culinary sleepover—a half-dozen cupcakes on the counter along with a note.

My latest creation: New York cheesecake cupcakes with berry compote filling. Decadent, sexy, and perfect with champagne. Hope you're not eating alone! XO, B.

I squealed with delight. "Oh, my God! These are my favorite!" I snatched one and tasted it, closing my eyes at the delicious flavor. "So good."

"What's going on?" William asked, walking into the kitchen.

"Beckett stayed over last night to bake in the AGA and watch Laird." I took another bite, unable to resist. "He left me these cupcakes, and they are to die for," I mumbled.

William raised a brow. He'd never seen me so enthusiastic about food, but he'd be a convert when he tried one. "Here, taste this," I said and fed him a bite. He took it, licking my fingers as I placed the morsel in his mouth.

His eyes widened. "This is delicious. Beckett made these?"

"Yeah, aren't they great? I know cupcakes are cliché these days, but this isn't all he can do. He's an amazing baker." I took another bite, polishing the cupcake off.

William looked thoughtful. "Beckett? That's interesting."

"How so?" I eyed the cupcakes, deciding whether I should eat another now or later.

"I've been thinking about a dessert endeavor." William lifted a cupcake and ate another bite. "These are good. Oh, I almost forgot. I have something for you."

"A present?" I asked.

He'd left half the cupcake uneaten, and I wondered if he was going to finish it. If not, maybe I could…

"You might say that." He reached into his coat and pulled out a monogrammed handkerchief. Setting it on the counter, he carefully opened it. I forgot about the cupcakes when I saw the Patek Philippe watch he'd given me upon returning from London. I'd left it at his penthouse when we broke up. Beside the Patek Philippe was my ugly Walgreens watch. "I didn't know what to do with these, so I thought I'd ask. What time is it, Catherine? Is it…"He glanced at the Patek Philippe. "Eleven forty-two? Or is it…" He looked at my black plastic watch. "Is that eleven fifty-eight? It's hard to tell if that's an eight or three."

I slapped him playfully.

"Which one?" He dangled both watches in front of me.

"William, I know what time it is. It's morning. And it's before noon. I think that's good enough. Not everything needs to be exact. And don't make fun of my plastic watch. I've had that one for four months now, and it's done a good job."

"I imagine a fine Swiss timepiece from your *boyfriend* will do a better job. May I?" He gestured to my wrist. I held my arm out, and he slid the watch on and closed the delicate clasp. There was a jolt of electricity between us, even in a gesture as simple as this. I felt the connection coursing through me.

"I'd like you to look at this at precisely eleven forty-two every morning and think about me touching you… like this." He leaned close and kissed my neck, making me shiver. "Like this…" His hand drifted down and gently caressed my breast. My nipple was instantly hard beneath his hand. "And like this…" His hand traveled leisurely down my body, leaving a path of heat wherever he touched.

Finally, he delved between my legs, cupping me, and rubbing my sex. He must have felt scorching warmth emanating from my core, even through the material of the dress and my tights.

"Every morning, think about my touch, Catherine."

"William…." I blushed, feeling a familiar stirring. Of course, I knew, despite my embarrassment, I would do exactly as he asked.

"I have something for you too," I said with a smile. I took my plastic watch from the counter and said in the same tone he'd used a moment ago, "Hold out your hand."

With a bemused expression, he held out his left wrist, on which he already sported an impressive Rolex.

"No, the other arm."

He offered his right arm, and I strapped on my cheap watch. It suited him, as it was a man's style. I was a little surprised William went along with this. He probably found it amusing. He had a wicked grin on his face.

"I want you to look at this at least once every day," I said, "and realize that you don't always have to be on time. I just want to know where you are."

William laughed, throwing his head back. He gave me a deep, genuine smile. "What are you doing to me, silly girl?"

"Exactly what you do to me. Will you promise?"

He shook his head. "I adore you, Catherine Kelly. Yes, I will do as you ask. I promise."

I hadn't thought about the gesture, but it suddenly meant a lot that he had accepted it and promised. I was giddy with the closeness I felt, the love I felt. William pulled me to him, embracing me, and whispering, " I love it. Thank you." His mouth found mine, and he kissed me deeply, showing me how much my small gesture meant.

"Maybe I should give you cheap gifts more often." I looked into his eyes and knew this was the moment. I wanted to tell him. *William, I love you.*

He kissed me again, passionately, his hands running up and down my back. Perhaps we wouldn't make that trip to Milwaukee after all...

Then, I felt something vibrate against my arm and pulled back.

"Damn," William said, pulling his phone from his coat pocket. He glanced at it and stepped back. "Shit. I have to take this. Yes?" Holding the phone to his ear, he walked from the kitchen into my living room.

All the happiness and pleasure I'd felt drained out. The day had been perfect so far. Finally, I'd been happy—happier than I had been in so long. I'd been content, and I'd felt safe with William. I didn't want it to end.

I looked at the beautiful watch William had given me. It was a perfect reminder of him. My gaze traveled to the remains of the cupcake William had been eating. I could hear him speaking in a low voice, so I took a bite. Laird had followed us into the kitchen and wagged his tail hopefully, so I fed him a morsel.

"Pretty good, isn't it?" I said. "Want more?"

I tried not to eavesdrop on William's conversation, but it was difficult not to hear. His voice rose. "Damn it! I can't."

I froze, listening now.

"Now is not a good time." There was a long pause. I wondered what the person on the other end was saying. Was it George? Someone else?

"Are you sure?" William sighed loudly. "No, it's has to be me. I'll go myself. It's the only way." Another pause. "I understand. I'll call you from the jet."

I clenched the counter as my stomach dropped. The jet? He was leaving? *Now*? Hadn't we talked about this? Hadn't he said he'd keep me informed?

And what about our day—our plans? I didn't know how this relationship would work if it was always like this—if I would always take a backseat to William's demands.

William strode into the kitchen. He'd been running a hand through his hair in frustration. It was tousled and going in all directions. His jaw was set, his eyes steel grey and somber. "Catherine…"

"I heard," I said without preamble. "You're leaving." I turned away.

"It's not what you think. I don't have a choice. I have to go."

I rounded on him, angry. "Why you? There's no one in your empire you can delegate this to? I don't even know what it is. I don't want you to go. Not today." I could feel tears ready to spring forth. Every time I tried to tell him how I felt, we were interrupted.

William pulled me close, and I sank against him. "I know, baby. I'm sorry. Trust me, if someone else could take this on, they'd be on the jet, and you and I would be on our way to Wisconsin." He stroked my hair.

"Where are you going this time? London?"

"Much nearer actually. Napa." He held me close, and I pressed my cheek to his chest, inhaling his scent and listening to the steady beat of his heart. I heard him take a slow, deep breath. "Come with me."

I clenched my jaw. I wanted nothing more than to go. I would have gone anywhere with him. Except there. Except Northern California. I hadn't been back since I moved to Chicago, and there was a good reason. I would refuse him. I hated to do it, but…

"I need you with me, Catherine," he said. "I can't do this alone." He took another breath, and I felt his heart accelerate. Tension filled his body, and his heart raced. I looked at him, concerned. I loved him, and his fears were mine now. His jaw was clenched, his expression deadly serious. "They think they found my brother. Alive."

TO BE CONTINUED…

Catherine and William's story continues in

A SIP OF YOU
THE EPICUREAN BOOK 2

Available now!

ABOUT THE AUTHOR

Sorcha Grace is an adventurous eater, beach lover and author of scorching contemporary erotic romance. She is also the nom de plume of a nationally bestselling author who publishes in another romance genre. Find her on Facebook and Twitter.

www.facebook.com/SorchaGrace
Twitter: @SorchaGrace